Praise for *Radar Girls*

"*Radar Girls* is a fresh, delightful romp of a novel featuring the little-known women of Hawaii recruited after Pearl Harbor to staff the islands' radar stations. Heroine Daisy is thrown into the deep end guiding in wounded Air Force pilots and listening for Japanese attacks, while juggling family troubles and a budding romance, but she and her radar-girl gang of irrepressible friends live up to their work, their duty, and their code name Rascal in sparkling fashion. Sara Ackerman never disappoints!"

—Kate Quinn, *New York Times* bestselling author of *The Rose Code*

"*Radar Girls* is a transporting, evocative novel with a unique slant on Hawaii in the immediate aftermath of the attack on Pearl Harbor. Ackerman skillfully tells an absorbing story while also crafting an ode to friendship and the strength of women faced with crisis, giving unsung heroes a triumphant and resonant voice."

—Kaui Hart Hemmings, *New York Times* bestselling author of *The Descendants*

"In *Radar Girls*, Ackerman again delivers a powerful story about a little-known piece of women's history with compassion and an unforgettable cast of characters. Daisy is a heroine to cheer for as she gives all she has for her country, the man she loves and, most importantly, herself."

—Noelle Salazar, bestselling author of *The Flight Girls*

"The perfect escape, *Radar Girls* delivers a pitch perfect combination of fascinating history and unforgettable characters. I loved being transported to Hawaii and learning about these adventurous, smart women who answered the call of duty at a critical time. Sara Ackerman weaves together a wonderful story about friendship and love set against the turbulence and fear of a nation at war."

—Elise Hooper, author of *Fast Girls*

"As warm as the Hawaiian sun, *Radar Girls* made me love the islands Daisy and her friends stepped up to protect in World War II. Their work to safely guide ships and planes in the Pacific theater was heroic, and one more proof that there were no 'women's' and 'men's' jobs, just a job to be done for the good of all. Brave, determined and fun, the WARDs preserved the beauty of their home, and the big-hearted generosity of the people who live there."

--Anika Scott, bestselling author of *The German Heiress*

"I loved this engaging look into a fascinating, little known slice of WW2 history, the creation of the Women's Air Raid Defense (WARD). The lush tropical paradise of Hawaii, left reeling in the aftermath of the horrifying attack on Pearl Harbor, provides the perfect setting for this captivating story of friendship, heartbreak and true love. Highly recommend!"

—Karen Robards, *New York Times* bestselling author of *The Black Swan of Paris*

Also by Sara Ackerman

Island of Sweet Pies and Soldiers
The Lieutenant's Nurse
Red Sky Over Hawaii

SARA ACKERMAN

RADAR GIRLS

mira

ISBN-13: 978-0-7783-3204-6

Radar Girls

Mira
22 Adelaide St. West, 40th Floor
Toronto, Ontario M5H 4E3, Canada
BookClubbish.com

Printed in U.S.A.

For Todd, the truest of loves,
and the WARDs, an inspiration to us all

RADAR GIRLS

1

THE SKY FALLS

December 7, 1941. Waialua, O'ahu.

On Sunday mornings, while everyone else was singing and praying to the Lord above, Daisy could be found underwater with the pufferfish and the eagle rays. Not that she had anything against God, in fact she spoke to him often, but you couldn't eat the Bible.

She stood with her toes buried in the cool sand and surveyed the water. Clouds blocked the low sun, but a few beams shot out, creating blue islands of light. The big question of the day was whether to swim toward Hale'iwa or to Mokulē'ia. A swell had filled in during the night and the low rumble of surf on the outer reef cut through the quiet. Going north would be more protected, so she decided on that.

Just before she dove in, her borrowed horse, Moon, whinnied loudly. The animal reared up, straining at the rope that tied him to the ironwood tree.

"What is it, boy?" Daisy said, looking around for any stray dogs or something that could have spooked the animal.

There was nothing out of the ordinary to be seen, just open beach and bushes. She walked back to the nervous horse and stood next to him, speaking in a calm voice. "Just relax and eat your grass. I'll be back soon."

Moon snorted and swung his head away from her. His neck was still slick with sweat from galloping down the beach. She had known he was fast, but to feel him under her bare legs like that was something different altogether. He was speed and power and grace all mixed up in one big, beautiful horse.

Daisy had taken a risk in riding him this morning. Nalu, the old horse that she often rode, had a swollen knee when she arrived at the stables. Moon happened to be in the next stall and had pranced around with a look that said, *get me out of here*. He and Daisy had developed a deep bond over the past few months, solidified by the basket of guavas that she brought to work every day. She had been itching to take him out on her own. Tall, black and spirited, Moon was without a doubt the most beautiful horse she'd ever met—and the most expensive. She was smitten, to say the least. As long as she was back before church let out, no one would ever know.

Daisy felt bad leaving the horse on the beach in an uneasy state, but she needed to be the first one out. The Chun brothers often beat her to the best spots and she wanted to give them a taste of their own medicine. Last Sunday, she had come home with an octopus, an *ulua* half as big as she was, and three lobsters. They had eaten well this week, and her mother had even put on an apron and made her famous lobster casserole. It had been a long time since she'd last made it. Daisy dared to hope that maybe her mother was turning a corner, but hope had let her down over the years.

December brought cooler water, and her skin prickled as she dived in. Visibility was only about fifteen feet because of the swell, but it hardly mattered because she knew every contour of the reef, all the resident fish families, and even the local blacktip sharks that patrolled the coastline. With each kick, the knots in her back loosened. Working six days a week took a toll on her, but who else was going to earn the money? Certainly not her mom, Louise. And without the money, there would be no food and no house.

As Daisy moved along, clouds gave way to sunlight that warmed her back. Schools of yellow tang and *manini* parted around her, glowing. Her route took her out about a hundred yards, before she veered right along a ledge that dropped onto a sandy floor. Tufts of red *limu* grew out of the cracks, and spiny *wana* dotted the coral. She kept an eye out for shell trails.

Then, all around her, the water hummed. She tasted fuel on her tongue. She popped her head up and scanned the horizon for any signs of a ship. But soon it was obvious the sound was not coming from the sea, but rather the sky. Several planes buzzed just overhead before banking and heading toward the pineapple fields. Then another. And another. Must be more military training. But on Sunday? She dived and continued on. With the swell also came current, and she fought to stay on course.

It took her twice as long to reach her destination, though along the way she plucked two hand-sized tiger cowries hiding in a crevice. Those often brought a good price. When she reached part of the reef full of lobster holes, Daisy set her spear on a coral head and put on her gloves. Lucky thing the tide was low. The first few holes were empty, but she finally caught sight of a set of spindly antennas. Her heart dropped. That hole was off-limits. Last time she'd nearly had her arm taken off by a moray eel as thick as her torso. She passed by the other holes again, stuck her hand in a few, but came up with nothing.

Hungry and tired after a long week at the ranch, she decided to head back to Moon. The current had picked up and she fought to make any headway, dreaming of scrambled eggs, steamed watercress and Portuguese sausage. As she approached the beach, the water started buzzing again. She kept swimming and kicked down after a *pāpio*. Military maneuvers had ramped up lately, but she never paid them any mind. There were more immediate things to worry about.

By now, the buzzing had turned into a deep vibration of the water all around. When she came up for air, she found a rock to stand on to see what was happening. From behind the ironwood trees, less than fifty feet over the water, a plane with red circles under its wings zoomed toward her, passing directly over her head, followed closely by an olive green plane with a white star on its side. The kind she was used to seeing—a P-40 Warhawk.

The *rat-tat-tat* of gunfire had her diving back into the water. What kind of idiots were these, shooting real guns over a residential area? Anger bunched in her chest.

Unless?

From shore came a loud whinny. She saw Moon rear up on the rope, his front hooves pawing at the air. Daisy half swam, half ran toward the beach, desperate to get to him and calm him down. The lead plane suddenly pulled up its nose, flew straight up and banked around. They were both heading back toward the shoreline, weaving only a dozen feet off the water. She dived to the bottom again and held on to a rock for as long as her lungs would allow. After coming up for air, she made a mad dash for Moon. To hell with the planes. She was almost to him when the rope snapped. She reached out, her hand closing around the frayed edge, burning as the rope slipped through. And then he was gone.

"Moon! No!" Daisy screamed.

He was tearing down the beach toward Hale'iwa at a full gallop. She took a few desperate strides after him.

Above, the two planes rolled and twisted at impossible angles. There was no mistaking the fact that this was no drill. She dived behind the massive ironwood tree, cowering in its folds. She choked on her breath. Her whole body trembled. *Stay calm.*

For a few seconds, it sounded like the planes were heading away, but moments later, they returned. She risked a peek. This time, the Japanese plane was in hot pursuit, and the P-40 had a line of smoke pouring from its engine. *Please, God, let him make it!*

They were headed right for her, yet she couldn't pull her gaze away. As the Japanese plane was steadily gaining on the Warhawk, the American pilot pulled into a barrel roll and miraculously reversed the Zero's advantage. Whoever he was, the man knew how to fly. Then, quick bursts of gunfire ripped open the Zero's fuselage and shattered the canopy. Daisy saw the Japanese pilot slump forward as his plane burst into flame and fell toward the sea. She ducked back behind the tree just as the explosion cut through the sky, rattling her teeth and piercing her ears. A loud splash and the sound of metal crashing on rock told her everything she needed to know.

She tried to stand, but her legs wouldn't lift her. In a panic, she looked down to see if she'd been hit by something. But all her body parts were intact. As she tried to catch her breath, Daisy watched the crippled P-40 skim the trees, heading toward the airstrip just down the way. She thought of the Japanese pilot, locked away in his watery grave. She thought of the American pilot, and was thankful for his survival.

And then she thought of Moon, terrified and frantic and running wild. She prayed he didn't get himself hurt. Even as it was, she would be fired. No question about that. Unless she could come up with a brilliant reason why she'd taken him—and then lost him.

Ironwood cones cut into her bare thighs. A few minutes passed, and she tried to stand again. This time, her legs obeyed and she walked out onto the beach. Not thirty feet offshore, the plane lay in several charred pieces on the reef, smoldering. The cockpit was underwater and the smell of burnt metal mixed with salt water and gasoline. She felt sick to her stomach.

Where had the Japanese plane come from? And more important, were there more? Maybe she should have paid more attention to the warnings.

She thought about going after Moon again. She owed him that much. This had happened on her watch and the poor horse had been terrified. But then she thought about her mother. Daisy took off running toward home. There was no point in trying to catch up with Moon, anyway. He would be long gone. Her mother, on the other hand, was likely to have worked herself into a bad state—if she was awake. You never knew with her.

Halfway to the house she shared with her mother, a distant roar came from somewhere behind the mountains. Or was it just the sound of huge surf that had a way of bouncing off the cliff walls?

Daisy stopped to catch her breath and make sure she wasn't imagining things. Time slowed. The beach was as lovely as ever, sand white and fine and scattered with broken shells. Ironwood and coconut trees in equal abundance rustled in the light trade winds. Squinting, she noticed a raincloud had moved off the tip of Ka'ena Point, causing a rainbow fragment to form just off the ocean.

The sound grew louder, like a swarm of bees had taken up residence between her ears. The ground began to rumble. She started off again down the beach as fast as her lungs allowed, moments before a wall of planes appeared over the Wai'anae Mountains. Some were mere feet above the cliffs while others stayed high. They were stacked and rowed so neatly, they seemed to be in a motion picture. Daisy beelined up to the trees and doubled over. She spit up salt water. Every single one of the planes had red circles painted on their wings or sides. A whole sky full of Japanese planes. Hundreds. And not one American plane in sight.

2

THE BUST

Their shack, as Daisy referred to the house, was nestled in a cluster of bent ironwood trees, all by its lonesome. Set back far from the beach to protect it from a direct blast of onshore winds, it still took a constant battering and the salty air and elements had done a fine job reclaiming it. Windowpanes had been blasted opaque, you could see through the back wall, and flowers had taken up residence in the gutters. The siding had gone from forest green to pale green to peeling gray, the roof turned to rust.

When he had first started working up at the ranch, Daisy's father had somehow persuaded Mr. Montgomery to sell him the small parcel of beachfront property for the price of a bag of sand. Most likely because it was in no-man's-land between Waialua and the ranch. And because her father had been the best horse trainer in Hawai'i and everyone knew it.

She flung open the front door and ran inside. "Mom?" she called.

All quiet. She tiptoed across the *lauhala* mat in the living room, avoiding the creaking floorboards. Her mother spent much of her life in one of two states—sleeping or staring out to sea. The bedroom door was cracked and a lump lay under the blankets, pillow over her head. There was no point in trying to wake her, so Daisy ran back outside, hopped on her bike and rode for the stables.

The air was ripe with burnt sugarcane and a scratchy feeling of dread. She bumped along a dirt road as fast as her old bike would carry her. That plume of black smoke above Schofield caused her heart to sink. So many Japanese planes could mean only one thing. An attack or invasion of some kind was happening. But the sky remained empty and she saw no signs of ships on the horizon.

By the time she reached the stables, she had worked out what to tell Mr. Silva—the only person at the ranch who was even close to being a friend—and beg that he help her find Moon. Whether or not he would risk his job was another story. Jobs were not easy to come by, especially on this side of the island. Daisy counted herself lucky to have one. When she rounded the corner by the entrance, she about fell over on her bike. Mr. Silva's rusted truck was gone and in its place sat Mr. Montgomery's shiny new Ford, motor running and door open.

As far as old Hal Montgomery was concerned, Daisy was mostly invisible. She had worked for him going on seven years now—since she was sixteen—but she was a girl and girls were fluffy, pretty things who wore fancy dresses and attended parties. Not short-haired, trouser-wearing, outdoorsy misfits. And certainly not horse trainers and skin divers. Nope, those jobs belonged to men. There was also the matter of her father's death, but she preferred not to think about that.

Should she turn around and hightail it out of there before he caught sight of her? He'd find out eventually, and he would be livid. Daisy pulled her bike behind the toolshed and slipped around the back side of the stables, peering in through a cloudy window. The tension in the air from earlier had dissipated and the horses were all quiet. A tall form stood in front of the old horse—Nalu—she was supposed to ride. It was hard to tell through the foggy pane, but the man looked too tall and too thin to be Hal Montgomery.

Horsefeathers! It was Walker, Montgomery's son. A line of perspiration formed on the back of her neck and she had the strong urge to flee. Not that Daisy had had much interaction with Walker in recent years. He was aloof and intimidating and the kind of person who made her forget how to speak, but he loved Moon fiercely. Of that she was sure. Just then, he turned and started jogging toward the door. His face was in shadow but it felt like he was looking right at her. She froze. If she ducked away now, he would surely catch the movement. She did it anyway.

She had just made it to her bike when Walker tore out of the tack room with a wild look in his eye. He had a rifle hanging across his chest, and he was carrying two others. He stopped when he saw her. "Hey!" he said.

"Oh, hello, Mr. Montgomery."

He wore his flight suit, which was only halfway buttoned, like he'd been interrupted either trying to get in it or trying to get out of it. His face was flushed and lined with sweat. "Don't you know we've been attacked? You ought to head for cover, somewhere inland."

He was visibly shaken.

"I saw the planes. What do you know?" she said.

"Wheeler and Schofield are all shot up, and they did a number on Pearl. Battleships down, bay on fire. God knows how many dead." His gaze dropped to her body for a moment and she felt her skin burn. There had been no time to change or even think about changing, and she was still in her half-wet swimsuit, hair probably sticking out in eleven directions. "What are you doing here?" he asked.

"I was worried about the horses," she said.

"That makes two of us. And goddamn Moon is not in his stall. You know anything about that?"

Taking Moon had been about the dumbest thing she could have done. But at the time, it seemed a perfectly sane idea. The kind of thinking that got her into plenty of trouble over the years. Why hadn't she learned? She looked at the coconut tree just past him as she spoke. "I have no idea. Perhaps Mr. Silva has him?"

"Mr. Silva went to town last night to see his sister," he said.

She forced herself to look at him, feeling like she had the word *guilty* inked onto her forehead. "Looks like you have somewhere to be. You go on, I'll find Moon. I promise."

Her next order of business would be scouring the coast and finding that horse before Walker returned. There would be no sleeping until Moon was safely back at the stables.

"I sure hope so. That horse is mighty important to me," he said.

Tell him!

She was about to come clean, when he moved around her, hopped in the car and slammed the door. He leaned out the window and said, "Something tells me you know more than you're letting on, Wilder."

With that, he sped off, leaving her standing in a cloud of red dirt and sand.

In the stables, the horses knew the sound of her footsteps, or maybe they smelled the salt on her hair. A concert of nickers and snorts erupted in the stalls. Daisy went to the coatrack first, and slid on an oversize button-up that she kept there for chilly days. It smelled of hay.

"How is everyone?" she said, stopping at each one to rub their necks or kiss their noses. "Quite a morning, hasn't it been?"

Peanut was pacing with nostrils flared, and she spent a few minutes stroking his long neck before moving on. Horses were her lifeblood. Feeding, grooming, riding, loving. She only wished that Mr. Montgomery would let her train them—officially, that was. Without being asked as a last resort by Mr. Silva when everyone else had tried. Lord knew she was better than the rest of the guys. When she got to Moon's stall, all the blood rushed from her head. The door had been left open and two Japanese slippers hung from the knob. She had hidden them in the corner under some straw—apparently not well enough.

Damn.

Just then she heard another car pull up. The ranch truck. A couple of the ranch hands poured out, making a beeline to the stables. Mr. Montgomery followed on their heels with a machete in his hand and a gun on his hip. Daisy felt the skin tighten on the back of her neck. His ever-present limp seemed even more pronounced.

When he saw her, he said, "Where's Silva?"

No mention that they were under attack.

"In town," she answered.

"What about Walker?"

"Walker just left in a big hurry," she answered.

One of the guys had his hunting dog with him. It was a big mutt that enjoyed staring down the horses and making them nervous, as if they needed to be any more nervous right now. Daisy wanted to tell him to get the dog out of there, but knew it would be pointless.

"The hosses in the pasture need to be secured," Mr. Montgomery said.

"Do you need my help?" she offered.

"Nah, you should get out of here. Get home. Fuckers blew up all our planes and now paratroopers are coming down in the pineapple fields. Ain't no place for a woman right now."

Daisy wanted to stay and help, but also wanted to get the hell away before he noticed that Moon was not here. "Yes, sir."

He stopped and sized her up for a moment, his thick brows pinched. "You still got that shotgun of your old man's?"

"I do."

"Make sure it's loaded."

On her way home, Daisy passed through Japanese camp, hoping to get more information from Mr. Sasaki, who always knew the latest happenings. A long row of cottages lined the road, every rock and leaf in its place. The houses were painted barn red with crisp, white trim. On any given Sunday, there would have been gangs of kids roaming the area, but now the place was eerily empty.

"Hello?" she called, letting her bike fall into the naupaka hedge.

When she knocked and no one answered, she started pounding. A curtain pulled aside and a small face peered out at her and waved her away. *Mrs. Sasaki.* She was torn, but chose to leave them be. With the whispers of paranoia lately, all the local Japanese folks were bound to be nervous. She didn't blame them.

This time when Daisy ran up to the shack, her mother was sitting on the porch drinking coffee from her chipped mug. She was still in her nightgown, staring out beyond the ocean. When she was in this state, a person could have walked into their house and made off with all of their belongings and her mother would not even bat an eye.

Daisy sat down next to her. "Mom, the Japanese Army attacked Pearl Harbor and Wheeler and who knows where else."

Her mother clenched her jaw slightly, took a sip of her coffee, then set it down on the mango stump next to her chair. "They said it would happen," she said flatly.

"This is serious, Mom. People are dead. Civilians, too. I don't know how many, but the islands are in danger of being invaded and there are Japanese ships and planes all around. They're telling us to stay inside."

A look of worry came over her mom's face. "You should go find a safer place to stay, away from the coast."

"And leave you here?"

"I'll be fine."

"I'm not leaving you."

Her mom shrugged.

She knew Louise couldn't help it, but a tiny part of Daisy was waiting for that day her mother would wake up and be the old Louise Wilder. The mother of red lipstick and coconut macaroons, of beach bonfires and salty hugs. The one who rode bikes with her daughter to school every day, singing with the birds along the way. The highs and lows had been there before, but now there were only lows and deeper lows.

After some time, her mother finally spoke. "Men, they do the dumbest things."

"That may be true, but we're at war. Does that mean anything to you?" Daisy said, her voice rising in frustration.

"Course it does, but what can we do?"

She had a point. Aside from hiding in the house or running away, what other options were there? Used to *doing* things, Daisy was desperate to help, but how? Their home was under attack and she felt as useful as a sack of dirt.

Louise leaned back. On days like these, she retreated so far into herself that she was unreachable. You could tell by looking in her eyes. Blank and bottomless. Mr. Silva always said that you could see the spirit in the eyes. Dull eyes, dull spirit. That Louise looked this way always made Daisy feel deeply alone. The onshore winds kicked up a notch and ruffled the surface of the ocean. She knew she should stay with her mom, but more than anything, she wanted to go in search of the horse. Moon meant more to her than just the job. She loved him something fierce.

Only one thing was clear: their lives would never be the same.

3

THE VISITOR

Each morning, when Daisy woke, it took a few minutes to register that her island home had been bombed and strafed and ambushed by the bulk of the Imperial Japanese Navy. Days passed in a blur. Martial law was declared and the death toll continued to rise. Worst of all was news of the youngest victim—a three-month-old baby killed by an errant bomb in Honolulu. She slept with the smell of fear and burning metal always nearby.

The first part of the day was spent scouring nearby beaches and coastline for Moon, while avoiding soldiers on patrol. Her heart was sick with guilt and worry, of war and missing horses. Mr. Silva knew the truth about Moon. She had told him the next day, unable to lie to the old man. Though she was surprised that Mr. Montgomery had not called her in yet to ask why her slippers were found in Moon's stall.

"If that horse ain't back by tomorrow, you gotta tell boss

man," Silva had said. The lie sat like a lead fishing weight in the bottom of her stomach.

Mr. Silva was the kind of old leathery cowboy you didn't argue with.

"But he'll fire me," Daisy said.

"You made your bed, girl. Talk is going around about evacuating folks to the Mainland. You and Louise would be safer there anyway."

The thought of leaving had never crossed her mind. "And you think it's safe to cross the Pacific Ocean right now? With all those submarines and who knows what else out there?" she said.

"Safer than being here."

Daisy sighed. He was probably right, as usual. And she was worried sick about Louise. If it came to running and hiding out in the hills—which was a real possibility—Daisy knew she could survive. Her mother, not a chance. Weak from lack of physical activity, thin as a reed and pale white, Louise wouldn't last a day. They had a machete, a fishing spear and a gun. A lot of good that would do.

Following Mr. Silva's advice, she rode her bike to the ranch early the next morning. Instead of turning into the stables, she followed a long drive lined with coconut trees up to the sprawling house. She'd tossed and turned all night, one minute seeing Mr. Montgomery understanding and forgiving, the next having her arrested and locked up for stealing. He was unpredictable that way.

Billy, her father, used to tell her that worry sucked the life force right out of your body. He had been full of sayings like that, and Daisy felt closer to him when she followed them, as though he was watching over her shoulder. As a girl, she had been to the Montgomery house for holidays and company barbecues, always mesmerized by the hundreds of jars of light hanging from tree branches, white-suited men strumming steel guitars and the little white pony, Taffy, who came to all their events. That all stopped after the accident.

Louise had always made a point to emphasize the word *accident*.

Daisy wiped those thoughts from her mind. She needed a clear head when facing her boss. She approached the wooden door tentatively and forced herself to knock on the smooth and solid *koa* wood. The maid directed her out back, where Hal was reading the newspaper with his morning coffee. The Montgomerys were a family of three-letter names: Hal, Peg, Dot. Only Walker was different.

Mr. Montgomery caught sight of Daisy over his paper. She saw his eyes, but then he dropped them and kept reading. Even at this hour, his mustache was waxed into place, and he was dressed in a beige linen suit. A mug of coffee steamed next to him, alongside a plate of malasadas, pineapple and Portuguese sausage. Her mouth watered.

"Good morning, sir," she said.

"You here with news?" he said, still reading.

"I came to tell you about Moon." Her heart hammered in her chest and she forced the next words out. "I rode him that Sunday morning, early. I'm so sorry, Mr. Montgomery—"

He slowly lowered the paper, and she saw genuine surprise. "You what?"

Had Walker not told him?

"Nalu was hurt and I figured I would take Moon out for a short ride, since he was antsy. But then the planes came and he spooked and took off down the beach. I never meant for this to happen."

He shook his head slowly from side to side. "You of all people know what that horse is worth, Miss Wilder. And

you thought you would just borrow him and no one would
be the wiser?"

"If the planes hadn't come—"

He stood up and faced her, eye to eye. "Looks like your
reasoning is faulty, girl, but that doesn't surprise me." He
poked a finger in her chest. "I got my people on the lookout, and they'll find him. If it turns out you did this for
the money, that little ass of yours is going straight to jail."

He may as well have slapped her. "I would never do
that!" she said.

"Regardless, count yourself out of a job. I don't toler-
ate stealing."

Though expected, the words stung. Living paycheck to
paycheck meant that she and Louise were just about out of
money. How would they get tickets to the Mainland? And
how would they survive once there?

She felt a wave of anger rise up. "You have my sincerest
apology, sir. But know this—it was an *accident*. Something
you know all about."

With that, she turned and hurried back into the house,
blinded by tears. She fumbled down the hallway. The aroma
of cinnamon wafted through the air. Turning into the
kitchen, she ran in on Mrs. Montgomery and her daughter, Peg, sitting at the table with a silver-haired man in
an army uniform. Both women looked as though they'd
come fresh from the salon, with pin-curled hair, coral lipstick and pleated skirts. The man saw her first, and raised
a thick eyebrow.

Daisy stopped short. "I'm so sorry. I was trying to find
the front door."

She spun to leave.

"Hang on," he said, and then to Mrs. Montgomery, "Is
this another daughter?"

"Lord no, she works for Hal cleaning the stables."

Worked. And she did a lot more than just cleaning the stables, though no one really cared.

"What's your name?" the man said to Daisy.

"I'm Daisy Wilder," she said, wiping the tears from her cheek and forcing a smile.

"How old are you, Miss Wilder, or is it Missus?"

"Miss. I'm twenty three, sir."

Peg waved her hand toward Daisy. "Miss Wilder is a dropout. I doubt she would be much help."

Daisy wondered what kind of help she was talking about. Ever since the sixth grade, when Daisy brought a cane toad with an injured leg into the classroom, Peg Montgomery had decided Daisy was unclean and a little too peculiar for friendship. That and the fact that Butch Anderson followed Daisy around like a baby duckling. At the time, Daisy had no interest in Butch, or boys in general for that matter, but it soon became clear that Peg did.

The man had kind eyes and a strong but quiet presence. He ignored Peg's comment and motioned to an empty chair. "Miss Wilder, come join us."

"Sir, I really should be going," Daisy said.

"Please? I was just explaining my reasons for being here to the ladies. And forgive me for not introducing myself, I'm General Danielson."

Lord, now she was trapped. Who could disobey a general? She sat down and crossed her legs, noticing for the first time a long black smear of bicycle grease on her pants. Wearing white never went well for her. She avoided eye contact with Peg and Mrs. Montgomery, instead looking at the tall glass of orange juice on the table in front of her. How she longed to gulp it down.

Danielson continued. "Now, I can't tell you much right

now, as it's highly secretive business, but I'm in need of able-bodied women that we can trust. Our boys are being shipped off for combat as we speak, and we need to replace them on the double."

"Is the work dangerous?" Peg asked.

"Not inherently, but it's technical, so we'll need you to pass some tests. And a physical."

Mrs. Montgomery patted Peg on the shoulder. "Peg here would be honored, Major. Won't you, dear?"

Peg fanned her face. Daisy was tempted to correct Mrs. Montgomery that he was a general, not a major, but held her tongue.

"So far, I have ten women committed in Honolulu, and I'm looking for twenty to start. But we'll be needing a whole lot more. How about you, Miss Wilder?"

Mrs. Montgomery coughed. "I know a bunch of women I can call. I'll have you twenty and then some rounded up by tomorrow."

"There you go, you don't need me, then," Daisy said, standing to leave. She heard a door slam and pictured the look on Mr. Montgomery's face if he found her sitting in his kitchen. It was more than she could bear.

"I think we could use you," Danielson asserted.

Daisy remained planted under his assessing gaze.

Mr. Montgomery came in, catching the tail end of the conversation. "We can get you better stock, General. Girls with a college education and a proper upbringing," he said.

A look of irritation passed over Danielson's face. "Miss Wilder looks perfectly fine to me. And you'd be surprised at how few women I've been able to round up. A good number of them already have kids, which won't work for us."

Whatever it was that Danielson needed them for, Daisy could not imagine being chosen. And yet the way the Montgomerys were all ganging up on her, making her sound like an ill-bred horse, made her want to know more.

"Can you tell us anything else?" she asked.

Mr. Montgomery shot her a look. "Miss Wilder cannot be trusted, so I think it's best she be on her way."

Danielson turned to Daisy, as if waiting for an explanation. There was no point in defending herself—not with this crowd—so Daisy turned and hightailed it out the door without another word, hopped onto her bike and flew down the drive, pedaling faster than her pounding heart. The wind felt cool against her burning face. All she could think about was getting home, packing their bags and looking for passage to the Mainland. She was done here, and the sooner they left town the better.

Once she made it a safe distance away, she slowed her pace. The flatlands here in Mokulēʻia soaked up the morning sun like a brick oven and her blouse stuck to her back. Even in December, the heat could be brutal. Just before town, she stopped under a monkey pod tree for a moment of shade and to collect herself. The horses and the ranch had been her life and she couldn't imagine her world without them. Also, being there tethered her to her father in a way that nothing else could.

She was off in a daydream, and hardly noticed the jeep approaching until it was upon her, a hair too late to duck off into the cane fields. Instead, she leaned over and pretended to fiddle with her shoe.

The car slowed and then came to a stop. "Miss Wilder, we meet again."

She looked up. "Sir."

General Danielson climbed out, leaned against the car and lit a cigarette. The smoke hung all around his face in the windless air. "Sounds to me like you could use a job about now."

She forced herself to meet his gaze. "You don't want me."

"What I want is to hear what happened with that horse straight from your mouth. There are always two sides to a story," he said, looking genuinely curious.

Daisy told him the blunt truth.

When she finished, he cocked his head. "Sounds like an honest mistake with no harm intended. Now, when I see a woman who works hard to earn a living—and I can tell by your hands that you do—I tend to pay attention. I'm looking for gals *exactly* like you."

She shrugged. "The work I do is simple."

"Can I give you a tip?" he said.

Clearly he was going to whether she liked it or not. "Sure."

"Don't believe everything you hear about yourself. It tends to be false."

She looked at him more closely, his creased forehead and thin lips. "I appreciate the offer, sir, but my mother and I will be evacuating to the Mainland, where it's safer. My mother isn't well and she needs me."

"You have a ticket already?" he asked.

"Not yet."

"Do you have any other family to help with your mom?"

The term *family* always filled Daisy with longing. When you lived in a place where four generations of people spilled out the windows of tiny plantation homes, you got a real taste of what the word meant. Daisy had none of that. Just a mother with an incurable sadness and some aunt in California whom she'd never met.

"Maybe."

"Well, maybe I could help you arrange passage for her?"

"Sorry, General. I need to go with her."

He looked her up and down, not in that way that some men did. She could tell he was simply taking stock. She suddenly felt self-conscious of her grease-smeared pants that fell inches too short, and the blouse with mismatched buttons.

"What if I told you the pay is good—$140 a month. You'll get your meals *and* you'll be considered an officer."

That got her attention.

"Excuse me?"

"You heard me, miss. Not only will you be serving your country, you'll be paid well to do so."

Double her salary at the ranch. Maybe she could build up a small savings. But could she send Louise off on her own? Granted, her aunt had been asking them to come for a long time now. "Can I think about it?" she said.

"This is important work, something you will always be proud of. Let me know by tomorrow. Here's my number."

As it turned out, there wasn't much thinking to do. She felt needed in a way she never had before. This was a chance of a lifetime to prove herself worthy, and she couldn't pass it up.

4

THE DEPARTURE

On a bright and sunny Christmas Day, Daisy stood with her mother on the docks at Honolulu Harbor. Instead of being serenaded with music and flower leis, the passengers—all women and children evacuees—were herded onto the SS *Lurline* like cattle. There were also wounded men carried in on stretchers. The ship's white hull had been painted battleship gray and converted to a troop ship almost overnight. In order to avoid torpedoes, the ship would follow a zigzag pattern across the Pacific. The Matson freighter *Lahaina* had been destroyed by a submarine the previous week, making everyone even more anxious than they already were.

Up until now, so much time had been spent readying her mother for the move, Daisy had scarcely had time to think about it. Though now, seeing Louise with her patched purse and red lipstick——something she hadn't worn in years—she looked like a child playing dress-up. The thought of Louise all alone on the crossing took the air right out of Daisy's lungs. Who knew if it was the right thing to do, but plans had already been made and they'd come this far. Daisy hugged her. "I'll come and get you when this is over. I promise."

Her mother had come alive some in the past days, being stubborn and ornery about what she wanted to bring. This was the most opinionated Daisy had seen her in years, and she prayed that it kept up. She'd take pigheaded over apathy any day.

Louise placed her hands on Daisy's cheeks, and looked up into her eyes. There was a light tremor in her touch. "Don't you worry about me. You just do your best at whatever this new job is and help win this war, you hear me?"

Her job over the past decade had been to worry about her mother, so not worrying would be like not breathing.

"I love you, Mom," Daisy said, pressing her face into Louise's freshly washed hair and inhaling hints of rose and beeswax. Her mother's hair had always been thick and blond with the perfect amount of wave, even in her decline. A sad reminder of what she'd once been, when women wanted to *be* her, and men plain old wanted her. When they finally pulled apart, Daisy turned and ran the whole way back to the train station, the loss pressing in on all sides.

This Christmas would be the worst on record, if you didn't count the year her father died. There were no Christmas lights in Waialua streets, no Douglas fir trees, and all the poinsettias in town sat on newly dug graves instead of tabletops. News had also been trickling in about more and more local Japanese civilians being rounded up and put in what they were calling camps. Some were told to leave their farms or be shot, while others were pulled out of classrooms and homes at all hours of the day and night.

With nothing to celebrate, Daisy instead took the time

to scour the shack. She washed all the linens, scrubbed the wooden floorboards, hosed down the *lauhala* mats, tidied up her mother's room and put away the clutter that tended to accumulate over the course of just one day while she was away at the stables. There was now a strange emptiness, an indentation in the air where her mother had once dwelled. A house takes on the personality of its inhabitants, and Daisy felt almost disrespectful to relocate things or throw them out. But Louise was gone and everything was about to change.

The new year seemed like it would never come, and yet now that it had, Daisy paced back and forth on the deck second-guessing her outfit and worrying about the so-called intelligence test all the girls would have to take. She looked at her watch. General Danielson had said he'd arrange for transport, and now that transport was late.

Dressed in her only skirt, a pleated number with a coffee stain hidden between the folds, and a white buttoned blouse, she wished she was wearing pants. Her blond hair was cut short, above her shoulders, and she had tried to pin some curls into it last night, but rinsed them in the morning because they were all going in opposite directions. On the rare occasion that she ever curled her hair, she'd had her mother to help her.

Out front, an early morning rain squall hung over the water, cloud tops tinged pink from the sun. The seas had flattened out, reflecting the clouds back up to the moody sky. Normally, she would be on her way to the ranch, and she longed to go back. She missed the horses and Mr. Silva. Working with animals came naturally to her. Working with people did not. Where might Moon be at this very moment? Anyone who knew horses would know he was something special, and anyone on this side of the island was likely to know he belonged to Mr. Montgomery. Which made her wonder: Where the hell was Moon?

Daisy wished she could drive herself to town. The Wilders did own a car, but it sat rusted in the carport with four flat tires and a dead motor. It had been her father's, but Louise was not able to keep it running and eventually she gave up. Daisy always intended to fix it, but she never had the time.

An engine cut through the lull of the shore break, and a moment later a red Pontiac pulled up the drive and into the yard. A horn blasted. Daisy peered over the railing and then jumped back and flattened herself against the wall. The Montgomerys. Danielson must have some clout, but there was no way she could endure a ride to Honolulu with Walker Montgomery and his sister. Absolutely not. She'd have to feign ill. The horn honked again. She considered running down the beach and into the water instead of climbing in the car with those two, but then she thought of General Danielson and his kind way. Of his reassurance that he did in fact need her.

You can do this.

Daisy hurried to the car. "Are you my ride?"

Walker glanced around the yard. "You see anyone else around here? Hop in, we're late."

She did as told, sliding onto the soft leather seat. Peg did not turn around but Daisy thought she might have mumbled a *hello*. Thankfully, the motor was loud enough that it would be hard to speak over, and the car creaked and groaned as they bounced along the unpaved driveway faster than was prudent. She kept trying to think of something reasonable to say but could not find any words.

Peg wore her hair rolled up on both sides and Daisy wondered how long it had taken her to get ready. She tried not to look at Walker, but failed. His shoulders took up half of the front seat, and he chewed his gum in double time. He was one of those men born with an overabundance of everything manly. Dark five-o'clock shadow even after he'd just shaved, square jaw, low radio-announcer voice and hands the size of baseball mitts. When he turned his face one way or the other, his olive skin glowed in the sunlight. Daisy looked away.

Walker had always been *that older Montgomery boy*, the one every young girl on their side of the island had a hankering for. He could throw a football farther, ride a horse faster, shoot a gun straighter than the other boys. Daisy had always avoided him because he was the only boy who caused her heart rate to jump, and she did not like the feeling. The bottom line was simple: Walker was 100 percent off-limits.

They passed through town, snaked their way up Kaukonahua Road and came upon Schofield Barracks—which still carried the scent of burning buildings. Daisy had not been here since the bombing, and could not tear her eyes away. Wheeler Field was a black mess of airplane carcasses and splintered hangars. The runway had been cleared, but there were still damaged planes everywhere.

"Unbelievable," Daisy said to no one in particular.

Walker met her gaze in the rearview mirror. "Thirty-six men killed and a whole lot more wounded. A boatload of aircraft destroyed. Those Japs knew exactly where to hit us."

"All that black…" she said, remembering how the smoke over Wahiawa had nearly blotted out the sun.

She knew from the boys at the ranch that Walker had broken his hand during a polo match and had been unable to ship out with the *Enterprise*. He was now on desk duty, which he said he hated. Thank goodness all the carriers had been at sea during the attack.

Peg reached over and put a hand on Walker's shoulder. "My big brother here singlehandedly took down one of those fighters, and nearly crashed into our house while doing so."

Daisy perked up, leaning forward. "Wait, were you in one of the P-40s that took off from Haleʻiwa?"

"I was."

It felt good to finally have something to say. "There was a gunfight between one of those pilots and a Japanese warplane directly over my head while I was diving. The Japanese plane fell not thirty feet away from me. I can't believe that was you," Daisy said, every detail etched in her mind.

"Believe it," he said.

She almost mentioned Moon being spooked by the planes but thought the better of it. "I'm no expert in air combat, but that was some impressive maneuvering."

"Walker is good at everything," Peg said.

"How did you know to be up there?" Daisy asked.

"My buddy PJ called in a panic and told me about the bombing, how all our fighters at Wheeler had been nailed and wanting to know about Haleʻiwa. Turns out he and a friend had flown their P-40s out there the day before and left them. I told him to meet me as fast as he could get there."

Daisy remembered his disheveled look that morning at the stables. "So after that fight, you drove to the stables? How did you fly with your hand?"

"I did what I had to. And I had to grab the guns. At that point I had no idea it was too late. We all thought they were coming back."

That was the curious thing—that the Japanese Navy had not returned yet.

"General Danielson seems to think it's just a matter of time. It's why he needs us," Daisy said.

Peg shot her a look. "I wouldn't get your hopes up. My friend Helen's uncle knows a thing or two about what we'll be doing. The work is technical and mathematical and you need to be sharp as a brand-new razor, he says."

"Aren't you a little nervous, then?" Daisy asked.

From what she remembered, Peg had nice penmanship but she was far from the brightest girl in class. The words seemed to fly right over her head.

"Today's meeting is just informational, and for weeding out gals who are not fit," Peg said.

Walker fiddled with the radio but didn't say anything. Daisy rolled her window down all the way, letting the cool wind blast her face. More than anything, she wanted to apologize to Walker for stealing his horse. But not in front of Peg, not now. She let her mind wander to the mysterious assignment ahead and if she would be cut out for it. She could gallop a horse bareback, but give her a written test and she'd break out in a cold sweat and forget her own name. Failing the test would be a horrible embarrassment, a disaster.

They rode in a painful silence much of the way, until Peg said to her brother, "Thelma's going to be there, did she mention that?"

"Nope. Haven't spoken in a while."

"Don't let that one slip away, Walker."

"Lay off, Sis. I have enough to worry about right now."

Daisy kept her focus on the pineapple cannery out the window, but her ears were tuned in. The car accelerated some and Walker turned up the radio. Peg gave him a sideways glance and shook her head. Daisy got to wondering: *What kind of woman would land Walker Montgomery?*

5

THE PALACE

Walker let them out at 'Iolani Palace, which was a good twenty minutes out of his way. Peg gave him a peck on the cheek, then marched right past Daisy toward the Palace, not saying a word. Daisy felt like a servant or an obedient dog as she trailed after her. She smoothed her stained skirt and hoped for the best.

The Palace stood like a stone fortress, with layers of history folded into each rock. As they walked across the threshold, Daisy felt the hairs on her arm stand on end. Once a home for the queens and kings of Hawai'i, it later became a prison for Queen Liliuokalani during the overthrow, and now was being used by the military for secret trainings. A sense of importance hung in the air, of grand things past and present. It was an honor to be here, that was for certain.

They were directed to a room with blackout boxes in the windows and armed guards by the doors. It felt like a strange place to be training to serve the American government. There was a musty smell to the place that was partly masked by a roomful of women wearing perfume. Daisy hated perfume. It made her nose tickle and her eyes run.

Peg seemed to know everyone, and hugged and kissed most of the women there. They were a well-dressed bunch, with hats and rolled-up hair and loads of lipstick and stylish A-line dresses. But what stood out the most was their whiteness. Living in Waialua, Daisy was used to being surrounded by Japanese, Chinese, Portuguese, Filipino and Hawaiian neighbors. Here, there were only a few—though no Japanese women—and being surrounded by so many *haole* felt foreign.

After signing in, she walked straight to the back of the room, avoiding all eye contact as she went. There was one open chair between a Chinese woman in a sky blue *mu'umu'u* and a fresh-faced beauty who looked like she could have still been in high school. They both nodded as Daisy sat. The chattering of women's voices reminded her of the school cafeteria, a place where she hated going because she never knew where to sit and half the time ended up outside eating alone under the big old monkey pod tree.

The woman in the *mu'umu'u* stuck out her hand and said, "I'm Lei Davis. I haven't seen you around."

Daisy shook. "I live all the way out in Waialua. Pleased to meet you. I'm Daisy Wilder."

"And here I thought I knew everyone in this town."

Lei was the kind of woman who might have been twenty-four or thirty-four, her skin was that luminous. Daisy could go only by her confident demeanor, which leaned toward mature.

The other girl, who looked part Hawaiian, gave her a wide smile with two perfect dimples and bright red lips. "Gosh you're tall. You look like a swimmer."

"I do swim, but I'm not a swimmer."

The girl gave her a funny look, then laughed. "That sounds like a paradox to me. By the way, I'm Fluff Kanahele, and I'm studying to be an English teacher—or at least I was, before this whole calamity happened."

A moment later, General Danielson and another man strode in and the conversations ceased. Daisy felt jittery but also excited to finally learn what was in store.

Danielson made it a point to slowly look around, as though memorizing every face in the room. "As you already know, we are here to take over for the men who are needed on the front lines. Each and every one of you is going to be doing some of the most important work any woman in this nation has ever done. But before we go any further, I need you all to take an oath of secrecy. What you'll be learning is highly confidential and should it fall into the wrong hands, devastating. This means no talking about what you do outside of this room. Not even to family. You are to tell anyone who asks that you are simply doing clerical work. Period."

A lady in the front raised her hand. "Even our husbands?"

"Even your husbands. Does anyone have a problem with that?" he said.

No one uttered a word.

"Good, I thought so. As a few of you already know, you will be working in the Air Defense Command Center at Fort Shafter. For now, we're calling it the Women's Air Defense. You will be a detachment of Company A, Signal Aircraft Warning Regiment, Special by Executive Order 9063. This here is Major Hochman. He'll be training you today on the plotting board."

He gestured to the man next to him and then toward the large round table in the center of the room, with a map of the Hawaiian Islands painted across its surface. Daisy had been wondering about it and how it played into their work. So this was a plotting board. But what exactly were they plotting?

Major Hochman, a redhead with a smattering of freckles, greeted them in a Southern lilt, "Thank y'all for being here. I imagine you have a lot of questions, so bear with me. We're going to get you up to speed on everything you never knew you needed to know about radar and keeping our skies and waters safe." He laughed at himself. "That was a mouthful. But in all seriousness, your being here is essential to the war effort, so don't you forget that."

Being acknowledged as essential was a new feeling for Daisy. She liked this man. He was a different breed from many of the men she worked with, who saw her more as an ancillary being rather than of central importance. And Mr. Montgomery himself would not be caught dead calling her *essential*.

He went on, "You'll be learning to take radar readings and keep close tabs on every moving object out there. Not even a mosquito is going to get past us this time. And don't you worry, we know that none of you have experience with radar. Hell, we are still learning about it ourselves."

That got a few sighs of relief. He then called on three women in the front row to stand. "Now, a few procedural things to get out of the way. These are your supervisors, Joyce Bird, Tippy Sondstrom and Vivian DuPont. They've had some forward training and will be assisting as you learn. Today they'll be fitting you for your uniforms."

Fluff said aloud what Daisy was thinking. "Why would they fit us before even testing us?"

"It seems backward," Daisy said.

Lei shrugged. "I doubt they have a bunch of dresses lying

around. Maybe they need time to sew them? They're thinking ahead, at least."

"Whatever the reason, I'm glad they have faith in us," Daisy said.

The women were dressed sharply in navy blue dresses. As far as uniforms went, they looked like something Daisy wouldn't mind wearing. They had plenty of pockets and a nice fitted waist. Not a whole lot of extra material and frills. There were all shapes and sizes here, though Daisy could already tell she was the tallest.

"You're like a giraffe," Tippy said cheerfully, as she wrapped a tape measure around Daisy's bust, at her eye level.

Daisy gave her a wide smile and said, "And you're like a pony."

That shut her up fast. People always commented on Daisy's height, as if they had a God-given right. But you never heard anyone saying, *Why, look how short you are!*

Next, they posed for photos for their identification badges. "You will wear your badge at all times while on duty, which commences now," said General Danielson.

He then handed out civil service applications and pens. "You ladies will be considered officers."

"How can we be officers without any military training?" a brunette with a neat bob asked.

Hochman glanced over at Danielson, who said, "Mainly for your safety. If captured by the enemy, they will have to treat you according to international prisoner of war standards."

A few murmurs rose.

Hochman held his hand up. "Not that we expect that to happen. What we're doing here will see to it. Next time those Japs come our way, we'll be waiting. This new technology is going to help us win this war, my friends."

He gave them time to fill out their applications.

What about the test? None of this mattered unless she could pass the test. Her palms began to heat up.

Instead of raising her hand, she asked Lei, "Do you know anything about this intelligence test they're supposed to give us?"

"I know we have to pass an Intelligence background check, and an army physical. But no one said anything about a test."

"Wait a minute, there's no test?"

"These men are desperate for help, so I doubt it."

Daisy could hardly believe her good fortune, but it sounded too good to be true. She raised her hand. "Excuse me, sir. Will we be taking an intelligence test?"

Everyone in the room, including Peg and Thelma Bird— whom Daisy had seen only in newspaper photographs— turned around to look at her. Peg whispered something to Thelma and they both laughed. Thelma was a curvy blonde who looked like she belonged in Hollywood. Her polka-dotted dress bunched around her bust and her rear end in a way that Daisy's never would.

"You'll be taking an exam tomorrow. But don't you worry, we will be training y'all in everything you need to know. Some of you may find that you're naturals at the plotting and filtering, and those who aren't, well, there's more than enough work to go around."

Daisy could have sworn she heard Peg say, "Good luck."

Her cheeks burned and that old familiar feeling of failure lodged in her throat.

They wasted no time getting down to business, and Major Hochman arranged the women around the table alphabetically. There were twenty in all and they went around and introduced themselves, beginning with Jo Ann

Abramson from Nuʻuanu, who'd hid out in her basement with her dog, Lucy, for two days before her husband finally returned, to Betty Yates from Louisiana, who lived in the navy yard. Some of the women were married to prominent businessmen, a few were military wives whose husbands had recently been deployed, and others were students at the University of Hawaiʻi, like Fluff.

Betty ended the round of introductions by saying, "As soon as Indochina was seized, my husband, Chuck, and I knew this was coming. We got ready for it as best we could, collecting food and blankets, even whiskey. But I'll tell you what. Nothing could have prepared me for seeing what I've seen in the past two weeks. That first day I followed a truck full of bodies stacked like logs. They had been burned to a crisp and smeared in oil. None of these boys deserved such a horrific death, and I will do whatever is asked of me to prevent another attack like this on our soil." Tears streamed down her face.

Daisy fought back a sob. She had been spared from seeing much of the death and destruction, but that raw terror of the dogfight overhead, and of being within a stone's throw of the fiery crash, had left her with a heavy feeling of unease that pressed in from all sides when she least expected it.

A few of the other women nodded and Libby Fontaine added, "A bomb went right through my neighbor's roof, killing their son and taking the arm of their eleven-year-old daughter. This was in Mānoa, mind you, far from any military bases. You bet I will fight however I can."

"Me, too! I'm a crack shot with a rifle and I'll take down as many of those bastards as I can," said Rita with fire in her eyes.

The room buzzed. Their determination was catching and Daisy felt the stirrings of something like hope. These women meant business. The lives of their families were at stake. Major Hochman looked nervous to interrupt, but did so anyway. "Ladies, I like your gusto, but we need to get started. There's a whole lotta information to impart."

It took a little while, but the group settled.

"Now, how many of you know anything at all about radar, or have even heard of it?" he asked.

A few women raised their hands tentatively. Daisy was one of them. She had her fascination with Amelia Earhart to thank for that. Last year, she had hung on every word about how the Brits defeated the Luftwaffe by using this fancy new technology. They had known the Germans were coming, and that changed the course of everything. She also knew that the Hawker Hurricane and Spitfire took down a large number of Heinkels and Messerschmitts, but now was not the time to announce that.

Hochman continued. "For those of you who don't know, RADAR stands for *radio detection and ranging*. This is revolutionary, gals. Using radio waves, we can detect aircraft in the sky and ships on the horizon and in general any moving object within a certain range. I'll get into the technical details soon, but on O'ahu alone, we have six stations set up around the island. These stations are sending us information and you are going to be using it to track any and all incoming aircraft."

Thelma raised her hand. "What about ships? Will we be tracking ships, too? Seeing as it was the ships that brought the planes that attacked us." She seemed very pleased with herself for asking such a smart question. Daisy knew it was unreasonable and premature, but she did not like the woman one bit.

"Our radar can detect ships and planes, both." Just then, a tall, dark-haired officer came in and was introduced as

Captain Tet Burgess, the man responsible for getting all the radar stations up and running on the island in record time. "He'll be helping me get y'all oriented today."

Captain Burgess was a bit standoffish and gave off a threatened scent. Maybe it was the ratio of women to men in the room. Daisy had a hard time focusing on anything other than his immense, hawk-like nose. Together, the two men went back and forth rattling off information about the radar stations and their locations—Kawailoa, Opana, Ka'a'awa, Koko Head, Wai'anae and Fort Shafter, which would also be headquarters. They pointed these places out on the giant map on the table, which was overlaid with a large grid.

"The numbers on this vertical axis are your corridors and the coded names there on the horizontal axis are your latitude. When a plane is picked up by one of our receiving units, they will call it in and you will be placing an arrow on the table to mark its location using one of these," Burgess said.

He picked up a metal pole with a rubber tip at the end of it. It reminded Daisy of a shuffleboard stick, not that she ever played, but she watched the men at the stables now and then. Mr. Montgomery loved shuffleboard, which meant everyone had to.

"Now, a few of you are sitting where there's a headset. You ladies will go first. Who has one?"

Daisy looked down. Just her luck, there on the edge of the table was a headset with a mic attached, the kind Mrs. Freitas, the telephone operator, wore. "I do," she said reluctantly.

"Good. Now, what's your name?" he asked.

"Daisy Wilder, sir."

"Miss Wilder, you will practice receiving a radio reading from an Oscar—which is code for the radar fellas at our stations—and you will be plotting it."

"Do we have a code name?" Daisy asked.

Major Hochman, who was leaning against a pillar, said, "You ladies are Rascals. Code name, that is."

Some of the women giggled. Peg and Thelma exchanged looks. "Perfect," Thelma said.

Thelma was the kind of woman who had probably never gone without. The kind who grew up with a mom *and* a dad, most likely a houseful of siblings, with dogs and horses and peacocks running loose on their beachfront estate. Girls like that could afford to be rascals.

Hochman emphasized. "Again, this stays in the room. Everything stays in the room. I know that women like to talk, but these are different times."

Assent came from all corners of the room.

"Of course!"

"Our lips are sealed."

"Never."

Daisy surveyed the table. Running north to south, the areas between the gridlines were marked with a number, east to west a name. *Martha, Nathan, Omega* and so on. She wondered how they arrived at their code words. Any location in the whole island chain could be easily narrowed down to a position within the grid. She looked for her house in Waialua. It fell in the tiny square of *12 Martha*, and here in Honolulu, they were *16 Nathan*. Maybe she could do this after all.

"So here are the very basics. You will get a call from an Oscar telling you that an aircraft has been picked up, and its location." He held up a small plastic green arrow. "This goes where the coordinates are. Green means you received the reading within five minutes. You'll change the arrow to yellow at ten minutes and red at fifteen. Shall we try it?"

The phone in front of Daisy's lap rang, causing her to jump. "Hello?" she said into the receiver.

The other women were watching her intently, as if their lives depended on what she did next. She had never been a big fan of speaking on the telephone, but that would have to change.

A deep voice said, "Rascal, this is Oscar at Koko Head. We have a bogey at 12 Clementine. Visual says it is a P-40 Warhawk, bearing southwest. Over."

When Daisy went to speak, nothing came out. Her mind had gone dry.

"Do you read me, Rascal?" he said.

She looked to Hochman, who nodded encouragingly. How on earth was she supposed to respond? When her voice finally returned, she said, "Thank you, Oscar. Will that be all?"

Where had that come from? Was she taking lunch orders?

"Affirmative. Oscar out."

She set a green arrow on the map and pushed it out with a poker to the grid that matched 12 Clementine, fiddling with it until it pointed southwest. Her hand shook slightly. "Here you go."

Burgess sighed, as though she was a lost cause. "Remember to answer with, 'Army, go ahead, please.'"

Give me a break, she wanted to say. "Yes, sir."

"And if the response does not begin with the word *flash*, then you respond, 'You have been connected with the wrong number. Please hang up and make your call again.'"

Hochman then took over. "Next we need to see if we can identify the aircraft. You will tell your shift supervisor, who will give the info to Major Oscar. Major Oscar oversees the whole room and he—or she—will consult with liaisons from the navy, marines, army and everyone else who has planes flying in these islands. If it can't be positively identified, we sound the air-raid alarm and send out the fighters. Got that?"

Thelma went next, and didn't fare much better. She answered fine, but kept saying the names and numbers backward. And when it came to Fluff's turn, she threw in a little chitchat with the Oscar, to which Burgess said, "Business only."

Afterward, Fluff looked around and said, "We're off to a great start!" and Daisy realized she was serious.

And so it continued. More calls and plotting and practicing moving the pips. A pip consisted of a five-sided block marked with altitudes, a square block that indicated the aircraft type, and a green-and-red arrow on top that signaled whether the plane in question had been seen or heard, or both. They learned the exact locations of the radar stations, and about corridors where planes would likely be coming from, though that was tricky to predict. They were told that, with experience, many of them would move up in the ranks to a position known as filterer. Daisy had no idea what a filterer was, but she decided then and there that she wanted to become one.

By the time afternoon rolled around, Daisy's brain hurt from such intense concentration. That and being around so many people at once. Everyone was on their best behavior, but personalities were squeaking through. There was the one girl who could not refrain from raising her hand and asking question after question. Daisy wanted to strap her arm to the table. Another insisted on telling whoever had the poker stick where to place the arrow. She simply could not stand to watch anyone fumble. And then there was Thelma, who thought the whole room ought to know every minute detail of her life. That her Chihuahuas were named Snap, Crackle and Pop; that she was allergic to shellfish and had been covered in hives on the morning Pearl Harbor had been bombed; and especially that Walker Montgomery was soon to be her man.

Just before leaving, they were issued gas masks and helmets that should be carried with them and stored carefully while at work. The masks were uncomfortable contraptions that strapped onto your face and had a can dangling beneath them. Just looking at them made Daisy short of breath. They were also given badges—number twenty-two for Daisy—and an armband that said *noncombatant.*

General Danielson told them as they walked out the door, "Rest up, eat a healthy breakfast and be ready to take the test at 1000 hours."

6

THE DRIVER

Outside the Palace, Daisy had to squint into the afternoon sun, which was blinding after being in a darkened room much of the day. The light slanted through a banyan tree and a troupe of mynah birds screeched and squawked, oblivious to the fact that their home was now a war-torn state. She wondered how many birds and fish and animals had been casualties of the attack. Nobody mentioned those in the papers.

Walker was waiting out front right where he had dropped them. He was staring straight ahead and unaware of all the women streaming around the car. Daisy trailed behind Thelma and Peg, enjoying the warm feeling of fresh air on her skin. When they reached the car, Peg went around to the passenger side, Daisy opened the back door and Thelma said, "Walker?"

Only then did he turn. "Hey there, Thelma."

He didn't get out, didn't say anything else, just awkwardly sat there.

"Did you fly today?" Thelma asked, standing close to his window and twirling a piece of hair.

"Nah, we had ground training. New planes."

"Will you be staying here in Hawai'i or leaving?"

Walker started the car. "It all depends," he said.

Thelma seemed desperate to keep the conversation going. She bent over, showing a valley of cleavage. "Well, now we'll be helping keep you boys safe."

"Glad to hear it. Say, we need to get going," he said, starting up the car.

"I'd love to—"

"See you later," he said, waving as they drove off. As much as Daisy was not taken with Thelma, she felt a tad sorry for her. The least Walker could have done was get out and show a little affection. Wasn't that what boyfriends did? Though Daisy wouldn't know firsthand because she had never officially had one. Peg swatted as him. "That wasn't very nice."

"What?"

"You haven't even seen her since the attack. You should have greeted her properly."

He shrugged. "I said hello."

"Come on, be a gentleman. You know how she feels about you."

He stepped on the gas. "Lay off, would you? I'm not in the mood."

Peg didn't push it. And Daisy could have sworn his neck flushed red as the fish scales in her freezer. She enjoyed the breeze, pressed against the leather seat as they raced along Kam Highway going twice the normal speed. Was this how all pilots drove?

By the time they reached Wahiawa, she felt herself nodding off. For the sake of not looking like a fool, she tried to stay upright and alert, but her head felt so good resting on the soft headrest. The past few weeks of being on edge all day and tossing and turning all night were catching up. What seemed like a few seconds later, she felt something moving up her leg. She froze. The room was dark, and there was someone standing over her, whispering in Japanese. He was tapping her with his rifle. In one motion, she slapped the gun away and tried to roll out the bed.

"Whoa, whoa, whoa, take it easy! You're dreaming, Daisy."

Her eyes shot open. *Oh God.* Walker had his arm slung over the seat and was looking at her with concern.

She wiped her chin and bolted upright. "I'm sorry, I fell asleep. I thought you were—"

"You're home, you're safe," he said. "Don't worry, we're all having nightmares and we're all exhausted."

For the first time, she noticed the shadows beneath his eyes, and a hollow red-rimmed sadness in his face. Daisy scooped up her helmet and her gas mask and slid to the door, wondering why he was being nice to her.

"Thanks for the ride. What time should I be ready in the morning?"

"I have to go in early, so we'll be leaving here at five."

Peg groaned, but early mornings were Daisy's favorite. Everything was calm—the water, the horses, the sky. It was the reverse of sunset, and she loved watching the colors turn from ink to orange to blue. And anyway, she could use the extra time at the Palace to study. "See you then," she said.

Instead of going inside, she kicked off her shoes, tossed her stuff into the grass and ran down to the beach. Gray storm clouds filled the Kaua'i Channel and she guessed she had about ten minutes before the rain hit. By habit now, she scanned the sky for planes, but saw none. At the water's edge, she stood up to her ankles and felt her worries drain out into the wet sand. Warm foam tickled her legs. One thing she loved about the ocean was its ability to always soothe her. Calm water, choppy water, cold water, warm water. All liquid forms of salvation.

Old horse blankets now hung over her bedroom, bathroom and kitchen windows, so Daisy was able to turn on the light and cook dinner and take showers at night. It had taken her a while to nail them down so not one speck of light escaped. Living on the beach on the north side of O'ahu, she didn't want to be responsible for guiding any enemy planes ashore. She'd left the living room windows alone, unable to cover the view of the ocean and the jalousie windows that let the breeze wash through the house. Most of the time, she now slept in the living room with the baseball bat and shotgun by her side.

Loneliness moved in at night, sending roots down through the floorboards and into the soil beneath the house. As poor a companion as Louise had been, her presence was a trusty backdrop. Another soul, always around. The world felt strangely void with her mother away.

Without fail, every morning, Mr. Macadangdang's roosters woke Daisy up at four ten on the nose. Today was no different. She rolled over and looked out the big window. The darkness was absolute. No stars, no moon, no sky. How would they make it to town in the dark without headlights? She hadn't thought about that yesterday. Civilians were not to be out on the roads unless they were on official business, so she was lucky to ride with Walker. You had to be ready to show your identification card if stopped. And the threat of being shot was still a reality. Following the rules was now essential.

After looking through her wardrobe, Daisy realized her mother had never hemmed her other skirt. So all she had were pants. None of the women had worn pants yesterday and she could bet that none of them would be caught dead wearing pants today, or ever. Well, too bad, Daisy had nothing else to wear. She picked out a red-checkered blouse to go with her slacks, but she looked too much like a sailor or a barmaid. Instead, she opted for a green-and-yellow floral top that highlighted the gold in her hair.

Before all of this happened, in the mornings, after a quick dip in the ocean, she got dressed without a care in the world. Horses didn't mind whether you were in a dress or a burlap sack. Slacks, button-up work shirt and a shake of her head. Cutting her hair short had been one of the more liberating things she'd done in her life. Poor Louise had cried when Daisy came out of the bathroom, scissors still in hand, mounds of hair on the floor. She had been sixteen.

"This is all because of that damn Amelia Earhart woman, isn't it?"

That December, the whole island had been abuzz about the lady pilot who had arrived on the SS *Lurline* with her own airplane. Rumors swirled that she was going to attempt a solo flight to California, though she neither confirmed nor denied them. Instead, she paraded around the islands on her own terms. Daisy had listened to her radio broadcast from the University of Hawai'i, and had been instantly drawn in. A woman who made her own rules. On January 11, when the paper announced her takeoff time would be 4:40 a.m. and she was really doing it, Daisy listened to her reports from across the Pacific every half hour that "everything is okay." She suddenly had a new hero, a woman to look up to.

When Walker rolled in, Daisy was waiting in the dark, tracing constellations with her eyes. All clouds had cleared the sky and stars shone like tiny fireflies. The upper two-thirds of his headlights had been covered over, dimming them to small slits. A small swath of hazy light shone out. She dashed over and opened the back door.

He surprised her by saying, "Peg is home sick, why don't you sit up front?"

Her mind raced to find a solution. Maybe she should tell him she had come down with a god-awful stomach bug. Or that she had found another ride later on, so she wouldn't have to wait so long at the Palace. But then she'd be stuck here and in grave trouble for not showing up for duty.

"If you insist," she said.

Inside the car, she pulled her sweater tight around her. The morning had a chill to it and now she felt even colder. Being around Walker tended to blank out her thoughts, and now was no different. She sat there like a mute fish, every now and then opening her mouth to say something but nothing came out. Soon, her cheeks started heating up, then her neck, and then the backs of her arms.

"Do you have the heater on?" she finally asked.

"No, do you want it on?"

Maybe she was coming down with something. "That would be nice, thank you. So what's the matter with Peg?" she asked.

"A bad bout of asthma. Every time she tried to stand, her lungs seized and she turned blue in the face."

Daisy frowned. "How awful. Is there something she can take?"

"She inhales Adrenalin, but it turns her a bit wild and then she sleeps for a whole day."

"Has she always had it?"

"Always. It gets worse when she's nervous."

Daisy was glad she didn't have asthma, or she'd likely be on the floor right now, dead. "I'm sure the war doesn't help matters. And this new job."

"And the test. I know she was worried about the test."

She turned to him. "Really? She seems so self-assured."

"My sister comes across that way, but inside she's just like the rest of us," he said.

Just like the rest of us? Did he honestly think that he was anything like Daisy or the plantation workers or most of the population of O'ahu? Him with all his money and good looks and family name?

"I don't blame her for being nervous. There's a lot to be worried about right now, the test being the least of it," she said.

"You can say that again."

They were driving at half the speed of yesterday, but still too fast for comfort in the dark. If there was a cow or a dog in the road, surely he wouldn't see it in time. Daisy stared into the dark, wishing they had this new radar affixed to the car. But no one else was on the road, which helped. Every so often, Daisy caught a whiff of fresh-squeezed citrus mixed with spice. The smell was not entirely unfamiliar, and she realized it reminded her of the stables, along with the smell of horse and woodsy-sweet kiawe pods. She had never attributed this particular scent to Walker, but looking back, he belonged to the stables. Most days of late, he was there, either riding or grooming or working. His cowboy hats hung in a row in the tack room, and his boots lined one corner of the wall. She had always moved around him, mostly invisible, mostly intimidated. And now, his smell was taking her right back. Lord how she wanted to lean up against any of those horses, press an ear to their warm sides and listen to their breathing.

As they passed Wheeler Field, small breaks of light were visible. Workers on the island were repairing aircraft and rebuilding on round-the-clock shifts. Over the Pontiac's motor, they could hear the sound of plane engines revving. Pretty soon, Walker's left leg started bouncing up and down like it had a mind of its own. Daisy could feel his tension clear over in her seat. She knew she ought to say something, but had no idea what to say. She thought back to her own time of loss.

"It must be hard on you," she managed.

He didn't answer for a solid minute, just kept driving, chewing his gum and tapping his leg wildly. A light, misty rain dotted the windshield and Daisy rolled up her window. Walker kept his down, and leaned out so his face caught the rain, then he slicked back his hair.

"I lost some of my best buddies up there. We were caught with our pants down, you know? Most of those men never even had a chance. They left families behind, wives, daughters, sons, fathers."

"I'm so sorry."

"Nothing will ever be the same," he finally said.

Daisy knew the feeling. "No, it won't."

They chewed on that for a while. Daisy remembered back to the day she found out about her father. They had just had a big Kona storm and the beach was littered in flotsam. She was out digging through driftwood and giant ropes from ships, hoping to find a few Japanese glass fishing balls to add to her growing collection. Out of the side of her eye, she caught a form standing at the edge of the yard looking out to sea. Right away, Daisy knew something was off. Maybe it was the way her mother sagged, as though her spirit had bled out into the sand. When Daisy approached Louise, she could feel her pain from several feet away. A cloud of anguish as real as an ironwood tree. *Your father is dead.* That cloud had never left her mother, and with Daisy it ebbed and flowed with the passage of time. She could still be fine one minute, and be in tears the next. Grief did that to a person.

Coming down the hill toward Pearl Harbor, Daisy was thankful for the darkness. Seeing the mangled ships and blackened buildings was enough to split your heart. It was not what Walker needed right now, that much she knew. He had the radio tuned to KGU, and they were listening to staticky Hawaiian music at top volume. It was better than the alternative.

On several occasions, she felt a pressure to say something smart. Something that would distract him from reliving that morning over and over in his head. She knew that drill all too well. But in the end, she kept her mouth shut. Conversation with Daisy Wilder was sure to be low on his priority list. Nothing she could say would matter.

A few blocks from the Palace, he turned the radio down and said, "Want to know a secret?"

Had she heard him correctly? "Excuse me?"

He slowed the car. "There's a secret to taking tests. You want to know what it is?"

"Well, sure, why not?"

"Go with your gut and never second-guess yourself. As soon as you read the question, whatever the first thing that comes to mind is, go with that. Works like a charm," he said, tapping his temple with two fingers.

He seemed so cocksure. "That might be easy for you to say, since I'm sure you did well in school and you're probably book smart. But I left school halfway through my tenth-grade year, and even then my teachers had long given up on me."

The worst was Mrs. Severson with her pointy glasses and smoker's breath. She had once asked Daisy why she even bothered coming to school. *Some folks just aren't cut out for learning, and you're one of them.*

"There are so many ways to be smart, and doing well in school is only one of them. This test will be different. It'll be more about how you think than what you know, I can almost guarantee it," he said.

"How would you know that?"

"I've taken my share of military tests, trust me."

A tiny spark of hope lit in her chest. "Really?"

"I've seen what you do with the horses. How you can make even the most stubborn animal eat right out of your hand. It's a kind of genius."

The word *genius* had never been used in the same breath as her name. A blush ran up her neck. They rolled to a stop in front of the Palace. She felt a kind of victory for having survived the ride in without making a fool of herself. And he'd not even brought up Moon.

"When you grow up with horses, it comes naturally," she said, reaching for the door handle.

"I've grown up around horses and I could never have the effect that you do."

Something about the way he said it made her turn. In the dim light, their eyes met. She could have sworn his lips were turned up in a smile. Her heart melted just a little. Then, he gave her a small punch in the shoulder. "Now go kick some 'ōkole."

Despite the blatant staring and mumbles about her pants. Despite the fact that she had left the house without eating breakfast and now her stomach wouldn't stop growling. Even despite the intelligence test scheduled for 1100 hours, Daisy felt giddy. It was an unusual feeling, like a school of fish swimming round and round in her chest, tails brushing up against the wall of her heart. Her mind kept returning to that look in Walker's eye.

When training started, Daisy made sure to sit away from a headset, to give other girls a chance at speaking with the Oscars and plotting aircraft on the board. Fluff was next to her, and after eyeing Daisy up and down, said, "I wish I could look so sporty."

Daisy looked around to make sure Fluff wasn't speaking to someone else. "I train horses, so pants make sense to me."

"You remind me of one of those fashion models who could get away with wearing a square piece of burlap and still look good."

Daisy laughed. "You're funny."

"I'm serious."

"Most people usually tell me I look like a man in these."

"I don't think so at all. Women brave enough to wear pants always impress me. It's like you have a special brand of confidence."

"More like practicality."

Fluff smiled sweetly. "Just take it as a compliment."

They fell back in where they left off, fielding calls from Oscars and placing arrows on the board. All the women got a chance, and some seemed to have a knack for it, while others took a lot longer. At 1000 hours, General Danielson arrived with the intelligence tests in hand. Daisy thought of Walker's advice, wishing she could have an extra helping of his confidence.

The paper smelled like fresh ink. As soon as she read the first question, she knew she was in trouble. *Who was*

Marie Curie? She knew the name, but could not for the life of her remember what Marie Curie was known for. When that was done, she then moved on to a section that made a lot more sense, and had her answering practical questions. After that it was rearranging sentences, and she reminded herself to *go with your first thought*. She saved the math for last, because math was the one thing that came easily to her.

As time went on, others began to set down their pencils and hand in their tests. Daisy tried to tune them out, but the scratching of chairs on the cold linoleum was distracting. And she needed focus. She took a few deep breaths and thought of the ocean and the blue silence of the beach. It had been years since she had done math homework, but once she got sucked in, the problems began to work themselves out in a logical manner. When she finally set down her pencil, she was spent.

Lunch was delivered by two older women in Red Cross dresses. Egg salad sandwiches, with crunchy pickles and a tangy potato salad. Daisy wasn't used to being served lunch. She usually filled her tin with rice and dried fish and *poi* and ate under an ironwood tree near the beach, alone. The women were chattering like a flock of sparrows in the morning. She was squished between Betty and Fluff.

Betty seemed to know a lot of insider information. "They say our living quarters will be ready on the first of February."

"Don't you live nearby?"

"It's a ten-minute drive. And since Chuck is on the ship most of the time, I may as well stay here. I'll visit when he's on liberty."

Daisy wasn't too keen on moving to Fort Shafter and living with a bunch of strangers so far from the ocean, but she had committed. She could always return home on her days off to get her saltwater fix.

"Which ship is he on?" Daisy asked.

Betty beamed with pride. "The *Enterprise*. He's an SBD Dauntless pilot, leader of his squadron."

Walker was on the *Enterprise*, and Daisy wondered if the two men knew each other.

"Aren't they away now?"

"No, they just came in after two weeks of protecting our islands. And I'll tell you what, there is no feeling better than watching your man walk down that gangplank safe and sound and having him wrap you in those strong arms." She closed her eyes for a moment and sighed.

Fluff said, "Those pilots are something else. Does he have any available friends?"

Betty waved a finger. "Honey, you don't want a pilot. Course, I wouldn't trade Chuck in for anything, but you have to have nerves of iron to stay sane. Every single day, you're on your knees praying he'll come home alive. Now that we're at war, I hardly sleep."

Daisy thought of Walker. As hard as it was for the wives, it must be equally hard for the pilots. Though they were at least doing something, not just sitting around biting their nails. And even though she could tell that Walker was shell-shocked, he was the kind of man who jumped right back into the fire. Thelma was going to have a rough time with that one. Betty looked at Daisy. "What about you? I don't see a ring on your finger."

"I'm not married."

"Do you have a beau?"

"No."

She knew this subject was bound to come up in a room full of women, but didn't feel like elaborating. So what if she was single? She had no desire to stay at home cooking corn casseroles and waiting for her husband to come home. Her dream of having her own little ranch allowed no room for that. The other thing was, you had to have a man *want* to marry you. Which had never even come close to happening.

Thelma sat on the other side of Betty and apparently had been listening, since now she leaned over and said, "Now, don't take this the wrong way, but wearing pants may not be the best way to land a husband."

Betty sat up straight and said, "I think she looks fabulous. You ask me, the reason she doesn't have a man is because she lives out in the boonies."

Fluff nodded in agreement. "My guess is Daisy will be fighting off the men soon, pants or no pants."

Daisy wanted to hug them both. Here they were defending her and yet they hardly even knew her.

"I'm not in the market for a husband, which makes it easy to wear whatever I want," she said with as much confidence as she could muster.

Thelma smiled, lips red and shiny. "Just trying to be helpful."

"I can take care of myself."

"That's not what I've heard," Thelma said, turning in her seat to face the other way.

Daisy was left with her mouth open. It was school all over again. Maybe she wasn't cut out for this. But resigning on her second day would admit defeat. She'd made a promise. And promises were meant to be kept.

7

THE RESULTS

The following morning, all the women circled up alphabetically around the table. The room smelled musty, most likely from the lack of light and the rain that had fallen all night. Daisy was in a foul mood already because Walker had been mute the whole drive in. He had dark circles under his eyes, and his demeanor had changed from friendly to gruff. A few minutes into the ride, she wished she had climbed into the back seat. Peg was still home sick, so it was still just the two of them. She hated to admit it, but a part of her had been looking forward to the drive in and listening to him talk. His voice had a gravelly texture with a dash of pidgin every now and then.

Now, they waited for their tests to be handed back. General Danielson and Major Hochman had the honors. Tippy and Joyce, two of the supervisors, were pouring coffee, and Daisy downed hers in eight seconds flat. The burn distracted from her thoughts. Most of the women were quiet, though a few squeals and quiet moans escaped. *Wilder* was next to last, and when Hochman handed her the paper, she kept her eyes on the island of Oʻahu on the grid in front of her. Her heart was thumping along at race pace. When she couldn't wait any longer, she flipped it over.

Daisy Wilder: 96 percentile.

She stared at the paper for a few moments, trying to make sense of what she was seeing. Her left eye twitched. It was impossible. General Danielson began to speak to the group.

"Now, given that this is what's known as a standardized test, your score reflects how well you did among others in the country taking this test. One hundred being the top, if you scored say, 96th percentile—" he glanced at Daisy and she felt her face flush red "—then that means you did better than 96 percent of the population—including both men and women in the army. And by the way, that was our highest score in the class."

The room suddenly felt sweltering. She fanned herself with the test. Whoever had graded it had obviously made a mistake. Maybe she should alert them.

"Who got a 96?" Thelma asked.

He gave Daisy a little salute. "The honor goes to Miss Daisy Wilder, who earned a perfect score on the math section, I might add."

Fluff and Betty stood up and clapped madly, making way too much of a fuss. Daisy wanted to climb under the table and disappear, though a piece of her wished that Peg Montgomery was here to witness this. Some strange miracle had happened, but she wasn't complaining. Many of the others congratulated her, but Thelma wasn't one of them. Her mind flipped back over the questions, and her uncertainty with so many of the answers. And yet, Walker's words had stayed with her. *Never second-guess yourself.*

Hochman added, "Now, you are all getting the same training, but some of you who have shown aptitude in certain areas will be moving up from plotter to filterer soon after we hit the ground at Little Robert next week."

"Next week?" one of the girls said.

"Yep, that's when you'll be officially taking over for the boys."

Right around the corner. A whole lot of responsibility. And they still had so much to learn. Daisy's mood had flipped 180 degrees since getting the test back. Never had she scored highest on a test, though school tests had always been about subjects while this one was more about thinking. She was also looking forward to tomorrow, when they would be learning about the radar stations and aircraft vectoring. There was a good chance she was the only woman in the room who knew what the word *vector* even meant. This was the next best thing to flying a plane herself.

When training ended for the day, the sky was black and raindrops the size of guppies fell in large puddles. The girls all stood bunched up in a steamy huddle just outside the door, waiting for a break. Talk centered on the capture of Manila and how it felt like the Japanese were on an unstoppable rampage across the Pacific. Bets were placed on how soon they'd return to Hawai'i. Only now, maybe they had a way to stop them. Daisy sure hoped so. Walker pulled up a few minutes later.

Fluff spotted him right away and nodded. "Who does *he* belong to?"

Thelma said, "That's Walker Montgomery, my boyfriend." She looked directly at Daisy.

"Is he the polo player?" Tippy asked.

"Yep. And the pilot. And the son of Hal Montgomery.

And the most handsome man on the island," Thelma said with a wink.

She blew a kiss to Walker, who lifted his hand in a curt wave.

Daisy felt incredibly uncomfortable. Walker was waiting for her, but walking out there in front of everyone and driving off with Thelma's sweetheart would not win her friends. And Thelma was not the kind of woman she wanted for an enemy. It was plain enough she already looked down on Daisy. For a moment, she considered running back inside, pretending she forgot something. But that would only prolong things. The fact was, Danielson had enlisted Walker's help, and Walker was a man of his word.

"That's my ride. See you all tomorrow," Daisy said before she darted off across the swampy grass, holding up her slacks so they didn't get wet. One thing was for sure, pants were far easier to run in than a skirt.

By the time she reached the car, she was drenched. She went for the back door, figuring it was closer, and what did he care anyway? They probably wouldn't talk the whole way home.

"What do you think I am, your chauffeur? Come around to the front, Wilder."

He was good at giving orders, and she followed them like an obedient dog, out of habit more than anything. She also wanted to remind him that her name was Daisy, not Wilder. But all the guys at the ranch called her Wilder. She was one of the boys, so she could hardly blame him.

He had the heater cranked up and all the windows were fogged. "How can you see anything?" she asked.

"Hello to you, too."

A sheen of moisture coated his face, along with every other surface in the car. Daisy could feel the dampness on the seat against her thigh. The roads had turned into streams and giant mud puddles, and the sun was in hiding. Mist clung to the mountains in white clumps. Ever since the attack, it had felt like the weather was in mourning along with the rest of the island.

Walker pulled out a pack of Doublemint gum and offered her one. She took it. "So? How'd it go?" he asked.

Daisy knew what he meant, but suddenly felt bashful. "More of the same. We learned—well, I can't tell you what we learned, actually. But we learned a lot."

"I meant the test."

She looked out the window at the cannery, taking in the smell of burnt pineapple. "I took your advice and went with my first guess. It actually worked."

"Don't sound so surprised. You did well, then?" he said.

"I did."

"What was your score?"

If there was one thing Daisy hated to talk about, it was herself. With so many interesting topics out there, why waste a breath on the dull stuff?

"What about you? Did you get up in the air today?" she said.

He chuckled. "Why are you dodging the subject?"

There was a strange familiarity between them, as if by proximity and shared horses, they knew one another. Their lives had always moved in the same orbit, only he was more of a star and she, a tiny planet. Was Walker Montgomery somehow becoming a friend?

"I'm not. I'm just curious," she said.

"So am I."

She could tell he wasn't going to let up. "I scored in the 96th percentile, which I'm told is quite good."

He pounded the steering wheel and let out a whoop.

"Good? Damn, that's eight points higher than I got. And here I was giving you advice."

With her mother gone, it felt nice to have someone to share her little victory with. And yet she still wondered how he could even speak to her. "Your advice is why I did well."

"I had nothing to do with it. You don't give yourself enough credit," he said.

"I'm just happy I passed." She shrugged. "Say, can I ask you a question?"

"Shoot."

The words tumbled out. "Why are you being nice to me? After what happened with Moon, I feel absolutely terrible. I had no right to ride him without your permission and... Well, I'm wondering why you don't hate me for it." She felt herself choking up.

He ramped up his gum chewing. Bounced his left leg. After a few moments of silence, he said, "Sure, I was pissed about you riding Moon without asking. But I know you love him as much as I do. And after hearing your side of the story, I realized it wasn't your fault. It was the damn Japanese. If it weren't for them, Moon would still be here." He turned her way and she felt her cheeks heating up.

"I'm going to find him," she said, risking a look.

His five-o'clock shadow had grown to more of a beard than a shadow. "We've already looked on every square mile of the North Shore, and Dad has feelers out around the island," he said.

"I'm sure you have. But what if someone found him and is keeping him? Then all your looking won't help." It was the only logical explanation.

"Word travels. We would have heard something by now," he said.

"I have an idea," she said. It was more of a notion that

she was not going to give up, and Moon *had* to be found. An idea would come. It had to.

"Want to share it?"

"No. But just know that I haven't forgotten about him."

He didn't press her, probably because he had no faith. Moon had been gone almost a month now. Time was not on their side. Whenever she thought of the lost horse, she felt a sharp stab of guilt.

Daisy thought back to the time their cat, Lola, went missing, when she was seven or so. Up until then, wherever Daisy went, there was Lola. Curled up in the crook of her arm in bed, in the tree fort twenty feet up, even on the beach. Lola would weave herself along the edge of the sand in the bushes while Daisy built sandcastles and driftwood forts. One day after school, Lola wasn't in her usual spot on the old log at the bottom of the driveway. She didn't come home that night, or the next, or ever. Even thinking about it now filled Daisy with a deep sadness. That was the moment she understood that love had a hidden downside. The more you loved something, the more you hurt when you lost it.

When they hit Schofield, Walker said, "You hungry at all?"

Daisy shook her head. "I've been overeating at the Palace daily. From the amount of food they bring us, you'd never know there were rations going on."

"Mind if we stop at Kemo'o for an ice cream?"

"I don't have any change on me," she said.

"My treat."

Kemo'o Farms used to actually be a farm. A pig farm. You could smell it from miles away. Now, they were known for their fat steaks and their location on Lake Wilson, which wasn't a real lake but people liked to fish there nonetheless. Daisy much preferred the ocean. But she wasn't about to tell that to Walker. He seemed so eager to stop there, it was endearing.

When they parked, she got out quickly, so there was no confusion about him having to open her door for her. They walked in side by side and up to the soda fountain. An older Hawaiian woman in a palaka *mu'umu'u* and bright red lipstick smiled brightly at Walker.

"Mr. Montgomery, long time no see! Bumbye, I was starting to worry about you," she said.

He held up his hand. "I got into a little accident on the polo field, and well, then the world went to hell on us. Glad to see you open for business and looking well, Luana."

"We're open, all right. Soldiers are lining up down the road to get in here, even the generals. No alcohol, of course," she said as she set down two napkins. "Your usual?"

"Yes, ma'am."

"And how about for your lovely lady friend?"

Daisy and Walker both answered at the same time, then fumbled to speak over one another.

"Make it two—"

"We just carpool—" Daisy felt herself turn beet red. She had never been referred to as someone's *lovely lady friend*.

"Do you like root beer floats, Wilder?"

The woman's gaze bounced back and forth between them. "You two not an item?" she asked skeptically.

Before either of them could respond, she turned to scoop the ice cream, leaving Daisy and Walker to sit with her words at the cool stainless steel countertop.

Walker seemed more amused than anything. "I drive her into—"

Daisy shot him a look.

"—work, on base."

"I didn't realize we had women in the military. What do you do?" Luana asked.

"Oh, I'm a secretary. Just filing and answering phones. Pouring coffee for the men. That kind of thing."

Luana sized Daisy up and shook her head slightly. "I wouldn't have pegged you for a secretary type."

Daisy smiled sweetly and shrugged. "Someone's got to do it."

Walker leaned a little closer to Daisy, though not quite touching. She suddenly wanted to close the gap between them, and feel the weight of his arm on her skin. There was a strange, magnetic sensation whenever they got close. A tickle to her insides.

Luana poured the root beer and slid them two chunky glass mugs. Walker picked up his and said, "Cheers, to your success today. And Godspeed to our boys."

Their eyes locked.

Daisy clinked her glass to his. "Godspeed to our boys, and to you on your next mission, whenever that may be."

As soon as she spoke the words, she realized it was going to be hard to see him go.

The following day was just as dreary, so it didn't matter that they were sequestered away in a room in the Palace. Daisy wore pants again, with her only other presentable blouse, and she earned more lingering looks of disapproval. Being at the stables around men all day, she never felt out of place, yet here, among women in dresses and heels and lipstick, she felt like a *pāpio* in a school of yellow tang. Having short hair did not help matters. It had grown some in the past few months without a cut, but still. Daisy was an anomaly. Always had been.

Now that the group had a fair understanding of plotting

basics, Major Hochman moved on to detailing the radar stations on the island. There were six stations, marked with large red circles on the map. Opana was on the North Shore near Kahuku Point in a landscape of dunes and whipping wind. On the morning of December 7, the boys stationed at Opana had picked up the Japanese planes, but mistook them for B-17 Flying Fortresses on their way in from California. The good news was, radar actually worked. Bad news, we could have been ready but weren't.

"We won't make that mistake again," Hochman told them.

The other stations ringed the island of O'ahu with their mobile long-range radar sets. Ka'a'awa covered the east, Koko Head south, Fort Shafter southwest, Wai'anae west, Kawailoa northwest, and Opana north.

"You'll need to know the exact location of each station so you will know your range. Who can tell me what range is, again?" Hochman said.

The man was patient as a tortoise, she'd give him that. In a painfully slow manner, he went over and over every detail. Daisy managed to count every freckle on his face. In the beginning, most of his questions went unanswered, though now a few of the girls had latched on and were able to throw out answers confidently.

He called on Thelma, who had her hand up. "Range is the distance from the radar station to the plot, or the aircraft in this case."

Thelma was quickly becoming the teacher's pet.

"Exactly. Now, at Little Robert, you'll have to mark the location—or set number—the condition, altitude, azimuth and range of an aircraft. Remember our SCR-270B has a range of 150 miles, give or take. You know the set number and condition, you know the range. What about altitude? Does radar tell you altitude?"

"No," a chorus of voices answered.

"And what does SCR stand for?"

"Signal corps radio," said Peg, who was back in action and had apparently been studying hard at home. Though Daisy wondered if Peg got away with missing all those days because of who she was.

"So how will you know if it's an aircraft?"

Daisy blurted out an answer. "Because it is noticeably moving. Nothing else will move remotely as fast as a plane."

"Righto, Miss Wilder."

For the first time ever, Daisy was actually enjoying being in class. Maybe it was because the stakes were higher and she was keen to know everything she could about the radar. Perhaps that was the secret. You had to have a genuine interest before you could fall in love with a subject. Daisy appreciated the logical nature of numbers in the same way that Fluff loved English. Though how could anyone fall in love with prepositional phrases or William Shakespeare was beyond her.

"Now, who here knows where the Japanese forces will likely be coming from? And which stations are likely to pick them up?" Hochman asked.

"Opana!" Betty called out.

"The tricky part is going to be discerning between friend or foe. We don't want any more casualties from friendly fire, so what you're doing here is critical. Speaking of friendlies, you ladies may also need to vector in some of our boys when called upon. I know it sounds real technical, but vectoring is simply when you tell a pilot to fly at a specific heading."

"How would we do that?" Fluff asked.

"Through UHF radio. Ultra-high frequency."

They continued doing practice exercises, learning how to speak with Oscars, which questions to ask, how to do line checks to make sure all was clear between command and the radar stations. Then they practiced vector simulations and simulations of Japanese aircraft moving in. All this talk of another air raid gave Daisy the jitters.

At high noon, two older Red Cross volunteers came in with lunch. Daisy was famished and nearly drooling as they set out trays of fried chicken, rice, corn salad and mandarin oranges. For dessert, they left several boxes of malasadas stacked high. This was more food than she ate in a month and she couldn't believe her good fortune. The noise level in the room quadrupled as everyone compared test scores and chattered about the news.

The girls all fell into groups so naturally, and Daisy circled the room looking for an opening. No one even looked her way. She was about to head outside when Betty waved her over. "Sit with us."

"Lord almighty, I need to know your secret," Fluff said.

Daisy thankfully squeezed in next to her. "My secret?"

Fluff was so pretty, her skin glowed. "I'm the girl who always had the lowest math score in the class. I know how to write a pretty sentence, but show me an equation and my brain shuts down."

The opposite of Daisy. "A lot of it has to do with how we're wired, I think. Numbers come easy to me, but I was the worst English student in my class. I was so bad at it, I used to skip all the time," she said.

"Where did you go when you skipped?"

"To the beach, either diving or fishing."

"I don't blame you, then. But most of this material is way over my head. I'm surprised they haven't kicked me out yet."

"They need us all," Betty said.

"Didn't I hear that you left school altogether?" Fluff asked.

Daisy nodded. "After tenth grade. We needed the money, and school was not my strong suit, so I got a job at Montgomery ranch helping clean the stables. My dad worked there. I did a little horse training, too, on the side."

Betty lit up. "I love horses! Maybe we can all go riding when things calm down."

"Do you still work there?" Fluff said.

Daisy was surprised the news hadn't trickled down to these two. On the first day, she'd overheard Peg saying her name to Thelma, along with *Moon* and *Walker* and *stolen*. She had assumed everyone knew by now.

"I got fired."

The girls both stopped chewing.

"I borrowed Walker's horse and he ran off," Daisy said. "They still haven't found him."

Fluff looked confused. "You mean the Walker who drives you in?"

Daisy told them the whole story, and it felt good to get it out, especially to people who didn't know the Montgomerys. When she was finished, Betty said, "Mr. Montgomery sounds like a mean old man. At least Walker seems to have forgiven you."

"Oh, I don't know about that. General Danielson asked him to drive me since I don't have a car—or at least one that runs," Daisy said.

"He doesn't look too sad about it."

"Maybe he just likes having someone to talk to on the way in," Daisy deflected.

"You two would make a fine pair," Fluff said.

Daisy winced. "He's taken."

"There's no ring on her finger, is there?"

"No."

"So, you've looked?" Betty asked with a sly smile.

She had.

Fortunately, Fluff changed the subject. "By the way, I have uncles and cousins all along the east side of the island, clear up to Kahuku. I can ask around about the horse. Sometimes people know things, but they won't say anything to a *haole*."

"That would be wonderful!'"

"Just help me with the math."

"You got it."

8

THE PENTHOUSE

Days began to blend into each other in a blur of coordinates and conditions and tracks and plots. The Women's Air Raid Defense—WARD for short, as they had decided to call themselves—was becoming a force to be reckoned with. Danielson had originally suggested Women's Air Defense, but no one wanted WAD for an acronym. *Zero Zeroes* had become the motto. By the end of the first week, they sounded like seasoned professionals when answering the Oscars' practice calls.

On the drives in, Walker was either lost in the dark corners of his mind, or asking Daisy questions no one had ever bothered to ask before. Being with him stirred a place inside she hadn't even known existed.

"If you could be anything, what would it be?" he said one morning.

"But I can't be anything," she answered.

He was clearly in a good mood today, head bobbing along to the radio. "But what if you could? Humor me."

She felt silly telling him. "I want to have my own little ranch and train horses."

"I should have guessed."

"Is there something wrong with that?"

"Not at all. You have the talent, skill and smarts."

But not the money or connections, she could hear him thinking.

Daisy did not want to talk about herself. "What about you, did you always know you wanted to fly?"

"Always. The business and the ranch were my dad's dreams, not mine."

"I've never been in an airplane," Daisy volunteered.

He laughed. "Are you kidding me?"

"Don't sound so surprised," she said, looking out the window at the endless rows of pineapple.

"You're serious."

"Very."

The smile spread across his whole face, forming those crowfeet she'd begun to look forward to seeing. "Now that you mention it, I could see you up there flying your own bird. You bear a keen resemblance to Amelia Earhart, you know that? Short hair, sporty, gorgeous."

That last word hit her like a wall of whitewater. Yet she did her best to appear unaffected. "I saw her when she was here. She started my fascination with airplanes, but more than that, I was taken with her fearlessness and the way she encouraged women to follow their dreams."

"You ever think of going to flight school?"

She shook her head. "It was purely a fantasy. My true love will always be the horses. Plus, I had to take care of my mom."

Walker tensed up. She could feel it clear across the car. "I'm sorry. That must have been rough on you."

Everyone in town knew about Louise, so it was no secret, but she doubted he knew the extent of it. No one did.

She shrugged. "The day my father died, my mother and I switched roles. I did what I had to, as would anyone," she said.

Walker focused all his attention on the road in front. He grew quiet.

Daisy sensed he had something else to say, but she wanted to keep things light. "Maybe one day you can take me for a spin up there."

She imagined him flying across oceans and far continents, ice-cold air coming through the cracks and the smell of gasoline on his hands.

"I still can't believe you've never flown before," he said.

"When would I have? I've been working six days a week since I was sixteen. And plane tickets are not cheap."

The gap in their upbringings stood between them, wide and glaring. Not that she was trying to rub it in. It just *was*.

"That's another thing I admire about you. You've always busted your 'ōkole and never once complained about it. Not even when my dad made you brand the foals. It was pretty clear that was hard for you, but you did it anyway. Without a word."

She looked at him. "You remember that?"

"I remember a lot of things."

"What else?"

He drummed his fingers on the wheel. "Hmm, let me think."

Daisy turned to see a burst of sun slipping through the clouds and lighting up Mount Ka'ala. These rides were turning out to be a lot like that sunshine, and making her feel close to Walker in a way she could not explain.

"This is from a long time ago, but it was the day my dad was trying to impress the mayor and took him and his wife out for a ride. But her horse bolted before we even got started and made a beeline for the beach."

He chuckled at the thought. "She was holding on to her hat with one hand and screaming loud enough for folks in Honolulu to hear. Everyone just stood in shock, but you jumped on Peanut and took off like a slingshot and somehow managed to stop 'em just before Kona launched her into the water. He was famous for doing that, remember?"

Daisy laughed. "He was a rascal, that one. And how could I forget? That woman had no right stepping foot on a horse. She was too high-strung."

"And you were so cool about it all."

"How old were we anyway?"

"It was before I left, so you were probably seventeen or so. In a way you seemed so much older than me, more mature I guess, but in another way so much younger," he said. "Our lives were different."

"Depends on how you look at it. They were also a lot alike."

For a while, she thought about all the small moments over the years that involved Walker. Not that they were ever doing things together per se, but both had been there, living, working, riding. Shared memories.

Walker said, "So back to the flying, once it's safe, I'm your man. Hell, I'll even teach you to fly if you want," he said. "We could start off right here at Mokulēʻia airfield and take a scenic tour up around the island, hugging the cliffs. You're going to fall in love, I promise."

Being in an airplane with Walker sounded too good to

be true. "Now, if the war will only cooperate," she said as casually as she could, though her insides were buzzing louder than a whole formation of bombers.

Falling in love was a frightening possibility—and not just with the airplane.

Daisy had managed to get herself scheduled on the first shift on the first day at Little Robert. She thought it might have to do with her test score and the fact that she memorized all the code names on the grid in one day.

With gas masks and helmets draped over their shoulders, the group piled into the back of a covered truck outside the Palace. They all wore their smart new uniforms and ID badges. As much as Daisy did not care for dresses, she had to admit she enjoyed feeling so official. So part of a team. And most of the girls had bold red lips. Fluff, never without her lipstick tube, had convinced many of the girls to wear their best fire-engine reds.

"We need to make a statement. It's our patriotic duty," she had told them, handing the shiny gold tube to Betty.

Her reasoning was that Adolf Hitler had banned lipstick in Germany, and in response, American women from coast to coast had begun wearing it in solidarity.

"Female power at its finest," Betty said, opening her compact and applying the red in generous strokes.

Daisy appreciated their fervor, but could not bring herself to wear it. "None for me, thanks." She hated lipstick. The plastic taste, the way it smeared whenever she touched her mouth, and how she felt like a clown when she wore it.

"This goes beyond the individual. What about doing it for your country? Or for us, your friends," Fluff said.

Daisy could not imagine walking around all day with bright red lips. Especially the first day on the job. "I think

I'm doing my part as a WARD here, so you'll have to take me as I am."

"Fine. But I'll win you over one of these days."

A cold wind whipped through the banyan leaves and up their skirts, making sure everyone knew it was January. As if they could have forgotten. Rain for weeks. Closed flaps kept anyone from seeing them, or them from seeing out. Along with Betty and Fluff, Lei, Thelma and JoAnn were there, and Tippy, who would be shift supervisor. Major Hochman rode up front. "What kind of name is Little Robert, anyway?" Betty said, over the rattle of the engine.

"For some reason it makes me think of Peeping Tom. It sounds like a creepy man who is trying to pass himself off as innocent," Jo Ann said.

"Who knows where the name originated, but it sounds rather harmless, don't you think?" Daisy said.

Fifteen minutes later, the truck skidded to a stop, hurling everyone into one another. Betty landed in Daisy's lap, Lei smashed her face into Thelma's shoulder, and Fluff fell onto the floor in a pile of limbs and blue material. "Now I know what it's like for those poor cattle on their way to the ships," she said.

They hopped out with a hand from Major Hochman, and stood in a line on the pavement beside the truck. Daisy looked around for anything that resembled a command center, but saw only a concrete warehouse with a two-story wooden building sitting on top of it. A few kiawe trees stood out among the rocky and muddy terrain, with a shed here and a warehouse there. The whole place had an abandoned feel, but maybe that was how they wanted it.

"Where's Little Robert?" Betty asked.

Major Hochman pointed to the structure. "Welcome to the Shafter Mudflats, gals. This here is known affectionately as the Penthouse. Now, be careful not to step off of the wood or you'll be in up to your teeth."

"*That* is the Information and Control Center for the whole Pacific?" Thelma said.

Hochman checked his buttons, smoothed his red hair. "For now. Come on, Colonel Nixon is waiting for us. Trust me, we don't want to keep him."

Daisy wasn't sure what she had been expecting, but this ramshackle building was not it. The moment they set foot on the walkway, the sky opened up, pouring out raindrops the size of alfalfa pellets. There was no way to hurry, so they carefully navigated the thin, slippery planks of wood for what felt like a mile, then up a short flight of stairs. By the time they reached the door, everyone was soaked, well-styled hair now plastered to heads, mascara running down faces. Daisy finally felt at an advantage with none of that to worry about.

A heavy blanket hung across the entrance and they ducked under it and walked down a dark passageway, then out through another blanket. Daisy brought up the rear, and when she entered was faced with an unexpected scene. The insides of the building were as modern and shiny as the outside was ugly. They were in a room with a big table covered with a giant map of the Hawaiian Islands, this one much larger than the one used for training. A grid covered the whole thing. Plotting stations were set up around the table, with four chairs on the short sides and eight on the long. Each spot had its own headset and mini-switchboard to connect the plotters to Oscars around the island.

Captain Burgess stood on a raised section with a bull-dog of a man looking down on the table. He waved but the other man did not. Uniformed men of all shapes and sizes manned the stations and telephones. They stopped what they were doing and gaped at the women. A troupe of monkeys may as well have waltzed in wearing tutus and party hats. Someone in front of Daisy mumbled softly, "Have they never seen a woman before?"

Major Hochman touched his hat in a salute to the bull-dog man. "Nixon, I've got your next shift here."

Nixon glanced at the clock on the wall behind him, then said, "God help us, boys, we have a truck full of Bettys here to take over for you. Brief them on your current plots. You're relieved of duty."

Technically, there was only one Betty, but no one was about to correct him.

"Highly trained and ready for work, sir," Major Hochman said.

The men stood and pushed out chairs, took off their headphones. One young fellow saluted the women, then motioned them over. He couldn't have been more than nineteen and had an angry field of pimples on his cheeks, but he bounced around with enough cockiness for them all.

He pointed to a marker on the map, north of Ka'a'awa. "This here is a transport, bearing West at 250 knots, bound for Kān'eohe. Confirmed friend. Any of you hotshots want to take it on?"

Fluff stepped forward and reached for his poker. "I will." The blue uniform suited her, conforming to her tiny waist, and enhancing the sea blue of her eyes. Her confidence caught Daisy off guard, and apparently it did the same to Colonel Nixon, who was suddenly standing next to them.

"What kind of aircraft is she?" he asked Fluff.

"Um. Let's see. I guess it depends on what you are transporting—"

Fluff looked up toward a cobweb in the corner of the ceiling and twirled a lock of hair around her finger, obviously stalling. If only he had asked her a question about William Shakespeare or Walt Whitman.

"Flying Fortress, sir," Daisy said, unable to help herself.

Nixon looked her up and down, his eyes level with her mouth. "Was I asking you?"

"No, sir."

"How did you arrive at that, Miss...?"

"Wilder. Daisy Wilder. Because those are the transports that have been landing here. And because of her speed."

He spoke coldly. "You happen to be correct, but you are also out of line." Then, so all could hear, "Ladies, a few ground rules will keep you out of trouble. First, if you don't know the answer to something, the proper answer is 'I don't know, sir, but I'll find out.' Second, don't interrupt me when I'm speaking to someone. And third but not last, if you think like a man, speak like a man and act like a man, you should do fine."

Fluff rolled her eyes and looked to be fighting a laugh. Daisy gave her a stern look. She was familiar with Nixon's type, and you didn't want to cross them. In her experience at the ranch, there were two kinds of men: those who liked women and those who didn't. No amount of smarts or competence could change that fact.

"Oh, and one more thing—don't touch my coffeepot." He then motioned for a few other men to come down from the balcony. "This is Captain Owens, our pursuit officer. He handles the intercepts when we can't identify a flight as friend. And this is our signal corps radar officer, or who we call Major Oscar. He's in charge of keeping our radar coverage optimal and coordinates with all the Oscars out there. And Lieutenant Dunn here is my second-in-command. These are my right-hand guys. Now get to work."

Major Oscar, a.k.a. Major Judd, was all arms and legs

with hunched shoulders, but his smile lit up the room. "Any radar questions, direct them my way."

The women scattered like buckshot around the table. Other men in the room offered a mix of welcome and *this is my territory* and flirtation. One in particular did not budge from his seat until Major Oscar stood behind him and coughed. "Joe, I know this is tough, but we have to give these ladies a chance," he said.

Joe set down his stick and slowly stood. As he passed by, Daisy heard him mutter *damn skirts*. It was men like him who made her want to excel at this gig. Private Beers didn't appear to share his disdain, and pleasantly showed them how to adjust their headphones. He began to explain the grids and codenames, but Major Hochman said, "Thank you, Private, but these ladies know the drill."

The room smelled like fresh-cut timber, burnt coffee and chalk. Phones rang off the hook. It was somewhat dingy, with all the windows boarded up, but at least they had a little more space to move around in. And although the room was unfamiliar, the table was just a larger version of their training table. Daisy swapped places with a private named Reed, who had a marker off the coast of Wai'anae.

"This is a squadron of fighters. F4F Wildcats. They go out several times a day for training when they're at Pearl," he said.

"Navy?" she asked.

He nodded.

It might be Walker. Strange that she could know his exact position in space and time. She pictured him up there in his suit and leather helmet, eyes scanning the horizon for any signs of the enemy. Those eyes. They undid her in a way that felt very dangerous. "Ma'am?"

She snapped out of it. "Yes?"

"There's a call coming in. Would you like to be the first to answer?" he said.

Where at all possible, wire lines were used over radio. And it had been explained to them that it depended on their position around the plotting table, and if they were idle or not, who would take an incoming call.

All eyes were on her.

She picked up. "Army, go ahead, please."

"Flash—Rascal, this is Oscar. Do you read me?"

"Loud and clear, Oscar."

A whistle came through the line. "Now, wait a minute. Who is this speaking?"

Apparently not all the Oscars had been informed.

"This is Signal Corps Command Center and you're speaking with Rascal badge number twenty-two. I'm ready to take your reading."

He must have placed his hand over the mouthpiece, but Daisy could hear him anyway. "What the dickens, Jim, there's a female on the other end of the line. What do I do?"

Another voice said, "These are the new recruits they stuck us with. Be a gentleman and give her the info."

"Here we go, Rascal, I hope you're ready for this. 1–bimotor–5–very low—seen—Opana station—N–2–W."

Daisy quickly translated in her head, *One bimotor plane was seen flying very low five miles north of Opana observation post heading west.*

And so it began.

The WARDs worked in six-hour shifts at Little Robert around the clock. If the Oscars sounded surprised when women first answered, they soon adjusted. Most of them, at least. A loud-talking one with a funny accent refused to give Fluff coordinates.

"Look, lady, lemme talk to your boss. This bird is out of pattern and I got a bad feeling," he'd said.

"Call me Rascal, and I am perfectly capable of handling the situation. We've been trained thoroughly," Fluff responded.

"I want to talk to a man."

"You're out of luck, then, because right now, I'm all you've got."

He hung up and promptly called back on another line. This time Lei got him. "Oscar, you can call back as many times as you want. We are all women here. Sorry to disappoint you."

He finally gave in, but not happily.

Soon, though, the calls became business as usual. Plotting air and surface craft accurately was everyone's first priority. The longer time passed without an invasion, the tenser people became. Frayed nerves could be seen everywhere, from the band of men with rifles combing the streets in Waialua to the talk that all of the local Japanese families in Hawaiʻi would be rounded up and shipped off to Molokaʻi. Walker, who had grown up with Japanese neighbors and classmates, said, "That's the dumbest, most ignorant thing I've heard so far. These people are Americans."

Molokaʻi already had the burden of housing the leper colony on Kalaupapa, and now this. On such a small island, where would they all go? Never mind the fact that most of them were loyal American citizens.

"I guess that's what happens when you have people making decisions from halfway around the world," Daisy answered.

Walker was back flying again, and his schedule had him on night duty, so the Montgomerys' butler, Mr. Bautista, drove her and Peg in most of the week—part of the Montgomery contribution to the war effort. Though Peg was out again today with another bout of asthma, poor thing. It had become clear that the woman was either on top of the world, or with one foot in the grave. No in between. A little bit like Daisy's mother. She was tempted to bring it up with Walker, but didn't dare.

Mr. Bautista had been working for the Montgomerys as long as she could remember. He spoke with a heavy Filipino accent and had a contagious laugh. He spent half the ride grilling her about the war, asking questions about her work that she couldn't answer and the other half telling stories about his time on the sugar plantation. With Peg not around, his whole demeanor changed and he seemed far more relaxed.

"Miss Peg says you do important work."

How much had Peg told him?

"All military work is important," she said.

"You flying planes, like the mister?"

"No, I'm afraid it's not that exciting."

"Driving submarines?"

She laughed.

"Maybe breaking Japanese code?"

"Mr. Bautista, we do clerical work in an office, mainly answering phones. That's all I can say. Can we change the subject, please?"

He grinned. "You girls are up to something, I know it. Miss Peg, she walk around like she big lady in town now."

Surely Peg knew better, but Daisy could just imagine her, feeling even more important than she already did.

"Just doing our small part."

Daisy and Fluff both found themselves a half hour early at the Palace. Skies had cleared and morning light brushed the horizon with lazy strokes of pink. They went for a walk around the block to pass the time. Fresh air and sunshine had never felt so good.

"What do you think about Colonel Nixon?" Fluff asked.

"At first I thought he was going to make our lives miserable, but he hasn't been *that* bad. How about you?"

Fluff picked a yellow plumeria and stuck it behind her right ear. "He's hard to read. I was certain he hated me that first day, but now I'm not so sure. It's Lieutenant Dunn who's interesting. Though his confidence can be a bit much. I catch him watching me a lot, and he makes no effort to hide it."

"That's no good."

"He's probably just not used to having so many gals around all the time."

"Still, he shouldn't be—"

Her words were obliterated by the wail of an air-raid siren, loud enough to send vibrations running up the backs of her legs and through her spine. They both covered their ears and ducked into the closest doorway, which happened to be the YWCA on Richards Street. Fluff clutched Daisy's arm and looked into her eyes with pale terror. "Is this it?"

The next instant, a dark sedan pulled to stop and the door swung open. "Get in!" said Lieutenant Farrow, one of the nice young officers who had been helping drive them to Little Robert each day.

They followed orders and he tore off before Daisy even had her foot in the door. At King Street, he made a right without even slowing down.

"Do you know what's going on?" Fluff yelled.

"Air-raid sirens. That means air raid."

Obviously.

"I mean do you have any insider information?"

"No, ma'am."

Daisy scanned the skies. Coconut trees and clouds. A

flock of pigeons. No Japanese planes in sight—yet. She wasn't sure what would be worse. An air raid or an invasion. Probably an invasion because then you would be face-to-face with the enemy, hear their voices, taste their spit. Lieutenant Farrow began to swerve like mad through Chinatown, nearly taking out a few pedestrians.

Pretty soon, Fluff had her eyes squeezed shut.

"Watch out!" Daisy screamed, as they narrowly missed an old woman carrying a bunch of bananas.

They careened over the bridge in Kalihi. Beads of perspiration covered the back of his neck. He seemed intent on getting them killed before the Japanese did. Fluff held Daisy's hand and they rode in silence, too scared to speak. Eventually, they made it to Fort Shafter and the moment they stepped out of the car, the sirens stopped.

Just a scare.

Fluff looked ready to collapse. "Lord, that was a doozy."

"Where did you learn to drive like that?" Daisy asked as she shut the door.

He smiled as though nothing had happened. "A moving target is harder to hit. Remember that."

It did not take long for the women to discover how true that statement was, because many of them could not even hit a stationary target. General Danielson thought that every WARD ought to know how to fire a .45-caliber pistol and arranged for shooting practice in the hills up behind Shafter.

On a rare sunny morning, the women arrived at a large field at the base of the Ko'olau mountain range, flanked by a rocky hillside on the left, and a forest on the right. From the sound of it, only a couple of gals knew anything about guns. Daisy being one of them. Four hay bales each painted with a big X were lined up as targets.

Fluff frowned. "I'm worried I might shoot my foot off."

"Don't aim at your foot, then," Daisy told her.

A couple of marines had been designated as teachers, and the main one, a stern-faced man named Sergeant Guthrie, showed them—in minute detail—every nook and cranny of the weapon. When he passed it around, Thelma reached out first to grab it, and her arm dropped under the weight.

"It feels like a bowling ball," she said, using both hands to hand it over to Peg, who could also barely lift it.

"There's a huge amount of pressure that happens when you fire, so the gun needs to be heavy enough to contain that," Guthrie said, spitting out a wad of chewing tobacco.

He then proceeded to show them how to stand, hold, aim and fire. With every shot, he hit the center of the X.

"He makes it look easy," Lei said.

When it got to be their turn, Peg, Betty, Vivian and Fluff went first. The targets seemed awfully far away, and now the trade winds were kicking up a bit. On the first round, Vivian ended up on her rear end in the grass. A little dazed but laughing, she brushed herself off and stood right back up and tried again.

"My hands are shaking so badly, I can't even aim," Fluff said.

"Relax those elbows," Guthrie barked.

By the end of the round, only Betty and Vivian had even come close to the X, and only once each. Next up were Daisy, Thelma, Lei and Rita. And though Daisy felt fairly comfortable with a shotgun, the pistol turned out to be an entirely different beast. Without a shoulder to press the gun against, aiming was a whole lot more challenging. But at least she was able to keep her arms steady. On their first shots, she and Rita hit the hay bale, but missed the mark.

Guthrie nodded. "Good job, ladies. Now make sure those front and back sights are aligned."

A couple of more tries, and Rita hit the bull's-eye. "Like I said on day one, I'm a crack shot with a rifle. Just needed a little getting used to this little guy," she said with a shrug.

Thelma and Lei were not so lucky and their bullets kept whizzing past the hay bales.

"I hope there aren't any unsuspecting pigs in the bushes back there," Fluff said from the sidelines.

Or people, Daisy thought. She lined up another try.

Moments later, a billow of dust erupted from the rocky hillside. Suddenly, Thelma was rolling around on the ground clutching her thigh.

"I've been shot," she screamed.

Daisy, who was closest, ran over and moved Thelma's hand aside. A large red welt had formed, with purple spreading out from the center.

"The bullet must have ricocheted off the rocks. It's just a bruise, no skin broken," Daisy said, in her best horse-soothing voice.

By the time Guthrie made it over to inspect the damage, Thelma was sitting up and had calmed down. Even still, she refused to look Daisy in the eye. The rest of the girls were all crowded around, peering down at her with concern.

"Whose bullet was it that hit me?" Thelma said, looking directly at Daisy.

"I think it was yours," Daisy said, though she couldn't be sure.

"I'd hate to think it was someone else's."

Fluff put her hands on her hips. "That bullet was definitely your own. I saw it."

A few others nodded in agreement and Thelma had no choice but to back off. But it was clear that Daisy would have to watch her back at every step. Some of these women she could trust, and some she couldn't.

9

THE DRILL

Sand hides things. Hoofprints, shells, crabs, tears. But the ocean does an even better job. Burnt airplanes and Japanese submarines, lost hopes and secret dreams. Every afternoon, after being dropped off by Walker or Mr. Bautista, Daisy put on her swimsuit, walked out to the beach and sat at the edge of the ocean, her body in dry sand, feet buried in wet. Sea-foam crackled and tickled her toes. She knew she wasn't supposed to be out there, but no one was there to stop her.

The ritual was to watch the sun slip into the ocean or behind the clouds, then swim as far as she could underwater. Over the shallow grooves of *limu*-covered rock, slipping between coral heads and across the fields of sandy rubble. Her goal was to make it to the outer reef without a breath. A lofty goal, but she could usually do it, except she'd noticed lately with all the time in the car and sitting around the table, her lungs rebelled.

On this particular afternoon, before her swim, she picked

up a stick and began drawing in the sand. A sun. A bird. A horse. She thought of all the times she and her father had created whole murals across the beach, only to watch them erased by waves. On some days, the shore was filled with herds of horses, and others, undersea worlds of humpback whales and dolphins and tiger sharks. *Don't think too hard about it,* her father would say. *The drawings are already there in the sand. We just uncover them.* Lord, she missed him, especially now. Having her father around for this war would change everything. He would make her feel safe, in that way that he always had.

Daisy let the stick work its magic, not really paying attention to what she was doing. Her mind was on Little Robert and the fire hose training they'd done earlier in the day. The damn thing had weighed more than all of the girls put together, but somehow they'd managed to hoist it on their shoulders and douse an imaginary fire. They had all danced around hugging each other when they succeeded. Even Daisy, who never hugged anyone.

When she looked down at her sand drawing, she was surprised to see a heart with the letters D and W inside. Had it been there all along? There was no point to dreaming about Walker, but lately he seemed to be hovering always at the edge of her mind.

In an act of rebellion, she stripped down naked and dived in. She usually waited until dusk for skinny-dipping, but the ocean never minded. Nor did the bats or the fish or the herons. With a strong but relaxed kick, she propelled herself to the beginning of the sandy rubble before coming up for air, lungs near bursting. Dense squalls of rain populated the horizon and she thought about how precipitation affects radar and can cause false readings. Were the girls in the Penthouse picking up this rain?

The rest of the way to the reef, she lay on her back, kicking lazily. Raindrops came down and she opened her mouth to catch them, tasting the sky. She made it to the reef, looked around for cowrie shells and eels, and then headed in at the same leisurely pace. All the tension and pressure and intense focus of the past weeks dissolved into the salt water and she began to feel more refreshed than she had in a long time.

As she neared the shore, she heard something, deep and low. She stood up and looked out to sea for planes, but soon realized the sound was coming from the beach. Coming from Mokulēʻia, a dark horse galloped across the open sand. For a moment she thought it was Moon, but when the animal moved out of the shadows, she saw a rider in the saddle. As luck would have it, she'd left her suit hanging from a branch of driftwood. By all estimates, there wouldn't be time to make it to shore and run up the beach without being seen. The alternative was to swim back out to sea or dive down and hold her breath while whoever it was passed. Thankfully, the water was dark enough to cover her.

She stayed in place and sank down with just her nose above water. Within a minute, she recognized both horse and rider. Wind and Walker. A shiver ran through her. Walker was not the kind of man who missed things. He'd probably spotted her already. Daisy disappeared beneath the surface anyway. Held her breath. One minute. Two minutes. Her lungs screamed for air and she finally had to come up. Wind stood on the beach right next to her suit. A dusting of rain came down, turning them both a glowing orange.

"Is that you, Wilder?" Walker called.

She realized she was backlit by a setting sun. "What are you doing here?" she asked, keeping low.

During the past ten years, Daisy had never seen Walker

ride the beach in front of the house. He had when he was younger, but that stopped after her father died. Now, everyone left them alone. Mr. Silva said it was because of her mother, who for a while had taken up target practice with the coconuts out front. She had made Daisy do the same.

"Last I checked, the beach is public," he said.

"The beach is off-limits now with martial law. You could be shot."

Walker laughed. "I can see it's stopped you."

"Technically, I'm not on the beach."

"But you had to walk down the beach to get in the water. So, *you* could be shot."

"They seem to have forgotten this little stretch of beach."

"Actually, I have orders to patrol it when I'm off duty. Me and a few of the guys out here. Keep an eye out for submarines or anything suspicious," he said.

That would certainly put a damper on her naked swimming. "I'm always on the lookout."

He glanced down at her suit.

"If you have the whole beach to patrol, you'd better get going," she said.

In his faded jeans and blue plaid shirt, he looked every part the cowboy, molded by the wind against his face. He made the switch from flyboy well.

Walker nodded at her suit. "Do you always do this? Skinny-dip, I mean?"

"It depends."

"On what?"

"On my mood, and how calm the water is."

She sometimes believed the mercurial nature of the sea mirrored her life.

"Not to ruin your fun, but with the new patrols, you

may want to keep your suit on. I'd hate for any of the other boys to surprise you," he said.

Here they were, having a perfectly normal conversation, and she was naked. Her bare shoulders cooled in the breeze and a line of goose bumps ran down her spine. Exposed as she may be, she sensed no threat. Then she spotted the heart she'd drawn in the sand just to his left and her breath stopped. A heart with their initials in it. She willed him to ride on. If he looked down, he would see it. If he saw that, her life would be over. Swim her out to sea, tie a rock to her foot and let her go.

"I'll keep that in mind, thank you," she managed to say.

She thought he was about to leave when he said, "Say, would you be willing to do a few patrols, too? On horse-back? We could use the help."

"I don't have a horse."

"I could bring you one. Any one you want, in fact. Now that polo is out, and you're gone, they aren't getting ridden half as much as they're used to."

It seemed too good to be true.

"What would your father say?"

"My father has enough to worry about. He won't know."

"I would like that. Though in February we move into the new quarters at Shafter, so I'll only be out on my days off."

"I'll let you know when we need you."

"We don't have a phone."

"I know where you live."

Riding the beach would be a dream come true, even if it meant being on watch for the enemy. Riding with Walker, complicated. But there was no way she could refuse him. "Perfect."

He looked her in the eye. "You know what's perfect?"

She could barely answer. "What?"

"All of this." He swept his hand. "The shadows on the cliffs, the low tide, calm water, light rain." With that, he kicked Wind and took off at a gallop.

She could have sworn she heard the words *and you* as he disappeared down the beach. But that was impossible.

The following day, during shift one, Lieutenant Dunn ran a training for the girls on aircraft types. Knowing flight speeds made all the difference in effective plotting, and was essential for filterers, he told them.

Dunn wore his uniform seemingly one size too small. He clearly spent time working on his physique, and made a point to flex his biceps every chance he got. You could tell he thought that having a captive audience of women was the best thing since the invention of jet engines. Being new to Little Robert, the women were still on their best behavior. Crammed into a small room off the main plotting room, they sat at full attention. Daisy felt claustrophobic without windows to look out, and reminded herself to breathe.

"Most importantly, we are here to prevent getting caught with our pants down again." He looked around at all the powdered faces. "Or our skirts down, I guess you could say."

He cracked a smile and a few of the women laughed. Fluff, Lei, Betty, Thelma and Daisy sat up front. No matter how hard Daisy tried to avoid Thelma, the woman always managed to be near. Betty had said, "She's keeping her enemies close."

"Anything and everything that flies in these islands is now being tracked. You ladies need to know what it is you're tracking, which is my job today. Now, can anyone tell me what kinds of aircraft we got flying around out there?"

A few names were thrown out. *P-40s. B-17s.* These were the planes most mentioned in the newspaper.

He scanned the room. "Anything else?"

Daisy wanted to answer, but looked around to see if anyone else had something to add. She hated to seem like a know-it-all. Then, Fluff surprised them all by saying, "A Hawk?"

Dunn stepped close and touched her shoulder. "The Curtiss P-36, you are correct." His hand lingered a few seconds too long, but Fluff seemed too pleased with herself to notice. "Now, you got your bombers and your fighters, your reconnaissance planes and pursuit, and you'll also be seeing some flying boats and transports. When the carriers are near, we also have the carrier-based naval bombers. There can be a lot of birds in the sky, and you need to stay on top of all of them," he said.

He began to list the various aircraft on the chalkboard, giving basic descriptions and operational uses and speeds. "In general, a cruising aircraft flies at a constant airspeed in a constant direction. If you know the established flight patterns, then you can more easily determine if you're looking at friend or foe. When something deviates from normal, that's a red flag."

Most of the women scribbled furiously in their notebooks. Daisy already knew the names of most of the planes, but enjoyed hearing technical details about each one. The Grumman F4F Wildcat, for one, was not as fast as a Zero, but sturdy as hell and equipped with a homing device that would help her pilots locate their carrier in poor visibility. It was exhilarating to put her once-useless knowledge to work.

Dunn sauntered back and forth as he spoke. "Now, the Douglas SBD Dauntless dive bomber, she's a beauty. We lost a whole squadron of them at 'Ewa on the seventh, but three days later, SBDs from the *Enterprise* took down a Japanese sub, bless their hearts."

By the end of the morning, the women knew every possible plane in the blue Hawaiian sky. They knew the speed difference between a fighter and a transport, and they knew that air traffic was likely to increase whenever the carriers pulled in. And even though Dunn seemed full of himself, the man knew his stuff.

Just after sunset, when the shift was nearly over and the girls were all dragging from being there double time, a reading came in from the waters beyond Kaʻena Point. Tippy Sondstrom, who had been hovering around the table like a nervous mother, gave it to Daisy to plot. Whatever kind of aircraft it was, it was moving fast. Daisy was certain it was a fighter. All the other plotters had an eye on her flag, which stood out because it was not in the usual flight corridor.

A few seconds later, another call came in. There were two more on its tail. Colonel Nixon requested coordinates and bearing and Captain Owens delivered them to the liaisons. All chatter ceased. While they waited, Nixon began to pace, his footsteps booming through the whole building.

The air force liaison finally received an answer, and said grim-faced, "Not ours."

Then navy reported, "Not ours, either."

It seemed like an hour passed before the marine liaison said, "Nope."

All eyes were on the civil aeronautics guy, who looked ready to cry. "No one's claiming them."

Nixon turned to Owens. "Sound the alarm and send out the pursuit planes." He addressed the Rascals. "Grab your helmets and gas masks and put them on. This could be the next wave."

You could taste the fear in the room, and yet the women all stood, calm and orderly, and strapped their gear on. No one said a peep. The helmets were hard-shelled, but Daisy wondered what help they would be against an air raid.

Maybe to keep off the ash, but that was about it. A moment later, the air-raid siren wailed from somewhere just outside the building, the uneven tone chilling.

Dunn yelled, "Be ready for anything."

The whole scene took on a feeling of being in an outer space movie, with alien creatures sitting around a table holding poles with funny tips. Only Nixon and a few others kept their gas masks off. Daisy wasn't sure if she'd rather be here in the midst of it, knowing what was possibly coming down on them, or at home, blissfully ignorant. Good thing Louise was away.

Plotters around the room kept their cool. More calls came in, while the men conversed in hushed tones. When the next reading came in, the objects in question had made a sharp turn to the east, bringing them closer to the coastline.

"I got a bad feeling about this, boss. Someone shoot the buggers down already," one young man said.

Nixon glared at him. "And what if they're ours? Keep your mouth shut if you don't have anything useful to say."

Dunn circled around the table, helping the girls adjust their masks and tighten their helmets. When he got to Daisy, his hip pressed into her back. He cinched her straps so tight the mask sucked at her face, then bent down so he was two inches away.

"There you go, doll, a perfect fit," he said.

He did the same to a few others, mainly the young ones, including Fluff. Each time, using a different name. *Sugar, Hon, Doll.*

Daisy scanned the board, looking for some kind of answer to the unknown bogies. Betty had just begun to plot the *Enterprise*, where the aircraft carrier had been picked up by Opana.

"What if they're from the carrier?" Daisy asked.

"Navy denied that," Nixon said.

The location made sense, but she didn't push it. She was having trouble breathing and felt light-headed and tingly. More than anything, she wanted to rip off her mask and take a deep breath, to run out the door and head for the ocean. She hated the feeling. *Stay calm,* she ordered herself. But no matter how hard she tried, she couldn't get a full breath. Her heart took off racing. Finally, she pulled the mask down and fanned her face with a code card.

"Rascal, put that gas mask back on. That's an order," Nixon said in a steely voice.

Betty reached out and placed a hand on her arm and kept it there. "We're going to be okay. Trust me on this."

The warm touch was a soothing balm.

Lei, who sat on her other side, whispered, "You can do it."

Daisy slipped her mask back on. The rubber smelled like chemicals and the tinted glass made it hard to see, but more than anything, she felt a rush of affection for these two friends who were rooting for her.

Five minutes passed, then ten. She was able to control her breathing just enough to not fall apart again. Over the years, Daisy had paid close attention to any weakness or sign that she could have inherited her mother's frail mind and unstable temperament. So far, so good. There had been the usual worries and fears, but nothing that screamed *hysteria.* Now she began to wonder. And then a call came in. Nixon picked up faster than she'd ever seen anyone lift a receiver. Sweat matted the front of his shirt, even though it was cold in the room. He nodded a few times and then slammed it down.

"Turns out they were navy after all. For some reason they had their fighters all marked as landed. Damn left hand doesn't know what the right is doing," he said, never once looking Daisy's way or acknowledging she'd been correct. Then the all clear sounded, sweet and loud, and nothing else mattered.

10

THE OPERATION

After four evening shifts in a row, Daisy slept in until noon. During that time, she had stayed with Lei in her two-story home in Nuʻuanu. The house was far nicer than any house she'd been in, other than the Montgomerys'. Tall ceilings, *koa* wood floors and a massive stone patio that spanned the whole front of the house. The best part, though, was that the maid, Asuka, always kept snacks on the table and set a tall glass of cool and pulpy orange juice on Daisy's bedside table in the morning.

Waking up in her own shack to the roar of the sea was nice, but she already missed Asuka. She went to the post office hoping for a letter from her mother. It had been over three weeks since she'd left and Daisy had begun to worry, even though the mail was unreliable these days. When she saw the envelope addressed in Louise's slanted script, she tore it open immediately.

Dear Daisy,

I hope to God that you are safe and well. As you can imagine, our boat ride was not the luxury trip people dream of. We were stuffed into crowded rooms and kept below deck most of the time. I nearly suffocated. Even worse, the captain swerved all over the ocean as though he were drunk. They said it was to keep us alive, which I guess is a good thing. I'm surviving California, but barely. Its damn near freezing here and your aunt keeps the windows open for fresh air. Aside from that, things are fine. I read the newspapers every day, praying for no more attacks and that those submarines go back to where they are from. I trust you are in good hands and am proud of you for staying and doing your part.

Love always, Your Mother

She never got personal mail, so this felt special. No post-cards from long-lost friends or loving grandparents. Only bills. Daisy read the letter three times. Yes, her mother was grumbling, but grumbling was better than silence. And she was reading the newspaper and praying! She sounded like a regular person. Maybe the war would be enough of a shock to Louise's system to wake her up to the world around her.

For the first time in weeks, the sun shone in full winter glory, turning the greens greener and the blues bluer—one of the things Daisy loved most about December and January. These were the moody months, where the weather flip-flopped on a whim. With all that rain, golden mushrooms had popped up all over the yard, too. Fairy stools, Louise used called them. Daisy sat in the overgrown grass, leaned against a tree and took it all in.

She thought about the fairy tales her mother used to read to her. *Thumbelina* was her favorite. Daisy loved to lie in the grass with her head on her mother's lap. Upside down, Louise's plump lips reminded her of red sea anemones and she could have stared at them all day long. As her mother read, one hand would run through Daisy's hair. There had been nothing in the world that Daisy loved more. But that Louise had disappeared long before the war.

One thing Daisy had noticed was that being around people all day sapped her energy. Give her an empty beach and a horse any day. Though she had to admit, she looked forward to seeing Fluff and Betty and Lei and was beginning to understand the notion of female friends. Unlike the men at the stables, the girls strung together more than two sentences, and always wanted more details. They asked where her mother was, and why she'd left and how Daisy was faring living all alone in the boondocks. How they came to have a house on the beach. Who was the closest neighbor. What kind of toothpaste she used. Fluff in particular grilled Daisy on her car rides with Walker, and found it unfathomable that a man and a woman could simply be friends.

"I promise you, I work with a bunch of men and none of them are interested in me. They hardly even notice I'm there," Daisy said.

Fluff gave her a look of disbelief. "So you think." The other girls also spilled their own secrets, and Daisy was touched by their vulnerability. Lei couldn't conceive and wanted a child more than anything—and now her *haole* husband seemed to have lost interest in her; Betty's hair fell out in large clumps whenever Chuck shipped out for any length of time; Fluff had suffered a recently broken heart by a man who, unbeknownst to her, had a family on the

Mainland. Why did it seem to be a rule of life that people were most attracted to what they could not have?

After a productive afternoon of mowing the lawn and trimming the naupaka hedge, Daisy checked the drying aku, which had been in the sun for four days now. Her father had taught her how to make a screen box and shown her just how much brine solution to soak it in. To top it off, Daisy liked to smoke it for added flavor. Usually, she waited for darkness and stars, but nighttime fires were a thing of the past.

She built a small fire with kiawe wood on the edge of the beach, and within minutes, she was intoxicated by the sweet and tangy smoke, swirling skyward. She was so focused on turning the fish and tending the coals that she failed to notice the two men on horseback until they were nearly upon her.

"Wilder," one said.

She jumped.

"You sending smoke signals to the enemy?" the other said.

"Just smoking fish, Dex."

"Not a good idea. I suggest you put that fire out before you get yourself blown up by the military."

"Who put you in charge?" she said, unable to help herself.

"We're part of the guard now."

Dex and Johnny Boy both worked at the ranch, and both had rifles slung over their shoulders. Dex could rope anything that moved and Johnny Boy was stronger than a bull. She looked beyond them for any sign of Walker, but the beach was empty.

She stood. "I'll put it out."

Johnny Boy smiled. "How about a few strips of that aku? Smells pretty *ono*."

The aku was food for the next week, and it was hard to come by now that none of the Japanese fishermen could take out their boats. But Johnny Boy had a mean streak and she didn't want to set him off.

"Where you been lately?" Dex asked.

"Oh, you know, here and there."

"More there than here, looks like," Johnny Boy said.

"I have a new job in town," she said, not wanting to get into it.

"Sounds like Junior is driving you and sister in for some kind of hush-hush operation. You know something we ought to know?"

Again, Daisy wondered what Peg was saying around the ranch.

"I'm not sure where you get your information, but they need typists and people to answer the phones. Boring clerical work—the kind that us girls are really good at," she said with a forced smile. She pulled off a skewer and handed it to Johnny Boy, still smoking. "Now, I need to get back to work."

He eyed her up and down, then took the fish. "You be careful, Wilder, out here on your own."

Daisy nodded to the shotgun, which was leaning against the ironwood. "Oh, I'm not alone."

Back at Little Robert, the pace had picked up considerably. Strengths and weaknesses were beginning to show, but the beauty was someone always picked up the slack. Betty helped Fluff pin chits on a board, showing what type of aircraft it was or whom it belonged to. *25 IS BOMBER! MAKE 34 NAVY! 5 IS NOW OATS! OATS* being *operational air traffic*, and the number corresponding to the flag on the table. Dunn had assigned the role to Fluff when it became clear her plotting was way off base and not improving.

But she had the neatest handwriting of the bunch and for some reason deemed it necessary to use exclamation points on each plotted flight. The most interesting ones were always the UNIDENTIFIED! Those got everyone's hackles raised, with *bogey* becoming an all too familiar term.

"What exactly is a bogey?" Fluff had initially asked.

"It can be one of two things," Dunn happily explained. "Either a false radar blip or an unidentified aircraft. In both cases, you need to take it seriously."

As much as Dunn liked to circulate around the table and find reasons to give a pat on the back or a squeeze to the shoulder, Nixon remained gruff and standoffish. He always had a cup of coffee in one hand and a notebook in the other, and never lightened up. Some of the girls had assigned him the code name *Joe*, for the coffee. "His poor wife," Fluff said, one day during lunch.

Lei lowered her voice. "Thelma said his wife died."

"How would Thelma know?" Daisy said.

"Her father has a hand in everything in these islands," Lei said.

"Do you know how she died?" Daisy asked.

"Nope."

"Poor Nixon, no wonder he's such a sourpuss," Betty said.

Daisy found herself sticking up for him, though she wasn't sure why. "You have to admire his dedication. I don't think he ever sleeps or leaves. I want someone like that defending our islands."

"I've never seen the man smile. That says something about a person, doesn't it?" Fluff said.

Louise never smiled. Maybe some people lost the ability along with their loved one. Betty brightened. "What do you say we make a bet! First gal to get Nixon to smile wins a prize."

"What kind of prize?" Fluff asked.

They all looked around, waiting for someone else to offer suggestions. Daisy had nothing to give but dried fish or cowrie shells. "Maybe just seeing a smile on his face will be reward enough. It'll mean we've cracked his armor."

"What fun is that?" Betty said. "I say the winner gets ten dollars. We get ten girls and each puts in a dollar."

Parting with a dollar would hurt, but at least Daisy had a decent paycheck coming.

"We'll call it Operation Smile. Top secret and need to know only," Fluff said.

They shook on it.

Two days until the WARDs were to move into new quarters at Fort Shafter, Daisy still had not encountered Walker. She was going crazy on the inside, hoping to ride a patrol with him on the beach. A man had never inhabited so much space in her mind, and it was unsettling. She also knew from Peg, who told Thelma who told JoAnn who told Lei, that he was back at home after a few nights of staying in the barracks.

Light winds and huge surf brought a dense layer of haze to Waialua. As the sun drew nearer to the horizon, the whole beach flamed up into dizzying reds and oranges. Salt coated every surface possible—windows, dishes, skin. Daisy sat on the porch and watched. Several fighters flew high above the waves, their telltale stars barely visible. No one came down the beach and she decided he wasn't coming. Again. The very moment she had made up her mind to swim, she heard a commotion in the bushes off to the left. Crashing branches and snapping twigs.

She grabbed the shotgun. "Hello?"

From between the ironwoods came a palomino that she

immediately recognized as Honey Girl. Walker sat atop, with Nalu on a lead behind him.

"It's just me, Wilder. Put that thing down," he said, taking off his hat. None of the guys ever did that for her, and it gave her a flush on the inside.

In a rust-colored plaid shirt and faded blue jeans, he looked all cowboy and no pilot. His hand must be all healed up, too.

"What are you doing in the bushes? You scared me half to death," she said.

"We came down the cane road, thought it would be quicker. Nalu spooked when he heard the planes."

"Horses and fighter planes don't mix."

He nodded. "Point taken."

"Why do you have Nalu? Isn't he injured?"

"His leg is all healed and I thought maybe you'd want to do a patrol with us. I know it's late, but a few things happened and I lost track of time. I could use the help."

After a quick change into riding pants, Daisy led Nalu over to a stump and climbed on. At sixteen hands, he was one of their taller horses. He was also a bighearted animal, and if you weren't careful, he'd nuzzle and lip you silly. Thank goodness he hadn't bolted away like Moon.

Low tide made for easy riding and Walker and Honey Girl took off at an easy trot. In all the years at the ranch, she had never ridden alongside Walker Montgomery. After he graduated high school, he'd joined the navy, something that angered his father to no end. Old man Montgomery wanted him to run the family business, but everyone knew that he and Walker had a falling-out of some kind. Since then, Walker's presence at the ranch had been sporadic.

"They say something big is going down in Singapore," he told her.

"Does that mean the Japanese forces are focusing their attention elsewhere?"

He slowed so they were side by side. "Not necessarily. They have ships and subs all over the Pacific, so we need to stay vigilant. How are you with that shotgun?"

"Pretty good."

She was more than pretty good, but she didn't want to boast.

"We want to keep you safe."

The way he said *we* sent a flutter through her rib cage. Without another word, he moved into a canter. They flew down the beach in a smooth glide with Walker out front, but just barely. Nalu did not like being behind and little by little, edged closer. He had a fine jump in his step and Daisy relaxed her inner thighs to make it easier on him. Though he moved well, he wasn't Moon. When they pulled up alongside Walker, Walker hunkered down and shifted into a full gallop. Daisy and Nalu matched them. They flew along until they reached a rocky outcropping up the way, right around the bend from where Moon disappeared. Walker slowed before she did.

A haunted look passed over his face, but he got off and led them through the rocks to the other side. The charred remains of the Japanese Zero sat half-submerged in the shallows, right where she remembered them to be.

He stopped and stared. Daisy stood next to him.

"The weird thing is, I remember every minute detail of that morning. The layout of the clouds, and where the rain squalls were. The slant of sun rays shining through. Sometimes when I close my eyes, it starts up again in my head, spooling out like a motion picture. I smell the smoke and hear the gunfire." He paused. "And I won't forget that guy's face for as long as I live. He was smiling at me."

Walker trembled slightly. Without thinking, as she would with a spooked horse, Daisy put her hand on his shoulder. She wanted to say something, but could think of nothing helpful. Her breath was slow and even, which often helped calm the horses. Sometimes she wondered if it was normal to base everything on your interaction with horses, but that's mainly what she had. Walker's skin felt hot to the touch.

"I know it doesn't make it easier, but he came here and shot up your island, killed your friends. You were just minding your own business," she said.

"The whole thing stinks. But I guess that's war for you."

Daisy had always wondered. "What made you want to become a pilot? You had so much going here with the ranch."

"You're not going to believe me, but it started by watching the gooney birds soaring around. Seemed like a pair of wings could give you freedom like nothing else. As you know, my dad can be overbearing—" he turned her way and studied her face for a few seconds "—and I wanted something that was all my own, not his."

Daisy was surprised that a man like Walker would take inspiration from a bird. But she understood. She loved the albatross, too.

"How was the training?" she asked.

"Grueling. At the time I thought it was overkill, but now I see that they prepared us well. Not only did we get drilled on Morse code and navigation, we learned hand-to-hand combat and psychology."

"They teach you psychology in flight school?"

"Oh yeah, in case we're taken captive. Americans are soft and lazy by enemy standards. We'd be toast. The training toughened us up, and then some," he said.

People always talked about the Japanese toughness and

discipline, and now they'd shown it at Pearl. "You were hardly soft and lazy."

"Compared to them I was."

"Not anymore. I've seen it with my own eyes," she said.

Beyond the rocks, they hopped back on the horses and kept going. Walker rode alongside her and they talked about everything under the sun. He had a unique talent for seeming so genuinely interested in every word that came out of her mouth, whether it was what kind of fish she caught for lunch, or how things were going at Little Robert and life with the girls. No man had ever been so easy to talk to, nor had she ever wanted to talk to one endlessly like this. It was like being with a girlfriend, except she didn't get dizzy daydreaming about kissing her friends. She would have kept riding all night if they could.

And then he surprised her with, "Can I ask you a personal question?"

Hadn't they already been talking about personal things? "Sure."

Walker pulled up on the reins and came to a stop, she followed suit. "How come you aren't married off yet?"

The water lapped at Nalu's hooves. Daisy thought about making up some lie that would make her not sound like such a failure in the love department, but opted for the truth. "No one has asked. And taking care of my mom, it's not like I had a lot of opportunity to date. Even if there had been fellas out here to date."

"Fair enough."

She quickly added, "I'm not opposed to the idea, with the right person, of course."

One side of his mouth went up. "So a man would have to pass muster?"

A storm was going on inside her, as she tried to maintain her cool. "He would."

She risked a look and their eyes met. For a moment, she thought maybe he would throw his hat in the ring, but instead, he said, "You should know we're heading out on a mission sometime in the next few days."

Daisy's heart dropped to the sand. "Where to?"

"They don't tell us until we leave. Safer that way."

One thing she knew about missions was that plenty of pilots never returned. Their eyes met. Betty's words immediately came to mind. *You don't want a pilot.* All at once, a terrible thought struck her: it was too late, she already did.

11

THE QUARTERS

After the WARDs completed a morning shift, a truck came by to drive them to their new quarters. For a girl always chosen last for teams, being asked to room with Betty and Fluff had felt better than a burst of sun on a cool winter's day. It warmed Daisy's heart from the inside out. The houses were nothing special, and to some of the girls, they probably seemed spare, but they were freshly painted and tidy looking, with ti leaf and red ginger ringing each one. House 375A had two bedrooms, and since there were three of them, Fluff and Daisy took the big room, with two twin beds. Betty, they all decided, should get the queen on the off chance she could smuggle Chuck in when he was off the ship.

No men allowed. The orders had been clear, but the girls were discovering that people sometimes looked the other way in matters of the heart. Especially with the military wives. An unspoken code. And rather than stay in a tiny room on the far side of base by herself while Chuck was gone much of the time, Betty had wanted to room with the girls. Their previous house had been converted to a bachelor officer's quarters, and she hated being alone. An unfortunate quality for a navy wife.

There was a metal bucket full of sand on the front doorstep. It reminded Daisy of the one she used to keep with hermit crabs and sea cucumbers. But this one wasn't for crabs. Ever since the attack on London, when German bombers dropped incendiary bombs across the whole city, Americans began pumping out pamphlets on methods for handling these highly flammable devices. Water and sand should always be kept on hand. Living on the beach, Daisy never worried about it. Here, she was thankful for the bucket.

They spent the afternoon unpacking and moving the couch into every position imaginable. Daisy would have been fine with it anywhere, but Fluff and Betty had strong opinions about where it should go.

"The couch should always face the window," Fluff said, in a sweet yet determined voice.

"But it blocks the door, and we don't want to have to walk around it every time we leave the house. Plus, you should always have a solid wall behind you," Betty said.

They both turned to Daisy. "What do you think?"

"I think it doesn't matter."

"Oh, it matters. Imagine a stream flowing through the house. What path would the water take? You want to keep the water moving and not block it," Betty argued.

Fluff looked around. "I don't see any streams running through the house, do you, Daisy?"

Daisy laughed. "Nope. But I like her reasoning."

"It's Chinese. We had a servant back home who was from

China, her name was Yu Yan, and she was always telling my mom where to put stuff. Mom resisted at first, but eventually saw how brilliant her suggestions were."

"You had servants?" Fluff asked what Daisy was thinking.

"Sugar, where I'm from, everyone had servants."

"Everyone?" Fluff said, with a look of disbelief.

Betty fanned herself with a newspaper. "Well, maybe not *everyone*. My folks hired a bunch of Chinese workers on the plantation, and Yu Yan's husband was one of the heads. Mama needed help running the house, so she took her in. Best decision she ever made."

"I didn't know there were Chinese people in Louisiana," Fluff said.

"Not so different from here."

Hawai'i's plantations were full of their own villages that everyone called a *camp*. Chinese Camp, Filipino Camp, Japanese Camp, and even a Haole Camp, each with its own flavor.

Lei, who had opted to keep living at home, showed up a little later with a bouquet of fresh-cut gardenias from her garden, three large boxes and four bottles of red wine. She set the wine on the Formica countertop, which was seaweed green. "I know it's contraband, but this is top-notch stuff, gals."

Daisy knew the look of a person who had been crying all too well, and with Lei's puffy eyes and red face, there was no mistaking it.

"Are you all right?" Daisy asked.

Lei half smiled. "I'm fine. Anyone care for a drink?"

Betty brought four wineglasses out from the kitchen, which she had stocked full with dishes and cookware from her own home. Daisy had helped her fill the shelves with all kinds of utensils she had never even seen before, and felt ashamed to say so.

Lei opened the wine and set the cork down, then asked Daisy to pour it while she dragged over one of the large boxes and pulled out a portable phonograph and began leafing through a stack of records. Daisy followed orders and poured out the entire bottle. Fluff came out of the bedroom in a flowy white dress and laughed out loud.

"Feeling thirsty, are you?"

"Did I do something wrong?" Daisy never drank wine. Never drank, period.

"Those are just some hefty servings, that's all."

Lei put on a record by Andy Cummings, who serenaded them in the background with "Waikiki" in that deep and swoony voice of his.

Betty raised a glass. "To us and our boys, may we keep these islands safe from any more attacks."

Lei added, "And may this war end as fast as it began."

"Speaking of our boys, Walker said they are leaving on a mission any day now," Daisy said.

"That's the scuttlebutt. I just hope I get to say a proper goodbye to Chuck. Seems like us wives are the last to know anything," Betty said.

Fluff glanced at Daisy with twinkle in her eye. "Walker is one of *our* boys now, is he?"

"He is a pilot on the *Enterprise*, so yes."

"That's not what I meant."

Betty jumped in. "Don't say I didn't warn you. You're likely to end up with a broken heart if you fall for a pilot."

Daisy looked into her glass, swirled it and took a big gulp. The wine went down more smoothly than expected. "All that time in the car together, it's only natural that we've ended up friends."

"He ever take any friendly detours on the way home to watch the submarine races?" Fluff asked.

Daisy swatted at her arm. "Don't be ridiculous."

"What's ridiculous about it? Two extremely attractive, single adults who happen to enjoy each other's company. I asked around, and word is, there has been no official engagement. Sounds like Thelma might be making more of it than it really is."

This was news.

"Mmm-hmm." Lei nodded in agreement.

"Don't let Thelma hear you say that," Daisy said, looking toward the open window, as if their voices might carry down the lane.

"Why are you so intimidated by that woman? Yes, she has money, but so what?" Betty said.

"I don't know. She's smart, too. And gorgeous and worldly—"

Fluff swung her hips around to the music. "And boring. Nor is she as smart as you, my lovely plotting wizard."

Daisy felt the wine in her legs, running through her blood vessels and weakening her knees. A rather pleasant sensation that detracted from all the unwanted attention.

"That woman is so full of herself, there ain't room for another person in there. Walker is a fool if he wants her, in which case you wouldn't want him anyway," Betty said.

Daisy's resolve was slipping. But if she admitted out loud that she had a thing for Walker, then it meant putting her heart out into the world. There would be no going back. Sharing the intimacies of her life with other people felt risky.

She took another sip of wine. "What makes you think I want him?"

Betty looked offended. "You think we're that dumb?"

"How about because you float out of the car whenever he drops you off. Or how your voice gets higher whenever you mention his name. It may not be obvious to you, but it's obvious to us," Fluff said.

They all nodded in agreement. These gals were not going to give up.

Daisy sighed. "So maybe I have developed an innocent crush on him. It's not like I'm going to act on it. And this stays between us. Walker's whole family hates me, and the last thing I need is for Peg to get wind of this."

"Jane Eyre said it best. Wouldn't you rather be happy than dignified?" Fluff asked.

"I've never read Jane Eyre."

"Well, you ought to. You could learn a few things about life and love. I'll lend you my copy."

Daisy wasn't about to point out that Fluff herself was un-attached and recently brokenhearted.

"And I don't give a horse's tail about being dignified. So I guess the answer is yes," she said.

"Which is precisely what draws Walker to you, I'm sure. Men love a wild streak. Something they have to tame," Betty said.

"Even if he liked me, nothing could ever happen be-tween us. His father fired me for stealing Moon and they think I'm a dumb hick. The Montgomerys would never allow their son to be with someone like me."

A breeze wandered through the house, stirring up the air. Mrs. Montgomery had always made it clear that Daisy—and even her father—were hired help and several steps below them in importance. Sure, they got invited to the Christmas party, but so did everyone else.

"We need to ramp up our efforts on finding that horse. Then they won't have any valid reason," Lei said.

Fluff told them, "I put it out there to my family. Uncle T says that up until December 7, the Pineapple Derby was still going strong in Kailua. I guess there are some unsavory characters involved and a lot of money being made. If Moon fell into the wrong hands, he'd be worth a pretty penny."

Lei opened another bottle and poured, though Daisy's glass was still half-full. Her body was glued to the chair and her head felt wobbly. She held her hand over her glass, "No more for me." Lei poured anyway.

"I think we need to run another top-secret operation," Betty said.

Fluff clasped her hands together and squealed. "Yes! We'll pack a picnic and go around the island on reconnaissance."

Despite her struggles with technical details, Fluff had really taken to the clandestine nature of their work. She couldn't keep her quadrants straight or figure out a range arc, but she knew every code name on the table, from Alfred to Kendrick to Zachary, and had begun to attach code names to everything and everyone. Nixon was Nancy and Dunn was Dorothy and Danielson, Daddy.

"We'll go on our next day off. I'll drive," Lei said, as though the trip was nonnegotiable.

Fluff squinted in concentration for a few moments, then said, "Operation Equine!" So this was what happened when a bunch of women got together for wine. They talked about men and concocted schemes to get themselves into trouble. Sitting here in this room was like a big warm hug, and before she knew it, Daisy's eyes were tearing up. For a few moments, it wasn't about the war and the fear and the latest rumors, it was about the four humans sitting in this small wooden house.

They all looked to Daisy for approval. How could she deny them?

"I love it!"

Sometime in the blackest hour of night, Daisy woke to a strange sound. She remained motionless under the covers.

Had she been dreaming? A loud rustle in the bushes just outside nearly stopped her heart. Sleeping in a different bed for the first time in her life was bad enough, now this. She should have brought the shotgun, but had figured they were on a US military base and well protected. It was a windless night, not even a whisper of a breeze. Across the room, Fluff snored away. Moments later, a low guttural noise came in through the window, followed by the tiniest *meow*.

Her whole body relaxed. She tried to go back to sleep, but every time she began drifting off, the cat would meow again. The animal seemed to know the exact second Daisy was going under. Tomorrow was a big day and she needed her sleep. She had half a mind to yell or bang the wall or even shine a light, but that would only cause a commotion and wake the whole neighborhood. After what felt like hours, she finally got up and tiptoed down the hall, through the living room and out the front door, guided primarily by her hands. Outside, there was enough pale moonlight to see outlines of trees, automobiles and large objects. Daisy went around back. She was barefoot and in a cotton nightgown, and the cool air pricked her skin.

"Here, kitty, kitty," she whispered.

She watched for any signs of a shape moving about, but saw nothing. Food might help her cause, but that would surely wake up Betty and Fluff. "Kitty!"

Going back to bed would solve nothing, so Daisy sat down in the grass and waited. Every now and then, she whispered to the cat, but it remained stubbornly hidden. With a parched mouth and a small headache at the base of her neck, oh, how she just wanted to sleep. She lay back in the grass. Between the clouds, clusters of stars shone through and she looked for constellations. If there was one thing you could count on in life, it was the night sky, and even more so, the North Star. Even behind the clouds, you knew the stars were shining.

For a time, she was caught somewhere between wake and dreamland. She swore she felt a sandpaper tongue licking her face and soft fur rubbing up against her arm. And then she was in a plane with Walker soaring over Kahuku Point. He let her take the controls and she was feeling very proud of herself when a round of bullets hit the fuselage. First one engine sputtered and then the other. The plane took a nosedive.

"We're going down!" she screamed.

Walker kept his cool. "Pull the nose up, nice and easy."

Nothing happened. The ocean below was a blue blur coming up fast. "I can't!"

"Daisy you can. Up!"

Something was hitting her on the side. Were they being shot again? No, it was just Walker leaning forward and tapping her. "Why are you hitting me?"

Daisy cracked her eyes. She was lying on her side in the damp grass and there were two black boots in front of her face. The plane had crashed but she was alive!

"Where's Walker?" she mumbled.

A hand gently shook her on the shoulder. "Ma'am, wake up."

In the predawn murk, she noticed the outlines of the house and everything came crashing back to her. She bolted upright, covering her chest with her arms.

"Rough night last night?" he asked.

"This is not what it looks like. There was a cat out here making a lot of noise. I came out to see what the fuss was and I must have fallen asleep."

Her heart still thumped along from the plummeting plane. Gunpowder tickled her nose.

"Who's Walker? That the name of your cat?"

Suddenly, Fluff was standing next to the man. "Yes, yes it is."

He kept his eye on Daisy. "Normally, I have to report this kind of thing. Breaking curfew is serious business."

"I'm sure you can see it was an honest mistake," Fluff said.

Daisy was annoyed. "This is our yard, not the street. So technically, I haven't done anything wrong."

He held out a hand to help her up. "How about this— you ladies keep Walker inside at night. That way there's no temptation to go out after him. And no confusion."

Fluff laughed out loud. "We'll do that, sir."

12

THE FLY BOYS

At 0800, the girls were sitting in their seats at Little Robert, ready to learn everything there was about vectoring an aircraft. Daisy was on her third cup of coffee, and had just swallowed her second malasada. On the mornings that Lei brought them, three-quarters of the girls in the room went around with sugar mustaches. Fluff was halfway through telling Lei about the cat named Walker when Nixon walked in. All conversation ceased.

"Hochman is out, so I'm taking over this morning," Nixon said. He did not look pleased.

Daisy looked closer, noticing Nixon, too, had a line of sugar crystals on his upper lip. For some reason, it made him seem more human. All eyes were on him, and he looked down at the papers he held, hands a little shaky.

"We're just waiting on two other fellows," he said.

The girls all sat tensely at their desks, until someone in the back started whispering, and then a few more, and pretty soon the whole room was an echo of chatter. Fluff picked up where she left off with Lei.

"The poor man probably thought he'd died and gone to heaven, with an angel in a damp white nightgown sitting at his feet."

Betty leaned in. "I was sound asleep, never heard a peep, but you can bet they'll be fighting for duty in our neighborhood now."

Lei attempted to seem interested, but there was a flatness to her smile. All of her gumption seemed to have been left at home.

"Is everything all right?" Daisy asked her, once again. Maybe it wasn't her place to ask, since Lei fell someplace between friend and mother and was the most efficient person around, but she couldn't help herself.

Lei simply said, "Fine."

She was not fine. Anyone could see that. In Daisy's experience, moods changed the chemistry in a room. Each one having its own signature and rubbing off on the people around them. Sadness was heavy and tasted like salt, making everyone feel weepy, while anger suffocated and pressed in with sharp edges, giving off a kind of invisible steam. From Lei, Daisy sensed resignation and a hollowness.

Living with Louise had required her to be an expert in body language. But it wasn't just that. Her father had taught her at a young age to pay attention not only to a horse's eyes, but postures and gestures and subtle cues they sent off. Humans were no different from horses. In that respect at least. She imagined herself in a room full of horses. Nixon would be the stallion with twitchy ears and tension around his eyes while Dunn would be the one flehmening and sniffing for pheromones. The girls would all be in various states of relaxation, with some, like Thelma, having their heads high and ears turned back, keenly listening in on others' conversations.

A few minutes later, two men entered the room, both in flight suits. Fluff stomped hard on Daisy's foot under the table as she watched Walker and another pilot shake hands with Nixon.

"Ladies, meet Lieutenants Walker Montgomery and Ed Skinner. They are going to help you understand what vectoring means to us here at Little Robert, and how important it is to a pilot," Nixon said, stiffly.

Walker seemed to grow more handsome each day, or was it a figment of Daisy's imagination? His eyes scanned the room and when they fell on her, a smile showed in his eyes. She shifted in her seat and felt a line of heat running up her spine. Something was obviously wrong with her. She found her reactions distracting and unsettling. Yet the more time she spent in proximity to Walker, the more she thought about him.

Nixon gave a brief intro. "Now, there will be times when we have pilots coming in that need help in navigation and maintaining their track, especially at night. With radar, we can do that."

This was the first time that Nixon had spoken to the girls as a group, and Daisy noticed that he rarely made eye contact with any of them. As he spoke, he kept turning his attention to the two pilots, as if they were the ones who needed to know this. Walker tapped his foot and nodded along to Nixon, but every so often, his gaze wandered toward the side of the room where Daisy sat. She made it a point to focus on Nixon. She wanted everyone in the room to know that she took this vectoring very seriously.

"There may be times when your guidance means life or

death for these boys. Would you two like to explain how they can best support you?" Nixon said to Walker.

Walker stood and put his hands in his pockets. You could have heard a feather fall. "Let me just start by thanking you all for volunteering to do this work. The fact of the matter is, we need you and we appreciate you being here."

Daisy thought he'd make a good politician someday. Nixon, though, remained unreadable but for the slight hardening of his jaw. Heads nodded, the girls sat up straighter in their chairs and a few spoke up.

"We're here for you."

"They'd have to drag my dead body off this island."

"Duty calls."

Thelma, front and center, said, "You can count on us, Lieutenant. For anything."

"Thank you, ma'am," he said.

Ma'am?

Skinner, a sun-tanned blond with bright green eyes, stood next to him and added, "I know that they've been holding out on you with this last job, and even that some guys think you can't hack it. That's why we wanted to come talk to you in person."

It was true. The WARDs had been transitioned to most other roles at Little Robert, aside from those of Nixon and Major Oscar and the liaisons. But up until now, no one felt they were ready or even capable of vectoring aircraft. But men were being siphoned out of the islands and into the Pacific at an alarming rate, and as with most things, necessity sometimes dictated.

Betty spoke up. "Oh, we can hack just about anything they throw at us, so you fellas needn't worry."

Walker gave a quick salute, then his eyes flashed to Daisy. "I don't doubt that."

A perceptible satisfaction spooled around her. Every single word that came out of his mouth felt meant for her and only her. She wanted to hold on to the feeling.

"A lot of people think that women are bad at science and numbers, but that's just plain wrong. You tell your pilot friends they are in better hands than they've ever been," Tippy called from the back.

Skinner turned bright red.

Joyce added, "And we've only just begun!"

A line of perspiration showed up on Nixon's upper lip, or maybe it was coffee, and he looked ready to bolt. Walker looked like he could use a little support right about then, but all Daisy could offer was a small smile. By volunteering to talk to a roomful of women, he knew he was stepping into a dangerous hive. The air buzzed with girl power.

"Can I see a show of hands, how many of you are military wives?" Walker asked.

Betty, Jane, Doris, Rita, Marilyn, Vera, Stella and Opal raised their hands high.

He nodded. "Thank you, and how many others have loved ones out there, fighting? Maybe a family member or friend?"

Since much of the town that Daisy grew up in consisted of Japanese and Filipino plantation workers, she didn't know anyone in the war. Except for Walker. Did he count as a loved one? Hands shot up around her. Her mouth went dry. For some reason, she felt like this was a test, that he was speaking only to her and wanted to see her reaction. Her hand felt heavy as a bowling ball. If nothing else, Walker qualified as a friend. Daisy raised her hand. Their eyes met and for what felt like a whole day, he didn't look away. She tried, but found she couldn't, either. The spot underneath her ribs hummed.

Skinner seemed to sense something had happened and took over. "So, I don't need to tell you what's at stake here. Now, going forward, you're gonna see a lot more air traffic, but nothing I can talk about specifically. My friend Walker here has a little story for you."

Walker ran his hands through his hair. "I'm not going to lie to you. Being a pilot can be scary as hell. You're up there all alone—or with one other guy—just you and the sky, until suddenly your plane is being riddled with gunfire. Immediately, you bank a turn so your wings are almost vertical and you beeline it for the ocean, straight down until you think your plane is going to come apart." He gave a sad laugh. "They tell you the wings will cave at 300 knots, and your airspeed is now close to 350 but the wings hang tight. The Zero is still on your tail, and now you fly straight up into the sun, praying to the Lord above that you don't stall out. After corkscrewing through the sky, you come back around and finally get a shot in that takes him down. You feel nothing but relief that you get to live another day. You can breathe again, until you realize you don't have enough fuel to get back to land. You don't see any other planes around and it's getting dark. What do you do?"

When he finished speaking, Daisy realized her own breathing had nearly ceased. All the other women in the room hung on his words. Fluff raised her hand and waved like an eager first-grader.

"Yes?" Walker said.

"Radio for help. Mayday, mayday, mayday! And you would tell them the type of plane, how many of you there are, the nature of your problem, your location, that kind of thing," Fluff said.

They had recently learned that you said "mayday" three

times in a row. This was the kind of thing that Fluff latched onto, though she still couldn't plot to save her life.

"And what if you've lost track of your bearings and there's no land in sight. What do you tell the controller?" Walker asked.

"Um."

"You should still be able to guess which way the islands are, based on the sun and the wind, and you would head that way," Lei suggested.

"But you're almost out of gas," Walker said.

Daisy raised her hand.

He raised an eyebrow. "Miss Wilder?"

Not ma'am.

"If you were within range, your plane would be tracked by one of the radar stations, and we'd have you plotted on the board. One of us would know your exact location, in which case we would send a rescue team straight away, so you could ditch if you had to."

He smiled. "Exactly. That's why it's so important for you to be accurate and to know your stuff. We depend on it. There will also be times when you need to direct bombers and fighters into blacked-out airfields through voice direction. You'll be their eyes and their ears, so to speak."

Walker and Skinner went over a variety of other scenarios that the women might encounter, and how they could help the pilots. Hearing it from his mouth—the cold and solitude of being in a fighter or a bomber—brought the weight of the WARDs' roles to life in a way that markers on a table never would. The lesson was sobering and inspiring and made Daisy want to memorize every relevant parcel of information. She vowed that on her watch, none of these boys would be lost.

When it came time for them to leave, Daisy felt the urge to stand up and hug him. An unusual reaction, but Walker seemed to cause all kinds of unusual reactions. As he walked out, she waited for him to glance her way, but he kept his eyes on the floor, leaving no opening for even a wave or a smile.

After the pilots were gone, Nixon drilled into them what he called the phraseology of flight. He had a tendency to add *ology* to the ending of words. As it turned out, he'd had been a freshly minted pilot in the Great War, in the 95th Aero Squadron, the first American pursuit squadron on the Western Front. Their mission was to rid the skies of enemy aircraft and escort bombers and reconnaissance flights. Needless to say, he knew a thing or two about air combat and the meaning of fear.

Vectoring was similar to plotting, only you were talking a pilot through the sky and to a destination. "So even though flight time is distance divided by speed, you have to take into consideration both magnitude and heading and wind. Air speed is hugely affected by wind. And here in the islands, we have plenty of it," Nixon told them.

"The trade winds," Fluff said.

"Most of the time. And don't forget, we say *met*, not *weather*. Speaking of, is there a WARD in the room who can recite the military alphabet for me?"

Thelma made a valiant attempt, but got hung up on *King*. Tippy couldn't get past *Oboe*. Then Fluff stood and in a loud, clear voice, rattled them off. "Able, Baker, Charlie, Dog, Easy, Fox, George, How, Item, Jig, King, Love,

Mike, Nan, Oboe, Peter, Queen, Roger, Sail, Tare, Uncle, Victor, William, X-Ray, Yoke, Zebra."

Daisy wanted to stand and clap, but Nixon just said, "Correct."

He then went over such terms as *continue present heading* or *turn left heading one zero zero*, which meant that the pilot was expected to turn to the desired heading. "Now, keep in mind, when you speak to pilots on heading, you say each number individually. It's two-eight-zero, not two eighty. Got that? And nine is always niner."

They learned more checklists and calculations that were rather technical, even for Daisy. Fluff and a few others kept raising their hands for clarification.

"I'm never going to get this straight," JoAnn finally said.

"With an attitude like that you aren't," Nixon shot back.

"You're right, sir. Sorry about that," she mumbled.

He went on. "The boys on board get five hundred hours of navigational instruction. They know their stuff. You need to know yours, too. Pure and simple, vectorology is providing navigational guidance to aircraft," he said.

Fluff, who had been taking notes diligently, set her pencil down. "Excuse me, sir, does this mean we can call ourselves vectorologists?" She was dead serious. If Nixon was ever going to smile, it would be now, but he only pressed his lips together and said, "You need to earn the title."

By the time they wrapped up training for the day, Daisy was feeling the effects of a poor sleep—stiff neck, heavy eyelids and foggy thinking. She went to her cubbyhole to gather her purse and gas mask, and saw a piece of folded yellow paper sticking out. Girls filed in around her, reaching for their own things. She hesitated to open it with everyone around, but curiosity won out. Beneath the note was a pink plumeria. No one was paying any attention, so she stuck the flower behind her right ear and opened the paper. The writing was neat and boxy, like an engineer's or architect's.

Wilder,

In case I don't get to say goodbye, well...goodbye, a hui hou! Stay out of trouble and take care.

Yours truly,

W

P.S. I'll miss our drives.

He had started to write something else, that began with *you*, and then crossed it out. Without thinking, she held up the letter to her nose and sniffed. Eyes closed. Was that sea salt and horse she smelled? Or just her vivid imagination conjuring up things? An image of Walker riding down the beach in his faded blue jeans came to mind, causing a swirl in her chest.

"What's that?"

Peg was standing two feet away, looking like a rat had gotten loose in her hair. Poor woman was always trying some new style and never quite succeeding. Daisy quickly folded the paper shut. Had Peg seen the writing?

"Nothing."

"Where'd you get the flower?"

"I picked it on my way in."

"Flowers aren't part of the WARD uniform. If we want to be taken seriously, we need to show them that we mean business. Show them that we're just like them," Peg said, with an annoying air of authority.

"Then why go through all the trouble styling your hair and wearing all that makeup? You think that is any better?" Daisy said.

Peg frowned. "A certain standard of feminine grooming is necessary."

"You contradict yourself. And we aren't just like them, but we're as good if not better. And I take this job more seriously than anyone, so I don't think one little flower will have any effect on my performance," Daisy said, proud of herself for taking a stand.

Peg turned toward her cubbyhole, and Daisy thought she was done, but she continued. "By the way, don't think that you have a chance with my brother. He has a tendency of being charming to everyone and in the process hearts are broken. Save yourself the trouble."

"Thanks for the warning," Daisy said, with half a mind to wave the note in her face. "But it's not me you need to worry about, it's Walker."

Peg frowned. "What's that supposed to mean?"

"Oh, nothing," Daisy said, then lowered her voice. "And while I have your attention, it sounds to me like you've been going around boasting about our new job. Both Mr. Bautista and Dex and JB seem to know more than they should. Whatever happened to our sworn secrecy?"

Peg's face went slack. "How dare you insinuate something like that. I haven't breathed a word."

"Well, you've said something, because they both asked me about our hush-hush and important work. I'd watch your step there," she said, turning a shoulder and marching off without waiting for a response. To hell with Peg.

The following morning in Little Robert was chaos. This mission that they had been hearing about for days now was clearly underway. The *Enterprise* was shipping out. Calls were coming in from Oscars around the island faster than the WARDs could pick them up. The women scrambled to keep order on the table. Dunn circled like a shark, assisting those who had questions.

"Can someone get more markers? We need more markers," he called.

The *Enterprise* appeared to be heading southwest, but beyond that, no one could say where she was going. Everyone had their hunches, though. "Somewhere in the wild blue Pacific, where the sea swallows the sky," Fluff said.

"Wherever she goes, I hope she kicks some serious butt," Betty said, to no one in particular.

Her husband, Chuck, had come by the house last night—despite strict rules about no men in the WARD quarters—to say goodbye. The minute he walked in the door, Betty sailed across the room and he lifted her up and swung her around. Chuck was tall and rugged with an easy smile and Daisy liked him immediately.

"You gals take good care of my little B, will ya?" he said.

Fluff said, "We have each other's backs. Always."

"Lord only knows how long we'll be away, but when we get back, I'm stealing her away for a few nights," he said.

Betty stared up at him. You could feel the love seeping out through their pores. "Daisy has a beach house she said we could use. The three of us are going to go stay there on our next two days off and I will scope it out," she told him.

He leaned in and kissed her. The two of them then disappeared into the bedroom while Daisy and Fluff did their best to continue preparing Betty's "Death Casserole," which was spinach and chicken dripping in mayonnaise and cheddar cheese. Her grandmother and great aunt baked it every time they went to a funeral, as it was always a sure thing. The unfortunate name had stuck.

"Maybe we should consider calling it something else," Fluff said to Daisy, who was chopping the spinach.

"I thought the same thing. Now is not the time to be serving Death Casserole to anyone."

"Do you think Betty would be offended?"

"She'd understand."

Fluff smiled. "What about Victory Casserole?"

"Perfect!"

"Speaking of perfect, those two make me homesick for a man. And not just any man. One that looks at me the same way Chuck looks at Betty."

Daisy slipped a cube of cheese into her mouth, savoring the sharp tang.

"Your time will come. I have no doubt," she said.

"Easy for you to say."

"What's that supposed to mean? You and I are in the same boat. But I'm not in any kind of rush," Daisy said.

"Precisely. But see, you genuinely don't care. And I do care and it's hard to pretend that I don't care, which makes me less attractive to the male species. It's some invisible law of nature."

Daisy shrugged. "We're going to have to work on it, then."

At Little Robert, once the bustle of the departing mission slowed, the women began honing their vectoring skills. Several squadrons of the Hawaiian Air Force, which had just been renamed the Seventh Air Force, remained at home to provide air defense for the islands, and drills were conducted where pilots radioed into Little Robert for navigation assistance.

Daisy kept a cheat sheet next to her with the phraseology Nixon had taught them. The first practice plane she guided in was a supposedly injured P-39 fighter pilot coming in from northwest of Oʻahu, beyond Kaʻena Point, to land at a blacked-out Wheeler Field. He was running low on fuel, too. Nixon stood behind her, coffee steaming onto the back of her neck. He seemed to have singled out Daisy for unknown reasons. Either he had no faith in her, or a whole lot of faith.

"Can I just direct him to Haleʻiwa?" she asked.

"Why would you do that?"

"Because it's closer as the crow flies, and there are no mountains to fly over."

Nixon leaned in and pointed to a spot on the map. "He can go through Kolekole Pass. Haleʻiwa has no medical facilities, so we don't send injured men there."

Daisy hadn't considered that. "Yes, sir."

Whoever the pilot was, he was doing a fabulous job of feigning injury and being unable to see in the dark. Even though Daisy knew it was fake, her palms began to sweat.

He moaned. "If I don't land soon, I'm going to have to ditch. Help me, Rascal!"

"What's your name?" she asked.

"Lieutenant Sanchez, ma'am."

"Okay, Sanchez, continue present heading. I'll be here with you until you land safe and sound, and a medic will be standing by," she said, glancing back at Nixon with a shrug, as she really had no idea what to say. But it sounded good.

"Tell him he needs to be above angels two to get through the pass," Nixon said.

"Angels two?"

"Two thousand feet. The pass is sixteen hundred feet but the mountains around it are four thousand. It's his only shot at getting through," Nixon said.

No one had mentioned *angels* as a measure of altitude above sea level, but their training was a crash course and then some.

"Just so you know, you'll be flying through Kolekole, so I need you to listen carefully to my every word, lieutenant."

A burst of static, and then, "Roger."

"What is your present altitude?"

"I'm at angels three."

"Perfect. Stay there."

They had learned that the higher you flew, the thinner the air was, and thus aircraft used less fuel at higher altitude. It had seemed counterintuitive, but so did a lot of things in Little Robert. Like Dunn and Nixon. Nixon was stern and gruff, while Dunn was personable and chummy, yet Daisy found herself avoiding Dunn and gravitating toward Nixon. Fluff was the other way around. She enjoyed the sugary compliments and was intimidated by Nixon's serious nature. But something about Dunn raised Daisy's hackles.

As Sanchez and his P-39 neared the pass, Nixon said, "Have you compensated for the inaccuracies of the azimuth?"

She'd been so nervous with him standing there, she couldn't think straight. "Not yet."

"Do you want to be responsible for this airman crashing his plane into the mountainside?"

"No, sir."

"Well, then, get on it."

A range cut—much less of a mouthful than *inaccuracies of the azimuth*. It was the job of the filterer to do this. Daisy and her team had not learned it yet. "We haven't been taught that."

She glanced up at him and noticed his face turning tomato red. "You know what scares me to death?" he said.

"No, sir."

"That we have a roomful of people here with absolutely no idea what they're doing. Instead of planning dinner and changing diapers, you gals somehow ended up in my command center."

Anger seared the back of her throat. *Planning dinner and changing diapers?* Her back went rigid. Daisy knew she shouldn't respond but the words poured out anyway.

"That's not a fair assessment. Nor is it accurate, since none of us have children. And we might be inexperienced, but it doesn't mean we aren't capable. We've only had a month to learn hundreds of codes, detailed maps, aircraft specifications, how to plot radar reports, and a dozen other things. Give us a chance, teach us, guide us, show us. But don't belittle us."

A voice came through the headset. "Excuse me?"

The pilot!

"Sorry, that wasn't for you," she said.

"Some poor bloke giving you trouble?" he said.

Nixon leaned in. "This poor bloke is Colonel Nixon, Sanchez."

"Colonel! Sounds like you have a firecracker on your hands. I gotta say I like her spunk."

Of all things, insulting Nixon over the airwaves with a pilot listening in. If Daisy still had a job tomorrow, she would be surprised. The voice of Mrs. White, her third-grade teacher, echoed in her ear. *Impulsivity is going to be your downfall. Mark my words.*

They still had a soul in the air who needed guidance. "Colonel Nixon, I apologize if I was out of line, but can you teach me how to do a range cut, so we can get Sanchez back here in one piece?"

"Sounds good to me," Sanchez said.

For the first time, Daisy noticed that the room had quieted and all the girls around the table were listening in. Nixon was cornered. His left eye twitched. But to Daisy's surprise, he pulled a chair over, grabbed a notepad and pen and started talking.

"So, you have a reading from Wai'anae and one from Kawailoa. The true position of Sanchez's flight is where the two range arcs intersect. Do you follow?"

"Yes, sir."

And that was how she learned to do a range cut.

13

THE MISSION

Civilians were allowed to drive on the roads again during daylight hours, but with fuel rations, you had to pick and choose your outings. Lei's husband, George, a businessman with Thomas & Sons, seemed to know a way around everything, and gasoline was no exception. As they careened down the Pali Highway toward Kailua, Daisy didn't even want to blink, the views were so spectacular. Green curtains of cliff to either side, all the way to Chinaman's Hat and Rabbit Island, and blue sky reflected even bluer seas, with white ropes of sand outlining the meandering shore. Fluff held her camera. "I love this old thing. I know it's a beast, but it takes fabulous pictures, and I want to record our day," she said.

This was the girls' first real outing together, and they were all thrilled to get off base and have some breathing room. To forget about life for a while.

First stop was the Kailua Track, even though all races had

come to a halt in December. The track had been closed for years, then recently reopened, and now closed again. Fluff's Uncle T worked there, managing the grounds and tending to the watermelon patch in the center of the racetrack, and he was to meet them at the stables.

"If someone has Moon, he's not going to be dumb enough to keep him at the racetrack," Daisy had said.

"This reminds me of the story "The Adventure of Silver Blaze," about a famous racehorse who disappears. Too bad we don't have a 'curious incident of the dog in the night-time' to help us. Though in your case, it was more of a curious incident of a dogfight in midair," Fluff said, turning sideways and leaning against the front door so she could see everyone in the car.

"What are you talking about?"

"Have you not read Sherlock Holmes, my dear Daisy?"

"Never. I hardly read."

Reading was not her strong suit.

"We really need to get you up to speed. Operation Equine is going to require us to be keen investigators, and there is no one better to emulate than Sherlock Holmes. His crime-solving methods were genius."

Fluff continued. "We need to approach it with a blank mind and think logically. Preconceived notions and making assumptions will only lead us astray. So let's get clear on the scenario. Tell us what happened from the beginning, and be as detailed as possible."

Betty lifted an eyebrow. "I had no idea we were sharing a house with Nancy Drew." Daisy laughed, but played along. There wasn't much to tell. Moon got spooked, Moon ran away. End of story.

"So as I see it, there are three possibilities. One, Moon is still roaming wild, but for whatever reason hasn't been located. Two, someone has Moon, either by design or by accident. Three, Moon is dead."

"If he was dead, someone would have found his body," Daisy said, not allowing for that possibility to exist in her mind. She could still feel the cadence of his hoofbeats on the hard-packed sand.

Fluff pulled out a leather-bound notebook and began scribbling. "Give me the names of those who know the horse."

"Me, Mr. Silva, who trained him, Walker, Mr. Montgomery and all the guys that work at the stables."

"You said he's a Thoroughbred. Where did Mr. Montgomery get him? And when?"

"About six months ago. He brought him in from the Mainland from a man named Gunner. The horse quickly became Walker's and now that I think about it, I remember thinking that maybe Moon was a bribe to get Walker back in his good graces. They'd had a falling-out years back."

Fluff's head bobbed against the window. "How did you know they had a falling-out?"

"Everyone knew. Then Walker disappeared for a while. I knew he joined the military, but then Mr. Silva said he was back on the island, but he never came around. And then once Moon showed up, he did."

"Hmm. Interesting. What was the falling-out over?"

"I'm guessing it has something to do with Walker joining the navy and not wanting to run the business," Daisy said.

By now, they were passing Olomana, and a marshy smell floated through the windows. The line of questioning seemed to be veering off course.

"No offense, but what does any of this have to do with Moon?" Daisy asked.

"We need to consider *everything*, as Sherlock Holmes

would have. Sometimes by sifting through all the facts, you come upon a vital piece of information you might overlook."

Betty twisted her thick blond hair into a bun. "Might you be taking this detective thing a little too far?"

Lei, who had been quietly driving and listening, said, "Let her continue," and then to Fluff, "You could have a future as a private investigator if we actually find this horse. I might even hire you myself."

For what? Daisy wondered.

"Oh, we'll find this horse all right and we'll clear Daisy's name in the process. Now, in your searching, did you find anyone who said they'd seen Moon?" Fluff asked.

"Not one person."

"That seems odd, given what a small town it is out there. A black Thoroughbred would stand out, wouldn't he?" Betty said.

Fluff said, "Did you go door-to-door and ask?"

"No, I didn't go door-to-door. We had just been attacked by the Japanese, remember?"

Betty was getting drawn in, "Could he have gone into the mountains and is up there enjoying his freedom?"

"Unlikely. Beyond the sugarcane, it gets pretty cliffy and then jungly. Horses prefer open plains and pastures," Daisy said.

"Then it stands to reason that someone has him. How much do you think he's worth?" Fluff asked.

"His sire is a famous racehorse from Maryland and all I know was that Mr. Montgomery paid upward of five thousand bucks for him."

"That changes everything. Now we have motive!"

Daisy sighed, missing Moon and his soft muzzle. "And Mr. Montgomery stood to make a lot more than that on betting. Moon was the fastest horse I've seen on the island. Walker wanted him for polo, but his father wanted to race him."

"Had he raced him yet?"

"Not that I know of."

Fluff squinted down at her notes for a while, lost in thought. Her hair spilled out across her shoulder in copper waves. She seemed so intent on finding Moon, it was touching. Here they were, spending a whole day helping Daisy, when they could be visiting their own families or relaxing. "I think that's a wrap for the time being. Now we gather more evidence," Fluff said.

Lei veered left, and the road went from paved to gravel to sand. Under a cloudless sky, they passed marshlands with cute little Hawaiian moorhens and long-legged stilts, an endless grove of coconut trees and a cluster of tin shacks with scrappy dogs and roosters roaming free.

"Are you sure we're in the right place?" Betty said.

Fluff motioned forward. "Keep going. Uncle T said it was just past the coconut trees."

Sure enough, they came upon a farm fence with two giant wooden poles. The sign hanging across the entrance read Kailua Track Horse Races. The place looked deserted but for a couple of horses and a dilapidated donkey grazing in a field. There was no gate, so they drove on in. As they putted through a grove of kiawe trees, the scent of nutty pods wafting in, a memory arose in Daisy's head.

Sitting on her father's lap, munching on buttered popcorn. The cheering and hollering around them was louder than anything her toddler ears had heard before. Dust and hoof thunder filled the stands. A voice on the loudspeaker announced a new horse, pulling ahead. Each time her father jumped up to scream, his excitement traveled to her through some invisible means. She wanted to remember more, but memories were such shifty things. Try to grasp one, and it slipped away. Nothing else came to her but a feeling of deep contentment.

Lei pulled over under a giant monkey pod tree near the stables. A gangly Hawaiian man who was shoveling manure stopped what he was doing and eyed them.

"Is that your uncle?" Daisy said.

"Nope. Uncle said he may or may not be here, since he had another job to take care of."

"He looks angry," Betty said.

Fluff hopped out and waved, "Hey, I'm Thomas Kanahele's niece. Do you know if he's around?"

"Do you see him here?" the man said with a hand shielding his eyes from the sun.

"I guess not. My friends and I just came all the way from Honolulu. Do you mind if we stretch our legs out and walk around a bit?"

"Walk all you want," he said, then resumed shoveling and humming a tune.

Most of the stalls had horses in them. They visited a stunning bay, a towering chestnut with a heart-shaped star and a gray mare who wanted snacks. Daisy had come armed with carrots, and quietly slipped her one.

"These are some fancy Thoroughbreds. I wonder who they belong to," Daisy said.

When the racetrack closed down fifteen years ago, Mr. Montgomery had shifted his focus to polo. Thus, she had no reason—or means—to ever come here. Now she was wishing she had.

"No idea. I was hoping there would be more people around to question," Fluff said.

"Not all investigation requires questioning does it? We

can still poke around," Daisy assured her. "And if nothing else, it sure is nice to hang out with some horses. I've been missing them like mad."

When they came back around, one of the horses in the pasture had moseyed on up to the fence and was watching them with a keen eye. Tall and dark, with a strong chest and nice lines, he was almost as handsome as Moon. *Almost.*

"Pretend you're not interested," Daisy said to the girls, stepping to the fence a little ways past him and pointing at a gray horse across the pasture.

"A bit like men, are they?" Fluff said.

Daisy could speak for horses, but not for men. "It depends on the horse. Some are open and affectionate, others spirited and aloof."

"Depends on the man, too," Betty said. "I never had to play any games with Chuck. We were 100 percent from day one and we still are, seven years later." She leaned her forearms against the fence and gazed up at mist gathering at the top of the Koʻolau Mountains.

"Don't look now, but here he comes," Fluff whispered.

A moment later, Daisy felt hot breath against her neck and a sniffing tickle. Good thing her hair was short, or he was likely to start nibbling. Dominant horses do the nibbling, and by the looks of him, he was used to running the show. Daisy turned slightly and held out a piece of carrot in her palm. He wasted no time eating it. While he chewed, she scratched the crook beneath his ear.

"You like that, huh?"

If there was one thing Daisy knew, it was how to make friends with a horse. Even a standoffish one, which she could tell he was.

"Hey! Who said you could fraternize with the hosses?" came from across the way.

The shoveler walked toward them. He was so thin, his pants were on the brink of sliding right off him, and he yanked them up on one side.

"Sorry about that. We couldn't resist," Daisy said.

"Hosses bite and dis bruddah will haul off and kick you, too. When you least expect it. Don't say I didn't warn you."

The way he said *hoss* reminded her of Mr. Silva, who spoke a fried-rice scramble of pidgin and proper English.

"Duly noted. But he seems like such a love beneath the tough exterior."

The man leaned his shovel on the fence and gave her a curious look. "I gotta say, I nevah seen him take to someone so fast. With most folks, he bolts."

"What's his name?"

"Eclipse."

She sensed an opening. "That's funny, since he reminds me of a horse named Moon. A big black Thoroughbred faster than the wind. Do you know of him?"

Creases formed on his forehead. "What did you say your name was?"

"Daisy Wilder, sir."

The *sirs* flowed out of her mouth on their own accord now, even when they weren't called for.

"Don't call me sir. Archie's my name. And I know of the horse. Montgomery Ranch, yeah?"

All this time, Eclipse remained behind Daisy.

"Right. But he disappeared on December 7 and there has been no sign of him anywhere."

"That rich *haole* has some good help and even better horses. My cousin Tommy works there, so I heard the story. What's your business with Montgomery?"

Daisy knew Tommy. A scrappy cowboy good with ropes. "I worked with your cousin until last month, helping with the horses. I did whatever they needed me to. Clean, groom, feed, exercise, even some training."

A lot of training, actually, but no one wanted to hear that from a woman.

Archie stepped closer and inspected her face. His breath smelled like sardines. "You're Billy Wilder's kid. Tommy's mentioned you. Your old man was a magician with the animals. A real shame about what happened to him."

She felt woozy at the mention. "You knew my father?"

With his burnt-leather skin, Archie could have been anywhere between sixty-five and ninety. "Tommy brought your father to help me now and again with the tough hosses, like Eclipse here." His *here* came out like *hea*.

Recognition dawned. "You're Archibald?"

"Das right."

Archibald was a legend in the horse world, and Mr. Silva mentioned him often. A paniolo from Waimea, he was known as the best roper in the Pacific, and could ride anything anywhere anyhow.

"You haven't heard any mumblings about Moon, have you? It seems odd that he would vanish into thin air like he has," Daisy asked.

Archie rubbed his prickly chin. "Why do you care so much about Montgomery's horse? There a reward up for him?"

Daisy explained that she was the one who lost him. "I love that horse and I will never forgive myself unless we can find him."

"Let me give you some advice, young lady—never say never. It'll ruin you."

Fluff, who was still standing next to her, started nodding in agreement. "Forgiveness is a virtue, especially when it pertains to ourselves."

Where did she come up with this kind of stuff?

Lei added, "Maybe we should offer a reward for any info on Moon. I'm surprised Montgomery hasn't yet."

"Walker suggested it, but his father said he had his people working on it and didn't want to be led on wild-goose chases all over the island," Daisy said.

"Tell you what. I hear anything, I'll tell T, but gimme your number in case," Archie said.

Betty rattled it off, and they said their goodbyes. For the first time since Moon ran away, Daisy felt like she'd gotten a break. A small one, but still. Archie might seem like an aging paniolo now out to pasture, but she could tell the man paid attention. All good cowboys did.

Around noon, they were coming upon the north end of the island between dizzying cliffs and white-capped ocean. Beaches along the way had been lined in barbed wire, and periodically they passed soldiers sitting atop jeeps or tanks with rifles and cigarettes in hand. The scenes felt staged, as if there should be a movie crew nearby, ready to film. In Kahaluʻu and Lāʻie they pulled in at two other small stables, but left without any new information.

"I still say we at least try to visit Opana," Fluff said, holding up her badge. "We can tell them we are scouting stations so we can be more accurate plotters. I want to see it up close and personal."

She had been bugging them all morning to swing into one of the radar sites along the way.

"You don't think they'll wonder why Nixon or Major Oscar wouldn't have warned them? And we aren't in uniform," Betty said.

"They won't care. They'll just be thrilled to meet us."

"How will we even find it?" Daisy said, though to be honest, she had a pretty good idea where it was.

"There's got to be a road," Lei said.

Betty sighed. "Just to get you to shut up, let's go."

After several wrong attempts, they turned up a dirt road cut diagonally into the side of a low cliff. Once they reached the top, and headed inland through dense foliage, they could see the tip of the antenna of the SCR-270 mobile unit above the trees.

"Would you look at that?" Fluff said affectionately.

It *would* be nice to see the station in real life. In speaking with the Oscars all day, you couldn't help but be curious about their location. More often than not, they'd be cursing the rain or the heat, but once in a while, one would mention the huge surf or a breaching whale, spotted out front. Ironwood trees lined a gulch on one side of the road, and around a corner, a gate came into view. Two armed guards stood in the road with rifles pointed at the car.

"Uh-oh," Fluff said.

Betty said, "Get your badges ready, and let me do the talking."

They rolled to a stop six feet from the men, with Lei waving her white scarf. "I'm not in the mood to get shot today."

"Oh please, they aren't going to shoot us," Fluff said.

The men approached both sides of the car. The one on Daisy's side looked about fourteen, with a thin layer of peach fuzz on his chin. "This is a US military installation. What's your business here?" he said.

Betty held up her badge. "We're from Shafter, part of the Air Raid Defense at Little Robert. We work under General Danielson and Colonel Nixon."

He motioned toward Lei. "What's with the Jap in the car?"

"She works with us. And she happens to be Chinese, not Japanese," Daisy said, annoyed at his ignorance.

"You sure about that?"

"Very," Lei said.

The two men exchanged glances. "This some kind of practical joke?"

"We're all officers with the Signal Aircraft Warning Regiment. Go on, have a look at my badge," Betty said, handing it over.

He studied the badge as though it were written in Japanese, then tossed it over the car to his buddy. "Looks real to me. What do you think?" he said.

The rest of them handed their badges over. The fourteen-year-old looked at the badges, then ducked down so he could see each woman in the car, then stared at the badges again. He seemed to be trying to come to terms with the fact that the car full of women might in fact be a car full of officers. Red creeped up his neck.

Betty offered a suggestion. "When you let us in, the Oscars will vouch for us. They know us."

That was a stretch. They might know their voices, though. Some spoke in smooth drawls, others clipped radio lingo, while a few New England boys omitted their *R*s altogether. Niner came out *ninah*. With those, you always had to ask them to say again to be on the safe side.

Still unconvinced, fourteen said, "You all look like you're on a Sunday outing. Why are you here, really? One of your husbands must have put you up to this."

Daisy read his name tag. "Private Hicks, do you know the army's penalty for disregarding a direct order from a superior officer?" she asked.

He frowned. "Court-martial."

"Do you want to be court-martialed?"

"No, ma'am." His voice had risen an octave.

"Then please let us through," Betty said.

He looked at his friend, who shrugged, then without another word, opened the gate.

Once they passed, Fluff burst into laughter. "You gals were brilliant! Those poor fellas stood no chance against you."

Daisy said, "Now what? We just waltz up and ask them for a tour? Don't forget there's a war going on." In her mind, this whole detour was not the smartest idea, and she had a feeling Nixon would not approve.

"I for one am not going to stop living just because there is a war going on. What good will that do anyone? You want to just sit in our house all day listening to the depressing news on the radio and twiddling our thumbs?"

"No!" was the unanimous response.

But there was an element of guilt that went along with enjoying yourself when a large portion of the world was suffering.

Fluff continued. "We deserve to be here. Consider it research to become better WARDs. Plus, these poor Oscars are stranded out here all day at the end of the earth. They could use a morale boost."

No one could argue with that. The unpaved road paralleled the cliff, and grew more rutted by the inch. Bodies flew in the air more than a few times, and a film of red dirt coated the windshield. Though Daisy had never been up here, the iron-rich soil prevalent on this side of the island made her feel right at home. Pretty soon they came to a circular clearing with a 180-degree view of the ocean. Two hulking military trucks were parked on one side, a canvas teepee-style tent on another, and the antenna trailer sat in the middle. All dirt, no grass.

"*This* is the station?" Fluff asked.

Daisy knew what she meant. The only impressive part was the antenna, which stood taller than a coconut tree. A head poked out from the side of the truck. Then another.

Betty jumped out and held up her badge. "Hello! We're Rascals from Little Robert, touring the radar sites."

"Well, I'll be..." one of the men said.

They were invited into the crude station, which felt more like the inside of a furnace, heated by the noonday tropical sun. Stripes of perspiration creased the men's uniforms and they all looked like they'd be better off in swim trunks. There were five of them in the cramped truck, which turned out to be the operations room. The other truck provided power.

"Welcome to the club. Best view on the island, if you don't mind centipedes in your bed and dirt in your oatmeal. They set us up here the day after the attack, round the clock, and it's been nothing but pleasure," said Bobby Ortiz, whose lightly accented voice sounded familiar.

"Things could be far worse, soldier," Betty said.

He grinned. "Oh, I'm not complaining. Just giving you a flavor of what it's like here. I'm the shift chief. Can I show you the ropes?" he asked, eyes settling on Daisy.

"Sure, we'd like that."

He lovingly pointed out an impressive array of equipment. The receiver, receiver trombone, spare receiver, spare parts kit, azimuth speed controls and the oscilloscope, which was where the signals came across on the screen.

"Oscilloscope. What a mouthful. I'll bet you can't say it five times in a row," Fluff mumbled to Daisy under her breath.

If Ortiz heard her, he didn't let on. "This baby is the star of the show—well, this and Big Bertha out there," he said, nodding toward the antenna.

He then picked up a pair of binoculars and handed them to Daisy. "We use these to read the azimuth angle, which is painted on the antenna turntable. Have a look."

Why was she always chosen to go first? A part of her wondered if her short hair and slacks had anything to do with it. That in their eyes, she was somehow more like a man. As if hair and clothing had anything to do with it.

"How tall is that thing?" Lei asked.

"Fifty-five feet. Nine dipole elements high, by four wide."

"What happens when it's windy?"

"So far so good. We haven't had to take her down yet. Last thing we need is another fuckup—" His hand went to his mouth. "Pardon my language. I'm not used to having ladies around."

Fluff waved it off. "We're used to it by now."

The antenna made one revolution per minute. They passed around the binoculars and listened to Ortiz expound on a lot of technical jargon, much of which went over their heads. Daisy was touched that he thought them important enough to share all this with. On top of being handsome and personable, the man knew his radar. After being there for well over an hour, and taking a few photographs with the crew, the girls finally tore themselves away.

They all considered the day a big success. Meeting Archie at the racetrack, the friendly team at the Opana radar site—once they'd gotten past the gate—and later, picnicking together in the shade of a māmane tree, nibbling on crustless egg salad sandwiches, saloon pilot crackers and chunks of pineapple. There was something to be said for a day of fresh air and friendship.

14

THE THIEF

Two minutes into their shift, Daisy felt a tap on her shoulder. Fully expecting it to be one of the girls, she flung the hand away. She was working on a range arc calculation.

"I'm busy," she said.

But it was not one of the girls. It was Nixon, a dark look in his eye. "In my office, Wilder." On the balcony, Dunn and Major Oscar avoided eye contact, suddenly very involved in their notes. The girls, however, all stared as they passed. Nixon slammed the wooden door shut and went to sit behind a large desk piled high with manila folders and coffee-stained books. Daisy remained standing. "I heard about your little joyride yesterday. Did you know I can charge you ladies with unauthorized entry of a military installation?" he said.

Oh boy. She knew it had been a dumb idea. But why was she the only one in trouble? "No, I didn't, sir. You must mean our visit to Opana."

"Damn right."

A plum pit formed in her throat. Her legs trembled. Being in trouble was nothing new, but Nixon intimidated her on a whole new level. He was school principal, boss, policeman and judge all rolled into one. Not only could he fire her, he could put her in jail, or the brig or whatever it was the military called it.

"There was no bad intent on our part. We were passing by and thought it would be a good idea to see the site firsthand, to get a better understanding of what we're dealing with."

"Passing by? You just *happened* to be driving along in the most remote section of the island?"

"We were on a mission, sir."

"If you were on a mission, you don't think I'd know about it? Nor do we send the WARDs on missions."

She told him about Moon and their hunt for information. A person with a heart would understand. But the jury was still out with Nixon. When she finished, he stretched and folded his arms behind his head, leaning back in the chair and looking out the tiny window. An awkward silence filled the room. Daisy noticed a framed photo of him with a sunny-faced blonde woman. Anyone could see that they were young and in love. They were both smiling. She at the camera, and Nixon at his lovely wife. She wondered how he'd lost her.

"Sir, if you don't mind my asking, why am I the only one in here?" she asked, figuring there was nothing to lose at this point.

"That's easy. Because the man I spoke to couldn't remember any of your names, but he said one of you was six feet tall and wearing pants. I'm guessing you were also with Fluffy and Yates and Davis. Am I right?"

Daisy held back a laugh. "It's Fluff."

"Fluff, Fluffy, I don't care. How can anyone be taken seriously with a name like that?"

His utter refusal to give any of them a chance was growing tiresome. "Have you ever bothered to have a conversation with the woman? I think that if you did, it might answer your question. She's intelligent and curious and kind."

An imperceptible flare of his nostrils told her all she needed to know. Well, too damn bad. Fluff was about the sweetest, most bighearted girl Daisy knew. She deserved better. Nixon made a note in the black wire notebook he carried everywhere, then said, "Let me remind you that this is not a sorority. This is the United States Army. Have you forgotten why you're here?"

"No, sir."

"Not for fun and games and definitely not to fraternize with the boys."

The insinuation shocked her. "You think we went there to fraternize? Would you like to know what I learned while at Opana?" He didn't answer, so she took the liberty of continuing. "Ortiz explained every piece of equipment in the K–30 down to the high-voltage rectifier. We now know that their antenna has very high gain, and the more gain, the stronger the *shout* and more sensitive the *listen*. We got a visual of the oscilloscope and a firsthand account of how the sweep signal passes through a calibrated phase shifter. He even let us turn the large hand wheel on the front panel so we could get an accurate measure of delay between transmitted and received pulses. It's through the trombone—"

"That's enough, Wilder," he said with a flip of his hand. "You're dismissed."

The word almost knocked her over. From the room or the army? "Dismissed?"

"Get back to work and stay out of trouble."

Trouble had a way of following her around these days, but she wasn't telling him that.

In the coming weeks, Daisy worked harder than ever to learn the required calculations to be promoted to filterer. She kept her head in the game and ignored all distractions— Nixon and his permanent frown, Thelma prancing around like a peacock, Peg dropping veiled insults almost daily, along with various other trainings that came up unexpectedly. Like how to carry a litter, or Morse code. For someone obsessed with code names, poor Fluff struggled with Morse, and Daisy had to work overtime to help her.

In the evenings, Betty showed them the proper way to make grits, how to fry your okra so it was just the right amount of crispy, and the secrets to New Orleans biscuits and gravy. Only problem was, Southern food loved its butter, which was damn near impossible to come by. Every so often, Lei would bring some over and Betty kept it under lock and key, rationing it out sparingly.

Radio and newspaper reports included nothing about the *Enterprise* or her mission, and the waiting was growing harder by the day. Daisy thought about Walker constantly, though she rarely spoke about him, and she could only imagine how Betty must be feeling. "This here is the problem with being in love. All anyone talks about is how love makes the world go round, but love also contains a big helping of pain and misery. When the party in question is taken away from you, for one," Betty said one night over hush puppies and pulled pork.

"Still, I'd rather be in love than not in love," Fluff argued.

"It's like a fever, rattling my bones—" Betty lowered her voice to a whisper "—and I'm afraid of what will happen if Chuck doesn't come back."

Fluff reached over and grabbed Betty's hand. "He *is* coming back. No *ifs*, *ands* or *buts*. Come on, let's pray," she said, grabbing Daisy's hand, too. Daisy was thankful that Fluff knew what to say, because she was at a loss for words. "Dear Lord, we pray that you look out for our loved ones out there fighting. That you hold them in your light and keep them safe from all harm. Please give them courage to face the challenges and fill them with the strength of a thousand men. In case you need to know, we're praying for two in particular, Chuck Yates and Walker Montgomery. Please bring them home alive, Lord. Amen."

Daisy noticed more blond hair in the shower drain, and sometimes she would hear Betty making tea in the middle of the night. Part of the problem was the eerie stillness that came over the house at three o'clock in the morning. That was enough to keep anyone up. How she missed the liquid sounds of the ocean. The one good thing about sleeping at Shafter was that Walker the cat—renamed Blanche once they realized she was female—made her rounds between the three beds each night. Black with white socks and a pink nose, she livened up the house with her feline spunk. In fact it soon became apparent that Blanche could chase her own tail for a good half hour.

"That cat is onto something. We should all learn to be so self-sufficient," Fluff said.

"Her brain is the size of a peanut," Betty said.

Daisy stuck up for Blanche. "Animals are smarter than we think. I wouldn't discount her."

"As long as she snuggles with me, I really don't care," Betty said.

Though the shifts were only six hours, working at Little Robert was draining. All that focus and the continuous pressure not to make mistakes. Nixon hovered, and since the visit to Opana, Daisy was extra careful not to draw attention to herself. Tension coated the walls and the tabletops, and everyone was still on edge about the next attack. None of the men spoke it out loud, but you could tell some of them lacked faith in the WARDs. An offhand comment here, roll of the eyes there.

One afternoon, Fluff seemed particularly pensive on the way home. "Does Lieutenant Dunn flirt with any of you?"

"Nope. I made it clear from day one I'm not open for business," Betty said.

"Me neither. But I see how he is around you," Daisy said.

Fluff seemed buoyed by the news. "I get the feeling he likes me, and I'm not sure how I feel about it. On the one hand, he's handsome and charming, but on the other, he might be a little old for me. What do you think?"

Daisy thought Fluff was being too generous in her assessment of the man. His overabundance of touching was enough to raise suspicion. That and the fact that Fluff was not the only one he flirted with. The way he prowled the control room reminded her of the roosters walking the dusty streets of Hale'iwa.

"Stay away from that one, honey. He's a BTO," Betty said.

"A BTO?"

"A big-time operator."

Daisy nodded. "I second that."

"Goodness, you two are harsh critics. He's been nothing but sweet to me since day one. At least he smiles and has complimentary things to say."

"What's he complimenting?" Betty asked.

Fluff got a dreamy look on her face. "My eyes, for one. He said a person could drown in them if they weren't careful."

Daisy thought back to Walker's comments on the various kinds of intelligence. While Daisy lacked in book smarts, Fluff clearly lacked in man smarts. Not that Daisy herself was any genius in that department, but when it boiled down to it, men were just animals, and she'd had some success with those.

"Nixon said we are not here to fraternize with the boys, and I'm pretty sure that includes Dunn," Daisy said.

"He's doing all the fraternizing. I'm just doing my job," Fluff said, looking hurt.

"Keep it that way," Betty said.

When they arrived home, Daisy went out back to collect the laundry on the line. Between the three of them, their clothes were as different as their personalities. Whimsical for Fluff, expensive and tailored for Betty, and practical for Daisy. She enjoyed the warm sun on her shoulders as she folded each item, and her thoughts once again went to Walker. She'd found it was easier to give in than to fight it, and allowed herself to imagine a ride on the beach. Only this time, it ended in a kiss. Once she had everything in the basket, she realized there were no bras and underwear. Inside, she hollered to Betty, "Where did you put all the undergarments?"

Betty poked her head out from the bathroom. "What do you mean? I hung them on the line."

"Well, they aren't there."

"Hang on."

Betty came out wrapped in a towel, another on her head, and they went out back. "Do you think Gwen or Florence might have taken them by mistake?"

Their houses backed up into the same weedy lawn, but each had its own rusted-pipe clothesline. Unless one of them was drunk in the middle of the night, it was highly unlikely.

"It would be peculiar if they had," Daisy said.

"Maybe they blew off. Did you check the hedge over there?" Betty pointed at the mock orange.

Not a stitch of wind. There was no way they could have blown off and clear across the yard, but she checked anyway. She was down on her hands and knees when Fluff came out.

"Did you lose something?"

"My underwear."

Fluff laughed. "Better not let Nixon hear you say that. But seriously, why are you looking in the hedge for them?"

"Actually, not just my underwear, but all of ours. Bras, too. I hung them all out this morning and now they're gone," Daisy said, standing up and brushing off the grass from her pants.

"I'll go next door and ask," Fluff said.

She was gone for all of two minutes and returned shaking her head. "Gwen said no, nor did she see anyone around. Did you check the washing machine? Maybe they're still inside."

Daisy trusted her memory. "I know I hung them up because I was specifically thinking how sad my underwear was compared to both of yours. And that it might be time for me to splurge on something prettier."

Until now, there had been no reason. And no money.

"There has to be a reasonable explanation," Betty said.

"Like what?"

"Maybe it's against military regulations to hang your delicates in public?" Fluff said in all seriousness.

"That's silly. And anyway, someone would have warned us," Daisy said.

"What about the young guard that found you sleeping in the grass dreaming about Walker. What if he took them?" Fluff said.

Daisy ignored the Walker comment because technically, she *had* been dreaming about him. "Why on earth would he take them?"

"I'm just thinking out loud."

Daisy was exhausted and went over to Blanche, who lay curled up in a pool of late-afternoon sun. One paw covered her eyes.

"He seemed harmless."

"Regardless. I'll question him when I see him. Remember, we don't make assumptions," Fluff said with her arms crossed over her chest for effect.

At some point in the blustery night, Daisy had to close the window because of a sideways rain blowing in through the window and onto her face. She tiptoed around until she found another blanket in a hall closet, and snuggled up under it. Fluff, who could sleep through just about anything, didn't even stir. After a restless half hour or so, just when she had begun to drift off, a loud siren rattled all the windows and shook the floorboards. She bolted upright. Fluff moaned.

"Air raid!" Daisy yelled, as she jumped up and ran to the dresser to grab whatever she could find to slip on. "Get up!"

The darkness was nearly absolute, but she heard Fluff rustle around and open the closet door. A moment later, Betty came flying down the hallway. "Wake up, wake up! Air raid!"

"We're up," Daisy said.

Gas masks and helmets all hung by the front door and they banged into the table and fumbled around grasping for them. Betty held the door open, and the three of them huddled together under the front eave. It felt about forty degrees, but that was the least of their worries. Something about that undulating wail haunted Daisy to the core.

"Damn it to hell, why in the middle of the night and why in the pouring rain?" Betty yelled.

Behind the screen door, back in the house, they heard a meow.

"What about Blanche?" Daisy asked.

"What about her?" Betty said.

"We can't leave her."

She had already lost one animal to the war, and refused to leave another trapped in a house that could be bombed or strafed at any moment. Was there a rule that said a human life was more important than that of a cat? In just several short weeks, Blanche had become an indispensable part of their makeshift family.

"You think she's going to let you just carry her to the shelter? In this rain?" Betty asked.

"I can try."

The minute Daisy opened the door, a small shape darted out past them, blurring into the inky night. So much for bringing Blanche with them. But at least she wouldn't be stuck inside. Fortunately, Betty had an umbrella and the three of them smashed together and made a dash for the shelter, which was just down the street carved into the edge of a hillside. By the time they got there, they were wet to the bone. Two others had already arrived.

"Watch your step, it's muddy in here. And there's bufos," someone said just as Daisy's shoe squished down.

Fluff shuddered. "Is that you, JoAnn?"

"Yes, and Tippy."

As more girls filed in, the wooden structure creaked and

groaned. Daisy, Betty and Fluff were pressed into the far corner, which slanted down at an unnatural angle. They hunkered together, shoulder to shoulder. Talk about being right in the thick of it. Visions of the dogfight overhead, and a sky full of planes, nailed Daisy to the bench. Her teeth began to chatter.

"Does anyone know details?" someone said.

"My guess is the enemy is retaliating for whatever our boys on the *Enterprise* have done to them," Thelma said from across the way.

At Little Robert, Thelma spoke incessantly about Walker and his bravery and how she couldn't wait to *walk into those arms* when he returned. So much so, that Daisy had begun to wonder if he had written Thelma a goodbye note, too. Could he be playing the both of them? The thought turned her stomach inside out.

Once everyone settled in, they strapped on helmets. The mood was dark as the moonless night. Daisy closed her eyes and worked on calming herself down. Lord, she wished she was at home and not trapped in this shoddy sardine-can shelter. She found it hard to breathe. Then Fluff screamed, jumped up and started stomping around, splattering mud everywhere.

"Get it off me!"

"Centipede!" someone yelled.

A new level of panic rippled through the cramped room. In Daisy's eyes, centipedes were nearly as terrifying as Japanese bombers. She'd had more bad bites than she could count; angry, swollen body parts and sleepless nights. When Fluff sat back down, she sought out Daisy's hand and held on tight. Within a few minutes, her heart rate had slowed and she was able to think straight.

They listened for the sound of engines or explosions, but

all they could hear was the splash of raindrops, an occasional bufo croaking and the sucking sounds of mud. After some time passed, small fires of conversation started up. *I have my gun and will shoot to kill. Have you heard they've made military zones on the Mainland and are rounding up Japanese people? Which Japanese? Any. What do you think about Sergeant Washington? Can I have your recipe for lilikoi pie?*

"Say, did you know the real reason for propellers on airplanes is to keep the pilots cool?" Fluff suddenly blurted out.

"Nonsense," someone said.

"Yes indeed. When they stop spinning, the pilots start sweating," she said. That got a laugh, and then jokes and funny stories began to circulate. Another hour passed with no attack and no all clear. Then someone said, "Wait, I hear something. Quiet."

A hush fell.

Meow.

"It's Blanche!" Daisy said.

They opened the door for the cat, but she refused to come inside. Daisy wove her way out, picked up the creature and brought her inside. Blanche settled on Daisy's lap, kneading and purring and content as a baby. When the all clear sounded ten minutes later, Blanche was the only one not happy to leave.

15

THE NEWS

In recent weeks, the girls were informed that radar stations had been set up on Haleakalā on Maui, Kōkeʻe on Kauaʻi and in Pāhoa and Kahuku ranch on Hawaiʻi. Local women of all backgrounds except Japanese had been recruited, crash courses were being given and churches and family estates turned into Information Centers. On Kauaʻi, with a smaller population to draw from, even high school girls were accepted into the WARD. General Danielson and Major Hochman spent much of their time island hopping and getting everyone up to speed. Having sites clear across the main islands provided a much wider net of security, and Daisy slept better because of it.

On a clear afternoon in late February, air traffic picked up considerably and the telephones started ringing like popcorn. Daisy and the WARDs were putting pips on the board as fast as they could.

Lei said, "This reminds me of being on shift at the cannery. You have to move fast or you could lose your fingers or even a hand."

Lei's parents worked on the plantation, and they somehow landed her a job at the cannery after school and during summers. Savvy and industrious, she'd worked her way up to supervisor by the time she was twenty. George had spotted her at a work party and wasted no time in marrying her.

"If these aren't American forces, we could lose a lot more than our fingers," Daisy said.

Fluff, who was in charge of coded chits to identify flights, scribbled madly to keep up.

16 IS BOMBER! 39 IS UNIDENTIFIED! 43 IS UNIDENTIFIED!

Nixon and the officers on the balcony circled together and spoke in hushed tones. Daisy stood up and pretended to stretch, moving closer and straining to hear. Whatever it was, something big was coming their way. Soon, she heard the words *surface craft*. Her pulse quickened. Twenty minutes later, Rascals from Kaua'i reported an aircraft carrier on its way across the channel.

Betty stood up and twirled around. "The *Enterprise*! They're coming home!"

All eyes went to the naval liaison, Ralph Cole, who sat with the phone smashed to his ear. The man had the best poker face in town, but Daisy detected a softening of his body, and creasing around his eyes. The news had to be good. When he finally hung up, he pumped his fist and yelled, "Ladies and gentlemen, we have a victory with a capital *V*! The Big E is a little scuffed up, and we had some losses, but enemy ships were sank, planes shot down and installations destroyed." He swallowed hard, eyes glistening.

The whole room erupted with cheers and squeals and hugs. Betty pulled Daisy in for a tight squeeze. Her cheeks were damp and she spoke into Daisy's hair. "I just *know* our men are okay."

Our men.

When the shift ended, two hours later, the girls raced home. A convertible roadster was parked out front of their quarters in the shade of a plumeria tree. The car had been the envy of every soldier and sailor on base, and Daisy recognized it right away.

When Betty saw it, she stopped in her tracks, going pale as milk. "I wonder why Elaine is here," she said, turning to Daisy and Fluff with a look of alarm moving over her face. Elaine was married to one of Chuck's pilot buddies, Ed, also on the *Enterprise*, though in a different squadron. Betty took off running.

"I have a bad feeling about this," Fluff said.

"Me, too."

Daisy thought about Walker, and how he could die, and no one would notify her. The idea nearly strangled her. She and Fluff picked up the pace and arrived to find Elaine sitting with an arm around Betty on the couch, heads together. In the kitchen, Rita Dogwood was filling a glass of water.

Daisy was afraid to ask, but had to know. "What is it?"

"Chuck was shot down," Betty said, tears streaming down her cheeks.

Shot did not mean dead, did it?

"Is he alive, honey?" Fluff asked.

Betty's lip quivered and she nodded. "They don't know for sure, but it doesn't look good," she said, gulping in air and folding over, sobbing.

The whole experience brought Daisy back to the day her father died. That sick feeling of knowing something was horribly wrong and your whole world was about to spin off its axis. And how the true agony of death was left to the living.

"What happened?" Fluff asked.

Elaine answered for her. "He was leading a division of dive bombers over an enemy airfield, bombing the crap out of them, and then he got taken down."

Fluff's face went pale. "Oh no!"

"Did he have time to bail out?" Daisy asked.

"Word is that he did, but in enemy territory."

She tried to think of something useful to say. "From what you've told me, Chuck is a fighter. If he's alive, he'll get through it."

Betty sat up with a faraway look in her eyes. "This can't be real. My Chuck cannot be dead."

Daisy had seen that look before on her own mother. It was the haunting face of loss. She squeezed in on the other side of Betty and wrapped her arm around her friend's waist. Words were not enough. They sat like that for some time, with Betty alternating between rocking back and forth, wailing and asking, "Are they sure?"

"They're sure," Rita said, softly.

"One thing to be proud of is that everyone's talking about how Chuck and his division wiped out an entire airfield on one of those islands—Roi, I think it was. Then on his second pass he encountered a pair of irate Japanese fighters intent on revenge," Elaine said.

Betty tried to smile. "Sounds like my boy."

"Were any others lost?" Fluff asked.

"There were others. I'm not sure how many."

Daisy kept thinking about how for every man down—on either side—there were loved ones smacked with the brutal truth of war. She wished there was some way to help ease the pain, but time was the only remedy for that. And even then, it never left you completely. Betty had a long road ahead.

To add to the bleak afternoon, Daisy was worried about Walker. There had been no mention of him, and it wasn't as though she could phone his house and say, "Hey, it's me, Daisy Wilder, calling to see if Walker made it home okay."

When it was time for bed, Daisy and Fluff pulled Betty's mattress into their room and slid it in between their beds. The minute they had the sheets on, Blanche sauntered in and started making biscuits smack in the center, then curled up, purring loud as a motor.

"Excuse me, young lady, you're taking up the whole bed," Fluff said.

Betty flopped down next to Blanche and curled her body around the cat. She was still wearing her uniform. "Let her stay. I want her here." Blanche sniffed her hand and then licked it with her rough pink tongue.

Once they were all tucked in, the night seemed eerily quiet. Warm. Not a stitch of breeze. Somewhere just outside the window, a cricket buzzed. Daisy rolled to the edge of the bed and looked down at Betty's dark outline. While she had been completely unequipped to help her mother grieve, she vowed to do whatever it took to see her friend through this. Not that she was an expert, but she knew that having someone by your side could make all the difference.

In a small voice, Betty said, "You never think it's going to happen to you, you know? You fret like mad, but some corner of you always believes it will be someone else's husband or father or brother. But no one is immune."

Daisy reached down and rested her hand on Betty's back, lightly stroking. Betty shivered under her touch. "I know it seems impossible right now, but you're going to get through this," Daisy said.

Betty whimpered. "I just want to go to sleep and never wake up. Why would I want to be in a world without Chuck? Tell me."

Daisy had no answer.

The following day, Betty insisted on working her shift. Overnight, enough tears had been shed to fill a swimming pool. But in the morning, Betty disappeared into the shower and came out of the bathroom forty minutes later with her hair neatly pinned up and her face made.

"I'm going to work. Do not try to talk me out of it," she announced.

Daisy admired her courage. She'd heard it said that grief came in a thousand shades, and this was clear evidence of that. While some people might collapse, others buckled up and marched on. Grief was akin to fingerprints, no two the same.

News had spread like wildfire about Chuck. When Daisy and Fluff and Betty walked in, the room fell into a hush. Then all the girls swarmed around Betty, hugging, squeezing and filling her with enough love to choke Daisy up. When the women had finished, Major Oscar and all the men took their turns. Even Nixon gave his condolences, and surprisingly, his hug was the longest.

"I think Nixon was crying," Fluff said later in the break room.

"I doubt it."

"No really, his eyes were all watery."

He knew a thing or two about loss. "Maybe this will soften him up," Daisy said.

Still no word about Walker, and the pit in her stomach had turned into a deep well. To confuse matters, today was Peg's day off, and Thelma had switched shifts with Ella

Wong. Ella had no idea why. Try as Daisy might, focusing on plotting was nearly impossible.

"Now would be a good time to ask Nixon about Walker," Fluff suggested over a cold Coke and leftover manapua.

"Nixon is the last person I would ask."

"Want me to ask him for you?"

"You would do that?"

"I have nothing to lose. That man will never take me seriously. At least you have a chance to impress him with all those speedy calculations that are always 100 percent accurate. He seems to *almost* like you," Fluff said with a shrug.

"He does not."

"Oh yes he does."

Back in the control room, Fluff marched right up to Nixon and said, "Excuse me, Colonel, we're worried about Peg's brother, Walker Montgomery, and wonder if you could tell us if he made it back in one piece."

He paused for a moment, then said, "From what I hear, his whole squadron is intact."

Fluff clapped her hands together and did a little jig. "This is wonderful news. Thank you, thank you, thank you!"

Nixon actually came close to smiling, then turned his attention back to his notebook. A few of the other girls had been listening in, and when Fluff passed Daisy with a look of glee, she felt self-conscious. Nevertheless, a whole garden of flowers had taken bloom under her rib cage.

Walker was alive!

16

THE GUESTS

Peg came to work the following day looking as though someone had taken an oiled horse brush to her hair—flat and greasy, no curls. Clearly something was up. Daisy broke into a sweat. She was dying to ask after Walker, but knew it would be pointless. A part of her wished she could go back to life before Walker Montgomery. The other wanted to walk out the door and hitch a ride to Mokulēʻia. Or the barracks at the navy yard. Wherever he was. Tomorrow she could find him.

The four of them had planned on driving out to the country and staying the two nights off at Daisy's beach house, but plans changed.

Fluff had said, "I ought to stay with Betty. I hate to leave her alone, but you and Lei go."

"Maybe we should all stay together," Daisy said.

"No, you go on home, see if you can talk to Walker. We'll be fine."

Daisy was thankful that Fluff understood. Early the next morning, Lei showed up with a bagful of bananas, freshly baked bread with guava butter and a neatly packed lunch basket. Daisy envied Lei's lifestyle, with Asuka providing all those wonderful treats. Food in the mess hall was hit or miss, but at least it was free.

They passed Pearl Harbor and the minute they started winding down Kaukonahua Road, with a deep ravine on one side and sugarcane fields on the other, Daisy picked up the scent of salt in the air. Regardless of whether she saw Walker or not, it would be nice to be home. If only for a night.

"It sure is lovely. I wish I could stay and enjoy it," Lei said.

"What do you mean?"

A heaviness came over her. "Some things happened this week that I have to deal with at home."

"What kind of things?" Daisy asked.

Lei had seemed out of sorts for the past couple of weeks now, so Daisy wasn't entirely surprised. She wanted to help if she could. But Lei was the type who was always concerned about others and never about herself. Daisy was coming to see that everyone wore their problems differently. Fluff laid everything out on the table. No guessing needed. Betty suffered in silence most of the time, while a good portion of her hair went down the drain. Lucky thing she was blessed with such an abundance.

"You really want to know?" Lei asked, keeping her eyes on the road ahead.

"I do."

"My dear husband has a gambling problem. Over the past few years, he's gone up and down. Losing money, then winning it back. Card games, horse races, even cockfights. The other day, I opened a letter by mistake and it looks like he took a loan out on our house and now is late on payments and the bank is threatening to foreclose. He never said a word. Can you believe that?" Lei said, with a shake of her head.

Married people kept secrets from each other. Daisy did know that.

"People lie."

"I feel so stupid. Here I was, going about my life with absolutely no idea of any of this. Sure, he'd come home sauced and smelling like a smokestack. I even got to sleeping in the other room on nights he went out. But he never let on that he'd lost more than a few hundred bucks here or there," Lei said.

"What does he have to say for himself?"

"He's ashamed, trying to rationalize it, but the worst part is, he twisted it around and last night he blamed me. Said it was my fault because of the way I'm accustomed to living. Maids, the latest automobiles, fancy dinners. Which is absolute hogwash. I don't need any of that."

The dark smudges under her eyes now made sense. The thought infuriated Daisy. "Someone needs to put him in his place, then. Do you want me to talk to him?"

A sad laugh. "Thank you, dear, but no. I'm meeting with our banker today to see how bad it is and what can be done."

It seemed a fact of life that people who loved each other inevitably hurt one another. Maybe love was not the answer after all. Maybe sticking with horses would be a smarter move.

At the house, overgrown grass, flowering dandelion and the bittersweet smell of burnt sugarcane greeted them. An albatross soared high out front. Lei stayed long enough for a cup of coffee and a quick look around and then she left Daisy with a whole basket of food and a bottle of wine.

"What am I going to do with this?" Daisy asked.

"Save it for our next trip out here."

The first order of business was jumping in the ocean and washing off all the layers of war from her skin. When she was finished, she lay on her stomach in the warm sand, watching crabs dig holes and scurry about. Every time the water washed up, a few of them disappeared, only to pop up again a minute later. Sun toasted her back and thighs, and she could have stayed there all day long. For lunch, she ate rice balls with flecks of seaweed and dried fish and chased them down with a lukewarm Coke. The solitude felt as refreshing as the deep blue sea.

In order to avoid thinking about Walker, she kept busy. For a good portion of the afternoon, she mowed the lawn, dug up weeds and set about washing the salt from all the windows. Another floorboard of the deck had rotted through, and she replaced it with a piece from under the house. The last one. Though now that she had a little extra money, she could afford to buy more.

When she was finished outside, she went into her mother's room. The walls had absorbed the sweet smell of rosewater, which hit Daisy hard with memories. So much had gone on in here. Love and sorrow and the disintegration of a once-vibrant life. As a girl, Daisy had loved to lie on the green-and-yellow Hawaiian quilt while her mother read to her, but later, a knot formed in her stomach whenever she entered. Now, she ran her hand along the dusty books on the shelf, sat on the squeaky bed and took it all in. Would Louise ever return? A loud voice inside said *no*.

As soon as the sun dipped behind the mountains, the air cooled. Daisy was tempted to go for a skinny-dip to the reef, but thought the better of it in case a beach patrol came by. Twenty minutes later, she was glad she hadn't. Two horses trotted down the beach. The sound of laughter carried in the wind. Not Walker, but Johnny Boy and Dex. No sooner had she retreated into the house, when they pulled up to the berm.

"Hooey!"

"Hey, Wilder!"

Daisy was in no mood to talk to these guys, or anyone for that matter. She remained in the kitchen, out of sight. The screen door banged in the wind.

"Got any more of that ono kine fish?" Johnny Boy called.

If she ignored them, and they knew she was in here, it would probably just rile them up. She stepped to the screen door. "I'm all out. Go see Mr. Sasaki. I bet he has some."

"Why don't you come out and say hi?" Dex said, like a whiny boy.

Johnny Boy jumped off his horse and onto the berm. She saw that he had a dark brown bottle in his hand. "Bumbye, I sure miss you at the stables. And those long legs of yours."

Dex laughed. "Don't be shy."

As if either of them had ever given her the time of day. These two were her least favorite men at the ranch, always a crude comment on the tip of their tongues, and careless with the horses. Her skin bristled with fear, as she suddenly wondered what the two men might be capable of. She remembered Johnny Boy's words from the last time: *you be careful out here on your own.* The shotgun was still leaning against the tree outside. Should she run? But there was no back door to the house, and Johnny Boy was suddenly at the bottom of the porch steps.

He held up the bottle. "Come have a drink with us, pretty lady."

Daisy went to the screen door and stepped outside. At

least this way she wouldn't be cornered if it came to that. "I don't drink, so you two can be on your way."

"Where's the fun in that?"

He moved onto the first step, wisps of liquor on his breath. Everyone knew that Johnny Boy was an ugly drunk. Daisy had heard stories, but never seen him under the influence. Now, she understood. The way he was looking at her, like she was a big, juicy piece of steak and he was going to take his time slicing it up into tiny pieces and savor every bite, gave her the chills.

She called out to Dex. "Please take your friend here, and leave me alone. What do you think Montgomery will do when he hears about you two coming over here uninvited?"

Johnny Boy came up another step, laughing. "So, invite us."

Daisy moved back, glancing toward the tree with the gun, metal on bark. Could she make it? Doubtful. Panic began to coil up her arms and legs. "I asked you nicely to please leave. And now I'm telling you. Get off my property!"

One more step.

He reached a hand out. Daisy shrunk back. And that's when she kicked the cane knife. She had been using it to hack down the sugarcane sprouting up in the backyard, and left it leaning up against the porch wall. With a duck and a swipe, she had it in her hand. "Don't make me use this. Now go," she said.

Johnny Boy stopped cold. "Whoa, easy there."

"You know I'm good with this thing. Now back the hell off."

"You always were a feisty one." He stared her down for a moment, mumbled something to himself, then spit on the step. "Just trying to be neighborly. You never know what a woman might need."

Daisy pressed herself up against the screen and watched him retreat down the steps. His jeans had slid halfway down his ass, and he yanked up one side. On the beach, another horse appeared, coming to a fast halt in the sand. Daisy hadn't even heard it coming.

Walker.

"What's this all about?" he said, hopping off and hurrying into the yard, hat askew and breathing hard.

"Just sayin' hi," Johnny Boy said.

"That true?" Walker asked Daisy.

Johnny Boy gave her a hard look.

If either of them lost their jobs because of her, they might try to retaliate. But Walker needed to know what kind of scoundrels they were. "If either of these guys sets foot on my land again, I'll shoot them. How's that?" she said.

A flush of anger crossed Walker's face. "You boys leave these horses with me, and get on home. We can talk about it later."

"But—"

"No *buts*, just go," Walker said.

Johnny Boy kicked the bush and sauntered off down the driveway. But by the way he moved, you could tell he felt no remorse. Like Walker had just inconvenienced the hell out of him and that was it. Dex followed without a word.

Walker came up and stood in front of Daisy. Their eyes met. Unable to stop herself, she crumpled to the top step. A quaking started up in her center and moved through her whole body, then rippling out limbs and discharging gallons of fear and anger. Walker sat down next to her. Gently placed an arm around her shoulders.

"I'm sorry," he said.

"What are you sorry for? Those two dimwits are the ones who should be sorry."

"Tell me what happened."

She did.

When she was finished, Walker said, "No woman should have to endure such treatment, and God only knows how far JB would have gone. I knew those two were trouble from day one. But you know my dad, he doesn't listen to anyone."

No, he didn't.

"I'm glad you came," Daisy said.

He leaned into her. "Me, too."

She felt a current where his skin touched against hers, a warm humming. Not wanting to ruin the moment with words, she leaned back into him. Safety and warmth and the faint smell of peppermint. He felt so *natural*. The onshore winds had subsided, and the water out front was slick as oil. She tried to push Johnny Boy from her mind. *Nothing happened, let it go.* Now, she knew she had to be better prepared. For an invasion of any kind—from home or abroad.

Walker reached behind him and produced a wilted clump of dandelions. "These are for you. Sorry, there was nothing else in bloom on the way here. And now they seem kind of inadequate."

No one had ever brought her flowers. She took them and promptly broke down. The kind of tears that came from a lifetime of hurts with no one to share them with, all bottled up. The crying wasn't about the cowboys, Louise, the war or even Walker. It was about crossing over into a place of vulnerability. About having people in her life now who mattered. Talk about bad timing. Poor Walker did not deserve this, but she couldn't stop.

He let her go for a while, then said, "Should I have gotten roses instead?"

Her laugh came out as a cough, as she wiped her face on her sleeve. "I'm sorry, I think this whole war business is catching up to me, you know? All day long, every day, there's this undercurrent of fear. Sometimes I don't even know it's there, but it's bubbling just below the surface. Sometimes just the smallest things make it spill over."

And I missed you.

"That wasn't a small thing," he said.

And I was worried.

"No, I guess it wasn't."

He nodded. "I wanted to find you when we docked, but I got knocked in the head pretty hard—a concussion—and doc ordered bed rest. Can you imagine that? Me, on bed rest?"

Daisy could have sat like this forever. His arm still holding her tight, staring out to sea. "Bed rest is not the worst that could happen. Tell me about it."

"A few more feet and I would have landed in the ocean and not on the deck," he said, pausing for a few moments. "But I didn't come to whine about my problems, it's just that I was hoping to go riding with you again soon. Funny how being out there in the middle of the Pacific—not knowing if you're going to live or die—really narrows what's important, you know?" He turned her way. They were treading on the edge, that narrow space between friends and something more. A place she had never been before, but recognized nonetheless.

She met his gaze. "How long are you supposed to take it easy?"

There she went again, blowing opportunities left and right. A big part of her found it hard to believe that she was sitting on her steps with Walker Montgomery, and surely this was some kind of misunderstanding on his part. Yet, here he was.

"I should be cleared in a few more days. Look, I promised my mom I was just going out for a short walk to get my blood flowing. If I'm not back soon, she'll send out a search party, but I had to see you. When do you go back to town?" he asked.

"Tomorrow afternoon. Lei is supposed to come get me."

"Let me take you in."

"Can you drive?"

"I can do whatever I want. Would it be all right if I came by earlier?"

"I have a lot to do," she said. The words belonged to that guarded part of her, still unable to make sense of what was happening, of what he wanted from her. She smiled to lessen the blow.

Walker stood and pulled her up. "For what it's worth, I thought about you a lot while we were away."

His expression was dead serious. Daisy found she could look anywhere but in his eyes. Suddenly, she was that skittish horse, ready to bolt at the first sign of intimacy. *Invite him over,* a voice inside screamed.

"Come at noon, and I'll feed you lunch. You could use some fattening up," she offered.

It was true. The bones on his face stood out more prominently. While Daisy had been plumping up on regular mess hall meals, poor Walker had been growing thinner by the week. War had that effect on participants.

After watching him lead the two horses down her driveway, Daisy brought the shotgun indoors and lay on the *puneʻe.* The only thing on her mind were his words: *I had to see you.*

17

THE PICNIC

Daisy took to the water the minute the sun came up. Dense clouds on the horizon and a mournful stillness meant another storm would be kicking in soon. At first, the water chilled her bare skin, but as her body worked against the current, she soon warmed. Straight out to the reef and then west along its inner edge, passing schools of *'omilu* and *manini*, an iridescent cuttlefish family and a turtle grazing on seaweed growing out of a crack in the coral. If only she could become one of them. Forget about all this human nonsense. Nature knew better.

An hour later, with three fish on her line, she came out a new person. Never mind that her body was covered in goose bumps, and she was shivering from cold, the world seemed righted again. She scaled and gutted the fish in no time, sliced two slabs, whisked up a lemony garlic sauce and put it in the fridge. Walker was in for a treat.

At 1000 hours, she hopped on her bike and rode to

Chock store to call Lei and tell her she had a ride. Humidity thickened up the air. Beyond the sugar mill and its rancid smell, down past the elementary school, she came to the small wooden building that sold a little bit of everything: fishing supplies, consumables, tools, toiletries and even some clothing. Myra Chock, ever the busybody, immediately bombarded her with questions. *Where you been? How's your mother? Did you hear we lost the* Houston? *Sank in the Java Sea.* Daisy had heard. In fact, working at Little Robert, she heard more than she cared to. But she couldn't tell Myra that.

"I've been staying with a family friend in town and assembling bandages and other odds and ends for the soldiers," Daisy told her.

"They pay you for that?"

"Some."

While she was talking to Lei, Daisy heard a car door slam, footsteps coming up the rickety steps. A moment later, Mrs. Montgomery walked into the store.

"Myra dear, I need some aspirin for my son and asthma medicine for my daughter. And can you please throw in a bag of coffee and some Camels and matches. The only thing that calms my nerves are these cigarettes," she said, waving her smoke across the room.

Daisy felt trapped. She hung up the phone quietly and stood there, immobile. There was no way out. Myra flitted about the store like a chicken, gathering goods.

"Hello," Daisy finally said, as cheerfully as she could muster.

Mrs. Montgomery jumped. "Oh. It's you."

A current of dislike ran between the two women, setting Daisy's hair on end. Or maybe it was the electricity in

the air from the incoming storm. Daisy opened her mouth
to say something, but nothing came out.

Myra asked, "How is your boy feeling?"

"The concussion seems to have affected his thinking."
Mrs. Montgomery looked directly at Daisy. "The doctor
says this is normal, that people change for a time after head
injuries, so you can't believe a word they say."

"Nah, they just need sleep. John used to bump his head a
lot in football," Myra said as she rang Mrs. Montgomery up.

"I just don't want *people* getting the wrong idea."

Daisy had the distinct feeling that the comments were directed her way. Though why Walker would mention Daisy
to his mother, she had no idea. Maybe Peg had said something. The barefooted high school dropout, hired help who
stole horses. Clearly not a good match for her dashing and
eligible son.

Daisy circumvented Mrs. Montgomery by walking
around a big table with stacks of neatly folded jeans and
Gob shirts. "Thank you, Myra. See you next week," she
said, in her most pleasant voice.

Noon came and went with no sign of Walker, and Daisy
began ruminating whether this counted as a date. She had
asked him to lunch, hadn't she? But only *after* he had offered her a ride to town. Either way, it certainly felt like one.
Maybe he changed his mind. A ridiculous twenty minutes
had been spent deciding which lock of hair to pin back, then
applying a coral-colored lipstick of Fluff's, only to dab most
of it off with tissue. Choosing what to wear had been even
more of a troubling issue. She finally decided on a pink-
and-white-checkered blouse with beige tapered trousers.

At 1230, she began wondering if the concussion had
made him forget about their plans. Or maybe Mrs. Mont-

gomery had been right, and he'd had no idea what he was talking about yesterday afternoon. The sound of an engine put an end to that.

The only way to properly prepare fish was over an open flame, though the clouds had marched closer, bringing darkness and the threat of rain. Daisy was outside tending to her fire, and when Walker came up behind her, she felt a vibration along her skin.

"Sorry I'm late. Mākaha foaled this morning and I got tied up helping Doc Wilcox," he said.

Mākaha was one of Daisy's favorite horses. "Was it a filly?"

"How did you know?"

She smiled up at him. "Just a hunch."

"Seems like your hunches are usually right, according to Silva."

She shrugged. "I pay attention."

"They miss you, you know. Silva and Hank and Cyril. Every time I show up, they ask how you're doing."

This was news. "Those old buggers? Besides Silva, they hardly gave me the time of day."

"Tough nuts, but they admired you."

"Well, tell them I say hello. And they might miss me but your mother sure doesn't. She made that clear today," Daisy said.

Walker's family was a big hurdle she wished she could forget about. But seeing Mrs. Montgomery had been a rude slap in the face.

"You saw my mother?"

Daisy spoke into the fire. "At the store."

He squatted down next to her, knee touching. "Tell me what she did."

"It doesn't matter."

"It does matter. I want to know. If I don't know, I can't do anything about it."

"Nothing you say or do will change anything."

He touched her wrist. "You're wrong about that."

Something about him always made her want to open up. "It was more innuendo than anything. She told Myra about your concussion and how you are not to be believed right now, and how she doesn't want *anyone* to get the wrong idea. She was looking directly at me as she spoke."

Walker lowered himself to a log. "Please, Daisy, try not to take it personally. My mother has a tendency to believe herself above everyone. It's not just you." He paused, a faraway look passing over his face. "She also holds on to things."

She knew he meant the accident and all the horrible things it brought with it. Dredging up old wounds was not what she wanted right now. There was already too much tragedy in the air.

"I'm used to it by now."

"I'll talk to her."

She shrugged. His mother was not going to change, no matter what. And Daisy wanted to enjoy what little time she had with Walker, before he sailed off. "I need to get the fish on the fire, so do what you think is best."

Walker insisted on helping cook the fish, and she let him even though she had a system. Daisy put him in charge of the frying pan while she washed and boiled the rice. This was not the cocksure Walker she knew. The way he kept lifting up one side of the fish with the spatula told her that cooking was not his specialty. But he seemed so concerned to getting it just right, it was endearing.

"I have to admit, that is the first time I've ever cooked a fish," he told her.

"What?"

He put his hand over his chest. "Swear to God."

"How does a man grow up so close to the ocean and not ever cook a fish?" she said.

"My mother and Lucinda never let me near the kitchen, said it was a woman's place."

Lucinda was their Filipino maid, who ran the house like an army installation. Daisy had always liked her.

"Is that how you see it, too?" she asked.

He cocked his head. "That sounds like a loaded question."

"Because it is."

"If that's where a woman wants to be. But suppose the woman wants to be a horse trainer or a pilot or an ace plotter and vectorologist, I say it's her call," he said.

She laughed. "How do you know about vectorologists?"

"Word travels fast aboard the Big E. A whole slew of pilots were talking about you gals, and how they might have had their doubts to begin with, but not anymore."

"Can someone please tell Colonel Nixon that?"

"He'll come around."

"I'm not so sure."

They sat on a blanket under the ironwood tree, Daisy noticing for the first time the age stains and unraveling threads. If Walker cared, he didn't show it. The fish was overdone but she kept quiet. Having him by her side was what counted. The sad truth was, Walker was her first houseguest. Partly because of Louise, and partly because there had been no one to invite.

"Can I ask you a question?" Walker said, when they had finished eating and were watching the shore break creeping up the beach with the rising tide.

"I suppose."

"How come you always avoided me when we were younger?"

The question caught her off guard. "I avoided you? I think you have it backward, Walker Montgomery. Whenever our paths crossed, I felt invisible."

Something dark passed over his face. He shook his head. "That's not true at all."

"It is and you know it."

At that moment, the skies intervened with a clap of thunder and a flash of lightning that lit up the whole western sky. A fat raindrop landed on Daisy's leg. And then another. They both jumped up at the same time and made a dash for the porch. By the time they made it under cover, they were both soaked. Daisy pulled a towel from the railing. It was still damp from her earlier swim, but she handed it to him. Walker dried his face and stepped closer. He placed the towel around her shoulders and pulled her in to a big, warm hug.

They stood that way for some time. It could have been minutes or hours, she wasn't sure. And then their eyes met. Beneath the weariness, she saw a longing as deep as her own. He hesitated for a fraction of a second and then brought his mouth to hers. Soft, with tenderness and a touch of fire. Butterflies took off in her chest. He pulled back slightly, eyes asking permission for more, and she granted it. His tongue parted her lips, moving slowly and surely.

Daisy was no kissing expert. It had been years since she had kissed a boy, and clearly Walker was no boy. He was a fully formed man who knew how to properly kiss a woman. He reached a hand up and coiled a lock of her hair around his finger.

"This," he said, pulling away. "Do you have any idea how long I've been wanting to do this?"

She really had no idea. "No."

"Oh, about a hundred years or so."

Just the edges of his mouth turned up. The very act of him smiling only for her, because of her, with her, completely undid Daisy. Her heart was full. His hands moved from her back to her waist. An inch or two taller, he pulled her into his warm, hard body. Hip against hip, thigh into thigh. He kissed her with hunger this time and she felt herself melting. Pretty soon they were up against the screen door.

"Is kissing allowed for concussion patients?" Daisy asked, when they broke apart.

"No one mentioned it being off-limits."

Heavy rain began to fall around them, peppering the tin roof. All the questions she'd had simply washed away, dissolving into the wet grass. Who cared about Thelma or his family right now? Nothing mattered but Walker standing here with his arms around her. Water blew in on them, until their legs were soaked. Daisy led him inside.

Walker got a serious look on his face. "Daisy, I want to go on record as saying that I told Thelma I'm not interested. Her father brought her out here the day after I got back—I think Peg put them up to it—and I made it very clear. Not that there was anything there to begin with but a whole lot of expectations. Everyone just assumed we were going to marry because of who she is and how much money they have. But *you* are the one who kept me up at night, the one I had to make it home for," he said, squeezing her hand.

A part of her believed him, while another part was still waiting to wake up. Now she understood why Mrs. Montgomery had been going on about his head injury. Another clap of thunder shook the house. Windows rattled and Daisy jumped. Walker pulled her close. An eerie midday darkness fell and shadowed his face, but she could feel a burning from his gaze. To quiet her thoughts, she kissed him. She tasted sea on his breath, which made her want him even more. His hands were everywhere—neck, collarbone, hips, ribs—leaving trails of heat in their wake. The whole room hummed, as though a cauldron of bats had taken up residence. So this was desire. There was a distinct possibility that she would never recover from this kiss.

18

THE PLANES

It was the rainiest winter in recent memory, of that Daisy was sure. The mudflats outside Shafter had turned into a swampland, several of the WARDs had contracted strep throat and everyone was trapped indoors for days on end. Even Blanche never left the house. The only ones who loved it were the cane toads. Daisy had not seen or heard from Walker since he dropped her off three days ago and was beginning to wonder if the whole thing had been a dream.

To be prudent, Walker had pulled over two blocks before the barracks, on a back street. He seemed to think it was entirely unnecessary, but Daisy insisted. There were eyes everywhere in the neighborhood and the coconut wireless was rampant with this many women living in one place. Words traveled fast on the trade winds. Nor was she ready to deal with Peg and Thelma blaming her for Walker's decision. Though they would anyway.

To make matters worse, they were now on the graveyard

shift, which for some reason happened to be when most air-raid sirens sounded. Usually a result of American pilots not properly identifying themselves. It stunk.

"Someone needs to tell those boys they're causing need-less panic," Fluff told Lieutenant Dunn one day.

"I'll take it up with Owens and the other guys," he said.

An hour into their shift on the night of March 5, Daisy was stirring sugar into her second cup of coffee when a call came in over VHF radio from Koke'e. Only every fourth word came through and the voice was muffled. Several of the girls crowded around to hear.

"Say again," the radio operator responded.

"Bogeys—bearing—coast—unknown—" followed by the hiss of static.

"I'll put money down that it's another one of our pilots not following protocol," Fluff said with her hands on her waist.

Daisy wasn't so sure. "He sounded concerned, more so than usual."

Major Oscar and Sergeant Jones, the naval liaison, had come down from the balcony. "What is it?"

"A garbled message from Koke'e. Sounds like they picked up something and I'm guessing whatever it was is coming our way," Daisy informed them.

"Call Opana and Wai'anae, tell them to be on high alert, paying special attention to the northwest," Major Oscar said.

Daisy and Betty sprang into action. Since losing Chuck, Betty worked with a new ferocity. Anything to do to help win this war, she threw her all into. On her days off, she had taken up knitting scarves for the pilots, and fashion-ing bandages from old socks. She canned guava jelly by the truckload and wrote them letters to boost morale. Though it was her morale that was being boosted. Helping others, she said, was a backdoor way to helping yourself.

The Army Air Corps officer leaned over the balcony and frowned at the mostly empty boards. "I don't like this," he said to no one in particular. "We have no operations or trainings in these waters, and neither does the navy."

A collective feeling of tension filled the room, so thick you could almost taste it. Daisy ordered herself to stay calm. Which was a silly notion, really. Trying to reason with fear was like wrestling a twelve-foot tiger shark for a *manini* on your line.

No matter how many times unidentified planes had turned out to be false alarms, each subsequent one evoked the same dread. It didn't help that word had been circulating among the male officers that reconnaissance and bombing raids were imminent. No one mentioned their source, but they seemed quite sure. Major Oscar started barking orders. "Someone call Nixon." He pointed to Daisy. "You, Rascal, go."

Daisy shrunk back. "Me?"

"My guys are all tied up."

Nixon lived next to Palm Circle, the heart of Fort Shafter, and was known for getting to Little Robert in five minutes flat. Still, Daisy hated to be the one to wake him up. The phone rang only once, and he answered, "Nixon."

"Colonel Nixon, sorry to bother you, but we got a call from Koke'e and we couldn't understand the message but it looks like we have two bogeys incoming. Oh, this is Wilder, sir, at Command Center."

A dial tone buzzed in her ear. Minutes later, Betty started waving her hand madly, nodding and jotting down notes. "Opana's got their echo. They think there's two!" she said.

Fluff placed an X in the standard, and in her neat, block

print marked it *UNIDENTIFIED*. Her hand shook as she wrote. Val picked up a call from the other Oscar at Opana. "Rascal, bogey bearing southwest twenty miles east of Koloa."

The women set markers on the board, and Daisy tried to collect herself as they waited for the next coordinates. Nixon strode into the room moments later. Aside from the pouches under his eyes, he looked perfectly put-together and ready for business. He came directly to the table.

"What are we looking at?" he asked.

Daisy and Betty alternated filling him in.

From the balcony, Major Oscar, who held a phone to each ear, called down, "No one's claiming them, sir. But we're still waiting for confirmation from air force."

Nixon's jaw hardened. "Any surface craft detected?"

"Not yet," Daisy said.

The creases in his forehead seemed to have deepened since yesterday. Without another word, he left the table and went to consult with the men on the balcony. Fluff came and stood behind Daisy, hands on her shoulders. She spoke quietly, "Do you think this is the real McCoy?"

It certainly felt like *something* was coming. Animals were designed to detect danger. Their heightened senses picked up vibrations and subtle changes in the air. Horses became uncontrollable, bees swarmed and deep-sea fish washed ashore. A Japanese attack was not a natural disaster by any means, but the atmosphere felt charged.

"We'll know soon enough," she said.

Ten minutes passed, and the planes continued a beeline toward O'ahu. Daisy watched the air force liaison approach Nixon with an anxious look on his face. Whatever he said caused Nixon to slam his coffee down.

Nixon alerted the room. "Air Force denied any knowledge of the aircraft, which means we need to prepare for an imminent attack. Sound the sirens and dispatch the pursuit planes. I also want a patrol out scouting for carriers, on the double, and shut down the naval yard. These fuckers are not going to get us again."

All the officers scrambled to their phone sets. The WARDs on duty were told to gather their helmets and gas masks, and have them on hand. Daisy grabbed Betty's for her, as she was glued to her headset. Whispers and murmurs circulated around the table. There was a feeling of organized chaos, and dare she say it, anticipation. This is what they'd been practicing for so long. Would they be able to hack it?

Generals and colonels and other brass began appearing in droves, all of them dripping wet. Every time the door opened, a cold fury blew in. There were so many bodies that nonessential staff were ordered into the break room. Daisy followed Fluff out, but Nixon called her. "Wilder, I want you to vector the pursuits. Get back in here."

She stopped cold.

Fluff turned and said, "Go on, you're the best one out of all of us for the job."

Daisy returned to the table and awaited instructions. She said a little prayer for everyone she knew on the island, humans and animals alike, and ended it with, *may this be another false alarm.* Danielson hovered over the board, and Daisy was thankful for his calming presence.

"You ladies are doing good work. I'm impressed," he told her.

Outside, the air-raid siren wailed its mournful song for a full minute. The sound sobered an already tense crowd, and no doubt had the whole island scrambling into wet, muddy and bug-infested shelters.

Betty commented, "These aircraft don't seem to be moving very fast. What do you think they are?"

Daisy helped her calculate airspeed. About 190 knots, which was below a B-17 or most American fighters. "Possibly flying boats."

So far, nothing else had been picked up by radar. Perhaps they were reconnaissance or forerunners of a larger fleet.

In the distance, the roar of fighter engines and the whine of ascent cut across the night.

"There they go. God bless 'em," Betty said.

Waiʻanae called in the pursuits, which had just shown up on their screen, and Daisy began tracking the lead plane and his two wingmen.

The pilot radioed in, "This is Warhawk two-six-niner. Black as tar up here, not a star or moon in sight. We're going to need all the support you can give," he said.

It had taken a little time getting used to the military lingo, using phonetic alphabet and code names and strange phrases. Daisy still felt like an imposter when speaking to the pilots, but she found that using the same matter-of-fact voice she used with the horses came in handy. It almost felt natural. She double-checked the bogey coordinates five times, then said, "Roger that. Fly heading three-zero-five. Incoming aircraft moving at one-niner-zero knots. What's your altitude?"

The fewer words the better.

"Angels three. Cloud bases are low tonight and the rain is spitting."

Daisy couldn't even imagine what it must be like flying around in the dark up there. A good thing they were heading toward Kauaʻi, otherwise they'd run the risk of plowing into the Waiʻanae range with any miscalculations.

Cigarette smoke and body heat mingled together in the

poorly ventilated building, steaming up the board. It was thick enough to choke on. Betty fanned herself with a pamphlet cautioning against venereal disease, which had mysteriously begun circulating the previous day. Someone's poor idea of a joke. Most likely one of the boys.

At any moment, Daisy expected a call to come in saying someone had made a mistake, the planes were ours. But that call still hadn't come. Now, the bogeys were more than halfway across the channel.

Nixon came down again and stood next to Daisy. "How far now?"

She pointed to the board, where Betty's and Val's markers and her marker were moving closer together. "Twenty-two miles."

"You need to tell him that!" he said.

She flinched. "Come in, Warhawk two-six-niner."

"Read you, loud and clear."

"You're closing in fast, twenty-two miles. Head zero-one-zero north and watch out."

Watch out? What kind of silly advice was that? How could he watch out when he couldn't see anything? Daisy wished Nixon had picked someone else. Pressure tended to make her stupid. Pretty soon, the planes were ten miles apart. A quiet came over the room, and the feeling that something big was about to happen. Beads of perspiration dripped down Daisy's neck, between her breasts, in the creases behind her knees. She wiped her face on her sleeve and reminded herself that she had prepared for this.

Betty sat to her left, nervously tapping her stick on the floor.

"Knock it off, Yates, you're making me crazy," Nixon growled.

She immediately stopped. "Sorry, sir."

The next reading from Wai'anae had the interceptors and one bogey on a collision course. The other seemed to be veering north. Daisy notified the pilot. "Eyes wide open, Warhawk two-seven-five. Bogey is within striking distance."

"Roger. In cloud soup out here. I've dropped down to angels two and am going in and out, but no lights sighted, though am getting intermittent sightings of Ka'ena Point Lighthouse."

Daisy thought that if our pilots couldn't see a thing, then neither could the Japanese. At least they had that going for them.

"Try to get above the clouds," Nixon said, leaning in Daisy's face to speak directly to the pilot. His breath smelled like stale coffee and sleep.

One of the downfalls of radar was that it didn't tell you altitude. One plane could be at five hundred feet and another at fifteen thousand, and they would both look the same on the oscilloscope. Another was that low-flying aircraft often went under the radar and were not detected.

"Tell him to stay with us," Nixon said.

"Stay with us, Warhawk."

The next readings showed the bogeys approaching O'ahu, one near Barber's Point and one just outside Hale'iwa.

"Turn around, heading one-eight-five. You passed them," Daisy said.

Word came in from the PBY Catalina pilots who were out hunting for Japanese carriers that so far they'd encountered nothing suspicious. Nor had radar across the islands picked up anything. Carriers might be able to operate without running lights, but as the girls had seen with the US ships, they showed up loud and clear on radar.

There was something remarkably unsetting about watching the bogeys approach the island from two directions, and pretty soon, the brass began to quarrel. By now, several more fighters had been sent up to intercept. None could see a thing.

"We need to open fire."

"Hickam and Schofield are standing by."

"Not with our boys up there, we don't!" Nixon yelled, face cherry red.

In the chaos of the Pearl Harbor raid, friendly fire from anti-aircraft artillery not only killed American pilots, but exploding rounds fell in neighborhoods across the South Shore, killing civilians too. When Daisy had heard this, she felt sick to her stomach. What a dilemma. She was thankful it wasn't her call right now.

"Wait until someone calls Tally Ho," Nixon said.

Tally Ho, she had recently learned, meant enemy in sight and engaged.

"Anyone not with a headset, put your helmets on," Danielson said.

Daisy would have gladly traded her headset for a helmet. Though in all honesty, what good was a helmet against a five-hundred-pound bomb? Her gas mask rested in her lap. No sooner had she placed the marker in the middle of O'ahu, when a loud explosion sent shockwaves through the Penthouse. Glass rattled, wood vibrated and people scurried toward the back wall. A moment later, another explosion, and then two more.

"Warhawk, we've been hit. Somewhere not far from Shafter," Daisy yelled into the radio.

The blasts sounded close, but not too close, possibly in the direction of downtown Honolulu. Bombing the heart of the city was unthinkable, bound to kill more civilians than servicemen.

"Roger that. I'm up at angels one, two, no clouds up here. The moon is shining and I'm getting glimpses of the city."

Nixon jumped onto the floor and took the radio from her. "Charlie Mike and be ready for more. Stand by for orders."

"Charlie Mike?" she asked. She knew the phonetics but had no idea what he meant.

"Continue Mission."

Betty reached over and grabbed Daisy's hand. If it bothered Nixon, he didn't let on. Soft and clammy, Daisy clasped as if her life depended on it. That warm hand did more to slow her pulse than any pill. They waited for more bombs to fall.

And waited.

And waited.

Finally, news came in that bombs had come down in a wooded area on Mount Tantalus, just behind Roosevelt High School. The blasts had flattened trees and left a smoldering crater, but there were no reports of injury. Radar tracked the enemy back out to sea until they were no longer visible. Suddenly, Daisy could breathe again, as a wave of relief poured into the room and swept away the tension that had risen to the ceiling. That was the thing with air-raid warnings, you never got used to them. Each one could be *the* one.

Nixon called everyone together. "Tell you what. Those bastards planned this knowing the moon would be full. But they didn't count on the weather and they sure as hell don't know we are watching them. Now we know how well our radar works."

And that us WARDs can vector and plot and do what needs to be done, Daisy thought. Of course, he would never say it out loud. A few cheers erupted.

"Now get back to business."

For the rest of that shift, Daisy checked the clock every two minutes. They were in continuous conversation with the Oscars around the island, and with every hour that passed without echoes, everyone let down their guard a few notches. It went down in the record books as one of the longest nights of her life.

19

THE SECRET

Two days later, on their first day off since the raid, the girls woke to find their lingerie missing from the clothesline again. Daisy's new underwear—which she'd found at Liberty House—Betty's fancy Love bra and Fluff's girdle. Why a twenty-year-old woman needed a girdle, Daisy had no idea, but Fluff claimed it improved her shape.

"What kind of lowlife would do this? What if he's a Peeping Tom, too?" Fluff said.

"How do you know it's a he?" Betty said.

Fluff frowned. "No way a female would do this."

The young guard who Fluff had questioned claimed ignorance, though assured her he would keep an eye out. Nothing had ever come of it.

Betty shrugged. "You never know. Maybe someone doesn't like us. Or they're jealous. Maybe they want to spook us. As if we need any more spooking."

No matter how you sliced it, it was an invasion of privacy. And Fluff was right, what if someone was out there sneaking around in the bushes watching them dress and undress, or listening to their conversations? The run-in with Johnny Boy had left her with an extra dose of caution. "It gives me the creeps. We ought to tell Vivian."

Vivian at Headquarters handled the barracks. She smoked her cigarettes using one of those elongated holders and seemed far more sophisticated than the rest of the girls. Ten minutes later, they were sitting in front of Vivian, telling their story through a haze of smoke.

She laughed at first, then said, "I'll call the FBI."

"I'm not sure it warrants the FBI," Daisy said.

As expected, the FBI said there was nothing they could do, so Vivian insisted they accompany her on a search of nearby quarters. Betty and Daisy both refused, but Fluff volunteered to go. After an awkward hour of searching, a procedure Betty claimed was highly illegal, Vivian and Fluff returned empty-handed.

"Well, that was awkward," Fluff said.

Vivian peered out the back door and said, "You need to set a trap. Hang out a bunch of bras and panties and wait in the dark for them. Then, when the culprit shows up, blind 'em with your blackout flashlight."

It was worth a shot.

Later that afternoon, Fluff and Daisy had just returned from the Fort Shafter pool—the chlorinated water a sorry substitute for the ocean—when a knock came at the door. Daisy was still in a towel, so Fluff answered. A man's voice floated in.

"Lieutenant, what a nice surprise. I'm Fluff Kanahele. I heard you talk at Little Robert that day."

Daisy's ears perked up.

"A pleasure, ma'am."

"Oh please, call me Fluff. Come in!"

Bold of Walker to show up here, but Daisy was happy to see him. She darted into her room and slipped into a sleeveless yellow dress with big bold flowers printed on it, something Fluff had talked her into buying. Smoothing down her wet hair, she walked into the living room. Walker stood just inside the threshold with his hands in his pockets. When he saw her, he swallowed hard.

"Sorry to drop in unexpected like this, but I was at Pearl and…well… I had no idea when you were coming back to Waialua," he said.

She felt a sudden case of jitters. "Did they clear you to fly?"

He smiled. "Got the green light today. Doc says I've made a remarkable recovery."

"I'm happy to hear. We need our crack pilots in top shape," Daisy said.

Fluff jumped in. "Did you hear about the fiasco the other night?"

"Boy did I ever. I would have liked to see our fighters ambush them in the Kauaʻi Channel, but at least the weather kept them from hitting their targets. How was it for you ladies?"

Daisy and Fluff looked at each other. "Daisy here directed that Warhawk like an old pro—"

"That is pure exaggeration!" Daisy said, cutting her off.

Walker seemed amused. "I told her from the beginning she had the brains and talent."

"Nixon was right there by my side. Nor did we intercept. Maybe someone better would have been able to make that happen."

"Not with those clouds. It was thundering at the ranch

and flooding the riverbanks. It would have been hard to see anything even during the day," Walker said.

Fluff excused herself, leaving Daisy and Walker face-to-face, though still an arm's length apart. This was new territory, and she had no idea whether to hug him or kiss him or invite him in for something. Juice? Beer? Necking? She could hardly think straight. Walker, though, seemed to know exactly what to do. He stepped toward her, tilted her chin and kissed her square on the lips. Daisy felt the kiss in the tips of her toes.

"I hope it's not a bother I just did that," he said, afterward.

"Did I seem bothered?"

He smiled. "Look, I know you aren't supposed to have men in your quarters, and my car out there is liable to stir talk, so I'll get to the point. Would you go on a date with me?"

Daisy had never been on a date. Not really. While she was still in school, Buddy Ah Sing had walked her home a few times, then later, at sixteen, she spent many an afternoon kissing Charles Kini in an abandoned sugar shack on the river, but his hands liked to wander and she finally tired of it. At nineteen, she had developed a crush on a cowboy named Cousin visiting from Texas. He walked her down the beach one night, asked her to *touch my member*, and then stormed off when she refused. Proper dates had not been part of her experience.

Walker mistook her silence for hesitance. "The timing couldn't be worse, but I'm not going to wait until the end of this war to take you out." He paused, eyes searching. "Say yes?"

"Of course I will."

They decided on the following Wednesday, the only

day they both had off. It seemed so far away, she considered telling him she was free this afternoon and would he please take her to a secluded beach and kiss her some more. Though Fluff would scold her for appearing too eager. The woman sure had a lot of rules when it came to men. *Never kiss them first. Let the fella do the asking. Turn them down every now and then. It makes them want you more. Don't give them too much on the first date.*

"It's settled, then," he said, his mouth curving up on one side.

"I'll look forward to it."

"That makes two of us."

Walker stole another kiss and then was gone.

Signs of spring began showing up everywhere. Mango blossoms adorned the trees, butterflies floated through the streets, and Blanche, it turned out, was pregnant. Spring had always been Daisy's favorite season. She appreciated the warm weather and calming seas, and loved watching the foals run around the field on their tentative new legs. Now, spring was a reminder that the world kept on spinning. Even in the midst of war.

"We aren't even supposed to have animals in here. How are we going to deal with a whole litter of kittens?" Betty asked.

"We'll give them away," Fluff said.

Daisy knew better. "You can't just hand out new kittens to people. They need to nurse until they're at least a couple months old."

Fluff clasped her hands together. "Then we'll raise them ourselves and keep them a secret. I can't think of anything better than a bunch of kittens to boost morale. Maybe they could help us get Nixon to smile."

"Be serious," Betty said.

"Animals can melt even the coldest hearts. Everyone knows that."

Daisy agreed. "She has a point. Having kittens around could lift all of our spirits."

Betty was the one who needed her spirits lifted the most, but Daisy didn't want to say it to her face. On the surface, she seemed to be coping well, keeping busy and tiring herself out so she could sleep, but anyone could see that half her heart was missing. She had lost weight and her uniform hung where it used to hug.

"Y'all, we are employed by the United States government. They pay us to follow the rules," Betty argued.

Daisy could not afford to lose the job, but how could she turn her back on Blanche? "As long as we keep them inside, no one will know. I say we keep them."

"Majority rules," Fluff said.

Betty sighed. "Fine, but you two can take the heat for it if we get caught."

"Speaking of caught. We need to set the trap for our lingerie thief. I thought I could have my camera and flashbulb handy, and stun 'em with the light. That way, we'll have proof," Fluff said.

After much debate over how to organize the trap, they decided to split the night into three shifts, and Fluff showed them how to use the camera. "How are we going to know when our shift is over?" Betty asked.

"The moon, silly. Daisy, when the moon is straight overhead, come get me. And I'll get Betty when the moon is forty degrees or so above the horizon," Fluff said.

They had recently learned that you could use your fist as a sextant, and Fluff had been thrilled with the news. Daisy thought that staying awake was hopefully optimistic, but she kept her mouth shut. The best vantage point was under the mock orange hedge, where they made a comfy nest out of blankets and pillows. At first, she was alert and reactive to every broken branch or whisper of wind, but soon found her eyelids kept closing. Eventually, she drifted off into a deep, dreamless sleep. When she opened her eyes, there was no sign of the moon and the sun had sent up early morning feelers of light. She bolted up, rubbing her eyes.

The lingerie still hung on the line.

At work, air traffic was slow, and Daisy went to the break room to grab a piece of the banana bread that Lei had brought in. She had a sore spot on the side of her head from her camping experience, and was rubbing it. To her surprise, Nixon was in there, cutting a slice for himself. Nixon never came into the break room.

"Good stuff," he said, wiping a crumb from his mouth.

"Lei's maid is the best cook in Honolulu. I'd put money on it," Daisy said.

"Are you a betting girl?"

She laughed. "No, but I stayed at their house long enough to know it's a fact."

He looked at her, then down at the banana bread, then back at her. "You gals stick together, don't you?"

"It's in our nature."

In just a couple of short months, Daisy had gone from loner to member of the herd. Bands of horses had a dominant mare, and she pondered who in the group would have that role. "Back in Indiana, my wife had a group of friends who called themselves *the mermaids*. No ocean around for miles." He shook his head at the thought. "But they loved the lake and met there for a few weeks every summer. No men allowed. I gave her a hard time for it, but she always came home glowing."

"Sounds like she was lucky in the friend department."

"She was lucky in a lot of departments...but one," he said.

Daisy could hardly believe she was standing here having a personal conversation with Nixon. "What happened?" she asked.

He opened his mouth to answer, when Thelma walked in. Instead, he wiped his chin with a napkin and said curtly, "Another time."

Then he left.

Thelma pretended to be cheery, but her eyes told another story. "Did I interrupt something?"

"We were just chatting."

She let out a sour laugh. "Chatting? With Nixon?"

"Trust me, I was just as surprised as you," Daisy said.

Thelma smacked her freshly painted lips. "Want to know what really surprised me? Seeing Walker's car outside of your house yesterday. He's not right in the head, you know that don't you?"

"So I've heard."

Daisy was tired of tiptoeing around the fact that she and Walker Montgomery had evolved into something more than just friends. What exactly that meant still remained to be seen, but they were two adults who *at least* enjoyed each other's company. Not to mention kissing.

Thelma persisted. "Why was he there?"

"Really, Thelma, is that any of your business?"

Her nostrils flared. "We were supposed to get married, so *yes*, it is."

"From what I understand, you two were never officially engaged. Sure, your families wanted it, but did anyone ask Walker? He's a grown man with his own opinions and feelings and desires. I heard it straight from the horse's mouth that marrying you was never his intention," Daisy said.

Thelma stepped back as though slapped. "Have you ever asked yourself why a man like Walker would have any interest in you?" She paused a beat, raising her chin for effect. "My theory is he feels guilty about your father and thinks he can somehow make it up to you."

All the blood swooshed out from Daisy's face. She reached out to steady herself on the table, blackness closing in from the sides and pinpricks running across her skin Had she heard correctly? "What did you say?"

"I said he feels guilty," Thelma said.

"Why would he feel guilty about my father?"

"Because his father was responsible."

Daisy grabbed her by the upper arm and twisted. "Why would you say such a thing?"

"Hey, let go of me!"

"Not until you tell me."

Her fingers dug into Thelma's flesh. Poor woman's arm was squishy and weak. Daisy gripped even harder, probably cutting off blood flow. She didn't care.

"I meant how Walker's dad shot him by accident on the hunting trip. Don't act so surprised," Thelma said, blue eyes watering.

Every cell in her being prickled. Thelma was wrong. "My father slipped down a hillside and shot himself accidentally. You have your story mixed up."

Thelma looked confused. "I thought you knew."

They stared at each other for a moment. Something like shock washed over Thelma's face. Daisy let her go. Her mind searched for threads of connection. Where would Thelma have heard that? It was not the kind of thing someone made up. Even someone as unpleasant as Thelma.

"This is news to me. Just a minor detail that no one ever mentioned," Daisy said, bent over from the force of the words.

"I'm sorry," Thelma said.

Daisy turned to leave. "I don't need your pity."

Unable to breathe or concentrate or stop shaking, Daisy went into the back office and told the shift supervisor, Tippy, that she believed she had food poisoning. She then slipped out the door of Little Robert without a word to anyone else. All she wanted to do was jump in the ocean or hop on the back of a horse and disappear. She had to think. But there were no beaches within walking distance, and even if there had been, they'd be blocked off with barbed wire. No horses, either.

Sweat trickled down her spine as the noonday sun cooked the asphalt. She walked along in a fuzzy haze, thinking back to the early days after the accident. Never quite understanding why her mother blamed herself. This changed everything. And if Thelma knew, then Peg knew, which meant Walker knew. And Louise.

Peg was not on shift, but Daisy knew where she lived. A big house on the corner that she shared with Thelma and two other WARDs. In recent months, Daisy had come to see that most of the women at Little Robert were friendly, no matter their age or background or color. There was an iron-clad sense of togetherness that permeated their ranks. The only ones who viewed themselves as above the others were Peg and her housemates. *High makamaka,* Fluff liked to say.

Daisy marched up the front steps and banged on the doorframe. Voices and cinnamon floated out from the kitchen.

Mary Morgan walked over, wearing an orange apron and licking a wooden spoon. "Can I help you?" she said through the screen.

"I need to speak with Peg."

"Peg is at her folks' place for the night. Is everything all right?" Mary said.

"No, everything is not all right."

It was only Saturday. Waiting until Wednesday was an impossibility. At home, Blanche sensed something wrong and wove herself between Daisy's legs in a figure eight pattern as Daisy downed a tall glass of water.

"I'm glad you're here," Daisy told her.

In a manner of minutes, she had changed out of her uniform, left a note for Betty and Fluff, and was speeding across the island in Betty's Oldsmobile. With Chuck gone, they had inherited the vehicle. Betty hated to drive, so Fluff and Daisy had been taking turns chauffeuring the group around. She hoped Betty wouldn't mind.

Daisy had no plan. No idea what she was going to say. Only that she was heading to the Montgomery house with her soul on fire. *Walker's dad shot him. I thought you knew.* What kind of lie had she been living her whole life? Going to Montgomery ranch every day, working for the man who shot her father. Being treated like a second-class citizen by a killer. Why would her mother play along? Storm clouds swirled in her head.

At the junction, she stopped the car. Ranch first or house first? If Walker was at the ranch, she could bypass seeing anyone else in his family. But maybe that was what she needed, to confront these people face-to-face. Taste the poison. She turned left toward the house and drove slowly through the coconut grove. A family of mongooses crossed in front of her. Her last time here had not gone over well, and this time was bound to be worse.

A strong west wind blew in, bending trees and stirring up

dust and buried emotions. She stood at the front door for a full five minutes before she knocked. When the door swung open, Peg stared up at her through bleary eyes. "Aren't you supposed to be working?" Peg asked.

"I need to talk to Walker," Daisy said.

Peg started to close the door in her face. "He's not here, sorry."

Daisy held the door. "Then I want to talk to your father."

"My father is not feeling well. He's not seeing anyone," Peg said, trying to shut the door again.

Daisy couldn't hold it in any longer and blurted out, "Is it true that your father killed my father?"

Peg froze, something shifting in her eyes. "Is that why you came to see Walker, to ask him that?"

"Thelma told me in no uncertain terms that Walker feels sorry for me because his father shot my father, which was news to me, but apparently this information has been circulating for some time. Answer me. Is it true?" Daisy said, terrified to hear the answer but needing to know.

"You're supposed to know. Your mother knows. I mean, I think she does," Peg said, fingers playing with the top button on her dress and eyes bouncing from the floor to the wall to the high ceiling.

Daisy had no words. She turned and bolted. The whole world had betrayed her, simple as that. She made it home and into the ocean, swimming until her arms burned. Underwater, no one could hear her cries. Nor did the fish care. The loss was bad enough—of both her father and her mother—but throw some betrayal on the flames and you had an inextinguishable fire.

Still wet and salty and spent, she sat at the kitchen table and began to draft a letter to her mother. At first she scrawled out every awful thought in her head, filling two sheets with questions and accusations and rantings. But after rereading, she tore them up. Starting over, she took her time in printing block letters, since her cursive was scratchy at best. She kept this one short and direct. Sending the letter was one thing, but whether or not she'd hear back was another story.

Dear Louise,
My heart is broken. I learned today that Daddy did not shoot himself, rather Mr. Montgomery did. You knew but did not tell me. I have so many questions for you, but the main one is: How could you lie to me all this time? As you can imagine, I feel like my life has been turned upside down and scattered to the wind. I would appreciate an honest answer promptly.
Your daughter,
Daisy

No sooner had she finished the letter, when she heard the dull thud of boots in the grass. In two seconds flat, she was standing behind the door with a butcher knife in hand. "Daisy, you in there?" Walker called, knocking on the wall and pressing his face against the screen to peer in.

She stepped away from the wall. "Go away."

He glanced down at the knife. "Peg told me you came by. And she said that somehow you didn't know what happened."

"I know now, so please just go."

"Not until we talk. I'll set up camp in the yard if I have to, but we need to talk this through. Would you put the knife down and come outside? Please?" he said.

She had no energy left. "Trespassing is against the law."

"Daisy, please."

"We can talk like this. Me in here and you out there,"

she said, setting the knife on the counter and folding her arms over her damp shirt, an old button-up that used to be her father's.

He spoke through the screen. "All these years, I thought you knew. There were a few times when I almost brought it up, but it never seemed the right time."

"How would I know? Your father told us and everyone that my dad slid down an embankment and his gun went off. *A most unfortunate accident* were his exact words. And now I've just heard from three people that they thought I knew," she said.

Walker softened his voice. "My father is the one who slipped and whose gun went off. He panicked, swore everyone to secrecy, even paid the ranch hands for their silence. Over time, it started eating away at me. I began to hate my father for making us hold on to this huge lie, and hated myself even more. Finally, I told my father he had to come clean or I would. We fought about it and I ended up leaving. But he told your mother, Daisy, I know he did."

As much as the truth hurt, what stung even more was the fact that Louise hadn't told her. And Walker. Walker was an accomplice. "In case no one noticed, my mother had gone off the deep end by then. I wonder why no one thought to tell me."

She could not look him in the eye, consumed with a twisting, suffocating shock. The idea that she could never be with Walker slammed down hard. Here was a man whose father killed her father and asked him to lie about it. And he had.

"Get out of here, Walker. And don't come back," she said, shutting the door in his face.

She listened for him going down the steps. Pressed her forehead to the knotted wood, imagining him doing the same on the other side. So close. Though the door, he said, "I'm not giving up on us."

"There is no *us*, Walker. There never has been."

20

THE DATE

Eyes nearly swollen shut, Daisy drove back to Shafter.
Walker had stayed on the porch for another ten minutes
and she swore she could feel the magnetic pull of his heart.
Once he was gone, she slid down with her back against the
door and sobbed. Heaving, air-sucking sobs. The first round
was for her father and all the lost years and love missed out
on. The next was for Louise, her broken mother. A woman
unable to perform her most important role. When those
tears had emptied out, she started crying anew for Walker
and what might have been. For the way he seemed to genuinely care, and those lips of his that she would never taste
again. Finally, she cried for herself.

When the tears ended, the questions started up again in
rapid fire. Had her father known he was dying? Did he suf-
fer? What if Mr. Montgomery had pretended to slip and
killed him in cold blood? Had anyone actually witnessed
the shooting? Who all knew? Had her mother reported this

to the sheriff? If so, why was Montgomery walking around a free man? Though she could guess that one. Mr. Montgomery was the most important man this side of Honolulu. He had everyone in his pocket, and his was the last word.

Daisy tried to sneak into the house, but Betty, Fluff and Lei were sitting around the dining room table eating boiled peanuts and drinking Primo beer. With Betty down and out, Lei had been spending more and more time at their place in the evenings. Partly to help out, but also to escape her own miserable situation. Heads turned at the sound of the screen door shutting behind the blackout curtain.

Fluff jumped up when she saw Daisy. "*Auwe* girl, what happened to you?"

The room was hotter than a brick oven. Daisy headed for the bedroom and fresh air.

"Come talk to us, sweet pea," Betty said.

No one turned down Betty. Not now. Reluctantly, Daisy stopped and leaned against the doorframe, the corner pressing into the back of her head.

Fluff popped open a beer and set it on the table. She patted the empty chair next to her. "Sit, and that's an order from your superior officer."

"Who made you my superior?"

"I did. Right now."

"It's sweltering in here. I can't take it," Daisy said.

"Where would you rather be?" Lei asked.

"Outside in the fresh air."

"Well, then let's go."

They gathered up the beer and peanuts, and set it all down on a beach blanket in the backyard. It was at least ten degrees cooler and the stars looked close enough to collect and put in mason jars. Daisy lay down on her back and stared up at the sky.

"Now, what's the matter?" Betty said.

Daisy told them everything, beginning with Thelma and ending with Walker. None of them knew that he had kissed her, so she told them that, too.

Lei smoothed Daisy's hair back. "Men like Montgomery make me want to retch. They think they own the world. But what they don't understand is that money can't buy goodness and truth."

"Or decency," Daisy said.

"Do you think he shot your father on purpose?" Fluff asked.

"I don't know why he would."

"What about the authorities? Do they know? We should march down there and tell them what really happened."

We. Daisy loved how Fluff immediately considered anyone's problem her own. A sign of true friendship if there were one.

"They already know. Walker made his dad go fess up. And if you don't mind, I'm worn out from crying and I've been round and round in my mind all day. Can we just look at the stars for a while?"

One by one, they arranged themselves with their heads together on the blanket—Palmolive soap, night-blooming jasmine and the faint smell of night mingling together. No one spoke. The collective breathing of the group soon fell in sync, causing a swelling in Daisy's chest like she had never felt before. A moment later, Blanche appeared, rubbing her head against their legs. Daisy reached down and stroked her, feeling the ever-growing bulge in her midsection. Any day now, the kittens would arrive.

At Little Robert, the first class of filterers would be announced at the end of the week. Aside from bragging rights, a filterer got to wear a red bar with a blue stripe pinned to the collar of her uniform. Out of the four of them, Daisy was the only one gunning for it.

"I'm not interested, nor does my brain work that way," Fluff had said.

Betty was too distracted. "I can't seem to focus for too long on any one thing."

And Lei had been chosen to be shift captain, in charge of scheduling and making sure rotations ran smoothly.

For the first time in her life, Daisy had been studying like mad. There was beauty in numbers and how with enough information stored in your brain, you could take unconnected plots and see a pattern. Now, she focused on memorizing the multitudes of codes, how to manage planes in distress—God forbid, and handling divergent echo interpretation reports. Studying also took her mind off the Montgomery mess, and waiting for her mother's letter that may never come.

Nixon had been worried about "turning the WARDs loose" and allowing them to run the show without oversight. There was no doubt the man was working himself to death. A rash had formed along his temple and down one side of his neck. "Looks to me like something's burrowing in there," Fluff said in the break room one day.

Lei lowered her voice. "That's what happens when you can't delegate. When you don't trust anyone to do the work as good as you would. It's a sickness."

"Maybe that's what's festering in his neck."

"I know it takes time to become experts, but we're fast learners. Someone needs to tell him that," Daisy said.

Fluff laughed. "That would go over well. Hey, Nixon, we'll take over from here."

"This war is going to change how women are viewed, mark my words. We are just as smart if not smarter than the boys, we've just never had the chance to show it. Look at all these recruiting advertisements and posters plastered everywhere—aviation, munitions, shipbuilding. It's our chance to shine, ladies," Betty said, holding up her Coke to toast.

Daisy tapped her coffee mug. "About time."

Fluff smiled. "By the time we get to Lizard, we won't even need them." Lizard was rumored to be their next digs, a state-of-the-art communication facility in a tunnel somewhere beneath Fort Shafter. Construction was going twenty-four hours a day, as it was in the shipyards, but they were still a month out from finishing.

Two filterers would be picked for each shift, and a handful of girls on Daisy's shift were interested, one of them being Thelma. Despite her personal shortcomings, Thelma was sharp. Daisy would give her that. After work at night, Daisy pored through calculations and manuals. She made note cards with code names and had Fluff test her. Fluff loved codes and code names, so they both benefited.

"You know, we've assigned code names to everyone but ourselves," Fluff said one night as they sat at the table with a bowl of macadamia nuts.

"What if we just use our first initial?" Daisy said, not wanting to get distracted.

Fluff lit up. "I would be Fox and you would be Dog. I love it!"

"And Lei is Love and Betty, Baker."

"They couldn't be more perfect!"

Fox, Dog, Love and Baker. Strangely, the names all fit. Fluff certainly was a looker, Lei took everyone under her wing, and Betty had been baking nonstop ever since Chuck went down. Daisy would have preferred *horse*, but dogs were loyal and intelligent and considered man's best friend. *Dog* was certainly better than *Victor* or *Yoke*.

"But we might need our last initials too, for clarity's sake, so we don't get confused with all the other gals," Fluff said, in a most serious tone.

"I doubt we have to worry about that."

"Just for fun. I'm Fox King and you're Dog William," she said, laughing.

William. *W.* Walker. Daisy could be thinking about anything—laundry, radar countermeasures, what shoes to wear—when Walker would appear in her mind.

Fluff snapped her fingers. "Honey, you have that faraway look again and I think I know why. It's William Mike, isn't it?"

Daisy nodded.

"Damn him. In my experience, men are not all they're cracked up to be. Some are easy on the eyes to be sure, but you can generally count on them either lying to you, cheating on you or dying on you," Fluff said, cracking a mac nut shell and slipping the nut into her mouth. "Man plus woman equals heartache. How's that for an equation?"

Daisy mostly agreed. "Men are negative numbers."

"They're absolute value inequalities."

"Calculus."

"Geometry proofs."

Fluff folded over laughing, though Daisy had to admit she enjoyed geometry. It was the only subject in the tenth grade that she excelled in. "So how come we keep coming back for more? I can't seem to get Walker off my mind, even knowing what I know."

"Human nature, I guess?" Fluff said.

"This is new territory for me. Boys have always been just that—silly boys. Walker is a whole other species and I never expected to fall for him like this."

"I don't think anyone expects it. That's why they call it *falling* in love."

A bolt of lightning shot through Daisy. Was this what had happened to her? Had she somehow fallen in love with Walker without even knowing it?

The following afternoon on the ride home from Little Robert, Fluff seemed extraordinarily giddy. Her cheeks were pink and she kept smiling off into the distance.

Betty nudged Daisy. "What's gotten into her?"

"I have no idea."

The minute they entered the house, Fluff announced, "Lieutenant Dunn is taking me out tonight for a bite. I know you two don't approve, but I'm going anyway."

Daisy frowned. "Wait a minute. What about our conversation about men yesterday? Have you forgotten so quickly?"

"Didn't I say it's in our nature to keep trying? Plus, Dunn is different. He's older and more mature and he seems to genuinely like me."

"Going out with a superior officer is not a good idea, Fox King. And you know how Nixon feels about it," Betty said, unbuttoning her uniform and grabbing three cold Cokes from the fridge.

"I disagree," Fluff said, flopping back on the couch.

"What if something goes wrong? Then you still have to work with the man," Daisy said.

Daisy saw his appeal. The easy smile and broad shoulders with tapered waist turned many of the girls to mush. But he was too slick, too friendly, too touchy. With everyone. They soon gave up trying to persuade Fluff to stay home. Options were limited on where one could go at night, and Dunn had told her it would be a surprise.

"Let's hope it's a good surprise," Betty said, as soon as Fluff walked out the door. Without Fluff home to lighten the mood, the evening unraveled like an old sweater. At seven o'clock, Betty pulled out a box of photo albums and broke down over every picture of Chuck. Her whole body quaked with sobs and tears wet the pages. Daisy sat on the bed with her for moral support.

Betty slammed her palm down on the pillow. "Twenty-six-year-olds are not supposed to be widows! Our life together was just getting started, you know? Chuck wanted to move to San Francisco after his next tour and open a restaurant. We were going to have three golden-haired children and a houseful of collies and I was going to bake pies and scones and sourdough bread. It's not fair," she moaned.

"Fairness is a figment of the imagination. I learned that long ago," Daisy said.

Betty's blue eyes were pleading. "*All's fair in love and war.* Whoever came up with such a dumb saying? It really should be *all's unfair in love and war.* And all is miserable and painful and awful."

"Maybe not *all.* Think about the wonderful times you had with Chuck and how much he adored you. You were one of the lucky ones, Betty. You had more love in a matter of years than most people get in a lifetime," Daisy said.

"Okay, so it's war I don't like, not love. All the senseless killing, it's not natural. Is it?"

"Seems like war has always been around, mostly because men are unable to come to agreement in other ways," Daisy said.

"Women should run the countries."

"Tell that to the men."

While last night Fluff was consoling Daisy, now Daisy was consoling Betty. And who knew who would be consoling whom tomorrow. On one day or another, they all held each other up. Everyone's turn would come. It was simply the way of the world.

★ ★ ★

In the morning, Daisy woke at the foot of Betty's bed, a thin blanket draped over her. She felt around for Betty's foot, but the bed was empty. Fresh-roasted coffee lured her into the kitchen, still in her nightgown and hair in all directions. No matter how early she rose, Betty was always up first. For the first time in weeks, she looked as though she had actually slept some. Not only that, but she hummed as she stirred batter in the big stainless bowl.

"I'm making banana pancakes," Betty announced.

Living with Betty had its perks.

"Were you awake when Fluff got back?" Daisy asked.

"No, but I peeked in when I got up to make sure she's here."

After freshening up some, Daisy returned to the kitchen where pale light filtered in through the branches outside. Their shift began after lunch, so there was no hurry. "How'd you sleep?" Betty asked.

The persistent ache in her chest felt less bothersome. "Better than I have in days. I think all that crying knocked something loose inside me." Betty nodded. "Hurts are cumulative, so a good cry is like a pressure-release valve. You might start off crying for one thing and before you know it, you've taken a walk down memory lane and are crying for things you thought you got over a long time ago."

There was a long list where Daisy was concerned. "Must be."

Betty set a bunch of bananas in front of Daisy to peel and chop. Banana pancakes had become a morning tradition on days off or later-shift days, and Daisy was thoroughly addicted. Betty made plenty extra for Fluff, who had still not risen. They ate and cleaned up. Fluff was still in bed.

"This is unlike her," Daisy said.

"Either she had a really good time or a really bad time. Or maybe she's come down with strep throat like Ming and Ruth."

Daisy washed a load of laundry and hung it to dry, then sat down and studied again. Betty cut up an old army blanket and stuck it in a box for Blanche's anticipated birthing session, which would be any day now. By ten thirty, when Fluff still had not come out of the room, Daisy went in to check on her. Fluff lay on her side, facing the window. Betty came and looked in on them.

"Fluff, are you awake?" Daisy said softly.

"No."

A bad feeling settled in her stomach. "What's the matter, are you not feeling well?"

"You could say that."

When Fluff half rolled over, you could see red scratches crisscrossing her arm and even a few on her face. Daisy felt the hair raise along the back of her body. "Honey, what happened to you?"

"Nothing."

This was so unlike Fluff, who never missed a chance to speak her mind. In this case, *nothing* clearly meant *nothing good*.

Betty came over and sat on foot of the bed. "Why are you all scratched up, hon? You need to tell us."

"I just want to sleep. Everything's fine, just leave me be," Fluff said, dully.

Daisy joined them on the bed. That metallic taste that filled her mouth when she thought about Johnny Boy flooded in. "You're stuck with us here. Neither of us is going anywhere until we know your story."

Fluff sighed, then propped a second pillow under her head. There could have been several nests in her hair, birds and all. "The scratches are from kiawe trees behind Hickam."

Daisy frowned. "What were you doing in the kiawe trees behind Hickam?"

"Trying to get home."

All these one-line answers were not helping. "How about you just start from the beginning and tell us everything. Think of me as Sherlock Holmes and Betty here as Watson," Daisy said.

Fluff tried to smile. "You guys were right. Dunn is a schmuck."

Daisy should have seen this coming.

"Go on."

"You're not going to give up, are you?" Fluff said, rubbing beneath her eyes with both fists.

"Nope," Daisy and Betty said in unison.

Fluff took a deep breath, then began. "After he picked me up, he told me we were going on a picnic on a secret beach to watch the sunset. I thought it sounded so romantic. I'd never seen him out of uniform and he looked so dashing in his linen button-down that matched the blue of his eyes. Once we got to the trailhead, instead of a picnic basket, he pulled out a burlap bag, which was fine, you know, since most guys don't own baskets. Anyway, we walked a trail through some marshy land and ended up at a tiny beach. It was lovely at first. He told me how he'd been wanting to take me out for a while now and how he finds it hard to concentrate when I'm in the room."

She rolled her eyes, which were now watering.

"Turns out the burlap bag had a bottle of whiskey and a tin of sardines and crackers. He set out two shot glasses in the sand and we toasted to the sunset. I thought nothing of it. I can handle a little whiskey. And we talked and talked and I thought it was going quite well, other than the fact that he was speaking to my breasts much of the time. I kid you not, his eyes dropped about every five seconds or so. I should have known what was coming next," Fluff said, rolling her head to look back out the window.

Daisy glanced at Betty, who shook her head in disgust. "And?"

"I was feeling a bit tipsy and charmed and suddenly he pulled me up to standing and started kissing me against the coconut tree. His kisses were a little rough, but I figured he was drunk and excited. I went along with it for a while, but a voice inside kept screaming that gentlemen don't act like this.

'Let's go for a dip,'" he said.

"I told him *no thank you*. He kissed me again, more tenderly this time, but pretty soon his hands were all over me. That's when I stepped back and said it was probably best to head home. We had only moonlight to see by. He apologized, said I was just so damn sexy, and then pulled me down so I was sitting on his lap. By then I was done. I just wanted to go."

Fluff stopped and asked for a glass of water, which Betty delivered.

"The bottle was next to him, and he took another huge gulp. It was clear he had passed beyond a level of common decency. After more groping, he unzipped his pants and forced my hand into his crotch." She held up a bruised wrist. "I knew the only way out at that point was to play along, so I did for about five seconds and then when I felt him relax, I jumped up and ran."

Daisy wanted to both cry and cheer for her friend. "Good for you."

Betty let out a big exhale. "Thank heavens."

"I ran along the path, but it was uneven and hard to see and I tripped and fell. He was coming after me so I crawled under a nearby bush and held my breath. He passed not four feet from me, muttering every curse word in the book. I knew I couldn't go back the way we came, so I waited for what felt like hours and then headed inland. Have you ever gone hiking at night?"

"Only beach walks," Daisy said.

"Well, I don't recommend it, especially around here. I ran into a swamp full of muck that nearly sucked my shoes off, then a thicket of kiawe, all the while not being able to see two feet in front of me." She pointed to the mess on her head. "I had to tear out chunks of hair caught on the thorns. And if that wasn't bad enough, a big fat rain cloud covered the moon while I was in the thick of it. Hours later, I made it to a road, and by some miracle that road led me back here."

"What did the guard at the gate say?" Daisy wanted to know.

"I told him I'm an officer and I'd been sent on a secret training mission that went afoul," Fluff said with a light returning to her eyes.

"You did not!" Betty said.

She nodded. "I asked him if he'd ever heard of Operation Whiskey Dog—that just came to me on the fly. Of course, he just gave me a funny look and let me through. I tell you, most of these boys don't know what to do when faced with a female officer."

Betty turned to Daisy. "If it were up to me, Dunn would be put on the next submarine out of here. What do you think?"

"Nixon needs to know about this," Daisy said.

Fluff grabbed her wrist. "No! Let it go, you two. No one is going to believe me over Dunn."

"We have to at least try," Betty argued.

"I should never have gone with him to the beach in the first place. And nothing really happened anyway. I managed to escape."

"And what if you hadn't?" Betty said.

The thought chilled Daisy. "The fact that you had to *escape* from your date says everything. If we don't stop him, he's going to keep at it with other WARDs. Who's to say he hasn't already?"

Fluff crossed her arms. "Absolutely not. I just want to forget about it."

"We don't have to decide anything right now. But let's disinfect all these scratches," Betty said, heading off to the bathroom and returning with a bottle of iodine and a handful of cotton balls.

They cleaned Fluff up as best they could and phoned Lei to find a replacement for her shift at Little Robert.

"What should I put down for a reason?" Lei asked.

"Sick and tired of men," Daisy said.

21

THE ADVERSARY

Betty and Daisy blew into Little Robert and straight to Nixon on the balcony. "Sir, we need to have a word with you."

Nixon frowned. "I'm busy."

"This can't wait."

He relented and ushered them into his office. Dunn was nowhere to be seen. Nixon sat down in his broad leather chair but made no motion for either of them to sit. The rash on his neck now bubbled with tiny white blisters that caused Daisy's skin to itch.

"This better be important," he said.

Betty and Daisy glanced at each other. Normally, Daisy would have let Betty do the talking, but something inside her had broken at the sight of those scratches on her sweet friend's body. "Sir, we'd like to file a complaint against Lieutenant Dunn on behalf of Fluff Kanahele. Last night

Dunn took her to a secluded beach and proceeded to fill her full of whiskey and try to have his way with her."

Nixon slowly shook his head. "And how do you know this?"

"From Fluff, of course."

He slammed his fist on the papers on his desk, nearly spilling his coffee. "This is the exact kind of crap I don't need right now. Men and women working together is a recipe for disaster. Didn't I say early on *no fraternizing*?"

Daisy pointed out, "That would include Dunn, then. He asked her out."

Betty added, "Sir, the problem is not that they work together. The problem is that Dunn tried to force her into sexual activities against her will. Which would be bad enough, but he also happens to be our supervisor."

"You say 'tried.' What does that mean?" Nixon asked.

"Fluff ran away. He even went after her, but she hid under a bush for half the night before finally climbing through a forest of thorns. You should see her right now. Her whole body is one big scratch," Daisy said.

Beneath those bushy eyebrows, she thought she saw a flash of concern. "If you don't believe us, stop by our house later and see for yourself."

Nixon's gaze went to the photo of his wife. "You take care of the girl and I'll have a talk with Dunn later. You are dismissed."

"Sir, please—"

He waved then toward the door. "Go on. I have a call to make."

Daisy was willing to take this above his head to Danielson or even Admiral Nimitz if she had to, but for the time being, she and Betty retreated back to their stations. Dunn, who was usually in and out of the main room all day, made himself scarce. And when he did come near, he kept his eyes on the board. Daisy would have spit on his shoes if he'd come close enough.

The following day, Daisy took the test for filterer at the end of her shift. Unlike the intelligence test, which was about thinking, the filterer test would be about knowing, and filled with highly specialized questions. When Daisy sat down at the desk and picked up her pencil, she could scarcely hold it in her hand. Despite a pep talk by Fluff, who knew more about test taking than the average person, her nerves came on like an earthquake. Thelma sat in front of her and the sound of her pencil scratching away on the paper made Daisy feel even worse.

For at least five minutes, she stared at the first question. *What are the altitude and azimuth of an object located due south and on the horizon?* This was an easy one. She knew the answer, but kept second-guessing herself. All around her, girls were furiously writing. She thought back on the conversation with Walker and his advice about going with the first thing that came to mind, and how he had referred to her as *genius*.

Daisy, you know this! She took a few deep breaths and forced herself to write. Once she answered the first one— *altitude is 0, azimuth is 180*—each subsequent question brought a new layer of confidence. This was not some pointless elementary school test. These questions were relevant and critical to their mission of winning the war. To saving lives.

For the first time ever, Daisy finished a test feeling as if she had done well. Quite possibly even aced it. Thelma had given her a smug look when they walked out, but at least kept quiet. Daisy started when she saw Dunn standing at the door, collecting tests, his body taking up half the space. She froze for a split second, and in that time, he managed to strip her down and tour her body with his eyes. There was no option but to pass. As she squeezed by, he pinched her side and whispered, "Watch yourself, Wilder."

Lei showed up with assorted boxes of Chinese food for dinner—lemon chicken, chow mein and assorted dumplings. Daisy knew it was to cheer up Fluff, but Lei also seemed on edge. They filled their plates and decided to make a picnic in the backyard and enjoy the moonlit evening and cricket songs. Daisy had yet to mention Dunn's words to anyone. Fluff had not wanted them to tell, and they had told, and now it looked like repercussions were already coming down.

They kept the conversation light, about weather and food and the latest social happenings about town, but you could sense an undercurrent beneath their words. In the nearby grass, Blanche was stalking a lizard or a mouse, her tail twitching.

Halfway through the dinner, Lei made an announcement. "I want to run something by you."

"We're all ears," Fluff said.

"George has been acting strange lately, going out at odd times and coming back rather full of himself. To tell the truth, I've been worried there might be another woman. But last night I heard him boasting that he would soon have enough money to pay off all his debts and then some."

"Anything specific?" Betty asked.

"That was all he said. But I'm worried he's going to get into big trouble, or worse, get himself killed."

"Can you ask him about it?" Daisy said.

Lei looked defeated. "Absolutely not. He flies off the

handle when I so much as mention money. I've never been afraid of my husband, but lately, I'm not so sure. I've been trying to go on as though everything is normal while I'm getting my ducks in a row."

"What kind of ducks?" Fluff asked.

Lei's mouth puckered. "I'm going to leave him."

A cane toad trilled nearby, sending an invitation out into the night. A lone male looking for a mate. The irony was not lost on Daisy.

"That's brave of you, but it sounds like he's left you no choice," Betty said.

Lei nodded, tears pooling in her eyes. "When the trust is gone, you have nothing."

"If you need to come stay with us, you can. We're on a military base. You'll be perfectly safe if he gets any dumb ideas," Fluff offered.

"Thank you."

Betty fumed, "If he so much as lays a finger on you, he'd have a truckload of angry WARDs to contend with."

"Don't worry about me," Lei said.

"How can we not worry about you, for goodness' sake? George sounds like he's turned into a shady character. And divorce is a big deal," Fluff said.

Lei shrugged. "I'm better off alone and moving forward than hitched to a scoundrel. Plus, now I have a purpose every day. Being a WARD has been an unexpected blessing."

That it was.

Daisy went into work with a pit in her stomach. In the middle of the night, her mind had taken off galloping on Dunn's words. *Watch yourself.* Had she heard him wrong? She went through a whole list of possible variations, none of which made sense. Regardless of what he'd said, the pinch and the look were enough to catch his meaning.

As she'd feared, it wasn't Nixon or Danielson who called the girls into the classroom, it was Dunn. Daisy slipped into the back row, behind Val and Joyce and Rita. Thelma sat in the front with her legs crossed and her hair done up in a fancy knot. Dunn called out the girls from the other shifts first, drawing the whole affair out much longer than he needed to. Waiting was something Daisy was good at—working with horses required a huge amount of patience—but right now her foot was tapping like a dying fish.

Dunn picked up the final two tests and stared down at them for a while. His eyes were a little too close together, giving him a rat-like appearance. "And finally, our last two new filterers are Thelma Bird and JoAnn Abramson. Congratulations, ladies."

JoAnn Abramson? Daisy knew without a doubt that she had scored higher than JoAnn. Nothing against her, but JoAnn could not keep her aircraft straight if her life depended on it. Sure, she was book smart, but put her under a little pressure and she caved in six seconds flat. Daisy had to sit on her hands to avoid hurling her pencil right at Dunn's face. So this was how it was going to be. While Thelma and JoAnn went up to collect their pins, Daisy slipped out the door.

Betty took one look at her face and said, "Oh hell."

The main room in Little Robert was close enough quarters where Daisy had to keep quiet. Being a sore loser in front of Nixon and Major Oscar and the rest of the girls would do nothing for her cause. But as soon as they hopped out of the truck after work, she told the whole story, starting with his comment the other day.

"Dunn fudged the results. I am certain that I scored

higher than JoAnn, and probably Thelma, too. He's screwing with me because we went to Nixon," Daisy said.

Betty kicked a coconut frond in their path. "Son of a bitch! We can't tell Fluff, though. She's already terrified to go back, and I don't blame her one bit."

"What are we going to do?"

Dunn wielded all the power.

"We'll figure out something."

They arrived home to a whole new Fluff. She was waiting for them at the front door with a huge smile. With her finger to her lips, she said, "Shh. Follow me."

She led them to the linen closet in their room. The door was open and Blanche lay on the blankets with a bunch of wiggling hairless kittens latched on to her teats. Daisy felt her heart loosen, all the injustice and hurts of recent days falling away. "We have five tiny new additions to our household," Fluff whispered.

Her face glowed like that of a brand-new mom. One who hadn't had the pleasure of going through labor and delivery. Her scratches had gone down some, but still showed. Which was good. Daisy wanted Nixon to see them.

"They all seem healthy, and Blanche has been licking them clean for hours now."

Blanche completely ignored the spectators and after a full round of licks, she laid her head down and sighed.

"We should leave them alone. She needs her rest," Daisy said.

In the kitchen, Fluff told them, "I'm going to add Kitty Midwife to my résumé. They all came out smoothly except for the last one. Only his upper body appeared and then he was stuck. Blanche was straining, I could see it in her eyes. Some kind of womanly instinct took over and I grabbed a washcloth, placed it over the kitten and gently pulled. Pretty soon, a leg or something released and he slid right out. The sweetest little being I've ever laid eyes upon."

As Daisy knew from horse births, a certain feeling released into the air and infused everyone involved with a sense of optimism about life. Perspectives shifted. Invisible but palpable, this feeling coated everything in a hopeful light. Soon, Dunn and Walker and the test faded, and the thrill of new life hummed around them. That night, they managed to bypass all work talk, and Daisy went to bed with a strange sense of calm.

22

THE DECISION

When faced with trouble, humans are known to stand and fight or run away. Daisy always considered herself a fighter. She'd rather stand face-to-face and deal with a problem head-on than run the other way. But right now, the lines were blurry on what to do. There were also other people to think about in this whole fiasco, not to mention her job as a WARD. The trickle-down effect of one slimy man and a bottle of whiskey.

Daisy had tried to reach Danielson, but he was on Maui doing more trainings with the WARDs there, and she couldn't get a straight answer when he'd be back.

When Fluff returned to Little Robert, Daisy and Betty made sure she was never alone in the same vicinity as Dunn. Several people asked about the scratches, to which she replied, "I had a run-in with a thorny tree." You could tell by their faces that they had their doubts about one tree inflicting so much damage, but no one pressed her. Dunn kept on being the same greaseball he usually was, and Nixon, though he hadn't done a thing, did seem to be paying more attention. Daisy caught him watching Dunn on several occasions.

Fluff still didn't know about why Daisy wasn't chosen as filterer. Daisy told her she'd mixed up two formulas, thus ruining all her chances.

"That sounds fishy to me, but if you say so," Fluff said, with her hands on her hips.

"I say so."

One afternoon, with only a few markers on the board, and a handful of girls in the break room, Daisy saw Dunn walk over to Fluff. She had her back to the room and was placing a chit on the board. In one swish of his hand, he grabbed her left buttock and squeezed, and then moved on as though nothing had happened.

"Whoa!" Daisy said loudly, spinning around to see if Nixon had noticed. But Nixon only jerked his head up at the sound of Daisy's voice. His gaze went around to everyone else in the room, who all stared her way. They were like a herd of cows when you drove through in a truck.

"What is it, Miss Wilder?" he finally said.

Fluff would kill her if she made a scene in the Command Center. "False alarm, sir. I thought I saw a rat."

Nixon looked surprised. "I've never seen a rat in here, and besides, a little rat never hurt anyone."

She knew she ought to stop there, but couldn't help herself. "That's not true, sir. Rats carry diseases that can kill you. They're dirty little animals."

Those in the room were still watching intently. To her surprise, Nixon held up his coffee, as though toasting, and said, "I'll give you that, Wilder."

For the rest of the shift, Fluff stayed within a three-foot

radius of Daisy. Some kind of radio equipment malfunction drew Dunn away, thankfully. But if this kind of behavior went on, their lives would be miserable. Daisy debated telling Nixon what she'd seen, but it would likely backfire. Among the pressure coming down from Nimitz, rumors of new missions in the Pacific and managing a whole division of women, Nixon's rash had doubled in size.

Throughout the next weeks, things hardly improved. Dunn played his usual charming self when it suited him, but made little digs at Daisy and Betty when he thought no one was paying attention. Thelma, on the other hand, wore her new pin like a fishing trophy and started offering unsolicited advice ad nauseam. Sadly, work had become something to endure, rather than enjoy.

They came home one afternoon to an envelope slipped under the front door. Fluff stooped over and picked it up, handing it to Daisy. Her name was spelled in large block letters on the front.

"My money says it's from William Mike," she said.

Daisy tossed it onto the table.

Fluff scowled. "Wait a minute. You have to open it right now."

Daisy started off down the hallway to see the kittens. "Not in the mood," she said.

The cats were little bright spots in a dark world. Two gray tabbies and three black and white like their mother, their sea-blue eyes had opened and they were suddenly interested in everything around them. Daisy was smitten.

"Fine, I'll open it for you, then," Fluff said.

Daisy came back and grabbed the letter. "You will not."

"Don't you want to at least see what he has to say?"

"It doesn't matter."

Fluff softened her tone. "You might say that, but you

don't mean it. Look, it's obvious you two really like each other—"

"*Liked*, past tense."

"Not in his case, I imagine. And don't hate me for saying this, I know you're hurt and you have every right to be, but sometimes it's better to let the past stay in the past. Did his father do something terrible? Yes. But Walker was a teenage boy, guilty mainly by association. A good man is hard to find, and he seems like one of the rare ones."

Hearing Fluff stand up for Walker burned her ears. Easy talk for someone who didn't lose their father right when she needed him most. But Walker was a good man, Fluff was right about that. Which made it even harder to walk away from him. She tucked the letter under her arm and said, "I'll read it later."

Later turned out to be as soon as she was done checking on Blanche and her mewling babies, who were now crawling all over the room with tiny paws and fuzzy tails. As soon as she touched the letter, it had begun sending bursts of heat through her skin. And now, no matter how hard she tried, she could not think about anything else. She tore open the envelope.

Dear Daisy,

I have so much to say to you, I don't know where to begin. So I'll start here: I'm completely torn up about not being able to see you. I think about you constantly and am on my knees asking for a chance just to talk to you one more time. I have something that I think could change your mind about me. So how about it? Please will you give me one more shot? If your answer is yes, please tie a ribbon (or rope or whatever you have) around the coconut tree out front tomorrow, and I'll stop in. If no, I'll drive on by.

Yours truly, Walker Montgomery

She read it again, lashes wet from tears. Did he not see the impossibility in their situation? As though this was something she could ever forget. Accomplice to a terrible lie, son to her father's killer. And yet Fluff's words, *he seems like one of the rare ones*, had taken up residence in a small corner of her mind. He did seem rare. And thoughtful and intelligent and honorable.

Could you fault a child for the actions of their parents? Daisy thought back to herself at fourteen. By then, her mother had descended into her tormented inner world, with only glimpses of her old self showing up. If someone had judged Daisy back then for sneaking scraps from the lunch room at school or taking an extra can here and there from the market, and then later for dropping out of school, what then? Would that be fair? She knew the answer. And yet this felt different.

Fluff had demanded to know what the letter said, and when Daisy told her, she said, "Betty has a big sash on one of those fancy dresses of hers. You could use that."

"That assumes that I'm saying yes."

"You have to say yes!"

"I'll decide in the morning."

Daisy spent the whole night flip-flopping around under her sheets. She would decide *absolutely not*, and then wake up later and change her mind to *yes, I have to see him again*. In the morning, over fried rice and a mug of steaming coffee, she remembered she had brought Moon's lead rope in with her to town, just in case. The rope was curled up in a basket in the closet. She could tie that to the tree, hear what Walker had to say and then decide. Before she changed her mind again, she found the rope, coiled it around the leaning trunk and tied a red bandanna to the end of the rope to make sure he spotted it. A strange desperation to see him again came over her.

They were back on the early afternoon shift now, and the truck came by at 12:30 p.m. on the dot. The day dragged like a wheel stuck in three feet of mud. As always, Daisy performed her job as best she could. But her heart wasn't in it. She stayed close to Fluff and far from Dunn. Nixon seemed preoccupied with his rash and had taken up wearing a cool wet cloth around his neck. There was a whole stack of them in the refrigerator, and Lei had the unfortunate task of keeping them stocked and washed.

"I don't handle the used ones with my bare hands. You never know if what he has is catching," she said.

Which was ironic, because toward the end of their shift, Nixon informed the girls that they'd be having a briefing on staying healthy.

"I hope he plans on sitting in," Daisy told Fluff.

She was eager to get back to the house in case Walker came by, and hoped they wouldn't run late.

The women all lined up at their desks like schoolgirls. Instead of Nixon, Dunn sauntered in.

"As you may or may not know, we have a big problem with VD in the military. Boys will be boys, but we all know that girls like to have a little fun now and then, too." He paused for effect, his eyes roving the room. "On account of that, we thought it might be helpful to give you all a little education. We can't have our WARDs spreading anything, it wouldn't look good."

Daisy whispered to Betty, "Look who's talking."

Dunn was on her. "Did you have something to say, Wilder?"

The room went quiet as a tomb.

"No, sir. I just asked to borrow a pencil," she said.

A bespectacled man in a white coat came in and set a cracked leather briefcase on the table. Thankfully, Dunn left. The doctor distributed pamphlets titled *Sex Hygiene and Venereal Disease* to each woman, barely making eye contact as he did. He cleared his throat and said a few words about avoiding sexual contact altogether and where to seek help if you did contract something, and promptly left.

Betty opened hers first. "Manhood comes from healthy sex organs. Did y'all know that?"

The pamphlets, which said they were prepared by the surgeon general, had a giant *VD* stamped across the front.

"'Even more relevant is that we guard against venereal disease by staying away from 'easy' women.' Don't gamble your health away, ladies," Fluff said.

Val read another line. "'Most prostitutes have venereal disease.'"

"Well, I guess that means we stop frequenting Hotel Street, then," said Betty.

Daisy threw hers in the trash.

It was dark by the time they arrived home. Dinner was leftover meat loaf and rice. Daisy kept waiting for the sounds of an engine. At nine o'clock, when Walker still had not come by, she decided to take a stroll in the fresh evening air. Stars were out in force. Daisy walked over to the coconut tree and immediately noticed something wrong. The trunk was bare. No rope, no bandanna.

She ran back into the house. "Someone took the rope down!"

Betty popped her head out of the bathroom, hair in curlers. "Probably Walker."

"Why would he do that? He said if he saw it out there

he'd stop in. There would be no reason for him to take it down," Daisy said, out of breath.

"Who knows, but I wouldn't worry about it," Betty said.

An uneasy feeling settled in her chest, but she tried to convince herself there was a reasonable explanation. *He'll come tomorrow,* she told herself as she drifted off to sleep.

23

THE STING

The minute Daisy and the girls stepped into Little Robert the next day, it was obvious something was afoot. The table was covered in markers and all WARDs on deck still wore their headphones. Deep in conversation, nodding and focusing and recording notes, they all but ignored their replacements. Junie Gonzales was pale as a cloud, and Daisy knew her husband was a dive bomber on the *Enterprise*.

"The carriers must be going out again," Betty said flatly.

Daisy rushed to put her helmet and gas mask away, feeling off balance and short of breath. "Please don't let it be the *Enterprise*," she whispered to no one in particular.

But it had to be the Big E. *Saratoga* was already off on another mission, and the *Yorktown* and the *Lexington* were at sea. Lord only know where the boys were headed this time, and for how long. She imagined Walker standing on deck watching the island grow smaller and smaller behind him—a green speck on the horizon, until it finally disappeared.

She slammed her locker door shut, harder than intended, and tried not to cry.

Earlier that morning, a guard had pounded on their door. When Daisy came to the screen, he held up the rope and bandanna, and said, "This yours?"

Daisy opened the door and swiped it from him. "Yes, it's mine. Why do you have it?"

"Sorry ma'am, you aren't allowed to have swings on the trees here. Someone broke an ankle last month. Just wanted to warn you," he said, tugging up at his pants and giving her a half smile.

"When did you take it down?" she asked.

"'Round lunchtime yesterday."

Daisy wanted to point out that the rope did not resemble a swing in any way, but he seemed too dense to know the difference. She wanted to wring his neck. But what mattered was that Walker now believed that Daisy had written him off, that she had no interest in giving him another chance. And now he was gone.

She spent the whole shift contemplating how to get a message to him. One that no one else would read. But that was impossible.

"What about asking Nixon to help us?" she speculated.

"Good luck," Betty said.

"Radio? Telegraph? Carrier pigeon? Smoke signals?"

"You're going to have to wait until they return."

In her mind, she composed the words she would say. *Dear Walker, I wish there were some kind of manual for how to handle this situation. All I know is that I want to see you again. Actually, that's not true. I also know that I appreciate the way you have so much faith in me, your strong and steady manner, and how you kissed me as if your life depended on it. Unfortunately, I think my life does depend on it. Please come back alive, and that's an order. Yours truly, Daisy. P.S. I put a rope on the tree for you, but a dimwit guard took it down.*

Daisy spent a whole week walking around, pretending to smile, but doing a terrible job. The feeling that she had somehow missed the most important moment of her life kept smacking her in the forehead.

What had Walker meant by having something that would change her mind? The whole thing stunk and she was mad at the war, mad at Walker, mad at her mother, mad at herself, but most of all, mad at Mr. Montgomery. The anger burned.

It was Fluff who finally pulled her out of it. "Do you know what you remind me of?"

"Who?"

"Eeyore from *Winnie-the-Pooh*. But you're less amusing and less fun to be around. And I'll tell you what—that gloomy, negative outlook is not going to help you at all."

They were hanging laundry on a windy morning, and Daisy couldn't keep her bra from flying away and her bangs out of her eyes. Part of her felt like lying down in the grass and screaming and kicking like a two-year-old. She felt so entirely out of control that it made her weak in the knees.

"What would you have me do instead? Any bright ideas?" Daisy asked.

"Actually, I do. First of all, you need to write Walker a letter and tell him everything you are feeling. All of it, hate, love, frustration, fear, desire. Don't hold back. Then you put the letter under your pillow and you say a little prayer to God, asking him to deliver your message to Walker in his dreams, while he's sleeping on that tiny bunk of his.

Then you thank God and leave the rest up to him," Fluff said, matter-of-factly.

Daisy sighed. "That just sounds like a lot of work."

Fluff crossed her heart. "I swear you'll feel better. Acceptance is one of those unassuming things that has real power. The sooner you accept things as they are, the sooner you can move on. It's out of your hands."

Daisy had watched Fluff go through the whole gamut of emotions with Dunn, and she seemed to be doing remarkably well. Maybe acceptance was her secret weapon.

"I'll write the letter tonight," she said.

In the morning, Fluff tore into the house announcing that one lace bra and two pairs of panties were missing from the line. "That's it! I'm setting up a sting operation every single night until we nab this fella," she said.

Tired of buying new underwear, Daisy said, "Count me in."

"Would someone actually go to jail for stealing underwear?" Betty asked.

Fluff put her hand on her hip. "It would depend on the judge and possibly any prior offenses."

"We need to be very smart about it," Daisy said.

"Oh, we will."

Instead of setting up a sleeping nest in the hedge across the yard, they placed a bell on the line. Whoever was on duty that night would be sleeping with their head next to the back door screen, camera on hand.

Betty thought it was a stupid idea. "The bell is going to scare them away long before we can get the camera ready."

"It's our only chance," Fluff argued.

Daisy was counting on their sixth senses to wake them if anyone was creeping around nearby. Sleeping animals sensed danger, so why not humans? "But if you do catch him in the act, stay inside. You never know what he might do if confronted."

"Whoever it is must be a real nut, so I agree," Betty said.

Fluff demonstrated how to use her camera, a boxy contraption with dials and buttons no one would ever be able to see in the dark. "You only have one bulb, so aim well and press here," she said.

Betty shook her head. "We're more likely to strike gold under Little Robert than to snag a photo of our thief."

"We have to try."

Four days passed with no action. Betty had slept half a night on the floor and called it quits. Going forward it would be Fluff and Daisy on rotation—a camera on one side, a baseball bat on the other. On the fifth night, Daisy found herself wide awake with a racing heart. She lay motionless and listened for any unusual sounds: an occasional coconut frond rustling; the faraway rumble of an engine; the almost imperceptible sound of grass underfoot. *Someone or something was out there.*

Feeling around clumsily for the camera, she worried at any moment she'd knock it over and make a big commotion. But her hand met it quietly. She rolled over and lay in wait. Clouds blotted out the moon, but there was enough ambient light to see a shadow moving across the yard. Too big to be any kind of animal. She held the camera up to the screen, ready to shoot. Her hand shook slightly.

The shadow came right up to the clothesline and stopped, almost as though he knew Daisy was there. She held her breath. *Come on.* A quiet eternity, and then the bell rang— high and shrill. Unable to see anything, she pressed down on the camera's shutter button. A bright flash seared into the night. The thief had turned halfway around before

Daisy could get a good look at him, and he had his arms up over his face.

"Get out of our yard, you creep!" Daisy yelled, grabbing the bat and moving to slam the door, lest he get the notion to come inside.

Feet pounded down the hallway, and Betty crashed into Daisy. Fluff followed close behind.

"What happened? Are you okay?" Betty said, looking slightly dazed.

Fluff scratched her head. "Did you get a shot or a look?"

Next door, someone opened the door and shined a flashlight. "Is everything all right over there?"

Daisy looked around. The man was gone, but her heart was still on high. "We're fine. Just a scare," she called into the dark.

"Are you sure? You don't sound fine."

"False alarm. Go back to sleep and we'll explain in the morning," Daisy called back.

Betty turned on the light, and they sat at the kitchen table. A moth fluttered near the crack in the blackout cloth.

Fluff's hair looked as though she'd stuck her finger in a socket, and her face sagged in disappointment. "Was it a false alarm? Who were you yelling at, then?"

Daisy handed her the camera. "He turned away in the light, but I saw enough to get a sense. I think I got a picture, too."

In the morning, they reported the incident to Vivian, who took a long drag from her cigarette and insisted on calling the FBI. Once again, the FBI said they couldn't help. She then called the military police and a young officer with peach fuzz showed up fifteen minutes later and took their statements.

"Was any, um, underwear missing after the encounter?" he asked.

"He was caught in the act, so no. All underwear is accounted for. This time."

"Get that photograph developed and maybe you'll have a case. Meantime, not much I can do," he said with a yawn.

Continuing on from there, they drove into Chinatown, where Fluff knew a photographer by the name of Tam Wong. The previous year, he'd been a guest photography lecturer at the university and he and Fluff had struck up a friendship. In the back of his herbal shop, Tam had a darkroom. When they arrived, the shop looked closed. They knocked and knocked and were about to leave when a door in the back swung open.

Fluff hopped up and down, waving. "Tam, it's me, Fluff!"

The man hurried to the front door and squinted though the dusty glass, recognition finally showing in his eyes. "Miss Fluff! Come in, come in," he said, opening the door and ushering them into a shop that smelled of roots and dried leaves and hundred-year-old soil.

Fluff explained the situation, and his head bobbled as he listened. "You give me one hour. I get your picture. One hour you know bad man."

While they waited, they walked up Nu'uanu Avenue and turned down Hotel Street looking for a coffee shop. The street was dusty, with wooden storefronts lined up wall to wall. Before long, however, they encountered lines of servicemen in front of several buildings and cottages. They stood in clouds of cigarette smoke and loud conversation.

"Boogie houses," said Fluff out of the side of her mouth. They'd heard all about the prostitutes, but Daisy wasn't prepared for the sheer numbers of young men in the area.

"They call 'em three-minute men. Three minutes, three dollars."

"Isn't prostitution illegal?" Daisy asked.

"From what I hear, they have an agreement with the police. As long as everyone follows the rules, the houses get to stay in business."

They crossed the street to avoid the lines, and found a hole-in-the-wall bakery with coffee that tasted like ashes. Daisy choked it down, just because she was nervous, along with two doughnuts and a pineapple slice. With each passing minute, Fluff seemed to grow more anxious. She kept looking at her watch and fiddling with a few loose strands of hair.

Tam was waiting out front for them when they returned. "Face showing! Good shot, good shot," he said with a toothy smile.

The photograph was sitting on the counter, giving off a vinegary scent. They crowded around it, heads together. Half the photo was black, but the other showed an arm partly blocking a face. There was no doubt about who it was.

Fluff put her hand over her open mouth and gasped. "Oh my word, it's Dunn!"

After the botched date and his antics at work, they had discussed him as a possible suspect. But even for Dunn, it seemed outlandish.

Betty smiled. "Would you look at that. Caught red-handed."

"Time to go see Nixon," Daisy said.

24

THE EXIT

When they arrived at work, Dunn was noticeably absent. Daisy slipped into the radio room, the break room and even cracked the door in Nixon's office looking for him. Fluff looked happier than she had in weeks. "I hope he's at home sweating over whether or not we got him on film."

Rather than confront Nixon on the spot, Daisy slipped him a note that said they had an urgent matter to discuss, and could they meet in his office *stat*. Ten minutes later, he tapped her on the shoulder without uttering a word, then continued on toward his door.

"You three have something you want to tell me?" he said.

"May we sit, sir?" Betty asked.

He motioned toward the rickety chairs. "Be my guest."

Daisy began. "Colonel Nixon, as you may or may not know, we've had some trouble with a thief stealing our lingerie from the clothesline while we're sleeping. Last night we set up an operation to catch him in the act." She produced the photograph, holding it for all to see. "I managed to get a photo of the man in question, sir. It was Lieutenant Dunn."

"Give me that," he said.

She slid the photo onto his desk. Nixon inspected the photo for some time, shaking his head. Fluff shot Daisy a look. He leaned back in his chair and looked over at the photo of him and his wife for what felt like five minutes. "I'll take care of it. Now get back to your stations," he said at long last.

It was a start, but nowhere near enough.

"There's one other thing," Daisy said, worried she might be pushing her luck.

"And what's that?"

"Would you have a look at my filterer test score? I think it was graded incorrectly."

She left out *by Dunn*.

"Why would that be?" Nixon said, shaggy eyebrows bunching together.

"Because I am certain that I aced it, and I think there was a mistake. I need to know for sure so that I can do my job correctly."

"I'll see what I can do."

Out in the hallway, Betty said, "He better do something about Dunn and your test or I'm going to raise hell."

"I guess we just wait and see if he has a conscience," Daisy said.

"And if he doesn't?"

"Then we pay a visit to Nimitz."

Fluff looked deflated. "Maybe I should just quit and everyone can just forget about this whole mess. I hate to put you all through so much trouble," Fluff said.

"This is not your doing. This is Dunn. And we'll make sure he does not get away with it."

Somehow.

Dunn showed up two hours later with pink on his cheeks, as if he'd been out running or playing tennis—or drinking. He stayed on the far side of the room and spent a lot of time jotting down notes and avoiding people. Daisy kept waiting for Nixon to say something to him, but Nixon went on business as usual. Air traffic was higher than normal, so that kept the place humming. On several occasions, Daisy had to talk herself down from marching over and giving him a thick slice of her mind.

When she had all but given up hope, Nixon suddenly walked over to Dunn and nodded toward the office. Dunn followed like a naughty dog who had just eaten his owner's new shoes. Betty gave her a sly smile. The two men had been gone for thirteen minutes and forty-three seconds, when a uniformed military police officer arrived at the door. Eyebrows raised around the room.

"Can you please direct me to Colonel Nixon's office?" he asked Major Oscar.

Once the man disappeared into the office, Betty said, "I'd love to be a fly on that wall in there right now."

"I hope this is what we think it is," Daisy said.

Fluff looked hopeful. "It has to be."

Moments later, the door opened. Dunn stepped out first—in handcuffs. Daisy stared in disbelief, heart pounding. In order to get out of the building, Dunn would have to march clear across the floor, passing the plotting table. Daisy stood. Then Betty. Then Fluff. And then Dunn put one foot in front of the other, moving within a couple of feet of the girls. His head hung, and there was no sign of that cocky demeanor he'd become so famous for.

"Good riddance," Fluff said quietly, as he passed.

Nixon watched from his office. Daisy turned and gave him a small salute. He nodded and shut the door. At that moment, even though they were underground, Daisy could have sworn the clouds above parted and a huge ray of sun was warming the hillside.

With Dunn gone, Daisy was able to concentrate on plotting again, and Fluff had returned to her usual bubbly self, flitting around the room, checking in on everyone and infusing the place with her magic. Major Hochman, who had been working in the field, replaced Dunn. All the gals were thrilled. Early on, he'd made an impression with his kind nature and Southern twang. He was patient, polite and brilliant. Half of the WARDs developed schoolgirl crushes on him, and Fluff was not immune. Fortunately, Hochman was happily married and spoke often of his wife, Jean, who brought them freshly baked coconut macaroons on a regular basis.

Time moved slowly for Daisy, who was on pins and needles with any news out of the Pacific, where an operation was supposedly taking place, and also still anxiously awaiting a response from her mother. Mail was unpredictable these days, so she had no idea if Louise had even received her letter. If only they could speak face-to-face.

"You should confront him," Betty told her one day.

"I wanted to wait and hear what my mom had to say first. Montgomery is not a reasonable man, and he dislikes me already. I want to be armed with information when I go there."

"Finding the horse would help," Betty said.

"I realize now none of this is about losing Moon. I think he wants me out of his life because I remind him of my father. Nothing I could do would win him over. Nor would I want to."

"He *is* Walker's father."

Daisy threw up her hands. "Why does it all have to be so complicated? My life before this was hard, but at least it was simple and predictable. Work, take care of Mom, dive."

"Would you really trade Walker for *simple* and *predictable*?" Betty asked.

Daisy still didn't think Walker was hers to trade, but she knew the answer.

On May 12 they moved from Little Robert to the new Information and Control Center. With everything hush-hush, the WARDs were told only two things: that they'd be able to walk to work, and that the place was code-named Lizard. It was good news after months of riding in the back of that stuffy truck and breathing exhaust, or navigating slippery wooden planks across the mudflats, in blackout conditions.

At 0700, Major Hochman and Major Oscar met everyone from their shift in front of the banyan tree at the end of their street and herded the women up the road. Daisy had never heard so many mynah birds in her life. Slanted sunlight spilled through the clouds, forming scattered pieces of rainbow. A typical spring morning, with weather that couldn't make up its mind. Daisy felt the same way.

"You have to wonder why they call it *Lizard*," Fluff said as they walked.

Betty chuckled. "I bet I could guess."

"If there are lizards in there, I'm rebelling."

Over the course of the past months, it had become increasingly clear that Fluff had an aversion to geckos. Whenever she saw one in the house—and there were plenty—she ran the other direction or asked Daisy or Betty to usher the filthy creature outside. Daisy loved geckos. As it turned out, so did Blanche.

A little over five minutes later, they arrived at the foot of a rocky hill. Hochman and Major Oscar stopped and waited for everyone to catch up.

"Don't tell me we're going to have to climb this mountain every day to get to work," Thelma said loudly.

Hochman smiled, smooshing together his freckles. "You won't be going over—you'll be going *in* it."

Major Oscar walked straight up to the rocks—which upon closer inspection had a large metal door carved into them—and pressed. The door gave way, revealing a well-lit tunnel that sloped downward and away from where they stood. "Welcome to Lizard, ladies. Watch your heads on the entry."

They stepped in. After thirty yards or so, the tunnel opened up into an enormous room. Freshly inked outlines of islands and grid lines and code names stood out against the shiny white board, which was considerably larger than the last one. There was also a giant grid with Oʻahu in the center up on the wall.

Fluff spun around, taking it all in. "Well, I'll be!"

"We must have done something right to have earned this," Betty said with a big grin.

Major Oscar showed them their new snack room, which had an L-shaped bar and full kitchen. You could even purchase snacks from a young private manning a cash register. Several radio and equipment rooms branched out from the main plotting room, with an interceptor room solely to plot US fighters sent out in pursuit of unidentified flights.

Daisy felt a certain measure of comfort knowing they were in an underground bunker, but the cool and thick air would take some getting used to. The smell of paint lifted off every wall and surface. After they put away their helmets and gas masks, Hochman and Major Oscar brought them back to the main room. The balcony stretched across one whole wall, and Nixon and several of the liaisons were setting up desks and testing equipment.

"Sir, I have your first shift ready to go," Hochman told him.

Nixon addressed them solemnly. "Morning, ladies. I wish I had better news to greet you with, but word has come in from the Coral Sea that we've lost one carrier, and another is badly damaged. There are conflicting reports, but the word is also that the Japanese have suffered heavy losses. Far more than we have."

The room swayed. All the excitement of seeing their new digs quickly fell away.

"Can you give us any more than that?" Peg asked.

"We're having a full briefing this afternoon, so I should know more tomorrow."

Daisy could not wait for tomorrow.

"Please sir, can you at least find out which carrier before then?" she asked.

There were three carriers out there, they knew that much from radio reports. The *Yorktown*, the *Lexington* and the *Enterprise*. Nixon nodded. "I'll see what I can do."

Meanwhile, Hochman walked them through the new equipment and changes in protocol and showed them where to find spare markers and pokers. It felt like moving from a tree fort in the yard into a real house. But Daisy heard only two out of three words he spoke.

Just before Hochman finished, Nixon came to the edge

of the balcony and held up his hand. "I have another announcement." He looked straight at Daisy. "Miss Wilder is being promoted to filterer as of today. Please congratulate her on the highest test score, which was apparently read wrong. She'll be helping to ensure plots are accurate, so we need to get her up to speed."

Cheers sprang up around the room. Fluff and Betty surrounded her in a group hug, with Fluff whispering that Nixon had almost redeemed himself. Lei came up and pinned the red bar with a blue stripe on her collar. Thelma did not look thrilled. And yet all Daisy could think about was the damn carriers.

Betty tried to reassure her. "Just because we lost a carrier does not mean we lost all the men aboard."

Sinking an aircraft carrier was no easy feat. Which meant it must have been some fierce battle. Which also meant aircraft loss. In this war, pilots were expendable. Everyone was expendable. And with each passing day, casualties accumulated on all sides. What would it take to win? she wondered.

Being a filterer meant working side by side with Thelma. Not a great prospect. Ever since their conversation about Daisy's father, Thelma had mostly left her alone, for which Daisy was thankful. She supposed everyone had a limit of coldhearted meanness.

In a side room, Major Hochman sat Thelma, JoAnn and Daisy down and explained the new IFF—Identification Friend or Foe—radar that would be installed in US aircraft assigned to combat. "The genius of the new device is that it picks up our radar beams and sends back a strong echo that shows up on oscilloscopes here on the ground. So we know instantly if the aircraft is one of ours."

"Whoever came up with that should get a big fat medal," JoAnn said.

He then closed the door, pulled up a chair and sat down backward on it. "Now, Nixon is going to have a talk with y'all soon, but I want to warn you about another possible raid on Pearl Harbor. The boys at Hypo are saying somewhere between May 15 and May 20. Which means you ladies are going to have to step up your game."

Three days.

"Will our carriers be back by then?" Daisy asked, though she was pretty sure she knew the answer.

"No."

"That leaves us as sitting ducks again, doesn't it?" Thelma said.

"Not exactly. This time, we'll be waiting," Hochman said.

Three minutes before the end of their shift, while Daisy was calculating the accurate bearing of a flight with readings from Opana and Kawailoa, Nixon came over. "Carrier down is the *Lexington*, most men survived. *Yorktown* was torpedoed but is still afloat. *Enterprise* was en route and did not engage. Will that help you sleep better?" he said to Daisy.

"Affirmative. Thank you, sir."

She caught Thelma looking at her, but put her head down and kept working. Nixon's words were a reprieve—for the moment. Another chance to breathe. If the *Enterprise* had been en route, where was she now? This war was nowhere close to being over, and the nail biting was torturous. Betty had been right—falling for a pilot was a bad idea.

25

THE BEACH

They did not have to wait long to find out more about the anticipated attack. Two days later, Nixon briefed the WARDs that the Imperial Japanese Navy was amassing battleships and carriers in its home waters, presumably to launch another assault. But now, instead of Pearl Harbor and Hawai'i as the main target, intel leaned more toward the Aleutians or possibly Midway atoll.

"However, we can't rule anything out. The entire Second Fleet has been silent for days now, which is never a good sign," Nixon said.

Daisy would have never imagined this life for herself. Speaking in code, the ability to recite names of half the ships in the Imperial Japanese Navy, and conversing with pilots with ease. But the fact that she hadn't seen a horse in weeks, or swam in the ocean, added an extra layer of strain. Which was why she invited the girls to spend a night at her beach house on their next day off—a Sunday. Who knew when they might get another chance.

They had no trouble finding kitten sitters, as every WARD on their block would show up at any hour of day or night for a visit. Most of the kittens were already spoken for, including one named Twinkletoes who had a tendency to spring into the air when she was the least bit excited. Daisy had claimed her for her own.

Betty packed a picnic basket and a cooler with bread and Spam, dill pickles, apple bananas and ginger ale. Fluff threw in a bottle of wine. With rations the way they were, only certain foods were available on any given day. Lei, their regular supplier of hard-to-find items, was too busy at home to join them. Daisy suspected there was more trouble with George.

Before they even hit the pineapple fields, Fluff said, "Yesterday, I had a nice conversation with Cheerio, and there's something about him that just seems so adorable. Can you help me find out more about him?" Fluff said, leaning forward from the back seat. Cheerio was a new Oscar who had all the girls talking.

"Have you not learned anything?" Betty said.

Fluff sighed. "One bad experience is not going to sour my opinion of men in general. I still have hope."

"Keep the hope, but avoid men we work with."

Daisy couldn't help but add her two cents. "I know what you mean about Cheerio, though. He always has something sweet or funny to say, and he seems genuine. Did he mention the bird to you?"

"Yes! What kind of man does that?" Fluff said.

Last week on a call, every time Cheerio tried to give the reading, a loud squawk erupted in the background. He kept saying in a voice like a warm blanket, "Easy there, mate." When Daisy asked about it, he told her he'd rescued an injured seabird and was nursing it back to health at the Wai'anae Radar Station.

"Still. Keep it professional. You know they don't like us getting chatty with the Oscars," Betty said.

Fluff ignored her. "Do you think there's a way to meet him in person?"

"Short of going out there and visiting the station, no. And look what happened with our last visit," Daisy said.

Fluff rolled down the back window, letting in the fresh morning air. "Don't you ever wonder what the Oscars all look like? Some of them sound so manly, like radio announcers, and others sound like someone's kid brother. I would love to get a bunch of mug shots and have to match the face with the voice," she said.

Fluff had graduated from filling out chits for each flight to taking readings, and she was very efficient at her job. Everyone moved along at their own pace, and though Fluff was not so mechanically inclined, her verbal skills were outstanding. "What if you went through all this trouble to meet him, and then discovered he was a real dog? Then what?" Betty asked.

She sat quiet for a while and then said, "Getting to know a man *before* you know what they look like could be a godsend. That way, you're basing everything on personality. And personality is what matters most in life."

"A noble idea," Betty said.

"And a true one."

"What kind of name is Cheerio anyways? It sounds British," Betty said.

Fluff shrugged. "I got the scuttlebutt that the other guys started calling him Cheerio since he uses the word so much and always signs off saying *cheerio*. I guess it stuck."

"We ought to set up a case file on him. You know, like Sherlock Holmes might do," Daisy said, half joking.

"Great minds think alike," Fluff said with a grin.

"I learned from the best."

Knee-high grass and fallen coconut fronds scattered about the yard gave the place an abandoned feel. That and the rusted-out car and tin roof. A hot rush of shame surfaced for about two seconds before Daisy remembered that she was among friends. From day one, none of these women had judged her—pants and all. They weren't about to start now.

After unpacking, the girls peeled off their clothes and made a beeline for the ocean, blue and flat and silent. Falling into its cool waters, they floated and frolicked and watched the albatross soar overhead.

"Have you ever seen an albatross chick?" Daisy asked.

"Never."

"Right now, they're adorable little fluff balls, but in later June, they'll have their full plumage and leave for a few years at sea."

Daisy used to spend hours traipsing through the dunes, counting the baby birds and creating a map in her head of where each one waited patiently for their parents to bring back squid and fish eggs for them. Now and then, she'd find one dead and run home in tears. Her father would say, "It's the way of nature. Those baby birds are now feeding the worms and the ants and the earth." His words always settled her.

Fluff stared up in awe. "Look at that wingspan. We could practice plotting them. Unidentified bogey bearing two-seven-zero and holding steady. Intercept needed."

"They're beautiful. A wonder they aren't picked up on radar," Betty said.

On the beach, they lay side by side, three hues of human. Fluff, with her naturally copper skin, Daisy the color of light ochre, and Betty, who was nearly as pale as the sand. Their bodies heated up within minutes, spring leaning toward summer.

Betty got up and pulled her towel four feet over, into the shade. "Let's pretend for the next few hours that there is no war, that all our loved ones are still living and breathing, and that this patch of sand is where we get to live for the rest of our days."

Fluff and Daisy joined her and time moved as slowly as a grazing turtle. Daisy enjoyed every minute of doing absolutely nothing. Just before lunch, they took a long walk on the beach, ready to dart into the bushes if any planes appeared overhead—Japanese or American.

Fluff was determined to see where Daisy once worked, and before they knew it, they were nearing Montgomery Ranch.

"Let's turn around now," Daisy said before they rounded the last bend.

"Where's the fun in that?" Fluff said, grabbing her hand and pulling her along.

It *was* Sunday. Maybe a sneak peek would be okay. "Just duck behind an ironwood if you see anyone. I don't want Mr. Montgomery to think there's a prowler on the loose."

They approached the edge of the field cautiously, rushing from tree to tree. From what Daisy could see, only the horses were there. A handful were out grazing in the pasture, tails swishing. Patches of dandelion dotted the field. The stables blocked part of the view of the driveway, so she couldn't be sure about vehicles, but there was a certain vacancy in the air.

"Why, it's perfectly charming! No wonder you didn't

want to leave. And this all belongs to Montgomery?" Fluff said, quietly.

"Every last blade of grass."

Betty, who wore a wide-brimmed hat to protect her fair skin, stole up to the fence. "Didn't you say no one is here on Sundays?"

"Mr. Silva checks in on the horses in the afternoon and feeds and waters them. Why?"

"What if you gave us a quick riding lesson?" Betty said with a wicked grin.

"Absolutely not!" Daisy said. At the noise, a couple of the nearby horses raised their heads and were now staring at the girls. Wind and Mākaha. Grass hung from their mouths.

"Hey, fellas!" Daisy said, just loud enough for their sensitive ears to hear. "It's me, your favorite carrot and guava slinger."

At the sound of her voice, Wind immediately trotted over, head high. Mākaha followed at his hooves. Soon, both horses stood at the fence with their muzzles in her hand, blowing and snorting and vying for rubs. Their soft whiskers tickled, sending warm tendrils up Daisy's arms and around her heart.

"Look at them. They love you, plain as day," Fluff said.

Daisy pressed her head against Wind, inhaling his earthy scent. "I've missed you beautiful beasts."

"They want us to ride them, especially the big dark one," Fluff said, eyeing the horse.

Daisy waved her off. "Enough with that. We aren't going to ride them. Talk about a foolish move. I'm already in enough hot water with the Montgomery family."

But the way Wind was looking at her, she knew Fluff was right. From across the field, two more horses made their way over. Nalu and Whiskey. And then Apple. Daisy thought about Moon. He would have been the first one over. She felt his absence smack in the center of her chest.

Could they?

It was still early, not even lunchtime. And Mr. Silva played cards at lunch with his buddies. He never missed a Sunday.

"You're quite popular with them," Fluff said.

"No one will know, and I bet these horses can keep a secret," Betty pressed.

Daisy glanced around. Listened for signs of life. It would be foolish and daring, but she knew that the odds were in their favor. Unless, of course, the Japanese showed up again.

"I won't be caught stealing horses a second time."

Fluff stroked Wind's neck. "Who said we're going to get caught?"

Before Daisy knew what she was doing, she had three horses lined up along the fence. Nalu and Apple were the two most docile creatures on the ranch, and would be perfect for Fluff and Betty.

Daisy briefed them on bareback basics. "We'll just do a big loop around the field. Stay in line with me and hold lightly on the mane without tugging."

They used the fence to mount, and once the girls were in place, Daisy hopped on Wind and gave him a gentle kick. The polo field was huge, and they stuck to the inside perimeter of the fence. All the smells of the place made Daisy feel more homesick than she thought possible. A heady mixture of manure and kiawe wood, salt and seaweed.

Behind her, Fluff squealed, "I'm in love already."

Daisy turned to see both friends glowing. The sun had gone behind a cloud, and was sending down beams of light around them. It was a scene straight from a painting. Being able to give them this day, this small fragment of joy, made it all worth it.

"Y'all want to pick up the pace?" Betty said.

Daisy kicked Wind a little harder. They rode past the stables, underneath a cluster of massive ironwoods, and clear across the field. She knew the horses would alert her to anyone approaching, but she still felt jumpy. They were halfway across when Wind's ears twitched. His head swung right. Daisy looked back toward the driveway and saw a cloud of dust rising up through the trees. *Horsefeathers!* They were on the wrong side of the field for someone to come. If she had been alone, she would have galloped across to the beach and been gone in a few breaths. But not with Fluff and Betty. Someone would get hurt. With no time to waste, she slid off Wind and ran back to Fluff.

"What is it?"

"Someone's coming. Hurry, put your foot in my hand and swing your leg over."

Fluff did as instructed, and then Daisy went to Betty. The car would pull in any moment. Daisy felt the same sense of panic as when Moon had run off. Their only hope was to hop the fence and lay flat in the knee-high grass.

"I thought no one came on Sundays," Fluff said.

Daisy ignored her and ran. "Follow me."

It felt like the longest run in her life. Barefoot and breathless, she hopped the fence and rolled down behind a clump of grass. Her heart thundered against her ribs. Betty and Fluff trailed ten yards behind, and right when they hit the fence, Mr. Montgomery's Ford rolled in.

"Hurry!" she called.

Obviously, neither girl was used to hopping fences, and

Fluff's dress snagged. "I can't get it undone," she said, frantically tugging and yanking.

Betty made it over and lay flat next to Daisy.

"Take it off," Daisy whispered.

Fortunately, the driveway faced the ocean, so unless Mr. Montgomery had reason to be looking this way, it was possible he hadn't noticed them yet. Daisy prayed. A moment later, Fluff wiggled free of her dress and joined them in her swimsuit. A car door slammed.

"It's Mr. Montgomery. Let's hope he doesn't notice your dress."

"Good thing it's green," Betty said.

They lay there for a few moments catching their breath, watching Montgomery. He pulled a bucket out of the back of the truck and went into the stables. Daisy looked over at her friends, wild-eyed and red-faced. Fluff in her swimsuit. Betty as flat to the ground as she could press herself. Daisy couldn't help but laugh.

"What's so funny, Wilder?" Fluff asked.

"You two. Us. Seems like we have a knack for getting ourselves into prickly situations."

"I'd be laughing too if this grass wasn't so damn itchy," Fluff said, a smile stealing over her face.

"Whose dumb idea was this, anyway?" Betty said.

"Yours," Daisy and Fluff said in unison.

Betty put a hand over her mouth and broke out giggling. Fluff followed suit. Soon, the three of them were in stitches, trying desperately to keep the noise down. Daisy got a mouthful of grass in the process. When the laughter finally stopped, she darted out and tore Fluff's dress away. The last thing they needed was for the cowboys to find a mysterious dress pinned to the fence.

"Come on, let's make a run for the beach while he's still inside," she said.

They half stumbled, half crawled through patches of grass, dried-out stumps and thorny lantana. At any moment, Daisy expected to hear a yell or a shout. But they made it. When they spilled out onto the sand, they tore down the beach without looking back. It wasn't until they made it around the first bend that they sat down in the sand to rest.

"You belong there," Fluff said once they'd caught their breath.

"Not anymore."

"We'll see about that."

After lunch, Daisy brought them into her mother's room because Fluff was interested in her book collection and they wanted a break from the afternoon sun. Daisy had no use for any of the old tomes, and Fluff was a self-proclaimed bibliophile.

"You're welcome to any of them."

Daisy opened the louvers and propped herself on the bed, kicking up her heels. The salt on her skin rubbed off on the bedspread. Betty and Fluff, still in their bathing suits, pulled out book after book. Fluff held one up and said, "*The Mysterious Affair at Styles*! This is a great book. Or this one— have you read *The Great Gatsby*?"

Daisy had not. Nor most of the other books in here. "Not yet."

As a girl, Daisy had always thought Louise so intelligent. She wanted to love books the same way, but her brain had other plans. She was off in a daydream when she noticed a floorboard raised up on the far side of the bed, half-hidden under the frayed skirt. It stuck up a good half inch above the rest. Curious, she leaned down and pressed on it. Nothing happened. The wood appeared too swollen to fit back in its spot.

"Hand me that letter opener, would you?" she said to Betty.

"What for?"

"I want to see what's under here."

They all crowded around as Daisy wiggled the metal between the wide board and the floor. This time, it came up easily. Her heart pumped faster when she saw what was in it.

"Well, I'll be," said Fluff.

Daisy held an envelope in her shaky hands. It was addressed to her mother, but unopened. She sat on the bed and the girls circled around her. The writing looked vaguely familiar, a tall and narrow block print.

"We should open it," Fluff said.

"No we shouldn't. It's not addressed to us," Betty argued.

Curiosity swarmed through her, fanning the inside of her chest. Daisy tore it open.

Dear Mrs. Wilder,

This letter is both an apology and an explanation, though I know neither can replace your tragic loss. By now, my father has come to speak to you, and you know the truth about what happened to Billy. It was by my bidding, as I demanded you get the facts. We also went to Sheriff Santos and reported the real story. He took our statements and filed them, changing cause of death to Accidental Death by Gunshot.

Mrs. Wilder, I understand why you want nothing to do with me and why you've refused to let me in, but I need to get it off my chest. I was there. I witnessed the accident. I saw my father slip down the hill and his gun discharge at the bottom. There was no malice, no intent, and despite our best efforts, Uncle Billy died swiftly with little or no suffering. Where things took a wrong turn was when my father asked the boys and me to lie for him. He was frantic and not thinking clearly. But when my father gets something stuck in his head, there's no swaying him. He convinced us it would be better for everyone involved, when really, it was better for him. For some odd reason he was worried he'd be accused of murder.

Not a day goes by that I don't think about Uncle Billy. He taught me everything I knew about horses. I miss him, and I would not be able to sleep another night without telling you how sorry I am. I wish I could do it face-to-face, and maybe someday I'll get the chance. If there is anything you or Daisy should ever need, please don't hesitate to ask. I will move mountains to make sure it happens.

Sincerely,
Walker Montgomery

By the time Daisy finished reading, she had dropped onto the bed next to Fluff, their knees touching. No one spoke for a full minute. The whoosh of wind through ironwoods was the only noise.

Fluff finally broke the silence. "Lord, this can't be good. Can you tell us what it says?"

Daisy handed her the letter. "Read it out loud, so Betty can hear."

Fluff read, swallowing hard between sentences. Her voice trailed off as she read Walker's name. She lowered the note and turned those big, beautiful eyes on Daisy. They were full of tears. "What a horrible burden to bear."

"Why wouldn't your mother tell you? Are you sure Mr. Montgomery told her?" Fluff asked.

"I'm not sure of anything," Daisy said. "Other than Walker was telling the truth about going to see my mom."

A fully formed image of Walker as a teenager emerged in her mind. The letter was hand delivered, not mailed. She had come home after a long day at the ranch and bumped into Walker coming out of her driveway. He rarely spoke to her, unless required to, and when he saw her, he stopped in his tracks.

"Miss Wilder," he said, awkwardly.

No one ever put a *Miss* in front of Wilder.

"Mr. Montgomery," she said back, tired and unable to muster up any politeness. "What are you doing here?"

He didn't answer at first, then mumbled something she couldn't hear, and said, "Just passing through."

She remembered him looking at her funny, and saying a few more senseless things before continuing on his way. Back then, he seemed so much older than Daisy. A real man. Her mother appeared to be out cold on the bed when she peeked in on her, and when Daisy asked about Walker the next day, Louise had no answers. For weeks, Daisy wondered why Walker had been in their yard, and then she forgot about it.

Now, she realized without a doubt that he had tried to make things right all those years ago.

26

THE MOONLIGHT

Daisy had once heard it said that when you can't sleep at night, it's because you're awake in another person's dream. She had no idea why she'd believe it, but if it was true, she wished the mystery person would let her be. All this time at Shafter, she had been missing her own bed, and now she lay awake to the sound of the ocean breathing, the night so still you could hear the crabs digging holes in the sand. She flopped around, curled and uncurled, and eventually got up and snuck onto the beach. It was hard to feel lonely under a sky full of stars.

The insomnia kept up for the next few days, leaving her bleary-eyed at work and cranky at home—going through the motions of life when her head and heart were elsewhere. She wished this mystery person would leave her out of his dreams. A good night's rest was more valuable than butter. She felt like she was hanging on by her teeth. Two things kept her sane: kittens and filtering.

Hochman had been spending the first hour of each shift teaching Daisy, Thelma and JoAnn. He explained the protocol for planes in distress and a checklist for when to call an air raid. Too soon and you panic an already jumpy population, too late and you end up under fire. JoAnn impressed Daisy with her recall ability, and Thelma had all but stopped the underhanded remarks and eye-rolling. Lizard, with its shiny new equipment, seemed to bring out the best in people.

So much so, that Fluff and Daisy decided to try something one day. They'd been told it was Nixon's birthday. All along, they had all suspected a soft heart beneath Nixon's tough exterior, and they wanted to test their theory.

"He's going to love it," Fluff insisted to Betty.

"You'll get us in trouble."

"I'm with Fluff on this one," Daisy said.

They dug up an old picnic basket, placed a towel in the bottom, filled an old tuna can with water and placed a kitten inside. This one was a sweet female named Cozy, on account of how snuggly she was. They brought her in in the late afternoon, on the shift change. Fluff snuck the basket into the office, and Daisy asked for a private word with him.

He eyed her suspiciously. "What's this about?"

"I have a situation I need advice on."

"From me?"

She nodded. "From you, sir."

When they opened the door and he saw Fluff standing at his desk next to a basket with a big red bow on it, he stopped short and grumbled. "Whatever you've got there, you can just take it back out the door. I don't need any presents."

Fluff looked hurt. "But, sir, it's your birthday. We went through a lot of trouble to find this, and think you're going to love it. So much so, that your life will be forever changed."

He stood ramrod straight. Daisy thought for sure he was going to insist they leave, but he said, "You ladies are a persistent bunch, aren't you?"

"When it comes to things we believe in—and people that matter to us," Daisy said.

He tensed.

"Come have a look!"

Nixon walked over to the basket, his neck red but not as flared up as it once had been. A second before he lifted the top, a tiny meow escaped. Fluff shot Daisy a worried look.

"Don't tell me there's a live animal in here," he said.

In one fell swoop, Daisy walked over and undid the bow, pulling Cozy out and setting her on his desk. All gray with a crooked tail, she was quite possibly the cutest of the litter.

"Colonel Nixon, meet Cozy. And Cozy, this is Colonel Nixon," Fluff said. Daisy held her breath as Cozy scampered across the desk toward the edge. Nixon scooped her up just before she went over, holding her up at eye level.

"That's a long way down for such a small creature," he said to Cozy.

"You're not allergic, are you?" Daisy asked.

"Lucky for you, no."

"I know it might seem like extra work for you right now, but the kitten needs a home and you are the perfect candidate. We know from experience that having an animal around is the best antidote for..." Fluff paused for a moment. "Well, for anything really. Aren't I right, Daisy?"

Daisy nodded enthusiastically. "Absolutely. They are automatic morale boosters."

Nixon set Cozy down again, and this time she sat and gazed up at him. He could not tear his eyes away, and yet he said, "I can't take care of a cat. Sorry to disappoint you, ladies."

Fluff wasn't having it. "Cats don't need much. For a little food and water, they give you love and companionship."

"We can help when you need it. And what if you brought her into work with you? To keep the rats away. Or she could be our mascot, like all of those dogs in Europe," Daisy said.

"This isn't a dog."

"A mascot doesn't have to be a dog. I've heard of donkeys or monkeys or even a lamb. Cozy would be perfect," Daisy said.

"Just hold her for a few minutes. Then decide," Fluff said.

Nixon appeared to be waging an inner battle, hemming and hawing. But he did pick up Cozy and brought her in close against his chest. He rubbed her cheek and Cozy turned up her purrs.

With surprising tenderness, he said, "You like that, huh?"

Fluff winked at Daisy. He had no chance.

After the visit to Daisy's shack, Fluff had torn through *The Great Gatsby* in record speed, even though it was her third go-through. In doing so, she became firmly attached to a notion.

"All those lavish parties. How brilliant would it have been to catch a Follies show?" Fluff said, nodding dreamily. "Say, we ought to throw a party. We can invite everyone at Lizard and all the Oscars."

"In the dark?" Daisy asked.

"Nor is our house quite Gatsby's mansion," Betty said.

Fluff smiled. "No, but you know whose is? Jackie Sweet! I bet she would go for having one. Her family has that giant beach house in Niu Valley. Think what good a party would do everyone right now."

Jackie Sweet, it turned out, loved the idea, and Fluff began making arrangements on the double. "We'll plan it for a full-moon night and have it out on the lawn. Uncle T and his band can play. Of course, people will have to bring their own booze. We'll begin early because of curfew." In the coming days, Fluff spent more and more time planning the party despite warnings of an impending attack or invasion. They set the date for May 26, a Tuesday. In their world, weekends were whenever you had days off. One evening, Fluff set up the kitchen table as an invitation station, where they copied card after card. Fluff had created the drawing herself and outlined it with a flower lei.

> You are cordially invited to the
> MOONLIGHT PARTY
> to be given by
> Fox King, Jig Sail and fellow
> VECTOROLOGISTS
> Blackout Passes and Homing Vectors Will Be Provided

The invite was catchy, with a no-snafu map to Jackie's beach house—which they called *the Objective*—and signs posted on coconut trees warning of Bogeys in the Bushes. Daisy and Betty diligently copied invitations until their palms were black with ink. As they worked, they listened to Radio Tokyo.

Back at Little Robert, they had been warned of the Japanese propaganda broadcasts, but that only made them more intrigued. Betty had rounded up an old shortwave radio from one of Chuck's buddies and so began their new nightly hobby—SWL'ing, a.k.a. shortwave radio listening. According to Hochman, you could not trust a word they said.

"But they sound so earnest," Fluff said.

"Why do you think they call it propaganda? It's meant to pluck your heartstrings," Betty said.

The Japanese were smart. They'd found a few English-speaking women to host the programs and relay the messages, which for some reason made them sound more heartfelt. And in recent weeks, American prisoners of war themselves had begun to read messages to their families back home. The show had suddenly become a whole lot more interesting. Coming from far across the sea, the reception was remarkably clear. But there was a false cheer leaking out from between the lines that did not match the firsthand accounts coming out of Japan.

"Hello, Mom, Dad and everyone... I hope you are well and happy. I am in good health and so far all right... I wish more than anything I could hear from you... We are taken good care of here. It's plenty warm, and the food is fine. Have Lana and Grant married yet? And Stella, tell her I miss her. Jack, too. I hope we will all be together soon and I pray for you every day. Please write! Your loving son, Felix."

It worked, to a certain degree. Daisy and the gals found themselves unable to pull away from the radio. When the announcer came on to read names, Betty always fanned herself with a magazine, leaned in and scarcely breathed.

"I know chances are slim, but a chance is a chance," she said on that first night.

Daisy would have done the same thing in her shoes. Hardly a day went by where Daisy did not think of her father. The fractures in her heart may have mended some, but they were still there, swollen and sore.

"I will listen with you every single night of this war, if it helps," Daisy told her.

"Me, too," said Fluff.

It was far easier to want to believe these stories than the ones they read about in the papers, where Americans were whipped to death and scalped with bayonets. Daisy and Fluff always tried to hide the paper from Betty when there was any mention of this kind of treatment. It was enough to cause Daisy to break out in a cold sweat, but it would ruin Betty.

During the next week, tension at Lizard rose even higher, if that was possible. Strict radio silence was ordered by Admiral Nimitz for any ship entering Pearl or plane coming in for landing. The Japanese had apparently been listening in on ground-to-air chatter, and through it learning of US carrier movements. When Nixon heard the order, he slammed his clipboard into the wall in a rare display of emotion.

"How do they expect us to do our job?" he grumbled to Hochman.

Delicately, as it turned out. The air force bombers and flying boats were still performing their scouting missions toward Midway, and most already knew the drill. Though air traffic was heavy, pilots had stepped up reporting their flights. Every now and then, though, a pilot for whatever reason did not follow protocol, and was required to break radio silence. Nixon made sure those got a talking-to.

Despite all of the added pressure, Daisy and the filterers managed their flights with cool heads and great accuracy. The military liaisons at Lizard had doubled and now more than ever they were on the alert for anything out of the ordinary. Most planes flew in established flight patterns, so a Japanese fleet should be hard to miss. Daisy was determined there would be no more foul-ups like Station Opana on December 7.

On the day of the party, Daisy received a call from Cheerio. "Morning, Rascal, looks like we've got a possible CV
incoming, two seven zero. Thirty miles out."

CV was military speak for an aircraft carrier.

Normally, contact would have been made by now.
"Roger. Is she alone?"

"Affirmative."

When Daisy hung up, Thelma sensed her excitement.
"What is it?"

"Maybe a carrier."

The word caused a ripple through her body. An airplane girl
through and through, Daisy had never been impressed with
ships—until she'd seen an aircraft carrier. That such a massive object could float was a major feat of engineering. Then
throw on ninety or so aircraft and a couple of thousand sailors
and send her out into the open ocean. Anyone would be hard-
pressed not to get choked up watching one come into port.

After the second reading, which brought the object directly in line with Pearl Harbor, Daisy ran to Nixon. "We
have a CV coming into Pearl!" she said.

Nixon conferred with Owens and then made an announcement. "The *Hornet* is on her way in. She was badly
damaged by an armor-piercing bomb. A plane flew in word
yesterday to Nimitz."

"Yesterday?" Daisy asked.

"Everything's on a need-to-know basis. You know that."

Daisy felt the sting of disappointment. She hated waiting, hated the feeling of helplessness, hated this whole stupid war. And she wasn't even a wife, so no one would be
waiting for her at the house if anything had happened to
Walker. No one would even think to tell her.

To keep herself distracted that afternoon, Daisy joined
Fluff and Jackie and a few other gals setting up the beach

house for the party. Whoever built the Sweet beach house
knew a thing or two about design. A two-story, white affair with long eaves and sprawling porches, the place was
about as perfectly situated as a house could be. Set back
from the water, amid heart-shaped milo trees and trellises
of hao, it oozed of lazy days and starlit nights. Thick, green
lawn stretched to the water's edge.

They set up clusters of chairs, tied red ginger and ti leaves
to the coconut trees, and created an assembly line where
they fixed egg salad and tuna sandwiches full of garlic pickle
relish that Betty had made. Lei had promised to bring trays
of sweet potato mac salad. Mayonnaise was hard to come by,
but Jackie had befriended one of the cooks at the officers'
mess hall, and he had snuck her two large jars. Everything
could be found if you were diligent enough, or knew the
right person. Even butter. Even beer.

"I know we said BYOB on the invite, but we can't have
a party for the boys without supplying some beer," Fluff
had said.

Once they were finished setting up, they all went into
the guest cottage and showered and changed. Watching the
other gals dress and primp still fascinated Daisy. While she
had let her hair grow out a bit, it came to just below her
ears and required little styling. Same with her dress. Simple, yellow and without frills. Betty had loaned it to her.
Though it did fit snuggly and adhere to what little curves
she had. Fluff wore a stylish aloha print dress with a wide
skirt, and Jackie an A-line seersucker. Jackie was finishing
up her last year at university with Fluff, and her father im-
ported automobiles. She was tiny and blonde and danced a
mean hula. Everyone adored her.

Fluff handed Daisy the lipstick tube. "We all have to wear
this. I know you don't like it, but do it for me."

"No, thank you," Daisy said.

"How about for the boys, then? A *screw you* to Hitler."

"You know how I feel about it."

"Just a dab."

Maybe it was time to play along, and make her friend happy. Teamwork, she was coming to see, required seeing things with a different lens. Daisy took the tube and painted her lips a fire-engine red. It tasted like crap.

"There, victory lips. How do I look?"

Jackie whistled. "I predict you're going to have a line of men following you around tonight."

"She only has eyes for one, and he's not on the island," Fluff said.

Guests began trickling in at around five. They had invited officers from Lizard and Shafter, a few of Chuck's friends from the naval yard, as well as boyfriends and husbands of WARDs. Even Nixon got an invite, though whether he'd come or not was a hot topic for debate. Daisy knew he wouldn't. Uncle T had set up with two other Hawaiian men under the hao trellis, sending steel guitar notes through the balmy afternoon. You'd never know a war was raging through much of the Pacific.

Not big on small talk, Daisy found herself awkwardly moving from group to group, always on the fringe of conversation. She wished she could share in the cheer, but her heart wasn't in it. Most of the buzz surrounded the *Hornet* and the sinking of the *Lexington*, but then she overheard something that stopped her in her tracks. Two men were standing near a small canoe that had been filled with beer and blocks of ice.

"They gotta repair her on the double. Otherwise *Enterprise* is the only flattop we've got for this next round," one said.

The other held up a bottle and clinked it against his friend's. "Watching her come into Pearl today was something else. Got me all choked up."

Daisy stepped closer. "Excuse me, did you say the *Enterprise* came into Pearl today?"

The man smiled. "Hello, sunshine, and who are you?"

He looked vaguely familiar, but she couldn't place him. "Daisy Wilder, sir."

His friend answered. "She rolled in at around 1500 hours."

She thanked them and hurried off to find Fluff or Betty or Lei. Within the last fifteen minutes, the crowd had thickened, but she finally spotted Fluff standing off to the side of the musicians, singing along. Daisy grabbed her arm and pulled her to where they could hear.

"The *Enterprise* is back!" she said.

Fluff's eyes went wide. "What?"

"They came in two hours after we left Lizard."

"Well, you know what that means!"

"What?"

"Walker will be here. I just know it. Peg is coming to the party and Peg will tell Walker and Walker will be dying to see you and he'll come. Remember what he said last time? That he thought about you the whole time he was away?"

"Yes, but this time is different."

"Listen to me. They say that in times of distress, the heart takes over. The only thing he'll remember is how he feels about you. And I can guarantee you, whatever he feels grew stronger while he was away."

But here were so many *ifs* involved. "What if he didn't—"

"Stop, I don't want to hear it!" A new song started up and Fluff pulled her out onto a grassy clearing. "Dance with me and forget about everything else, if only for a song."

Daisy was not a dancer. In fact, as an adult, she had never once had the opportunity to dance. "I can't."

"For someone so smart, you sure have a lot of limitations," Fluff said, not letting go of her wrist. "I'm not taking no for an answer."

They were barefoot, and the thick grass felt good against her soles. She took the last sip of the beer that someone had handed her earlier, and set it on a stump. Fluff was already hopping around and swinging her hips. Watching her, Daisy felt as graceful as a two-by-four.

"Relax, it's supposed to be fun," Fluff told her, just as Betty came over and joined in.

Within thirty seconds, the whole grassy area filled up with wiggling bodies. It took some time, but Daisy began to loosen. Maybe it was the beer, or maybe the carefree energy that moved around her. A brief window into normalcy. Though attending parties was far from her normal.

They danced a few songs and then went to cool off near the fishpond. The sun had just fallen behind Diamond Head, creating an orange halo around its flanks.

Betty had begun swatting at her arms and legs. "These mosquitoes will be the death of me."

"I seem to be immune," Daisy said.

"They would have me for breakfast, lunch and dinner if they could. I can already tell I'll be up all night scratching my ankles," Fluff said, then nodded toward the entrance. "Say, look, here comes a new batch of fellas."

A group of uniformed men walked across the lawn. The way they walked, all attitude and swagger, you'd have thought they owned the place.

"Pilots," Betty said.

Daisy went on high alert, but even from a distance, she could tell none of them was Walker. Suddenly, from behind, a voice said, "Someone told us this pond is full of moray eels. You gals seen any?"

That voice.

Fluff must have recognized it too, because she swung around. "Say something else," she ordered.

The man had shockingly blue eyes and an easy smile. "Rascal, we are on the hunt for unidentified subs in these waters. Any sightings?"

"You're Cheerio," Fluff said softly, as though he'd just walked in off the water.

He winked. "The one and only. And which lovely Rascals are you?"

The girls all introduced themselves, with Fluff turning a whole shade darker. She had such a radiant inner light, it was hard to imagine every man not falling in love with her. Except that Fluff did not believe she was worthy, and therefore attracted the wrong kind of man. A simple law of human nature.

Cheerio, however, could not take his eyes off Fluff. "My buddy and I had a bet going that we'd know who was who. So far, I've been wrong. But as soon as I saw you across the lawn, I had a feeling it was you. Only you're prettier than I imagined."

Fluff swallowed hard. Everyone at Lizard had a secret crush on Cheerio, mainly because he was so darn cheery. But he was also funny and smart and thoughtful. And now, they discovered, handsome. Shorter than Daisy, he filled out his uniform well. His features were all points and angles, with a sharp nose that perfectly fit his face. The overall effect was pleasing, and it was obvious Fluff thought so, too.

Her dimples deepened. "That's about the nicest thing anyone has ever said to me."

"Aw, come on."

"I'm serious."

There was something about a compliment coming from the right person that magnified it tenfold. Daisy had experienced the same thing with Walker.

"Just calling it like I see it," he said.

Right off the bat, he began asking them questions about their lives, especially Fluff. *Where are you ladies from? What do y'all do in your spare time? Are you married? Where's your favorite beach?* From the conversation, it appeared he already knew a fair amount about Fluff. Though chatting was discouraged between Oscars and Rascals, they found it nearly impossible not to. Some days, there was nothing more comforting than the sound of a human voice, warm and familiar.

Twenty minutes later, Cheerio was leading Fluff onto the grassy dance floor. Betty and Daisy found a table with Lei and a few other gals and sat and took it all in. The night was perfect. Gentle winds stirring up the smell of mock orange and salt water. Mosquitoes buzzed along with the music and someone had lit the lanterns and covered them in blue cloth.

Something about the way Cheerio held his hand across Fluff's waist, protective and tender, made Daisy feel like weeping. Fluff had endured so many jerks, she deserved someone who looked at her exactly as Cheerio was now.

"I have a good feeling about them," she said.

Soon, a couple of pilots came over and asked Betty and Daisy to dance. Daisy felt like declining, but then thought the better of it. After putting their lives on the line day in and day out, sharing a dance was the least she could do. Betty was game, too. Felipe and Charles were their names. Felipe swung and dipped Daisy around as though she weighed no more than a doll, while Charles, bless his heart, kept stepping on Betty's feet. They danced a few songs, until the musicians took a break.

Uncle T set down his guitar and came over to say hello, then said, "Can we talk for a minute? You, too," he said to Daisy.

"Sure, Uncle," Fluff said.

He nodded toward the back of the house. "Over there." They followed him to a rock wall that bordered the back porch. "You remember Archie, the old paniolo at the racetrack?" he asked.

Daisy and Fluff both nodded.

"Archie told me he heard something that may be related to your missing horse. There were two men in suits standing outside one of the stalls talking the other day, and words have a way of traveling in there. Thin walls, you know? Anyway, one of the men used the words *horse* and *Montgomery* in the same sentence. When they lowered their voices, he got curious and moseyed on up to the wall on the other side of the stall. They were arguing about a boat in June and how to get the horse on board. But here's the kicker. He swore one mentioned something about painting over the brand with tar."

Daisy's skin prickled. "Did he hear the name of the boat or a specific date in June?"

"No, but he's gonna do a little more reconnaissance. Archie might be crotchety, but he honest to God loves those animals more than anyone I know. Stealing a horse does not sit well with him." His big brown eyes locked onto Daisy. "And whatever you did made an impression on him because he seems more than eager to help you. Not his usual."

"Thank him for me. I love that horse, too," she said.

She thought back to that morning in December. It seemed like years ago, with Moon and his gentle nudges on her arm as she put his bridle on, of his long dark lashes and his particular musky smell. Finding him would fill a big gash in her heart.

As the full moon rose higher, the party kicked up several notches. Silver light on the water. Voices in the air. And the rustling of love in the surrounding milo trees. Fluff and Cheerio weren't the only ones who suddenly found themselves magnetically drawn together. As Daisy meandered around, she spotted Thelma, Rosie, Gladys, Helen and Fran all captivated by their very own sailor or soldier or flyboy. And at the tables, groups were drinking and laughing and making the most of a beautiful night. Who knew what tomorrow would bring.

But wasn't that just life?

Daisy took a lantern out to the fishpond and watched for the eels. Two spotted ones poked their heads out of holes, but none came out entirely. She missed the eels out front of her house. She missed the smell of the ironwood trees, missed Walker. Every time a shadow flickered, she turned in hopes to see him walking toward her. Eventually, she did hear footsteps in the grass. But it was Peg standing there in moonlight, not Walker. Daisy had seen Peg throughout the night, but purposefully steered clear. Her presence alone meant that her brother was alive, and that was enough.

"He's not coming, you know," Peg said.

Daisy was caught off guard by her bluntness. "What makes you think I'm waiting for him?"

"It's pretty obvious. You've had your eye on the entrance the whole night."

"Why are you watching me? Or maybe that's not the right question. Maybe I should ask why you hate me so much. You'd think it would be the other way around," Daisy said, sick of feeling this way around Peg. Always watched, always judged.

A fish jumped in the pond, making a small *plop*.

Peg looked a bit stunned, and before she could answer, they were interrupted by a peculiar sound. Daisy held a finger to her lips. They listened. A few seconds later, just beyond the pond, a groan. It sounded human. Peg and Daisy looked at each other in bewilderment. No one else had come out this way. Though now that she thought about it, the faint smell of cigarette smoke had floated past a few times.

"Hello?" Daisy called into the dark.

Another groan. And then a cough.

"Who's there?" Peg said.

A female voice slurred back, "Mayday, mayday..."

Daisy and Peg both rushed around a short hedge, through a clump of coconut trees and into a grassy clearing. In the center of the clearing, a lone figure sat in the grass. Daisy knelt down on one side, Peg on the other. The woman was cross-legged with her dress bunched up around her hips. Moonlight spilled in, illuminating her red dress and dark hair.

"Is that you, Vivian?" Daisy said.

A tall glass lay on its side next to her. "I came out to watch for bogeys, but the sky won't stay still and I don't feel so hot."

Peg grabbed her hand. "Come on, let's get you some water."

Vivian yanked her hand away, lay back and burst into tears. "I want my Donny to come home, and I'll just sleep here until he does," she wailed.

Don Dupont was an SBD Dauntless pilot on the *Yorktown*, and had been gone for some time now, but was expected back any day. "He'll be home soon, I know it," Daisy said.

"Everyone always says that, and you know what? It's bullshit, horse shit, cow shit, fish shit—you name it, it's just shit. No one knows who is coming back and who isn't until the carrier has pulled in and unloaded its precious cargo," Vivian said, alcohol vapors strong on her breath.

Peg sighed. "The two of us have been in your shoes, Viv. And living with this uncertainty never gets easier."

The words reminded Daisy just how much Peg loved her brother. And how they were all in this together. "You're right, Vivian, I shouldn't have said *I know he'll be home.* I apologize. I don't know, but I do hope, and hope goes a long way."

"Hope and prayer. They're all we have," Peg agreed.

"Come on, Viv, you need water," Daisy pressed.

"Coffee. I need coffee, and I need my man," Vivian slurred.

Peg and Daisy each took an arm and hoisted her up. They brought her through the back door to the kitchen and set her up at the breakfast nook with water and a plate of saloon pilot crackers. Peg brewed a pot of coffee. Vivian was a mess—smudged mascara, smeared lipstick and a trickle of dried vomit on her chin. Daisy found a rag and helped her wipe her face.

"I love you ladies, you know that?" Vivian said.

Peg winked at Daisy. "We love you too. Now eat up."

Daisy went to rinse out the rag in the sink, and when she turned back, Vivian had her head down on the table and was snoring lightly.

Peg remained sitting quietly for a moment, then said in a soft tone, "I don't hate you, Daisy. I never have."

Daisy felt blindsided. "I don't understand."

"To be honest, I think I resented the whole accident and the rift it caused in our family. Between my mom and my dad, and my dad and Walker. I always felt invisible, at school, at home, everywhere. When you don't know who to blame, sometimes that blame takes on a life of its own."

The words hung between them, ripe with feeling.

Peg continued. "And my brother is keen on you. No woman has ever gotten under his skin the way you have. He was a mess when you told him to leave you alone. As brooding and miserable as I've ever seen him."

Daisy couldn't help herself. "Really?"

"Really."

"Why is he not coming tonight?"

"Nimitz wanted to recognize some of the pilots on the *Enterprise*. Walker was one of them."

Pride swelled in her chest. "I'm not surprised."

Peg smiled. "Me neither."

Music drifted in through the open windows. Daisy thought what a strange triangle they made. Two women, one man and a tragedy that linked them all together. Maybe in a strange way, they could all help each other heal.

Daisy offered her a crumb. "I changed my mind, you know. About seeing Walker. But he left before I could tell him."

"It sounds like they won't be staying home long this time. I hope you get a chance to tell him," Peg said.

"Do you know anything else?"

"Only that something big is brewing."

27

THE REAL DEAL

Daisy walked into Lizard on shaky legs. Too little sleep and too much dancing. But a lot of others were in far worse shape. Over half the girls had called in for replacements for their shift today, claiming sudden illness, and Lei had literally dragged Daisy and Betty out of bed. Fluff had slept at Jackie's and been spared.

Halfway into the morning, Nixon announced a mandatory meeting at noon for all WARDs. "I don't care if they need to bring a sick bag in or come in a wheelchair, get 'em in here," he told Lei.

At about 1145, WARDs began showing up in varying degrees of disarray. Wrinkled uniform, smooshed hat, bleary eyes. They assembled in a large meeting room down an unused corridor. Even more than usual, the mountain above seemed to press in on them. Cool, dense air tickled the hair on Daisy's arm. General Danielson, Major General Tinder, the commander of the Hawaiian Air Force, and

Major Ernest Moore strode in wearing their pinks. Everyone fell silent.

Tinder went first. "Ladies, you've done a fine job so far in stepping in and taking control of our airspace. I commend you for that. As you know, we've had a few scares, a few snafus, in a period of relative calm. That is all about to change."

He paused, taking his time to scan the room and make eye contact with as many WARDs as possible. "You've heard talk about a major encounter, and we've been scrambling trying to figure out where the Japanese are planning their assault. Now, we have our answer. We're certain it's Midway."

Tall and dark, Tinder could have walked in off a film set. This whole affair almost felt like a movie, but Daisy had only to think about the charred and twisted remains of hangars and ships, or close her eyes and relive Walker's dogfight overhead, to remind herself that it was real. Tinder informed them of preparations being made, B-17s that were being readied and what kind of flight patterns to expect in the coming week. "All women and children living between Punchbowl and Liliha Street have been ordered to evacuate and stay elsewhere. You folks will be the only females in the area."

Murmurs echoed off the stark white walls.

Betty raised her hand. "If you're so sure it's Midway, what's the big danger here?"

"We have a lot of reasons for concern. One, with all of our forces fifteen hundred miles away, we're going to be sitting ducks. And two, there could be spillover here. Especially if the Japanese Navy comes out ahead. Hawai'i is the next stepping-stone to the Mainland. So you ladies need to be prepared," he said, glancing over at Danielson.

Danielson stepped forward, as stone-faced as Daisy had ever seen him. "From now on, helmet and gas masks are with you at all times. Hell, even in the bathroom. You ladies are going to be on your own. I repeat, there will be no assistance in case of an attack. I expect an order to be given shortly that no one is to leave Shafter."

At that moment, the back door opened with a loud click. Daisy turned to see Fluff slink in and sit in the back row. Daisy thought she detected the faint smell of coconut oil.

He went on. "You may be required to stay on posts for extended periods of time, in which case, it might be wise to bring your C rations to the tunnel."

While he spoke, his hands went in and out of his pockets no less than eighteen times, and his usual smooth voice caught on words. The explosions from Pearl Harbor were still fresh in everyone's minds. Daisy was quite sure there was no more powerless feeling than standing on the ground while enemy planes—whose main goal was to blow you to smithereens—flew overhead.

As if they weren't anxious enough, Moore then went into detail about litter-bearing and firefighting and where spare ladders and buckets could be found, and about a new yellow powder called Sulfanilamide to use in case of severe injuries. "It's the best thing we've seen yet for infection," he told them.

Important as this all was, Daisy checked her watch. She was antsy to leave Lizard and go find Walker, even if that meant marching down to the docks and hollering out his name. She'd drag one of the girls along for moral support. But in the next instant, her hopes were dashed when Tinder announced, "Operationally, aside from the B-17s coming and going, the *Enterprise* is leaving as we speak, and the *Yorktown* once she's patched up, hopefully in a day or two."

Without even raising her hand, Daisy said, "But they just arrived, sir."

He shrugged. "War waits for no one."

The anticipation of seeing Walker again, and hopes of telling him that she'd made a mistake, was rudely stamped out.

"Isn't the *Yorktown* badly damaged?" someone else asked.

"Nimitz has ordered that she sail in forty-eight hours. And you saw what those boys in the navy yard did with the *Pennsylvania* and the *Maryland*. We have God on our side."

A small cheer went up.

The first of June, all overnight passes were canceled and those with telephones were prohibited from using them. As promised, the B-17s left in the morning and came back in the afternoon. Radio silence was strictly enforced, so the balcony was crammed with military liaisons who knew every flight going in and out. A seaplane raid on O'ahu was still expected by some, so the shifts were double-stacked with WARDs.

"It's not as though we can go anywhere or do anything, so we might as well be at Lizard," Fluff said.

On June 3, Nixon called everyone into the main room. "CINCPAC just got a bulletin from NAS Midway. One of our PBYs spotted three different Japanese fleets seven hundred miles south of Midway. Main body is bearing 262, speed 19. Eleven ships," he said.

You could have heard a tear drop.

Fluff, who had developed a keen interest in picking up bits and pieces of intel from the Dungeon, the top-secret room where codebreaking took place, said, "But Hypo says the IJN will be coming from the northwest at 315 degrees, so this can't be the striking force."

Nixon frowned. "How can you possibly know that?"

"I make it my business to be as informed as possible. Knowledge is power, sir," Fluff said.

Daisy swore the edge of his lip went up.

"And what else do you know?" he asked.

Fluff looked around, realizing that all eyes were on her. She smiled sweetly and said, "I know that tomorrow is when the carriers are supposed to arrive at Midway."

He nodded. "You may be right about that. We'll find out soon enough. In the meantime, B-17s have been dispatched to bomb the crap out of them."

It was beginning.

That evening, Fluff flitted about the house like a sparrow, her whole being abloom. She had spent the previous night counting stars and kissing Cheerio until the sun came up, and apparently missed him already.

"Do you believe in love at first sight?" she said to no one in particular as she stared out the window at a blood-red sky.

Daisy corrected her. "Wasn't it *love at first sound*?"

Fluff shrugged. "You know how Betty always says when you know, you *know*? Well, I know. And boy can that man kiss, let me tell you—"

"No wonder you look like you put your lipstick on wrong," Betty said, walking out from the kitchen with a pitcher of fresh-squeezed lilikoi juice.

Fluff grinned so wide, a new dimple showed in one cheek. "My lips *are* a bit raw. But you should know that he was a perfect gentleman. I felt safe and respected and adored. How's that for a winning combination?"

"We could definitely use more Cheerios in the world," Daisy acknowledged.

"Oh, and guess what his real name is?"

"What?"

"Elmer."

"I think I'll stick to Cheerio," Daisy said.

"Me, too."

By all accounts, tomorrow would be a big day and the girls had to report in at 0400. Daisy was bushed and ready to crawl into bed, but Betty insisted they listen to a few minutes of Radio Tokyo. "Lili Marlene" was playing when they flipped it on.

Fluff groaned. "If I hear this song one more time, I'm throwing that radio out the window."

"You know what Axis Sally always says, 'Your husbands and sons just love it so much.' As if she has any idea," Betty said, shaking her head.

Orphan Ann crackled on when the song ended and in her teasing way, said, "Well, you boys fighting out there in the Pacific, that one was for you. We'll be waiting for you tomorrow, so be ready to get annihilated. Sea level is going to rise around that tiny rock you're protecting."

"Good Lord!" said Daisy, feeling light-headed at the words.

Whoever supplied Ann with intelligence knew their stuff. But they mixed in enough outlandish claims that you never knew what to believe. Just last week, she announced that the West Coast had been invaded and Japanese forces had made it all the way to Oklahoma.

"Now, for all you people wanting to hear word from your boys, we have two here tonight who have something to say. They're looking strong and feeling good!"

Betty turned up the radio and they all leaned in.

A monotonous man's voice came on. "I'm Bill Godfrey and I wish to say hello to my folks back home. My health is good, no major illnesses so far. Please send bar chocolate, cigarettes and playing cards to help pass the time. Say hello to Joey and Linda and tell them I hope to see them again soon. I know you're worried about me, but I hope hearing this message will lighten your heart. Love to all."

Even though they all sounded the same, it was hard not to get teary-eyed when you heard these men speak. The empty-tin-can tone in their voices spoke far more than the scripted words.

Ann came on again. "And here's our next guest."

"Ha. *Guest*," Fluff said.

The second he started speaking, Betty turned milk white and started shaking.

"This is Charles Yates, airman stationed in Honolulu, Hawai'i. Hello, Mom and Dad and Betty. I sure miss you and I'm hoping you are all well and healthy. We're holding up and getting fresh air. You don't need to worry, they're treating us just fine. Please send photographs and hold me in your prayers. All my love."

The message was over before they knew it, and Orphan Ann came back on reading a message from another prisoner of war not in the station. They heard none of it. Betty looked to be having a hard time breathing, and Daisy jumped up and grabbed a glass of water. Fluff was rubbing her back, saying, "There, there. Honey, Chuck's alive!"

Betty lay her head onto the cool tabletop and her whole body shuddered. "I know, but for how long?" she said.

Daisy felt her own tears rise up. "This is the best news we've had since the war started. Let's focus on the *alive* part. Remember what we talked about? *Alive* means *hope*."

In between sobs, Betty said, "I don't know how I'm supposed to feel."

"Feel it all. Happy, scared, relieved," Daisy said.

Betty lifted her head, her whole face smeared in tears.

"All this propaganda crap means nothing. I don't believe they're treating him well. You ask me, he's probably eating dirt and being beaten half to death."

They'd heard enough to know this was possible. Or even likely.

"We can't think about that," Fluff said.

"I know Chuck's voice. This was a hollow, broken version of him," Betty said, then started laughing through the tears. "But he's alive. My baby is alive."

Daisy knew there was no *one* correct way to behave when you found out a loved one was a prisoner of war, so they let Betty cycle through the gamut, sobbing one minute and on her knees thanking God the next. After a time, when her breathing had settled, she asked, "I need to get him back. How can we get him back?"

The pleading in her voice cut straight to Daisy's heart. "I don't know, but we will. At this very moment, our boys are bombing the crap out of the Japanese Navy. No way will we let them gain control of Midway or get close to Hawai'i. They've already lost the war. They just don't know it yet," she said, with full faith.

Fluff bobbed her head. "I agree. My money's on us—all ten dollars of it."

Betty wiped her face with a dish towel and let out a long sigh. Just then, Blanche wandered in with several kittens in tow. Jumping onto the table, she nudged her head into Betty's hand.

"You know you're not allowed up here," Betty said, stroking her shiny black fur. "But I'll let you get away with it just this once."

When she smiled, there was a light in her big brown eyes that had been missing for months. They moved to the living room and sat let the news sink in for a while longer. Daisy eventually fell asleep on the *pune'e* with Blanche curled up against her side, purring like an outboard motor. She dreamed of giant swells and sinking ships, and a sky full of Japanese aircraft raining fire upon Honolulu.

Though it was ink black and blustery outside, Lizard was brightly lit and brimming with people. The WARDs on shift looked exhausted, but instead of leaving as they normally would, they shuffled down the hallway to the lounge, where cots had been set up between the couches for naps. Fluff was immediately called into the radio room, while Daisy moved between the main board and the filtering room.

Markers covered the map, with remaining surface craft and aircraft on high alert, and patrols circling all of the islands. Somber faces went about their business, waiting for word of the Japanese striking force. No more sightings had been reported at Midway. Daisy was thankful for Hochman, who brought them hot coffee and spoke in the same relaxed drawl that he always used.

At 0800, Fluff tore into the room and went straight to Nixon, a paper in hand. Nixon had been on his secure line much of the morning. He read the paper, then spoke to the room. "Enemy carriers, 180 miles from Midway. And planes, too. May heaven help our boys."

Please, God, let them come back alive. Every single one of them.

Midway was three hours behind Hawai'i. Daisy could picture a pale predawn sky humming with airplane engines, and the heavy splashing of ship hulls against the waves. Despite her prayer, she knew that many souls would be lost today. Tension rose as they waited for more news. When word came from Midway's naval air station, it wasn't good. Most of the fighters on the island were damaged and the power stations destroyed, but at least the runways were still intact. And still not a peep from the enemy, who had a talent for showing up unannounced.

The day progressed in a blur of watching Nixon's face as he spoke on his secure line, plotting patrolling aircraft, hearing snippets from the radio boys and pilots, and generally being on tenterhooks. When they got word that *Yorktown* had been badly hit, the mood in the room reached a new low, only to drop further a couple of hours later when they heard she'd sunk. Daisy had been counting on the Japanese ships to be the ones sinking. *Come on, boys, we're counting on you!*

Some of the people in the room had been there for over twenty-four hours. Nixon had a sheen on his face and dark pouches under his eyes, while Major Oscar's face was wrinkled in that way when you just wake up from a too-short nap. The whole place smelled like fried chicken and cigarettes. Normally, smoking was prohibited, but rules had gone out the window. And the break room and hallway had become a rotating motel for sleeping women. All of their perfumes and body lotions mingled together to create one sweet and complicated scent of female humanity.

It was sunset hour, though you'd never know under all this rock, and Daisy was about to take her first real break of the day, when Fluff alerted everyone of a new call from Wai'anae. "We have what looks like a line of bombers coming in, Cheerio says."

The incoming aircraft had also shown up on Shafter's radar, though again, with radio silence, no one could say for sure what they were. Their speed would indicate B-17 bombers, who had not yet returned from their mission to Midway. Major Oscar and the air force liaison had been pacing the floor waiting for them, so all eyes were on their course. After the third reading, Daisy noticed one of the planes had fallen behind and was veering south.

"Do you think there's a problem, sir?" she asked Major Oscar.

"They'll call in if there is."

"And break silence?" No sooner had the words come out of Daisy's mouth, than the UHF radio crackled to life.

"Honolulu, this is Bulldog 6 coming in from Midway. Do you read?"

Daisy, closest, picked up. "Five by five, Bulldog. We've got you."

"How far out are we?"

"We have you ninety miles off of O'ahu. You're almost home!"

The connection cut out, then she heard, "...Low on fuel, not sure if we're gonna make it."

"How much do you have left?" Daisy asked.

His voice came across the airwaves all broken up. "We're flying on fumes...extra weight...two injured men and a medic aboard...heading?" he said.

She glanced up at Major Oscar, and noticed Fluff standing by her side. A few of the other girls in the room had tuned in, too. "Turn left heading two seven zero. You're a little off course," she said, forcing a calm voice. "If you need to ditch, we know your location and will have rescue to you on the double. How many are you?"

"Thirteen. Roger. Stay with me, Rascal."

The Flying Fortresses usually held ten men at most, and the extra weight would slow them down. Daisy wanted to ask him how it looked for America out there across the ocean, if any Japanese ships had been sunk and how many lives lost. But she knew she couldn't, not over radio waves, which everyone knew the Japanese were listening in on. Just as the Allies were doing to them.

While Major Oscar went to consult with Nixon and call for a rescue vessel, Daisy checked the readings. The bomber had corrected course and was now seventy miles out.

Fluff spoke up. "You all know I'm not religious, but I think these boys deserve a prayer. What do y'all say?"

Everyone nodded.

Her voice was loud and clear. "Dearest Father in heaven. We have an urgent matter that needs your attention. This bomber has thirteen very important men on board who need to get home to see their loved ones. Would you please give them an extra helping of luck right now? We need them all in one piece. Amen."

Short and sweet, and so Fluff. *Amens* bounced around the room, even from Nixon, who was now standing behind Daisy, his coffee breath wafting around her.

"Honolulu, I have a message for a Rascal named Wilder. Will you relay?"

A wave of panic hit her hard and she sat up taller. "You're speaking to Wilder, sir."

She heard muffled voices in the background and then the pilot came on. "We have a Lieutenant Montgomery aboard and he won't shut up about you. He keeps mumbling that he needs to get back to see you, over."

What was Walker doing aboard an air force bomber? There could be only one answer. "Is Lieutenant Montgomery badly injured?"

"He was shot up by a Zero and had a rough landing. Not gonna lie, he's been in and out of consciousness. But he's a fighter, and he's damn persistent," he said.

"Tell him that he needs to come back alive, and that's an

order. And tell him I will be waiting." Then to the copilot, "Please, fly this bird home safely."

A warm hand rested on her shoulder. She expected Major Oscar or Hochman, but it was Nixon. "Bulldog 6, this is Colonel Nixon. How's the visibility out there?"

Daisy wished she could see the sky and watch for their plane with her own eyes, not some relayed radar reading. She looked at her watch. 1850.

"Heavy clouds. But glimpses of an orange sky."

In summertime, the seas were calm and warm. If they ditched, at least they wouldn't be ditching into giant swells and whiteout frigid conditions.

"Godspeed, boys," Nixon said, heading back to the balcony to take a phone call.

Air felt scarce in the room. If the plane did not ditch, she'd be guiding them into a blacked-out airfield at Hickam, which was a whole other dicey matter. Hochman came over and asked if she was up to the task. "You bet, Major."

Minutes crept by like molasses. Daisy watched the board and the plotting of the other flights. Of all planes, why did Walker have to be on this one? Her imagination began creating scenarios. If his injuries had not been that bad, they would not have risked flying him back to Hawai'i, would they have? She wanted to ask more, but knew they had other problems to worry about. Betty, who had been plotting on the far side of the table, by Kahuku Point on the map, set down her stick and came over. For most of the day, she'd been shut away someplace in her own mind, though still functioning. Daisy had kept an eye on her, watching for signs of distress.

"At least they aren't in enemy waters," she said.

Like Chuck.

Enemy waters or not, Walker was injured. "But he's already hurt. If they ditch, it could kill him," Daisy said, feeling a tremor in her voice.

"Did they say what was wrong with him?"

"Just that he was shot up by a Zero and had a rough landing."

"Get on that radio and ask them again," Betty said.

"I can't."

"Why not?"

"It's not professional," Daisy said.

"Figure out a way," Betty said.

Just then, Fluff skidded back in on the cold linoleum, coming from the receiving room. "What's happening?"

Daisy held up a finger. Fluff could wait. And she had an idea. "Bulldog 6, this is Honolulu. Come in, Bulldog 6."

The now familiar voice came on right away. "Bulldog 6, read you five by five."

"We need to ready the ambulance for your arrival. Please report on condition of injured, starting with Lieutenant Montgomery."

Fluff's eyes went wide.

"Montgomery took several bullets to the shoulder area, and lost a fair amount of blood. And we think he may have a collapsed lung."

She felt pain in her shoulder and tightness in her chest. A wave of darkness rolled through her, but she mustered all her courage. She was simply not going to fall to pieces right now. "Have you dumped all ammunition, extra weight?"

"Affirmative." They heard yelling in the background and a *Goddamn it*, and then, "Mayday, mayday, mayday. Bulldog 6 is ditching. I repeat, Bulldog 6 is ditching."

Betty looked Daisy in the eye with such knowing that Daisy wanted to wrap her arms around Betty and squeeze, burying her face and shutting out the rest of the world. If anyone knew the feeling, it was Betty.

Instead, she yelled out to Hochman and Nixon, "Bulldog 6 is out of fuel, They're ditching!"

The men scrambled over.

"Bulldog 6, what's your altitude?" Betty asked.

"Angels one, zero. We have clear skies now, and Venus is bright as hell. Losing speed and altitude quickly. See you on the other side, Rascal. Bulldog, over and out," he said before the receiver went dead.

If there was ever a time to get the correct location, it was now. Minutes could be the difference between Walker living or dying, and same with the rest of the men.

Daisy shoved her chair back, sprang up and ran to the filterer table. "We need to do a range cut on the latest readings for Bulldog 6, from both Shafter and Wai'anae. They're ditching!" she called to Thelma, knowing that the oscilloscope at Wai'anae had its own peculiarities.

As she tried to make the calculations, her hand trembled. The plane's true position would be where the range arcs intersected. Also, airspeed would be significantly slower. Daisy knew the glide ratio of a B-17 was about sixteen to one, so she had to account for that, as well.

Thelma came up and looked over her shoulder, smelling of gardenia. "Are you okay?" she asked.

"Do I look okay?" Daisy shot back.

"What can I do to help?" Thelma said, sounding surprisingly genuine.

Daisy felt her throat bunch up. "Can you double-check these coordinates? I want to make sure I have them right."

Thelma dragged her wooden folding chair over and sat a couple of inches away. "Take a deep breath, Daisy. They're going to be all right."

"Walker may have a collapsed lung, and to crash-land in his condition—" She paused, pulling herself together. "Wait, you're right, and we are going to do everything in our power to see that plane in," she said, a moment before the lead on her pencil snapped. "Damn!"

Peg was suddenly by her side too, her face white as chalk. She handed Daisy a pencil from her apron. "I heard my brother is aboard that flight, and he's wounded."

"Yes on both accounts."

"How far out will they be when they land?"

"Nineteen miles, coming in at two-seven-eight degrees."

"At least they'll be close," Peg said.

"It's something," Daisy said.

After passing the position directly to Nixon, who didn't even bother to double-check it, Daisy collapsed into a chair under the clock. It was 0730. Fluff brought her a Coke and a Spam sandwich. "Here, you have to eat something."

The thought of eating made her want to retch. She watched Betty, who was now guiding in the first bomber to Bellows Airfield. The planes had to clear the Ko'olau Mountains before descending, and landing without running lights raised the level of danger exponentially. But Betty looked as cool and collected as an old hand.

Daisy recalled that first day in the Palace when no one had any idea what was in store for them. How they'd all fumbled answering those first calls. And how apprehensive and awkward she had felt, like the outsider she'd always been. Only to be swept in by Fluff and Betty and Lei, who could not have cared less about her slacks and boyish hair and general lack of refinement.

And Walker. Walker was the one who had more faith in her than anyone.

Damn you, Montgomery, keep breathing.

28

THE WAIT

They waited. And waited. There were more bodies crammed into Lizard than Daisy had ever seen. The other flights had landed safely, one at Bellows and one at Hickam, not far from where Fluff had fled from Dunn. An ambulance met the one at Hickam to transport a radio operator who had a nearly severed arm from flying shrapnel.

"He's an Oscar, he's one of us," Fluff had said, and offered another personalized prayer for the man.

Daisy stayed glued to her chair, counting the seconds until the rescue pilot called in. She knew that in addition to surface craft, a submarine in the general vicinity and a PBM Mariner seaplane were being deployed. A Dumbo Mission, they called it. When the girls had asked Hochman why, he told them the old planes used to resemble flying elephants, with wooden life rafts attached under their wings. They would drop them for the survivors until ships arrived. Now, the ability to make water landings speeded things dramatically.

Waiʻanae called in the PBM, and the pilot radioed in a minute later. "Mariner 6 to Honolulu, we've got a low ceiling and heavy rain, over. Check my bearing, please."

Nixon, who had been keeping a close eye on Daisy, mumbled *shit* under his breath. Low clouds and rain were not what they needed. Bulldog 6 had said it was clear, but weather in Hawaiʻi had its own mind. At least the winds were light. Daisy corrected the Mariner's heading by five degrees, working to keep her voice calm and steady. When she looked up, she saw that everyone in the room was focused on her. Peg looked as anxious as she did.

"You should reach them in approximately five minutes," Daisy told him.

If all went well.

"It's auspicious that both planes are number six," Lei announced. "It's considered a lucky number by the Chinese."

"They haven't been too lucky so far," Daisy pointed out.

There were so many variables in a water landing. Weather, swell size and direction, visibility, type of aircraft, pilot skill and experience, and boatloads of luck. The women had rehearsed this exact scenario numerous times. Only not with Walker as one of the souls on board. It felt different now, so achingly personal and surreal. A good portion of Daisy's heart was on that plane.

Hochman and Nixon paced behind the board, while Daisy sat perched on the edge of her seat. Phones were still ringing and coordinates marked. Bodies moved around her on the plotting table, but she scarcely noticed. When the next reading came in, it showed them slightly off where they ought to be.

"You're too far north. Turn around and head one-three-zero. And hurry!" she told them in a commanding voice that didn't sound like her own. Telling a pilot to hurry was not protocol, but she couldn't help herself.

He seemed unfazed. "Roger, searchlights on, seas calm."

Shining searchlights were a risk they had to take. There were no bogeys in the sky, so they had that going for them. The plane followed their standard search and rescue grid pattern. She looked at her watch. Nearly fifteen minutes had passed since the pilot first made contact. What was taking so long? She went over the calculations in her mind again. Had she somehow made a mistake? Nixon looked at her as though he might be thinking the same thing.

All of Lizard fell silent and she swore she smelled salt water and fuel. Heard the drone of an engine, dropping out of the sky, and the ensuing explosion. She shook her head, trying to clear the image.

Suddenly, the radio burst to life. "Honolulu, we've found them. Flare spotted and raft is intact. We're going in for a landing. Will report back soon. Mariner 6, out."

"Roger your last, Mariner 6, will do. Rascal, out."

The whole room broke out in cheers. But they weren't in the clear yet—at least Walker wasn't. She took a swig of the warm Coke and kept her rear end on the hard seat. Betty and Fluff slid their chairs over, and Lei, Peg, Thelma and half the WARDs on shift huddled around them. Some of the men, too.

Daisy closed her eyes for a moment, and imagined the ocean at night—dark and silky and bottomless. Miles out at sea, there would be gentle rolling swells and the smell of salt surrounding you. Currents with logs and sticks and coconuts created long trails of debris. And the occasional shark. She hoped the lifeboat could hold all thirteen of them.

Fluff whispered into Daisy's ear, "Have faith, honey."

No matter what happened, Daisy felt held up by a kind of sisterhood that she never knew existed. She could feel the caring soaking into her skin like a soothing balm. Whenever her mind wandered to dark thoughts, all she had to do was look around at their faces.

And suddenly, Mariner 6 came through loud and clear. "Honolulu, this is Mariner 6. All souls alive and now on board with us. Injured men will need immediate medical attention upon arrival, over."

Daisy sprung up and hugged the nearest person, who happened to be Nixon. His back was as solid as a fifty-pound bag of rice. When she pulled away, he was half crying, half laughing and wiping tears from his eyes.

"Goddamn it, they're gonna make it," he said. "Good filtering, Wilder."

And then his mouth broke into a warm and dazzling smile, full of pride and approval and something fatherly that touched a place in Daisy buried for so long. All this time, she'd known that beneath the steel exterior, there was a heart inside there somewhere wanting to come out. The plane was to arrive at Hickam. As soon as they heard this, Daisy asked Nixon, "Sir, may I be excused from duty?"

"Get the heck out of here, Wilder." He nodded toward the door. "And take backup."

"Thank you, Colonel."

She nearly yanked Fluff's arm off. "Come on, we're going."

"We can't just leave."

"We're cleared."

At the door, they heard footsteps behind them. "Can I

come with you?" Peg asked, her pale face dusted with red blotches.

Fluff glanced at Daisy, who nodded. "Of course," she said.

Fortunately, Tripler Hospital was not a far walk from Lizard. Halfway there, they heard the whine of an airplane engine in the distance.

"It has to be them," Daisy said, picking up the pace.

It felt good to breathe the fresh evening air into her lungs. A mixture of night-blooming jasmine and mock orange. Once their eyes adjusted, they navigated by spotty moonlight to Palm Circle. None of them said much. There was nothing to say. A singular unspoken sentiment surrounded them all.

Tripler was nothing fancy, just a two-story wooden building that looked more like an oversize plantation house than a hospital. They sank down on a grassy mound out front and waited for the ambulance.

"Cheerio said that the doctors here are top-notch. They patched up a few of his buddies like new. Lord knows, they've been through the wringer," Fluff told them. "And my friend Beatrice on staff here says they've become masters at reattaching limbs."

The thought gave Daisy chills. "How about fixing lungs?"

"I'm sure they're good at that, too."

Though none of them had any idea how one fixed a collapsed lung. Before long, they heard a siren drawing closer and closer. *Shouldn't there be two?* If Fluff and Peg were wondering the same thing, neither said anything. The thought sent Daisy into a cold fury and she felt like Moon had on that fateful day in December, wild with fear and ready to bolt. Instead, they went inside and checked in at the nurses' station. Someone had already called in the emergency, and nurse Gina Hayes informed them, "We're ready for him."

Fluff corrected her, "There are two of them."

Gina looked up from her clipboard. "There's only one. The other is going to the morgue. I'm so sorry."

Daisy's knees almost buckled. "Do you know which one?"

"All I know is the surgical team is scrubbing up and they've called in some kind of specialist from Honolulu."

Fluff led Daisy to a chair, and Peg sat down next to her, lip quivering. Daisy reached out and grabbed her small, cold hand. No matter what bad blood had gone on between the two of them, she knew how much Peg adored her older brother. This small gesture was the least she could do, especially since she was unable to form any words.

When the ambulance drove up, they all stood and went to the door. The blackout curtain hung heavy and black between them and the answer Daisy awaited. Men's voices carried in. A door slamming. A man backed in, carrying a litter. She looked down at the face. Arched eyebrows. Dark five-o'clock shadow. And then she fainted.

29

THE PATIENT

Daisy opened her eyes. Fluff and Peg and another woman in a nurse's uniform she didn't recognize all stared down at her with pinched faces. The light above them was blinding and Daisy closed her eyes again.

"Where's Walker?" she asked.

"Walker is in the emergency room. He's in good hands," Fluff said. "Sweetie, we need to take care of you right now."

"I'm fine."

The nurse said, "You just fainted, which tells me you're not fine. Have you fainted before?"

Her mind felt fuzzy. "Never. Excuse me but I need to see Walker. Did you talk to him?"

Peg and Fluff exchanged a look.

"What?"

"They were in a big hurry and we didn't want to get in their way, or excite him," Peg said. "And it looks like he has more injuries than just a punctured lung."

Daisy didn't want to know. "He's made it this far. Isn't that a good sign?"

They all nodded in agreement.

The nurse felt around on Daisy's wrist for a pulse, seemingly unable to find it. "Have you eaten anything today?"

Fluff answered for her. "I saw her eat a banana this morning, but once we got to work, the day went by in a blur. I can also guarantee that she's had enough coffee and Coca-Cola to send her to the moon and back. Isn't that right?"

Daisy nodded.

"What exactly is it that you ladies do?" the nurse asked, eyeing their uniforms.

"Top secret," Fluff said.

"No, really."

"Yes, really."

Oh, how she loved to say that.

Sometime later, after Daisy had force-fed herself half an egg salad sandwich and chunks of canned pineapple, a nurse from the operating room came out to speak with them. The doctors were going in to remove a bullet lodged in his thigh of all places. Another had gone through his upper arm, but that one came out the other side. As for the punctured lung—a pneumothorax—she told them that was likely caused by blunt trauma in the rough landing, not a bullet wound.

"How do you treat that?" Daisy asked.

"Needle aspiration and prayer. Sometimes in a last-ditch effort, they'll go in with a chest tube, but we aren't there yet. We'll let you know when you can go in and see him."

It was nearly eleven when the nurse returned, face expressionless. "Follow me."

Walker lay in a small room upstairs with three other men. All asleep. The first thing Daisy noticed was the bluish hue to his lips, as though he'd eaten a whole basket of blue-berries. His mouth hung open slightly and his long lashes rested against his cheek. He looked so utterly fragile. And pale. And heartbreaking.

Fluff hung back while Daisy and Peg moved alongside his bed. Daisy was tempted to climb under the sheets with him and infuse him with all the love she could muster. But they didn't want to wake him, so they just stood there. She burned the contours of his face into memory, said a silent prayer, gave him a feathery kiss on the forehead and left him to heal.

Daisy felt something on her shoulder, shaking her. She brushed it off, thinking it was Mr. Silva wanting her to shovel more manure out of the stalls. "Miss Wilder, wake up," a sweet voice said. "He's asking for you."

"Mr. Montgomery?" she mumbled.

"Walker."

She woke fully, realizing where she was. Unfolding her limbs, she climbed off the couch and followed the nurse, a different one, into Walker's room. Her lips were so dry they stuck together but she didn't care. She tiptoed in, so as not to wake the others. Walker's eyes were closed, and one arm and one leg were bandaged up thick. Daisy knelt down so she was a foot away from his face. "I'm here," she whispered.

His eyes opened and he turned toward her, the edge of his mouth turning up on one side. "Damn you're a beautiful sight," he said.

He was blue and unshaven and gaunt, but in Daisy's eyes, he was perfect.

She picked up his hand. "I've been here since before they brought you in. Peg too, but she went home at midnight to get a few hours of sleep. She'll be back."

"You and Peg? Together?"

Daisy smiled. "We talked things over."

He exhaled, then winced on the inhale.

There was so much to say, and yet all she wanted to do was sit with him and hold his giant, calloused hand. Tell him that she loved him, and then some. They were words previously reserved for only her parents and the animals, and she felt strangely shy about uttering them.

"Are you crying, Wilder?"

Her hand went to her cheek, which was warm and wet. "I was so scared I would never see you again," she said.

"Ah, hell. When the bullets started coming in, I thought I was a goner. But I told God I had a girl back home who had never flown in an airplane and I needed to make it back to see her, and how she shone brighter than the sun. Get down here with me, Daisy, would you?" he said, patting the side of the bed with his good hand.

Daisy.

Without hesitation, she slid onto the sheet, lying with her side halfway off the edge of the bed. Who cared if the nurses complained? She pressed her forehead to his cheek. That familiar Walker smell—horses and fresh grass and soap—mingled with iodine and sulphur. His skin burned to the touch.

"Did you change your mind about me?" he asked.

"I found the letter you wrote to my mother. I wanted to tell you so badly, but you were already gone." She ran a finger down the side of his face. "We can talk more later. Just know that I am not going anywhere."

Their eyes met.

"I love you, Daisy. I think I always have."

His voice trailed off, lids fluttered, and then he was out.

30

THE BOAT

June could be counted on to bring lazy trade winds, more mangoes than you knew what to do with and lychees by the truckload. The trees had their own business to attend to, and cared not about any war. Daisy and the girls had risen early to help Lei pick mangoes off her trees, and now Betty showed them how to make mango bread. They'd be taking loaves into Tripler for the patients. You had to carefully peel them to avoid getting a rash, and chop the dripping orange flesh into chunks. Kittens shot around underfoot, so they had to watch their step.

Walker was still in the hospital, but his lips were less blue and his wounds were healing without signs of infection. Daisy visited twice a day, at least, and lay on the bed with him. Still careful, but he now could wrap one arm around her. The mood in all of Shafter and all of Honolulu had shifted after the victory at Midway. With a good portion of the IJN at the bottom of the sea, the people of Hawai'i were sleeping more easily at night. Lizard felt lighter too, with Nixon smiling at least once a day now. Sometimes for no reason in particular.

When a knock came at the door one morning, Daisy expected one of the girls next door coming to visit the kittens, so stopped cold when she saw the outline of a man in a cowboy hat behind the screen.

"Wilder, that you, girl?" a raspy voice said.

"Archie?" she said, opening the door. "Come in."

He stepped inside, bringing smells of the racetrack with him—leather, alfalfa, hay—and held his hat against his chest.

"Uncle T told me where I'd find you. There's a boat leaving today at three. Sounds like your horse could be on it."

The clock read 10:38 a.m.

The docks at Honolulu Harbor were still bustling, though now with soldiers and livestock instead of Matson steamship passengers draped in *lei*. All five of them—including Peg, who had stopped by to help with the bread—had piled into Lei's car.

"You need us as backup," Fluff had demanded, when Daisy said just she and Lei would go.

"Plus, Moon technically belongs to me, so I might have more pull if it turns out to be him," Peg offered.

The ship in question was named the *Emmaline* and she was already being loaded. Betty had insisted they dress in uniform and carry their badges. "We'll tell them we're on official business."

Archie didn't know which pier *Emmaline* would be docked at, but she wasn't hard to find. They could smell the manure and sweat from a mile away. When they walked up, most of the animals had been loaded on already, but for a handful of sheep. Fluff peered into the hold and said, "You think they'll let us in?"

Two armed guards walked over to them. "Excuse me, ladies, what's your business here? This is a secure area."

"Not a chance," Betty said, under her breath.

Fluff held up her badge. "We're on a mission to retrieve a stolen horse and we have strong reason to believe he's aboard this ship."

The man eyed the badge, and then looked her up and down. He glanced over at the rest of them. "Haven't seen any horses loaded today."

Daisy felt her heart drop and was ready to turn and leave, when he looked beyond them and said, "Unless these fellas have a horse in that trailer," nodding to a truck and trailer backing in. The trailer had *Sinbad* stenciled on the side in red.

All the hairs on Daisy's neck stood up. She knew that truck anywhere. Black with wooden slats along the flatbed, the truck was a familiar fixture at Montgomery Ranch. Both doors opened, and Johnny Boy stepped out of the driver's side and a pudgy spectacled man from the passenger's.

Lei froze. "George? What are you doing here?"

Daisy glanced from Lei to George to Johnny Boy, her mind sticking all the pieces together.

George looked at his wife and the row of uniformed women standing next to her, then toward the entry to the docks, then over at the two guards. For a moment, Daisy thought he was going to make a run for it. Instead, he flushed red and stood there biting his lower lip. The guard asked to see their papers and George fumbled for them in the cab of the truck. The way his shoulders slumped and his hands shook, you could tell he knew he was in for it. Daisy went to the trailer and looked between the slats. "Moon, is that you in there?" The horse let out a loud whinny. She could see ropes going every which way, securing him so he couldn't move an inch. A big brown eye looked out at her.

"It is you! My big, beautiful boy. We're going to get you out of here, I promise!"

When she came away, she noticed Archie standing off to the side. He gave her a nod but made no move to get involved, just watching from the periphery, a guardian of sorts. Daisy whispered *thank you*. She stayed with Moon as the guard looked over the papers. No matter what happened, she was not going to leave his side until he was back at home in Mokulē'ia.

"These look to be in order," the guard said, handing them back to George, who got a smug look on his face.

All five of the girls started talking at once.

"No!"

"They're fake!"

"This is my horse!"

"You can't let them get away with this!"

Daisy stood in front of the trailer door with her arms crossed, and Peg joined her. "There is no way you are letting this horse on the ship, Private Logan. I won't let you."

Johnny Boy, who had been quiet up until now, said, "These broads have no idea what they're talking about. This ain't their horse, and we're putting him on that ship. He has a ticket." He glared at Daisy and spit out a hunk of chewing tobacco near her foot. "You going to let a female tell you what to do, Logan?"

Apparently it was the wrong thing to say because Logan raised his rifle. "I don't like your attitude, cowboy."

Daisy butted in. "How about we let the horse out and you can see for yourself."

George coughed loudly. "That's a bad idea. This is all a

big mistake and if you'll kindly move aside, we can get him loaded. We're already late."

Private Logan glanced at his friend, who nodded toward the trailer.

"Open it up," Logan said.

Johnny Boy didn't budge.

Lei came and stood next to Daisy and Peg, and said to her husband, "Go on, you heard him, you lying piece of filth."

When neither Johnny Boy nor George made a move, Daisy took matters into her own hands and unwound the chain and opened the doors. As quickly as she could, she unclipped the hooks that bound Moon into his cell. She kept a hand on him at all times. He tossed his head around, blowing and stomping and making a huge racket. Daisy could see why as soon as she caught sight of the bit, which was too small and too tight. Lei and Betty unlatched the ramp and let it down.

"We've got you. Easy, Moon," Daisy said in a low, steady voice. At the bottom of the ramp, when he saw Johnny Boy, the horse reared up and went wild, pawing at the air and whinnying loudly. Daisy managed to grab the lead and this time held on for dear life. She would be dragged through the docks and through downtown Honolulu if she had to. This horse was not leaving her side.

"It's over, Moon. We're going home," she said.

It took a moment, but he seemed to understand. She ran her hand along his neck. Lord how she'd missed his strong lines and coal-colored coat. Before Moon had vanished, Daisy had taught him numerous cues. As far as horses went, he was a fast learner. She motioned for him to lower his head and spoke softly. "Relax. No need to be afraid anymore."

Moon responded right away, dropping his neck down and placing his chin in her palm. Daisy risked leaning down and placing her forehead against his, and tenderly kissed his muzzle. He sighed. For a few moments, it was just the two of them. Woman and horse.

"I've missed you, my big love," she whispered, tears streaming down her face.

When she looked up, Logan and his buddy were restraining Johnny Boy and George. At long last, it was over.

After the bust, Archie had lingered on the docks and offered to help get Moon home. In anticipation of recovering the stolen horse, he'd brought a trailer from the racetrack. As he and Peg and Daisy made the long drive to Mokulēʻia, Daisy started off elated, but with each mile closer, she began to dread an encounter with Mr. Montgomery. Their lives were inextricably bound, but would he be able to see past his own self-importance?

"Maybe I should have stayed behind and let you two deliver him," she said.

Peg patted her thigh. "You're the one responsible for finding Moon. You need to be here."

"I'm nervous."

"So am I, but deep down, my father is a good man, Daisy. He wants to make amends, I know he does. He just doesn't know how. I think it's been easier for him to sweep it under the rug," Peg said.

Daisy wanted to ask more, but knew this was between her and Mr. Montgomery.

Archie chimed in. "The problem with that is, eventually the rug falls apart. You might think you've outrun it, but there's no escapin' da truth. Remember that."

With all those years under his belt, and lines on his face, Archie commanded a certain respect.

"Yes, sir."

When they pulled down the dusty drive to the ranch, that old familiar smell of horses and salt reminded her that this was where her heart resided. Lord how she'd missed this place. In the trailer, Moon began a series of loud whinnies and stomped hard on the metal.

Archie chuckled. "The boy knows his place."

Mr. Montgomery's car was right where it always was, next to the naupaka hedge, so clean and shiny, you could have eaten dinner right off the hood. A moment later, the stable door opened and he came outside, standing with his hands on his hips and squinting into the late sun. Daisy could hardly swallow.

Archie raised his hand, just barely, and nodded toward the rear. "We got some precious cargo here for you, Hal," he said out the window as he pulled to a stop.

Mr. Montgomery looked inside the cab, taking in the sight of Daisy and Peg next to each other, and looking a little confused. "What's this about?" he asked.

Peg climbed out, pulling Daisy along with her. "We got Moon back, Dad! He's alive and well and we have Daisy to thank for it."

He frowned. His gaze fell on Daisy. As much as she wanted to turn away and look anywhere else—the ocean, the field, the mountains, she held her ground. "I'd like to get him out of this trailer. He's been locked up for heaven knows how long," she finally said.

Mr. Montgomery didn't say anything, but walked around back and began unfastening the door. They all followed. His hands shook on the latch, and in that moment, Daisy realized how much the horse meant to him. She felt a stab of guilt. Moon's ears twitted and he raised his nose in the air as he walked down the ramp, sniffing all the familiar scents. His coat was still black as freshly cooled lava.

Mr. Montgomery held a leathery hand against Moon's neck. "Well, I'll be damned. I had all but given up hope. Where was he all this time?"

Peg explained the sequence of events as they led the horse over to the pasture and water trough. Her father's expression remained hard to read, and Daisy let her do all the talking. When they neared, several of the horses grazing looked up. Nalu, Daisy's other favorite horse, trotted over and the two began nickering and snorting. Some people said horses easily forget each other, but Daisy knew that to be false. Horses that were close never forgot. They were social beings, just like people.

They watched for a while, and then Peg said, "I'll leave you two alone. I think you have a few things to discuss."

Daisy gave Peg a look that said, *Don't leave me!* But a part of her knew this had to be done. Moving forward might require going backward in time, to the moment her life had spun off course. Lies and actions needed to be addressed. Mr. Montgomery cleared his throat. His hand went to his waxy mustache, smoothing it down with two fingers. He looked even more uncomfortable than Daisy felt, and moved so he was leaning on the wooden fence, one foot up. Daisy joined him.

They stared out at the horses in an awkward silence, and then he surprised her by speaking first. "You know, I loved your father. He wasn't just an employee, he was part son, part brother, and he worked five times harder than anyone one else at the ranch. I let him down in the worst possible way. I ruined more than a few lives along the way, and I want you to know that I'm sorry for everything. I know that a bunch of words can't fix anything, but there you have it."

A gust of wind swept in from the ocean. Daisy said nothing, and he continued.

"Lying about shooting Billy, well that hole was too big to ever climb out of. You probably don't remember, but I couldn't sleep, lost weight." He shook his head. "Lost my mind, really. I swear to you on a stack of Bibles I did not pull that trigger intentionally, but I was a coward and I worried what it would look like if I told the truth."

His voice caught and Daisy snuck a glance. Tears streamed down his face. This was a new Hal Montgomery, one she never thought she would see. "But Walker made you?"

"My son is a much better man than I am. He made me come clean. I don't think I slept a wink until then. But even still, the memory of that day haunts me and it'll be planted in my mind for the rest of my life. God's punishment, I suppose. I tried to make up for it by giving you work, but being around you made me think of how badly I had screwed up, and of Billy. And poor Louise alone in that shack. You have all their talents and then some."

The cadence of his voice reminded her of Walker, a chip off the old block, but one with a conscience. Maybe Mr. Montgomery had one too, somewhere under that thick skin of his, trying to push its way to the surface. None of this was new information, but he was making some sort of effort at an apology. She would give him that.

"As a girl, I always looked up to you and your family. You were the man who made our world go round. We lived and breathed Montgomery ranch. My father loved you, too. Which is why it made it even harder for me to fathom what happened. And then to find out like I did from Thelma, it felt like a bomb dropped directly in my lap. It wasn't fair," Daisy said.

He shook his head. "We all thought you knew, that Louise had told you."

"She never did."

"Everything she did was to protect you, so don't be too hard on her."

It wasn't her mother she wanted to be hard on. "If you

felt so bad, why fire me when it came to losing Moon? You knew I had no other options, and that my livelihood was wrapped up in the ranch. You could have made things better then, but instead you made them so much worse."

"I'm not proud to say this, but I thought that if you were gone and you two left for the Mainland, maybe it would be easier to forget," he said, pausing to wipe his cheeks with his plaid shirtsleeve, then huffing. "That was a mistake. I only felt worse. Not only for being a complete asshole, but for losing the best worker I have."

By now, Daisy's resolve was slipping. She wanted to sit in the grass and have a good cry and let the ground soak up a lifetime worth of tears.

"One thing I do know is that my boy loves you. And Peg, she cares about you. We all do. I know that sounds like a ridiculous notion coming from me, but it's the truth. When this whole war blows over, I want to have you back at the ranch," he said.

Daisy swayed with the weight of his words. Could she ever go back?

He held up a hand. "Don't give me an answer now. This is a lot for you to chew on, but I want you to know the offer stands. You and Walker can run the place. And you would be the lead trainer, like you should have been long ago. I can't fix my mistakes, but I can do my damned best to make up for it. I owe it to you and your mother, and to myself."

There was no way she could go back now. Time would be needed to settle into this new reality. But the war would not be over anytime soon, of that she was sure, and in that time, she would attempt to come to terms with things. Mr. Montgomery was Walker's family, after all. She would think on it, let the idea simmer and her heart mend.

Lead trainer.

Her dream.

A few days later, Daisy snuck in a box of malasadas to Tripler for Walker and his roommates. "Any word on Johnny Boy and George?" he asked.

The story had come out that Johnny Boy and George knew each other from the racetrack, as both men had a hankering for betting. On the morning of December 7, Johnny Boy had been on his way to church when he saw Moon in a field off to the side of the road, munching on grass. He knew what Moon was worth, and instead of taking him back to the ranch, he hid him away and contacted George. Even as the island was under attack. When brought in for questioning, Johnny Boy claimed he did not recognize the horse, and George blamed Johnny Boy for duping him. Daisy knew better. Both men knew exactly what they were doing.

Daisy sat on his bed with her legs crossed. "They're awaiting trial. Neither man can make bail, which was set suspiciously high," she said.

The Montgomerys having clout came in handy sometimes.

"Did you find out what their plan was for Moon?"

"From what I gather, he'd worked out a sweet deal. Deliver Moon to Kentucky and walk away with a pretty penny. JB and he would split the profit, though I doubt he was up-and-up with JB, who is not the sharpest guy around."

Some races had been shut down on account of the war, but not the Kentucky Derby. Heaven forbid people were not able to drink their mint juleps and wear those big fancy hats. Though Daisy had to admit, it would be a dream to attend one day and see the likes of Seabiscuit or War Admiral. She wondered how Moon would have measured up.

31

THE EXPLANATION

Daisy, this is where I tell you how badly I failed you and that I am ever so sorry. I fell apart and I left you with a heavy burden. Some of us are more fragile than others, and I'm one of those people with a delicate nature. I simply could not take the loss of my Billy. Nothing I say will ever make up for not telling you the truth when I learned it, but maybe this letter will help you understand. And Hal's son, Walker, did come by one day to tell me the truth. You'd have thought Hal himself would have been man enough, but no. Only his teenage son had the gumption. And trust me, I debated about telling you, but at that point you were already working at the ranch and I knew how much you loved those horses. I didn't want to take that away from you, too. I knew we needed the money, and I knew I was incapable of scraping what little there was left of me off the floor. I know that words fall short, but sometimes they're all we have. I hope you will find it in your heart to forgive me one day.

Your mother, Louise

32

THE ENDING

Late September 1945

The winds had shifted out of the south, heralding a Kona storm blowing in. Clouds brewed on the horizon, black and ominous, and the ocean kicked up small whitecaps in Pearl Harbor. Daisy, Fluff, Lei and Betty all stood near the dock, arm in arm. Waiting.

Celebrations had been going in earnest for days, now that the war was officially over and surrender documents had been signed aboard the USS *Missouri*. People were calling it V-J Day—Victory over Japan. Parades and marching bands filled the streets of Honolulu, and Daisy and the girls participated proudly. Lord knew it had taken longer than anyone expected, with years of suffering and brutality, but better late than never. Over four hundred thousand American lives lost and upward of sixty million total. Those numbers were nothing to be proud of. But the relief was palpable. You could taste it in the air.

News had also come of the official disbanding of the

WARD organization, since more military personnel would now be available to staff the radar installations and command centers around the islands. Operation Magic Carpet was newly underway, with carriers transporting men home who had been scattered around the Pacific and Southeast Asia. General Danielson, who had been transferred to California, sent a handwritten note to Lei—who was now chief supervisor—when he heard.

In my time, I've seen my share of fighter controls. I'm in charge of a handful right now, but you ladies in Honolulu should know that the one at Lizard, manned by the WARD, is in my opinion the best. The war might be over now, thank God for that, but you ladies should take pride in the fact that you were running the best Air Raid Defense system in the world. Hands down. When the threat was greatest, you rose to the occasion. Best wishes to all the girls remaining.

Yours truly,
General Danielson

For Daisy, it was bittersweet. As difficult as the war had been, these women had become family. They had held each other up through thick and thin. Heartbreak, apprehension, loneliness, you name it. But all things had to end. It was a rule of nature, a cycle of life.

Fluff, the eternal optimist, had said, "An ending is really just the beginning of something else, and the possibilities are endless. Think of it like that. Plus, it's not like we won't be seeing each other. I'll be on your couch every chance I can get."

For Lei, Fluff and Daisy, that might be true, but who knew where Betty would end up, and so many of the other military wives who were now like sisters. Daisy put it out of her mind. Any time now, the USS *Rescue* was set to arrive, and Betty had received a telegraph that Chuck would be aboard, sailing from Yokohama, where the POWs were being cared for and processed. Over three years in a prison camp and now he was free. The girls had been anxiously reading the papers, seeing photographs of overjoyed GIs getting their first glimpse at freedom, or a war prisoner savoring his first cup of coffee. Those were the lucky ones, if you could call them that. Bone-thin and gaunt, nevertheless they had endured.

Today, Betty was jittery and teary-eyed, and Daisy felt the same. Information had been scarce. All they knew was that Chuck and his fellow prisoners had walked and hitchhiked over five hundred miles from a camp near a place called Kobe. Betty had become preoccupied that he would not survive the crossing home.

"He didn't walk five hundred miles to die on a hospital ship. He'll make it back to you, Betty, I know he will," Fluff had assured her.

Daisy hoped she was right.

The women pressed up against the fence like caged animals for over an hour, waiting for the sound of a ship's horn. A crowd had gathered. Men, women and children milled about, some of them WARDs, some servicemen and others family. Anticipation clung to them, despite the brisk winds. A few minutes later, a loud blast came from the entrance of the bay. They all jumped.

"It has to be them!"

Sure enough, a white ship emerged, cutting through the chop. She had a long blue stripe across her hull, with red crosses adorning the smokestack and other parts of her massive body. There was absolutely no mistaking her mission. As she drew closer, you could see men on the decks waving madly.

Betty pinched her lips. "I do believe she's the most beautiful ship I've ever laid eyes on."

Daisy could hardly see through her tears, and knew the moment would be inked into her memory forever. "What a blessing."

"It's a miracle, is what it is," said Lei.

Pretty soon, the crowd began cheering and hollering and throwing flowers and confetti. Kids jumped and twirled. Women hugged. It took a while for the ship to tie off and ramps to come down. And once the men began disembarking, the girls made their way to the front of the line to get a good look. These were not the pilots and soldiers Daisy was used to seeing. They were so weary looking, and half the size of regular men. The first one off the ramp bent down and kissed the earth. Several others did the same.

Betty was hopping and biting her lip, and then she saw him. "There he is!"

Chuck didn't kiss the ground, but when he saw Betty, he fell into her arms and buried his face in her neck for a solid minute or two. Daisy had never seen two people pressed so close together, and soaking each other in. This was the kind of love that could sustain a person for years on end. There was not a dry eye in the whole shipyard.

33

THE SURPRISE

Two months later, Walker showed up at Daisy's shack at 0600 on the dot. He had told her he had a surprise for her, and to be waiting. "Bring a jacket," he'd said.

When she hopped in the car, he leaned over and gave her a long, slow kiss. The kind that stirred up her insides and lit up her toes. Daisy had been enjoying his soft, warm touch as often as time permitted. She was back full-time at the beach shack, with Walker staying every chance he got. She'd spent some of her earnings replacing the roof with red corrugated tin, putting up new boards on the salt-blasted ocean side, as well as brushing it all with a fresh coat of paint. Fluff, who had stayed true to her word and visited often, insisted she now call it a cottage. Betty and Lei agreed.

Walker handed her a bandanna. "Here, cover your eyes with this."

Daisy laughed, but obeyed.

They sped off down the road, and instead of heading

up through the sugarcane fields, they veered left toward Hale'iwa.

"You know that I know every single nook and cranny of this coastline, don't you?" she told him.

"A man has to try."

Daisy breathed in his scent as they rode along.

She wondered where they were headed, since they rarely went this way. Perhaps the Pali lookout, after a long, leisurely drive up the coast. Or maybe a dip in the calm blue waters of Waimea Bay. The 'oama were running, but Walker probably had no idea. He was still half cowboy, half pilot, with few fisherman tendencies. That was fine with Daisy. A man and a woman should retain their own passions.

Five minutes later, he pulled off the main road, heading toward the ocean. Daisy could smell the sandy soil and the sweetness of kiawe pods. She knew exactly where they were and what the jacket was for.

"Have you guessed?" he said.

Hale'iwa Field.

"Are you taking me up for a spin, Lieutenant?"

"Private planes are back in business."

She slid the bandanna off and saw a big smile lighting up his face. "Have you notified Shafter?" she asked. The last thing they needed was a pair of P-40 pursuits showing up on their tail.

He squeezed her thigh. "I'll let you do the honors."

On several occasions over the past few years, Daisy and the girls had been taken to Hickam and given tours of the aircraft. Seeing these birds up close and running her hand along the seams of the sun-warmed metal wings had felt almost dreamlike. They'd even been allowed to sit in the cockpit with all its levers and gauges and buttons. But never once did they go up in the air. Now, Daisy realized she had been waiting for this moment since the day she'd heard Amelia Earhart say "There's more to life than being a passenger."

Their ride today would be a bright orange Aeronca TC-65 Defender. Several of the schools in town used them for flight lessons, and Walker was good friends with the owner of one. Apparently, he'd flown her out here yesterday. Ever thoughtful and full of surprises. Daisy was more and more smitten with him each day.

Walker patted the side of the plane. "This baby survived the attack on Pearl Harbor, circling at two thousand feet before being shot at by Zeroes. A miracle Vitousek managed to land her. A beauty, isn't she?"

Daisy knew the story well. "Gorgeous. And she was one of the lucky ones, from what I've heard."

Several other civilian planes had been shot down after encountering a sky full of Japanese planes on what had begun as a quiet Sunday morning all those years ago. Two pilots missing, two dead.

Once inside and strapped in, Walker briefed her on their route and handed her the mic. "All yours, Rascal."

Daisy froze for a moment, but then experience took over. "Shafter Control Center, Aeronca N33768, at Haleʻiwa, ready for takeoff, heading north to circle island."

A man responded, "Shafter, all clear Aeronca. Have a nice flight."

Daisy could barely contain her excitement. The runway was bumpy and sand-blown, the propeller even louder than she'd imagined, sending vibrations through the back of her legs and rattling her teeth. But a rush of pure exhilaration coursed through her. She was flying!

"This thing must be like riding a tricycle after what you're used to," she said into the headset.

"Something like that."

Looking down over the reef, she could see every coral formation, patch of sand and rocky inlet. So many shades of blue. It all looked so Technicolor, and so much more beautiful than she had imagined. As they passed Opana, Walker came in close and dipped a wing. Two men poured out of the truck and began waving their hats madly. Knowing they couldn't see her, Daisy waved anyway.

"I sure miss talking to those Oscars. We might not have known a lot of them by face, but over time, they became almost like family. I suppose war has that effect on people," she said.

Walker turned so she could see his face, nodding. "When lives are on the line, it ups the ante like nobody's business."

They followed the coastline, passing Kahuku and soaring next to the green, sawtooth ridge of the Koʻolau Mountains and high above the milky-blue shallows. Where low clouds hung down, Walker flew around them. They were on the reverse route of the one Daisy and the girls had taken years back, when this whole thing began. She remembered how they ended up at Opana and shocked the pants off the guards. It brought a smile to her face. So much had happened in the time between.

Outside Mokapu and Kāneʻohe Bay Naval Air Station, flocks of seabirds—shearwaters, sooty terns and petrels—littered every square inch of rock. Daisy felt like she was finally one of them, loving the sensation of floating on air. But near Waimanalo, the plane suddenly lurched to the left and began a free fall. Her stomach went clear to the roof.

Grabbing hold of a bar on the inside of the plane, she yelled, "Whoa!"

Walker's amused voice came on. "Relax, that was nothing. Just a little thermal."

They soon leveled off, but bobbed around in a rough patch of air for a while. Daisy's palms began to drip as Walker swooped in next to the cliffs, buzzing so close she could see the flowers on the vines.

Damn him. "You're enjoying this aren't you? Watching me sweat."

She looked down to the foamy whitecaps far below. Tiny cotton balls. Maybe it was a good thing she'd stuck with horses.

"I don't have eyes in the back of my head, honey," he said.

"You know what I mean."

He laughed. "The Daisy Wilder I know doesn't sweat."

On the South Shore, the bumps subsided and they glided past Diamond Head and out front of Waikiki, with people dotting the beach now that the barbed wire had been hauled off. Now, only coconut trees stood guard. The calm air soothed her nerves. Beyond Waikiki and Aloha Tower, they approached Pearl Harbor. Sandy shallows flanked the narrow channel that led into her three lochs—west, middle and east. From their vantage point, out beyond the breakers, Daisy spied the crisscrossing runways and hangars, and Battleship Row, which once again was lined with hulking, metal warships. Walker, who had been pointing out sights like an overly eager tour guide, grew quiet.

Goose bumps prickled her skin. The sound of hundreds of engines roared in her ears, loud as buzzsaws. Daisy swung her head around, half expecting to see a swarm of Japanese planes surrounding the little Defender. Smoke filled the cabin. Ash in her mouth, Daisy squeezed her eyes shut. *Just a cloud, this is not happening,* she repeated to herself.

Walker's voice startled her out of it. "You okay back there, Rascal? Over."

She found it hard to speak. "Affirmative, Captain. Just a little choked up."

"You never quite get used to it," he said, dipping a wing. "Flying over Pearl, I mean."

Daisy saluted the blue water below. "Rest in peace, boys. Rascal, out."

So many souls lost. Hearts broken. Needless horror. And yet Daisy thought of the boatloads of grit, mountains of courage and undaunted spirit that went along with it. This was what she wanted to remember. The good in the world had come out swinging. *And won.*

★ ★ ★ ★ ★

AUTHOR NOTE

Though this novel is purely fictional and the characters are products of my imagination, it was largely inspired by true stories of the Women's Air Raid Defense (WARD), which was formed in the Hawaiian Islands by emergency Executive Order 9063 immediately following the attack on Pearl Harbor. I stumbled upon the story idea while researching for my novel *The Lieutenant's Nurse* and was surprised I had never heard of them. With little information available, I ordered a book called *Shuffleboard Pilots: The History of the Women's Air Raid Defense in Hawai'i 1941–1945* by Candace A. Chenoweth and A. Kam Napier that chronicles the WARD history and is full of fascinating details and vivid memories from the women themselves. As much as possible, I tried to weave their stories into my book: about training in 'Iolani Palace, hiding out in flooded air raid shelters, trying to catch the mysterious lingerie thief, and plotting husbands as they flew out to battle, some never to return.

The women whom I read about were courageous, intelligent, patriotic, fun, and full of heart. They were given a crash course in radar and codes, taught complicated calculations, and shown how to guide pilots into blacked-out runways or talk them home when they were lost. Their work was critical and essential to the war effort, and as soon as I finished reading *Shuffleboard Pilots*, I knew I had to write a novel about them so that the rest of the world would know their story. If you want to learn more, I highly recommend you read *Shuffleboard Pilots*.

The tagline on the front cover—*they brought the flyboys safely home*—came directly from a Kaua'i WARD, Beatrice Dang, whose son I corresponded with. "One thing my mom would say when I asked what she did... In a sassy way she said, 'When the flyboys got lost, we brought them home.'" I thought this perfectly summed them up.

I hope I have done justice to these amazing women!

In a few places, I had to take creative license and tweaked facts to fit the story—which is often the case in historical fiction. One such scenario is when Walker Montgomery is flying the P-40 out of Hale'iwa Field at the start of the book. Walker was a navy pilot and the P-40s at Hale'iwa were US Army Air Corps planes that had been temporarily moved from Wheeler Field. Lieutenants Harry M. Brown, Robert J. Rogers, John J. Webster, George S. Welch, and Kenneth A. Taylor were the brave pilots who between them took down nine enemy planes that morning.

As always, I would love to thank my wonderful publisher, MIRA Books, my brilliant editor, Margot Mallinson, and my amazing agent, Elaine Spencer. I still have to pinch myself regularly to make sure it's all real—that I now have four gorgeous books in the world, with a fifth in the works. So many people are involved in putting out a book, and I am so grateful to have such a supportive and awesome team rooting for me every step of the way. Also, to friends and family who were by my side as I brainstormed, plotted, wrote, edited, promoted, ruminated, lamented, and obsessed over my book. Your love and support have not gone unnoticed.

Also, I am extremely grateful to several expert readers who helped check for technical accuracy: Dr. Bill Wiecking; William S. Hochman, Lt.Col., USMC (retired) and Commissioner (retired) Marin County Superior Court; and Robert L. Dixon, Lt.Col., USAF (retired). I am honored that they gave me their time.

And lastly, to Hawai'i, thank you for being such a unique, special, and magical place. I am blessed to call you home. XO

Sara

RADAR GIRLS

SARA ACKERMAN

Reader's Guide

1. The WARDs answered the call of duty during a very intense time, just after the attack on Pearl Harbor, and the fear of invasion was real. If asked, do you think you would have stayed in Hawai'i and joined, or would you have preferred to evacuate to the Mainland? What other ways did women contribute to the war effort?

2. Did you know about the Women's Air Raid Defense program prior to reading this book? If so, how did you hear about it? If not, were you surprised to learn about it? Did you learn anything new about the attack on Pearl Harbor and its aftermath?

3. The four women, Daisy, Fluff, Betty and Lei, all came from different backgrounds, and yet became the best of friends. Which of the four characters do you identify with the most? Why? Do you have friends who have bonded through challenging life experiences?

4. The WARDs replaced men in an active war zone and faced plenty of skepticism, discrimination and outright hostility because they were women. How do you think they handled it? Have you ever encountered something similar in your own life? How challenging is it to work in a male-dominated field?

5. War is known to bring out the worst in people, but it can also bring out the best, and stories of courage and hope and survival abound. How did the characters in the book react to the pressures of war on their doorstep? Do you have any family stories of living through or fighting in the war?

6. How do you think becoming a member of the Women's Air Raid Defense shaped Daisy's journey?

7. Hawai'i was under martial law through much of WWII, which included blackouts, curfew and rationing. How do you think that would have affected you? What food and drink would you have the hardest time living without?

8. Do you think it will be possible for Daisy to forgive Mr. Montgomery? What about her mother? How much did Louise's mental illness affect the rest of her life?

9. After Dunn assaulted Fluff on their date, it takes the women catching Dunn in the act for Nixon to finally do something about it. How else could they have handled the situation? How would that same behavior have been treated today? Has much changed?

10. What similarities do you see between life during wartime and life during the COVID-19 pandemic?

11. What did you think of the ending and the final flight? Have you ever been to the Arizona Memorial at Pearl Harbor? Or other war memorials either national or international? Which ones? How did you feel being there?